The Feather of Truth

The Detective Ghazini Series

Book One

Ian Campbell-Laing

This is a work of fiction. All the characters, organizations, and events portrayed in this novel are either products of the author's imagination, or are used fictitiously.

The Feather of Truth. Copyright © 2015 Ian Campbell-Laing

All rights reserved.

ISBN: 1515369781
ISBN-13: 978-1515-369783

To my Mother.

The Feather of Truth   Ian Campbell-Laing

ACKNOWLEDGMENTS

This book, my debut novel, couldn't have been written without the support of my family and friends.

Firstly, to my dear mother, who had such a harsh life. She instilled in me the need to work hard for everything, never give up, always have an enquiring and creative mind, and treat everyone equally and with respect. "Everyone has a story to tell. Just listen," she said to me many times.

To my wife and son, who have such an incredibly dry British sense of humour and gave me much feedback—often brutally honest—about earlier versions of this book.

I choose my friends carefully. They have always treated me well whatever my circumstances and welcomed me time and time again—even when I gave them less attention than they deserved. They know who they are, and I am indebted to them for their insightful comments on earlier drafts of this book. Such friends are the antithesis of so-called "fair-weather" friends, who instead appear today but are gone tomorrow, after they have no further need for you.

Finally, my thanks to the Amazon team at CreateSpace who guided me expertly from draft manuscript to final publication.

~Ian Campbell-Laing, United States, 2015

PART ONE

Rien ne pèse tant qu'un secret.
Nothing weighs on us so heavily as a secret.

Book of Fables, Book VIII, Fable 6, 1678–79
~Jean de la Fontaine, French poet

CHAPTER 1
MOORGATE, LONDON, ENGLAND

April, 2025

Richard rubbed the sweat from his slightly moist hands onto his trousers as his eyes sought confirmation from the laser pen's projected screen image. As he narrowed his eyebrows, the energy from the photons of electromagnetic radiation illuminated his pursed lips and the few wrinkles on his forehead.

Vengeance demanded no middle course: he needed to obtain and exploit specific secret information. If access were denied, the bank would dismiss him for such a brazen, unauthorized act. If granted, his methods would have to be completely undetectable by the bank's intricate system of firewalls—or he would lose everything.

Without moving his head, he diverted his gaze to the top of the right lens of his reading glasses, informing him that his current heartbeat at ninety beats per minute was double that at resting, but his blood pressure had risen only by 10 percent. Richard briefly smiled. Not bad, considering, he thought. He ignored the small "+61²" contained within a circle next to it, signifying that based on the latest physio-actuarial studies, he should live until he was ninety-six years and two months old.

A green-coloured message appeared on the screen, disturbing his peripheral field of vision. Guided by man's evolution, its light entered the front of Richard's eye, at the cornea, transmitting an inverted picture of the image to his brain, which then turned it the right way up.

Access Confirmed.
Welcome, Chuck Jelleners.

Perfect! We are logged in. But now comes the trickier part, he thought. He smiled broadly, exhaled through his nose, and nodded his head. He didn't say anything out loud, because all conversations at this German bank were automatically recorded, even if you sat alone in your office.

Richard glanced down briefly at his glass-top desk, upon which stood upright his silver pen: five inches tall, an inch round, and supported by a three-pronged silver stand. Overhead and slightly ahead of him to his right, fluorescent yellow-tinged beams of light struck the pen, creating a shadow of a thin miniature rocket to its left and onto his desk. The pen projected a laser image of a keyboard onto the desk, and separately, the image of a computer screen suspended a foot away in front of his eyes.

Like an actor about to go on stage, he wanted to get his performance underway and take pleasure in, and be rewarded from the hours of preparation. This play, whilst having been meticulously planned and rehearsed by Richard, still also depended on other players' reactions.

Richard's long, slender, manicured fingers rested on the desk, waiting for their instructions to carry out his commands. His index fingers tapped lightly on the glass surface, just like tennis players who, when waiting to receive a serve, nervously and out of habit often twiddle their racquets in their hands and shuffle their feet in readiness to spring towards the impending projectile.

Even though the bank's security system, V-Trax, had completed its complex identification process to confirm Chuck's identity—using a synthesis of retinal scan scrutiny, fingerprint recognition, layered voice analysis, and keystroke pattern correlation—Richard still paused before proceeding. Inhaling through his nose the cold conditioned air, he held it for a few seconds, and then exhaled the warmer waste air through his mouth. He hoped the deep and slow breathing would provide an alert partner to his brain, as this cyber game played out.

He glanced down at his watch, a Patek Philippe rose-gold Complication: 7:30 p.m. He should be leaving work in ten minutes for his client dinner appointment. That would still give him just enough time to get what he needed before detection.

Even if he backed out now, he knew that he had just broken the bank's code of conduct information security and privacy rules. If discovered, he would be dismissed instantly "for cause" and lose the two million pounds in bank stock that he had accrued. Blackballed, he would also be denied a professional reference and would find it almost impossible to be able to work in the financial industry again. As confidence took over nervousness, he dismissed such outcome outliers.

His initial anger at Chuck—his arrogant, overbearing, self-entitled, deceitful American boss—was soon seduced by a desire for revenge against, and ruination of, him. Richard just needed to secretly access key information stored within two files of V-Trax. Richard's next action was to get past the intricate firewalls. If caught, he would definitely be spending considerable time in a cell at His Majesty's pleasure.

Richard watched the screen image. He had created a malicious worm, the G-H0st, to infiltrate the files. His hands were now gliding over the glass surface, his fingers rapidly and lightly tapping out codes of instructions. His intense, green, piercing eyes were fixed on the image in front of him. Like an experienced pianist, he rarely needed to look down at his fingers.

G-H0st zeroed in on the password for the first firewall. Richard had created a far subtler program than of old, which simply used a scattergun approach that tried millions and millions of potential passwords. Instead, his program utilized enhanced specific magnetic resonance detection.

The Feather of Truth   Ian Campbell-Laing

After twenty seconds, the screen flashed up the alphabetically-ordered constituents of the password.

bCCcDeeeghiiMNnPrrstuvXz

He thought, How odd! No numbers or symbols to make the password encryption more difficult to break?

A few seconds later, the completed password appeared.

NichtszuverbergenPiMCDXC

What did that mean? He wondered.

At first sight it appeared to Richard to be made up of two parts. Richard had studied Latin at his boarding school in the north of England and guessed that maybe the end section, "MCDXC," were Roman numerals. He knew that now wasn't the time to test his rusty memory. In a separate window, he typed in a Google request. Up came the number 1,490—which unfortunately didn't resonate with him at all.

The first section looked German. His fingers tapped in a translation request on Google in a lower corner of the screen.

In a small window, two similar translations for *Nichts zu verbergen Pi* popped up. He smiled as he read it, acknowledging that the programmer at the bank had a sense of humour.

Nowhere to hide, Pi.
Nothing to hide, Pi.

But the "Pi" reference seemed obtuse, initially. Private investigator? Any hacker would be pursued by a PI? However, it was spelt Pi, not PI.

Then Richard realized that the programmer was likely a mathematician. "Pi," often written as the Greek letter π, was used in maths and cosmology with its beauty being that when expressed as a decimal, 3.14159…, the digits never, ever repeat themselves. They never ended. It tied into the "Nowhere to hide" perfectly—the person who hacked into the system would be hunted down forever. The chase to find the hacker would never end!

And the "1,490" reference was obvious, now. Richard suddenly remembered that this German bank at which he worked was one of the oldest in Europe, being founded in the year 1490.

At the top right hand of the screen image, in dark blue, a half-inch-sized hourglass suddenly appeared, signifying that the first firewall was ready to be penetrated by G-H0st.

G-H0st then asked him:

Proceed—Y or N?

Caution, Richard. He paused. Via the password, the programmer was sending a very clear message to any potential hacker: the intruder had nowhere to hide if he penetrated this firewall.

However, Richard was convinced that the "nothing to hide" by the bank was a blatant lie, because he suspected that the system had plenty to reveal, and the bank itself had plenty to hide.

His right index finger lightly pressed "Y" on the glass-top keyboard image.

The hourglass started spinning, indicating the firewall had been penetrated. He had reached the next level of protocol of V-Trax. As chemicals flooded away from the frontal cortex of his brain, releasing its footbrake of reason, a feeling of unrestrained power swept over him.

Richard smiled. He took another deep breath, thinking, so far, so good. The first counterplay of retribution will surely be confirmed.

Before he exhaled, the loud noise of a thunderclap came from the pin-sized speaker at the top of the pen, and he jolted his head back. The screen image then went black, highlighting a small white dot that appeared at its center. He leant forward and squinted, as the overhead lights in his office brightened to counteract the sudden darkness.

Richard's mouth opened, his body tensed, but he remained silent. What the heck is going on?

The dot blinked once, and then white streams of light quickly radiated out from it, reaching for the edges of the screen. The pulsating streams vanished as quickly as they had been created. The screen went back to its original colour, and the hourglass reappeared. Richard had never encountered this before.

He wiped more sweat from his palms onto his trouser legs, trying to find a drier patch, and used the back of his shirt sleeves to get rid of the beads that had just appeared on his forehead.

From the speaker at the back of his high-back chair, he heard a female's familiar voice announce, "Bad posture. Please sit more upright!" He ignored her. From the corner of his eye, his attention was diverted to three digits that had just appeared in bold red type next to the hourglass:

180…

The middle of his eyebrows narrowed further.

Then it changed to **179**. He leant his head forward to less than a foot away from the screen image.

178…

Immediately, his nervous system jolted back his head and forced his body to become stiff. As he exhaled noisily, his brain automatically decoded this new information and elevated his mind to a higher state of alertness, preparing him to make the decision to either go for confrontation or cut and run. Simultaneously, glands caused over thirty hormones to be released throughout his body in anticipation of having to handle an impending threat.

Christ, this wasn't meant to happen. I have less than three minutes before the bank's system administrator is alerted of an intruder, and then I am done for. I will then surely have nowhere to hide.

His heartbeat had shot up to one forty-five. His pupils dilated, forcing in more light. As the veins in the skin on his arms and down his back constricted, he experienced a chilly sensation, which immediately made him briefly shiver and quickly raise his shoulders in a shudder.

She was repeating again, "Bad posture. Please…"

"OK, OK!" he shouted and pressed the "silent" button on the side of the chair to get rid of her persistence.

His body temperature continued to rise. He wiped more sweat from his fingertips, and he felt the moisture on the back of his neck sticking the skin to his shirt collar.

The countdown was unrelenting…**170**…**169**…**168**…The unstoppable decrease in value of the integers, racing towards zero, reflected the unforgiving increase in their importance.

CHAPTER 2
THE ROYAL AUTOMOBILE CLUB, PALL MALL, LONDON

Six months later

The immaculately dressed American woman sat inelegantly on the toilet seat in a cubicle of the ladies' restroom. Her dark blue Chanel silk skirt, panties, and stockings were pulled down to her calves. Her knees were much higher than her hips. Wearing thin blue surgical gloves, her slim hands worked quickly to complete the delicate operation.

On her lap rested her black Kate Spade leather shoulder bag, upon which she had laid out two large green grapes, joined together by a single stalk and nestling on a clump of soft facial tissues. Next to these was a small open cellophane jiffy bag.

As if directing a dart, the first three fingers of her left hand guided the syringe's microscopically thin needle into the middle of one of the grapes, entering at the point it was attached to its stalk. The thumb and index finger of her other hand kept the grape steady, and then they let go to grip the syringe. Her left hand's index and middle finger gently pulled up the white plunger, withdrawing one-quarter of a cc of the grape fluid. Using her thumb, these contents she expelled onto five tiny grey-coloured grains sitting at the right on the bottom of the cellophane bag.

She waited half a minute, whilst the fluid completely dissolved the grains.

Placing the needle back into the cellophane bag, she pulled the plunger, withdrawing the near-translucent, light green mixture. She expelled it back into the grape. She repeated the exercise on the second grape with the remaining five grains waiting at the other end of the bag. She leant to one side, allowing the light bulb overhead to highlight her work. She examined both grapes. No puncture marks could be detected on either.

Smiling, she wrapped the tissue around the grapes, and lifting open her shoulder bag, she carefully placed them inside one of the double pockets. Then she placed the syringe into the cellophane bag, expelled the air, zipped it up, and opening her knees, carefully dropped it into the water of the bowl of the toilet. She took hold of her right-hand glove at her wrist, and pulling it, it came away from her hand. She removed her other glove and released them into the toilet.

She then did a quick pee, and as she stood up, flushed the toilet. As she bent down to get dressed, she turned to watch the jiffy bag and gloves being flushed away by the water's circular vortex motion. She waited until the toilet refilled itself of water, to ensure none of its contents came back up. But she then flushed the toilet again, for additional insurance.

She smoothed down her skirt and exited the cubicle. She was still the only one in the ladies' room. She washed thoroughly her hands, and reapplied a spray of her hideously expensive Baccarat perfume to the inside of her wrists and behind her earlobes.

Her pulse was racing, so she forced herself to breathe heavily and slowly, in an effort to slow her heart rate down to a more normal level.

After checking her appearance in the mirror, she grabbed her shoulder bag and returned to await the arrival of her lover at their table in the Great Gallery restaurant.

CHAPTER 3
TEDDINGTON, SURREY, ENGLAND

April, 2025

Kofi Ghazini's family was of humble Nigerian descent. Two generations prior, they had arrived in Great Britain to start a new life. The family of five had brought only one suitcase and had the equivalent in today's money of fifty pounds in cash. One of the sons met and fell in love with a girl his own age, and driven by their innate physical desires, had embraced the folly of youth. At age sixteen, they withdrew from education to elope and explore a new world of excitement. They had struggled financially ever since. They were Kofi's parents.

Kofi's father, who had a drinking problem, went through a succession of low-paid, menial jobs and then tried his hand in setting up a local store. But through a combination of bad luck and misguided business decisions, he had been declared bankrupt earlier that year. After the government's derisory and short-lived handouts had been used up, the father felt worthless, humiliated, and had tried to commit suicide by taking an overdose of sleeping tablets. But he had failed at this as well, and had lapsed into a coma in hospital. Ironically, and perversely under the British National Health System, the government then fully paid for his care. A year later, five years ago now, Kofi made the heart-wrenching decision to switch off the machines that had kept his father alive in a vegetable state.

Kofi's uneducated, unskilled mother could only get a part-time job in the local B&Q hardware store. Earning just the minimum hourly wage, she was not able to bring up her son as she had wished. So, despite being heartbroken about giving away her only son, she put aside her personal desires and placed him into the care of the British Adoption and Fostering Services department. There, she hoped they would find a loving and reasonably well-off family that would take him in under their wing. But in a bigoted and ignorant world, with his personal embarrassing "secret" recorded in his personal health file, many families were reluctant to take him on.

After his father's death his mother married a drunk who abused her. Kofi's future looked grim. He turned his attention to crime.

CHAPTER 4
MOORGATE

Richard sat back in his chair with his hands clasped tightly behind his head and his mouth slightly open. Whilst the adrenaline in his body had subsided slightly, the muscles in his arms were still taut. Two areas of his brain were wrestling with opposing forces competing for his attention and acceptance: the powerful engine of his amygdala urging him to carry on with his quest for revenge, and his cortex acting as a foot brake, reasoning and reining him back. Skirmish or skedaddle. Press on or pull out.

He remembered wise words from his grandfather, Ben. "When reaching for the summit, know when to have the courage to pull back and try another day." He wondered for a moment if he should just get out of the system immediately, without accessing the secret data he needed, before he was detected. Definitely not, his amygdala, taking control, instructed him.

But what on earth was making G-H0st alert him that his presence within V-Trax would be detected in less than three minutes? This had never happened before. All previous uses of G-H0st on other advanced systems had always indicated that his presence was completely invisible.

Ten years prior, Richard and his roommate, C. L. Z., better known as "Sleazy," Stringlemaier, were studying in the United States at the Massachusetts Institute of Technology, commonly called MIT. There, these two rebellious intellectuals developed in their spare time a software program that they named G-H0st. It allowed them to hack into any corporation's system without that host system knowing that a breach had occurred.

They could snoop around for as long as they wanted, coming and going as they pleased through the secret back door they had created. It was as if the user's presence was invisible, almost ghostlike, and hence the name.

But their G-H0st program went further: it allowed the user, once in the system, to change and even backdate data totally undetected and then exit the system, leaving no trace. They could literally rewrite historical data. They weren't aware of any other system that could do that. It was then that they realized how they could leverage that functionality for the benefit of the less fortunate, whose voice is often unheard in society.

Richard and Sleazy, like many of the public, were angry at some of the pharmaceutical companies' refusal to offer the poor in underdeveloped countries reduced prices for much-needed drugs to combat malaria, AIDS, and other fatal diseases. So they decided to test G-H0st's potential on the system of a leading American global drug manufacturer, Scea Pharmaceuticals, an egregious price gouger. On taking over the rights of the drug Daraprim, used by AIDS patients to help fight infection, Scea immediately increased the price by 5,000 percent—from $14 to $750—when it allegedly cost less than one dollar to produce.

Richard and Sleazy accessed Scea's procurement sourcing system and increased the price by $3,000 on a random sample of high-value invoices received from suppliers. The drug company, typically dealing with tens of millions of value in invoices daily, did not notice the relatively small discrepancy on one original invoice for, say, $366,000, and automatically paid the increased price of $369,000.

The G-H0st virus diverted $3,000 of the total payment to a secret offshore bank account in the Caribbean island of Saint Lucia. To balance Scea's books, it then reduced the invoice back to the original amount, in this case $366,000, and deleted the $3,000 payment entry. The supplier had been paid the correct amount by Scea, but Scea's bank records would differ from their bank statements by the $3,000 it had overpaid. But this amount was unlikely to be investigated with any vigor internally by the bean counters and would be too small to be picked up by their auditors, who typically didn't review anything on a sample basis below their de minimus $5,000. The discrepancy would eventually simply be written off.

Also, by typically amending a six to a nine in the thousands column on an invoice—when glanced at quickly, the number was so similar—G-H0st added another layer of nondetection.

Over many thousands of invoices, the amounts added up, and Richard and Sleazy had managed in the first year to accumulate $20 million in their offshore account. Then, they sent anonymously all of that money to the Red Cross, for the express benefit of helping underdeveloped countries fight fatal diseases in children. Richard and Sleazy did not profit one dollar. That was their agreement whilst at MIT.

Not once were they alerted that the drug company's host system had detected their hacking. It seemed that they had gotten away with their game of pilfering from the privileged to profit the poor, and secretly had become the unknown modern-day Robin Hoods.

After leaving MIT, Richard had updated and enhanced G-H0st and occasionally tested it on other corporations. Outwitting his peers stimulated him intellectually and felt satisfying. He never copied data or stole money again, and considered the risk of being detected negligible. It was his hobby, and he simply wanted to develop the most sophisticated system ever built. Ego and arrogance drove him to play this technological game.

Chuck Jelleners ran the day-to-day operations of the Asset and Private Wealth Management division of this German investment bank, and Richard was his deputy. Outwardly, everyone thought that Richard liked and got on very well with his boss. In reality, Richard detested Chuck, whom he considered the antithesis of himself: Chuck was a diminutive, overweight, self-entitled, demanding, and brash American.

However, what Chuck lacked in intellect, he compensated by having a great deal of intuitive common sense. And this, combined with being cunning and devious, had advanced him to the second most senior person in the division. He was intolerant of the slightest mistake and dismissed anyone who criticized him. It was no surprise that his division had the highest staff turnover rates of the bank.

Richard had been at the bank for ten years and had been Chuck's deputy for the last three. He had survived because he made Chuck look good, and Chuck was totally dependent on Richard.

Richard looked back at the screen and saw the numbers continuing to fall. **167…166…**

Bloody hell, that's the first time the loud bang was invoked! He thought.

When he first coded G-H0st, he had set up the loud bang and white streaks on the screen to signify that the host computer into which he was hacking had set in motion a protocol process that, if allowed to conclude, would detect his virus within a certain estimated time frame. It was a warning to Richard to exit quickly. The loud noise signified evolution's "big bang"—the moment that physicists believe was when the universe was created from a tiny spec no larger than a pinhead, but stored within which was the mass of the whole universe as we know it today. It was the moment when time itself had been wound up, ready to start its ethereal clock. The white streaks of light expanding outwards created space and time. And so it was with V-Trax. GH0st at that moment had detected V-Trax's own big bang's response to Richard's cyber attack, uncoiling its protocol within the bank's computer networks and servers in search of the intruder.

155…154…

Clearly, technology has moved on, and this V-Trax system is altogether far more sophisticated than others I have encountered. But at least my G-H0st system big bang protocol worked and is alerting me of the impending danger.

He focused his thoughts. His confident instinct chose to back his powerful amygdala: he had never been a quitter. The brake pedal of reason from his cortex had lost out. He decided to go for it. It was now or never to get revenge.

Richard, obtain the information from V-Trax, and get the heck out of the system before the time is up, he thought.

Thirty seconds later, he saw the second grey hourglass appear: he was through to the edge of the second firewall.

Proceed—Y or N?

This time he didn't wait. His right index finger lightly pressed "Y" as the countdown continued...**131**...and the second hourglass started spinning. He had only just over two minutes left.

Then he saw the file for which he had been searching—the compensation file of the division. He quickly brought it up as a second window and sorted the numbers in the Excel sheets by descending order. He saw Chuck's name at the top of the list, not surprisingly, given he was second in command of the division, and he guessed that the CEO himself wouldn't be listed there.

His fingers froze the top left section of the spreadsheet and scrolled across to the total compensation column. He saw that Chuck had been given $8,525,000 last year, compared to $5,525,000 the previous year. Christ Almighty, that's utterly outrageous!

He glanced up at the timer. Only 115 seconds to go before he had to be out of the system to avoid being caught. And he knew that he should get out way before 0 seconds, just to be sure.

He then saw on the screen that in the New York office, Chuck was calling him on the videoconference line. He ignored it.

He heard a knock, knock on his office door. It opened, and Sam, his personal assistant, came in. Richard shook his head and raised his palm, showing two fingers, just like a vicar motions towards his flock at church when they are about to say a prayer. Sam took the hint, and he closed the door and waited for two minutes.

Then Richard heard his mobile phone ring. He knew it was probably Chuck, given the fact that he constantly e-mailed and called Richard day and night with tasks he wanted him to complete, almost always urgently.

God Almighty, how many distractions will I have tonight, of all nights! He wondered.

The timer showed **105** when the third hourglass appeared on the image, indicating he was at the edge of accessing the third and final firewall and inner sanctum of V-Trax's confidential data. He quickly wiped the sweat from his forehead using the sleeve on the back of his left arm. His heartbeat had climbed further, to 180.

Proceed—Y or N?

He tapped "Y" and quickly went to the second compensation file and typed in Chuck's boss's name, "CELSIUS MAYSMITH III."

He wasn't surprised by the enormous amounts—a multiple of Chuck's salary. *Well, with Celsius's intellect and leading the division to success, I guess he earns it,* he reasoned.

He typed in multiple diversionary commands in an attempt to install further complex layers of distraction to see if G-H0st detected a slowing down by V-Trax of his presence in the system.

Nope, the countdown continued. **60...59...**

He was about to get out of the system by the back door, when he spotted a confidential client index file that looked intriguing.

Following Oscar Wilde, he decided the only way to get rid of temptation was to yield to it and tapped the letter "A" on the keyboard image. His silver pen detected the movement of his iris and automatically and very quickly scrolled down a few of the names:

Ahmadi, Jamal

The current president of Iran is a client of our German bank? Interesting, he thought.

Ali, Muhammad (nee, Cassius Marcellus Clay)
Alda, Alan (nee, Alphonso Joseph D'Abruzzo)
Allen, Woody (nee, Allen Stewart Konigsberg)
Armin, Idi Dada
Andrews, Julie Elizabeth (nee, Julia Wells)
Asianov, Alexander (nee, Krasnoshtein)
Astaire, Fred (nee, Frederick Austerlitz)

Wow! There's no way these are or were all clients of the bank, surely? Is it possible?

He tapped the letter "B."

Bach, Johann Sebastian

Well, no surprises there, given it's a German bank started in the fifteenth century.

He quickly scanned further down the list…

Barney, Timothy Michael
Barnstable, Lord Canaan of

Oh, yes? The chairman of the RAC Interesting!

Barrett, **Victor **Daniel
Barton, Mischa
Bayer, Doug Ian
Beckham, David Robert Joseph

He smiled. Aha, the talented, handsome British footballer with the unusually high-pitched voice.

Beckham, Victoria Caroline (nee Adams)

With his "Posh Spice" wife who often looked bored during the Wimbledon tennis championships final. Although, conceded Richard, she did have a hand in styling the very pretty Range Rover Evoque, which Richard's wife drove.

Beckwith, Tamara
Bell, Lake
Benatar, Pat (nee, Patricia Mae Andrzejewski)
Best, Louise Elizabeth
bin Laden, Osama bin Mohammed bin Awad
Blair Ogus, **Lionel** Henry
Blair, Anthony (**Tony**) Charles Lynton
Blunt, Sir Anthony Frederick
Oh yes, he recalled, and the British traitor, Sir Anthony…
He scanned down further.

Bono (nee, Paul David Hewson)
Branson, Sir Richard Charles Nicholas
Brooks, Mel (nee, Melvin Kaminsky)
Brosnahan, Rachel
Brydon Jones, **Rob**
Buffet, Warren Edward
Burgess, Guy Francis de Moncey
Bush, Sr., George Herbert Walker
Bush, Jr., George Walker

Oh my God! Why has the bank got a file on these people—ex-presidents, British prime ministers, celebrities, singers, billionaire fund managers, IT geeks, spies, actors, actresses, dictators, hot-shot attorneys, sweet store magnates, teachers, and terrorists? What has it already done, or what is it planning to do with this confidential information?

He paused. Don't access your own file, Richard. That's too dangerous for this first visit into the bowels of V-Trax. Instead, access Chuck's file.

He entered "JELLENERS, CHUCK."

Up came the file on his boss.

30…In the corner of his eye, he spotted the timer that GH0st had programmed to flash continuously once it reached the half-minute remaining mark.

Christ, stop chuffing about, Richard! Get on with it and grab what you need and scarper. Think consequences. Why risk everything? But his instinct caused him to believe this might be useful and he should still have time, just. After all, information contains power.

He furiously tapped the command to download only a small section of the enormous file so he could look at in more detail later.

Time to complete download: 26 seconds.

Richard knew that it was going to be very tight. He now quickly rehearsed what he needed to do once the download was complete. His index fingers nervously tapped on the desk.

Download complete.

3…

Delete the shadow mirror password file—Y or N?

He didn't think. Automatically his right finger pressed "Y." He didn't want that trace of G-H0st found. He typed in the final code of command and waited.

2…

Log Out—Y or N?

He quickly tapped "Y" and leant forward as if his presence would speed up the command.

1…

Goodbye,

Richard was expecting the computer's final command to say "Goodbye, Chuck Jelleners." Why had it omitted the name? The screen went blank just as the timer showed 0.

Had he made it just in time?

He stared at the pen and took some more deep breaths. He reached out his left hand, and when he picked it up, automatically its thin, three-legged stand retracted neatly and silently into the comfort of the streamlined fuselage of the pen.

He synched the pen with his iPhone so that during the cab journey tonight, he could look on his iPhone at the data he had just seen. He then put the pen into the holder in his briefcase. He grabbed the laminated card with Chuck's retinal scan and fingerprint that sat on his desk and slid over its covering case. He tapped it twice, two-thirds of the way from the top, and it locked itself. If it were opened by anyone, it would now simply reveal a small vanity mirror inside. His clandestine work was partially completed for the evening.

Within less than a minute, his heartbeat had dropped to 140.

The door of his office opened, and Sam's face appeared looking concerned.

"Sorry, I was just finishing something important. Everything all right?"

"There's some security chap to see you, Richard. He's waiting outside the office. Shall I show him in? He says it's terribly important. He's packing a gun also!"

CHAPTER 5
MOORGATE

How could they have caught me so soon? He started sweating again.
"Oh, um…sure…Just give me a sec, then show him in please, Sam."
"OK, sure."
Richard closed his briefcase, zipped it up, and put it to the side of his desk. He grabbed the "Diversity as a Driver of Business Performance: Unlocking the Hidden Mosaic" presentation folder resting on the cabinet next to his desk, opened it, and started writing a note on one of the slides in the deck.

In walked the security guard who then waited near the doorway. He coughed to get Richard's attention. Richard slowly looked up and smiled to acknowledge his presence. He saw he was wearing the standard VCb security department uniform of black trousers, crisp white shirt with a VCb blue clip-on tie, and his name badge stitched onto the breast pocket of his blazer. Richard didn't recognize him. Judging by the gap between the guard's head and the top of his office door, Richard guessed that he looked six inches shorter than he, but noticed that his tight-fitting blazer showed he was very muscular and broad. His blazer was not done up, and as he moved towards Richard's desk, it flowed open to reveal attached to his belt was a gun in its black holster, a small mace spray canister, and a short, compressed aluminum baton. He was someone to be in your corner and not to confront.

"Might I have a word with you, Mr. de L'Isle, sir?" said the guard in his Cornish accent, pronouncing "word" like "wurd."

"No problem, officer. What's up? I do hope it's quick, because I was planning to leave for the night in a few moments, if that's OK, as I have had a very long day." Richard closed the presentation and pushed it to the side of his desk and started reaching over for his briefcase.

The guard smiled back as he listened to Richard's middle-class accent, symptomatic to him as evidence of a good education and a privileged life with no financial stresses—completely opposite to his own upbringing and blue-collar life.

He glanced at Richard's suit jacket, which hung on a hanger on the door. It looked tailored and expensive. Richard's legs were crossed over each other and stretched out a foot or so beyond the long, glass-top table, revealing the large soles of his black lace-up shoes. On Richard's left hand was an expensive-looking watch, and certainly not a type the officer could afford. The officer also had experienced a very long day and now still had to work the night shift to earn extra money for his family. The officer thought, We all work hard in this environment. How he detested and resented the privileged people whom he was destined to protect.

"It's about an unidentified cyber security access on your PC, Mr. de L'Isle."

Richard's amygdala reverted to a higher level of alertness, but the tone of his voice remained calm. "Oh yes, officer? In what manner do you mean, exactly?"

The guard wasn't sure if he detected some nervousness about Richard, and for a split second wondered if he could make some mischief—the only real satisfaction he ever got in his job of servitude. Then he thought better of it: he was also tired and still had a long evening and morning ahead of him. Perhaps another time!

"I'm making the rounds on all the floors. Just making sure everyone still at their desks saw the e-mail memo we sent and remembered to power down their PCs, because we're doing a security penetration test on all of them in the department overnight, sir."

He saw Richard look concerned. "Purely routine, sir."

Richard exhaled, quietly. His tense muscles relaxed. "Oh, yes, I do remember. Will do it right now. Thanks for the reminder, appreciate it."

"Good night, sir."

"'Night, officer, and thanks again for popping by."

The guard left, and Sam popped his head around the door again. "Just wanted you to know that I'm headed off now. It's the night I play in the band, do you remember? Anything you need?"

"No, thanks. We're good. Of course I remember. Just have a great evening. I will be off myself, shortly. And good job today, Sam. This diversity PowerPoint presentation you did for me is looking great. Very professional job as always, my friend."

"Thanks. You OK, Richard?" Sam noticed Richard's face was still flushed since he had popped in a few minutes earlier.

"Nope, am fine. Just concerned about trying to leave here sharpish so that I am not late for my client meeting. But thanks for asking."

"OK, very good. See you tomorrow, Richard." Sam turned and closed the door behind him.

Richard's shoulders felt tight, and he could still feel the back of his collar absorbing the sweat from, and sticking to the back of, his hot neck. He loosened his tie, undid his top button, and ran two fingers inside his collar to free it from his neck. His head felt a slight throbbing at his temples, so he reached for his iPhone, selected the health app, and placed it to his neck. 0.2 ccs of salicylic acid stored in the phone entered his blood stream.

Within thirty seconds, the drug was latching onto and inhibiting the enzymes in his brain whose chemical reactions were causing the nerve endings to register pain.

The Feather of Truth — Ian Campbell-Laing

He looked at his watch. It was 6:40 p.m. Time to get going. He had an important dinner engagement with Rebecca, which he knew would be very awkward indeed.

CHAPTER 6
TEDDINGTON

Detective Chief Inspector Kofi Ghazini was trying to relax in his favorite armchair, next to the fireplace in his small Victorian cottage overlooking the river Thames. The cottage had been his parent's house. It was seven o'clock in the evening, and he had been on the go for nearly twenty-four hours. He was looking forward to tomorrow, Friday—his fortnightly weekday off.

It was a cold and windy evening outside, and he took solace in a large gulp of his favorite warm beer, Black Sheep from Masham in the North of England. He had nearly finished his second pint since arriving home half an hour ago. He then leant forward and selected a log from the copper vat and placed it on the top of the charred embers in the hearth. He sat back down and patiently watched for the fresh log to rise in temperature, devour the air, and release its orange light and heat. He had turned off the central heating in the room: he preferred the comfort of this natural source of warmth in the room. The smell of smoke added to the aroma of vanilla and almonds from his rare book collection housed in the bookcase behind him.

At his feet were his two rescue dogs, both nine-year-old buff-coloured cocker spaniels. Buffy, the male, had been found in a cold garage, shivering and whimpering at the back of his cage, lying in his own waste, abandoned a week earlier by his owner, who had gone on the run after murdering another gang member. Remy, the bitch, had been mistreated by her drug-dealing owner—she would bark incessantly, out of fear, if any person or dog approached her.

Whilst they adored Kofi's housekeeper, Mrs. Bates, who looked after them in the day, Buffy and Remy couldn't wait to be curled up and in deep sleep in the warmth and tranquility next to their master once he had finally, after a long day, come home to them.

"Hmm. Just another month until my three-month sabbatical, old things, and then we can spend all day walking and hiking to our hearts' content in Yorkshire," he said and reached down to stroke Buffy's head where it rested on his left foot, on which Kofi wore a bright-green-coloured sock. Buffy sighed contentedly at the gentle stroking of the fur on his back and the deep soothing voice of his master. Kofi did the same to Remy, who got up from her basket and licked the back of his hand, demanding more attention.

"Provided of course I can wrap up my last case—the Goldschmidt drowning." Then he smiled at the thought of the TV crime shows that depicted a detective solving just one crime at a time, and then all neatly within the allotted hour of the program. In reality, detectives were always working on at least a dozen crimes at the same time, with each taking many months, even years, or for some, decades to solve. It required a certain organized brain to segregate each case from another and then be able to unravel their different individual webs of deceit.

It also took a great strain on one's mind: seeing such horrific injuries, mutilated bodies, crimes against children and the elderly, and disturbing sex acts was difficult to forget. As a consequence, many homicide detectives suffered from post-traumatic stress disorder, or PTSD.

In addition to the Goldschmidt case, Kofi had been working on a dozen horrific murder cases, but the chief constable of the Surrey police force had insisted on reassigning all twelve of them to other detectives and recommended that Kofi take a sabbatical. Initially, his pride had caused him to resist, but after the chief hauled him into her office and explained her rationale, he backed down.

She had been always concerned about Kofi, but not because of his quirky personality—he was a loner and preferred to listen to opera or watch history and science documentaries rather than socialize; whilst always being immaculately dressed in expensive suits, he wore odd brightly coloured mismatched socks; and his unusually deep voice, coupled with his habit of occasionally without notice saying a drawn-out "hmm" before a sentence, often unnerved people.

Outwardly, whilst he always looked tired, he appeared to be coping: he displayed the mildest and most courteous manner, never raised his voice, and using his cerebral brain, had in the fourteen years since joining the force become the most successful of all her detectives in capturing and getting convictions for murder.

But after examining his caseload and recorded duty hours and reviewing his last annual medical and psychological examination, which revealed he suffered from many typical PTSD symptoms—disrupted sleep patterns, crime scene flashback nightmares, eating erratically, and drinking too much—she was now fearful of him burning out at only aged thirty-five, especially after his horrific personal tragedy five years ago, in the year 2020. Her responsibility was to help him.

CHAPTER 7
FRANKFURT, GERMANY

Five minutes earlier in Germany, the sixty-five-year-old global head of security for the German bank sat in his office. It was nine o'clock in the evening, and he had been at his desk since six o'clock that morning. As always, he didn't feel tired. Udo Wassermann had started reading a three-page automated e-mail sent from the V-Trax system: "Management Exceptions Report."

As he digested the details further, he realized the implications. "Oh mein Gott! Wie konnte diese Schicht Protokoll Verletzung geschehen?" he said out loud. *Oh my God! How could this layer of protocol breach have happened?*

"Die Quelle muss beseitigt werden," he said quietly to himself. *The source must be eliminated.*

He knew he had to contact his CEO immediately and set in motion swift retaliatory actions. He looked at his watch. Damn! He realized that his boss, Klaus was just about to attend a meeting with the finance cardinal at the Vatican.

Udo decided to text Klaus instead of calling him on his cell and leaving a voice message. The text message would be encoded and would appear as gibberish to anyone reading it other than its intended recipient. However, even if someone managed to hack into it and decode it, the English text would still seem innocuous and would simply be ignored by the reader or any system monitoring it.

Udo spoke softly with a hint of a German accent. "Cell phone command…Encrypt the following text to Doktor K's private cell…Start of message: Two boxes of Sigmund's eggshells appear cracked…trying to replace supplier…End of message."

CHAPTER 8
MOORGATE

As he walked towards the cylindrical barriers of dark blue tempered glass, Richard noticed that his headache had gone. A quick glance through the lens of his glasses showed his heartbeat and blood pressure were back to their low normal readings. His skin temperature was only slightly elevated, but he saw that his life expectancy forecast had shortened very slightly.

He stopped and, putting his bags down, reached up and redid the top button of his shirt and tightened his tie back into place.

He picked up his bags, then as he carried on walking he analyzed the events of the last half hour. He slowly nodded his head in concentration. Yes, it had been a close call, but G-H0st appeared to have logged out without detection just before zero seconds. Over the past few weeks, G-H0st had been analyzing Chuck's keystrokes pattern, so that when Richard typed normally, it translated them into mimicking Chuck's propensity to stab at and press down harder on the last letter of a sentence with his right index finger, and of course spelt words in the American and not the English manner. The only slight doubt in Richard's mind was why V-Trax hadn't confirmed Chuck's name when exiting.

He took a deep breath and exhaled quietly. As he approached the middle barrier, he stopped and placed his feet in the areas marked on the ground and, stooping down, placed the palm of his right hand face down on the top of the glass panel. Briefly looking up to his right at the oval-shaped camera lens protruding at the end of an aluminum stalk, he spoke in a firm voice into the microphone, "Richard de L'Isle."

His identity confirmed, swiftly and silently the protruding horizontal arms of the barriers withdrew on either side of him, allowing him to proceed towards the three, ten-foot-high revolving exit doors.

Once clear of the barriers, he ambled on heading as usual towards the middle exit. Also out of habit, he glanced to his left to view the middle of the three large plasma TV screens in the lobby, checking to see what was on the latest news from the BBC. The other two screens, Bloomberg and CNN, he ignored. Tonight on the BBC, the well-known, seasoned, and acerbic political reporter Kirsty Sackur was standing in front of the Houses of Parliament interviewing the leader of the Opposition, Bill Turnbull. The sound was on mute, but what caught Richard's eye were the words scrolling from right to left in the grey band at the bottom of the screen:

Police are still investigating the circumstances surrounding the death of triple gold medalist and ex-Olympic Swiss skier, Joachim Goldschmidt, who died a month ago after falling through a frozen pond which he was ice-skating on, near his home in Haslemere, Surrey.

It caused the muscles in his legs to become briefly paralyzed. He stopped, and knowing there were numerous cameras in the lobby, he deliberately in an almost seamless motion moved his body from leaning forward to bending down to untie and retie the laces of his right shoe. He did it slowly to allow his face to become recomposed on the thermal image recognition cameras. As he stood up, he reached for a handkerchief from his jacket breast pocket and blew his nose. He knew that if V-Trax detected a yellowish colour on his forehead or a blue-purple colour on the tip of his nose—signifying that those parts of his face were cooler due to the blood draining from his extremities—it might be interpreted as him being fearful, potentially due to a recent sudden shock or having committed a misdemeanor.

Oh my God! he thought. I wonder if they now think that it may not have been an accident? He knew the Goldschmidt family well: they were neighbours of his. The police had been around to Richard's house many times to question him and his wife about the death. Richard hadn't heard anything for a few weeks, so he simply assumed that the police had been satisfied with their answers.

***

At a secure, remote location, an updated record of Richard leaving the building's barriers had been automatically stored on a massive encrypted storage disk system, as it did for any movement or activity for all fifty thousand employees of, and visitors to, any of VCb's fifty offices around the world.

VCb's sophisticated surveillance and security protection system, V-Trax, knew everyone's movements and discussions. It tracked what time you entered and left the building, and video recorded you in the lifts and meeting rooms. Along with all other VCb's employees, Richard's keystrokes on his computer, e-mails, and text messages received and sent on both his business and private cell phones, and calls made on his home landline were closely monitored. V-Trax knew when, and for how long, you were at the water cooler, the staff canteen, the corporate gym, the photocopier, and even in the restrooms.

V-Trax had the capacity to store forty terabytes, forty trillion bytes of data, in its one-hundred-square-foot computer rooms located in two separate, secret, bombproof locations: each storing the equivalent data to cover a million four-drawer office filing cabinets.

Richard briefly scanned the words on the TV screen rushing to enlighten the audience, and which had changed to:

Tensions heighten between Great Britain and Iran after Prime Minister Malcolm Quigley refuses to retract his statement criticizing Iran's new nuclear enrichment program.

And then to the more mundane and titillating:
Manchester United striker Ryan Cathedralis to take DNA test in love-child paternity scandal.

Richard enjoyed constructing anagrams of people's names and wondered if he could come up with something amusing for the philandering, overpaid footballer. After a few minutes he quietly whispered to himself. "Let's see…Arachnids Reality…Nope, no good." Then, "Carnal Ready Shit. Partly OK but not quite!" Soon he came up with, Randy Chaste, Liar…Nope, definitely not chaste." Finally he had it. "Here you go, this is more apt, Randy Liar, Cheats."

Richard didn't see any more references to the ongoing Goldschmidt investigation, but all of a sudden, he became distracted by what the reporter was holding in her hand. Given the advances in technology over the last decade, he was surprised to see her clutching an old-fashioned, oversized microphone with the letters "BBC" facing the camera.

Richard recalled that long gone were the days when one could only use a keyboard to type on, or a mouse to click, or simply a finger to touch a screen, in order to activate the computer into obeying your instructions.

Then came the "voice induced technology" era, which, in its infancy, used a basic iPhone Siri app that allowed one to speak simple commands like "Find me the nearest bar still open." Later, as a follow-up, that person's friend might say, "Find me the nearest hospital. Emergency here. Guy passed out completely drunk in the gutter."

After that, there was the novelty of creating a Word document simply by speaking into the microphone above a computer screen.

But now the world was at a crossroads, the dawn of a new age. The public would soon be able to control their laptops and desktop computers simply by "thought induced technology," which was becoming ever more advanced and available.

Richard recalled only recently that his wife, like many people, seemed shocked about this prospect happening so soon. Many were fearful of its implications. *Brave New World*. Big Brother. Conspiracy theories. It went on and on.

He remembered the conversation he had recently had with his wife. "Jens, actually, I'm surprised it's taking so long! Remember, it was over twenty years ago at the University of Minnesota, in America, that the boffins rigged up some electrodes onto the head of a helicopter pilot. He was able to fly a virtual helicopter in a 3D landscape screen by using *just* his

The Feather of Truth   Ian Campbell-Laing

own thoughts."

"Are you saying that soon a pilot will be able to fly a real helicopter, or God forbid, the plane that will take us to Zimbabwe for our safari holiday, just by *thinking* about it, while doing the crossword and having his first-class cheese-board lunch?" asked Jennifer.

"Yes, it will happen sooner than later, and it's really not such a leap of technology. Don't you remember when I told you about the soldier many years ago who stepped on an IED in Helmand in Afghanistan and had one of his legs blown off below the knee?"

"Yes, I think so. The IED was some sort of landmine, wasn't it?"

"Yes, it was an improvised explosive device, which is just a fancy name for a homemade landmine. Well, he subsequently had the latest high-tech prosthetic leg fitted. He was blindfolded and fitted with headphones listening to music, so he wouldn't be able see or identify any outside noise. He was asked to describe the feeling as he put that leg into three different buckets. He correctly identified what was in each bucket from the feeling alone."

"Yes, Richard, I recall watching the documentary with you on the Science Channel. The first contained hot sand; the second, freezing cold water with ice cubes; and the last one had a warm treacle-like liquid, or something like that, right?"

"Absolutely. The soldier's perception was amazing. He said he could *feel* the individual grains of hot sand flowing over the toes of his prosthetic foot, no different to when he put in his other natural foot!"

Yes, continued Richard in his thoughts as he now started to walk towards the exit. but what was even more remarkable was that the soldier's thoughts as he placed his foot into the separate buckets were beginning to be "understood" by the computer. The neurological brainwaves flowing from the solider through the electrodes attached to his skull were being decoded, and his actual thoughts were being displayed as words on the computer screen next to him—albeit crudely and not entirely accurately.

So, not only do we have e-mail, texting, Facebook, and tweeting that reveal our actions to whoever wants to read them, coupled with GPS on our mobile phones that knows our precise physical location, but soon with some more advanced technology, even our private thoughts, our secrets, would eventually be known to anyone who wanted access. And, remotely—without being hooked up to a computer. You won't know whose reading your thoughts or when!

When that day came for the general public, and it would come very soon, it was going to be mind-boggling with the terrible truth that one would not be able to think a lie privately without a computer recording and publicizing it. There would be no secrets, and nothing would be sacred. There would be no place to hide.

The Feather of Truth   Ian Campbell-Laing

He said quietly to himself, and sighed, "What a terrible thought." He then remembered the password of, and warning to, potential hackers into V-Trax: "Nowhere to hide." For many people in this new age of totalitarianism, this was the unwelcome face of capitalism, and already an unacceptable intrusion into one's civil liberties. Many thought the world was now at a crisis level. Lawsuits proliferated against such "evil" corporations that were deemed to have gone too far in "spying" on their employees and on stakeholders.

The German bank where Richard worked, Volks-Commerzbank—the People's Commercial Bank—was always referred to simply as VCb. Founded in the fifteenth century, it was one of the oldest and most respected European banks.

VCb was now casting off its previous conservative image and breaking ground in innovation, in its attempt to become the premier global bank in the world. It was eager to subjugate its aggressive American, British, Dutch, and Swiss competitors. But it had recently taken on more risk than some would deem appropriate or acceptable and had been admonished severely around the world by some of its banking regulators. It also had three cases of individual privacy law violations pending trial. Naturally, VCb intended to challenge these allegations vigorously using its considerable legal armory. If necessary, VCb would settle out of court, without admitting any guilt, and more importantly, without any details of its secrets getting into the public domain.

VCb's chief executive officer, Dr. Klaus Becker, knew that Udo had installed the V-Trax system worldwide without employees being aware of it. Klaus had felt compelled to have such a system, not just because of the near-fatal injury of a high-profile VCb client in the foyer of the London office building some five years earlier, but also because he wanted VCb to have total control over all of its employees and clients.

Udo also had all the glass at the bank be replaced by tempered glass, which is made at high temperatures that put the outer surfaces into compression and the inner surfaces into tension. Such stresses cause the glass, when broken, to crumble into small granular chunks instead of splintering into jagged shards. These granular chunks are less likely to cause injury. The perpetrator of the near-fatal injury was a young man with a history of mental health issues who had got caught up in an anticapitalist demonstration by a mob of disgruntled students. Had this information been known on the day in question, the perpetrator would not have been allowed access into the building.

The cameras above the access areas in the London lobby of the bank not only took a picture of the face of each person entering and leaving the VCb building, but by using the latest software, also examined four areas unique to all people: their iris, retinal profile, fingerprint, and footprint.

The Feather of Truth   Ian Campbell-Laing

Then through accessing worldwide databases, they were thus able to confirm the individual's precise identity. Additionally, with thermal imaging and physiological software, they hoped this should prevent potential nefarious behavior.

In addition, a year ago, V-Trax had secretly introduced a revolutionary module of biometric screening, which was hidden inside the entryway barriers. This produced a holographic 3D image of one's body. These were much more detailed than those present at major airports and government institutions, which used to show the person's near-naked and often unflattering outline, along with any metal objects. These biometric images were also stored within the V-Trax database.

Udo had assured Klaus that the V-Trax system was completely secret, with its data and images undetectable by anyone. However, the design of the system was not complicated, and based on the fact that information of whatever type always creates its own unique magnetic field, V-Trax then simply generated an equal and opposite field every one-hundredth of a millisecond to counteract the current information's polarity, causing the information to appear invisible when viewed by outsiders.

What Klaus and Udo did not know was that Richard's G-H0st system had identified the polarity timing difference and could view the information.

However, Richard was not aware that the only other person who had ever hacked into V-Trax and got past the all-important second firewall level had died rather unexpectedly on that very same day, in what initially appeared to be suicide. The police suspected foul play, but the case was eventually closed for lack of direct evidence.

CHAPTER 9
BLACKDOWN CLOSE, HASLEMERE, SURREY, ENGLAND

Jennifer de L'Isle had just finished reading to her two young sons their favorite bedtime story, *The Gruffalo*, and was now in the kitchen helping her eldest, James, with his homework. As expected, it was a battle to get him to focus on studying at home in the evening after school. She and Richard had discussed sending him to boarding school, to let the faculty deal with the hassle of homework and the exhaustion of trying to maintain discipline over a nine-year-old.

Jennifer Granville had met, or, more correctly, clashed with Richard de L'Isle at Oxford University; both were members of the Union's debating society, and they had taken opposing views on "This House believes that it is acceptable to use torture to obtain information from suspected terrorists." She won the debate with her opposing arguments.

When he had asked her out on a date, she hesitated, even though he was clearly an excellent catch: strikingly handsome and athletic, well over six feet tall, softly spoken, attentive, and a self-deprecating acerbic wit. But, he had a reputation of being unfaithful.

However, his charm soon disarmed her fears, and they became soul mates. When she witnessed at social events him ignoring flirtatious advances from other women, she concluded that he was trustworthy and the unfaithful rumors were unfounded, and probably created by her jealous rivals.

Jennifer came from a wealthy family who could trace their lineage back to the Norman Conquest of the year 1066. Her ancestors had settled in Cornwall and were handsomely rewarded with a castle and vast acres of land for their support of King William the Conqueror. Relatively speaking, Richard came from more humble and less aristocratic stock, albeit a very comfortably well-off family.

After gaining an upper first-class honors in English literature, Jennifer went to work as a trainee in marketing. A few years later, she and Richard married, and she soon fell pregnant. After having her first child with Richard, she never returned to the work force, preferring to play an active role in bringing up her children, and determined to earn their love and friendship through being there for them when it mattered. She planned on returning to the workforce when they weren't dependent on her.

For the last few years, she hadn't been remotely interested in any intimacy with Richard, which initially concerned her—especially when Richard had complained. But now it didn't bother her, and anyway, Richard hadn't pursued the topic again; he seemed to have accepted it as well. All well and good, she thought, because after a long day, the last thing she wanted to do was get all hot and sweaty with Richard and have to sleep in the damp patch of the bed.

She was comforted also, after reading an article that said, "A lack of interest in sex after producing kids is a common occurrence due to the hormonal changes women experience." But, the same article also mentioned that during this period in a woman's life, it was often accompanied with the feeling of being depressed.

Was she depressed? She wasn't sure. She couldn't see why she should be. She had a charmed life compared to most and was grateful for what she had. She was wealthy, lived in a manor house in a gated community, and had all the modern appliances. She drove a new Range Rover Evoque and went on expensive holidays. She recalled, when Richard and she were first married, the drudgery of doing the weekly grocery shopping. Now, when her fridge, freezer, or pantry detected that an item was running low, it immediately ordered it from the supermarket, and then within the hour through an inbuilt 3D printer, it appeared automatically in its assigned space in the appliance or cupboard. However, Jennifer wasn't yet convinced that the taste of the 3D printed edible product was yet as good as the real thing. Her house cleaned itself through an elaborate network of ducts that transported the dust to an external rubbish site underground, which, when combined with the soil, produced compost, which automatically was transported to the area of the garden that needed it. Windows were coated with a film that prevented smearing and never needed cleaning. And the age of folding one's clean clothes was now over – one simply placed the wrinkled clothes in a machine and a few hours later they came back neatly folded. Also, driverless cars were now the norm, the main obstacle being just getting used to not being in control of your car.

It seemed that she didn't have to lift a finger. But, to Jennifer that wasn't the point. She was exhausted looking after her three boys and never seemed to have much time for herself. She craved intellectual stimulation, but when Richard got home after work—and increasingly later each week—he was too exhausted to talk much.

Her best friend, Isabelle, had become concerned about Jennifer and had suggested she see a doctor, saying it may be something as simple as a vitamin deficiency, or wheat intolerance, or alternatively something more serious. But Jennifer stubbornly refused to see one.

When Isabelle asked her how many times did she and Richard "do it," Jennifer was initially too embarrassed to own up, so she lied and said, "A few times a week, I guess." Isabelle had seen through it all and said, "Jennifer, what tosh! You are the worst fibber!" She then confided in Isabelle that that side of the relationship was nonexistent. Isabelle had warned her that it wasn't healthy to have no sex life, and that Richard would easily be able to find physical solace elsewhere. Jennifer had told her most emphatically that Richard was too honorable a man and trustworthy to have an affair, and dismissed the idea completely. "We certainly don't have any secrets between us, that's for sure!"

All Isabelle had replied was *"Per-lease!* He's a man, for heaven's sake."

However, she had wondered why Richard had to attend all these dinners. It seemed to have been only in the last few months that he was coming home increasingly later, and more often than not, staying in town at his club, the RAC. She just assumed that it was part of his job as he became more senior.

Instead, what was concerning her most, presently, was the last visit at her home by the African detective chief inspector.

CHAPTER 10
MOORGATE

As he walked towards the revolving doors, the tiny microphone implanted near his ear picked up the sound of the signal of an incoming call: *Wife, home.*

He slowed down and spoke: "Cell phone, accept call."

"Hi, Jens, sweetheart, how's it going? You've not forgotten I'm seeing a client tonight, right, Sir James Campbell? I'll be staying in town, as it may be a late night."

"Nope, Richard, I remember."

"OK, good. How are the little terrorists today?"

"The boys are fine, Richard, albeit a handful as always."

Richard heard his wife give out a long sigh. "What's up, Jens. Everything all right?"

"Not really. Just wanted to say that the police were around our house again about the Goldschmidt drowning…"

Richard stopped walking, stood upright, and shook his head. "What on earth do they want with you again? Didn't you tell them what we discussed—that you found the poor man lying face down in the freezing water? You even called the police, for Pete's sake, to alert them!"

"Yes, I did. But they now have a new detective on the case. DCI Kofi Ghazini, who's outwardly amiable, very cerebral like *Inspector Morse*, but a persistent Rottweiler, just like that detective series *Columbo*. He asked me to go through my statement again. Apparently, a couple of things didn't stack up. He said he had talked to Mrs. Goldschmidt, who mentioned that our two families had a falling out last year. He wanted to know why I hadn't put that down in my statement."

"My God, Jens, didn't you tell him that it was over a stupid, silly dispute about an overgrown leylandii hedge that blocked the sun in our garden, and which they refused to chop down?"

"Yes, of course I told him that. Richard, I'm nervous…what if they really think—"

He interrupted her. "Well, don't you worry, Jens. It's good that they are being thorough. But I can't think why they would think it was anything other than an unfortunate accident. Especially after what we told them."

"Richard, I would prefer it if you were here with me if they question me again. Promise me you'll do that, OK?"

"Of course, Jens. Want me to call Policeman Plod right now and get him off your back?"

"OK. If you want, but remember to be polite, Richard."

The Feather of Truth   Ian Campbell-Laing

He heard her sigh again. "What else is up, Jens? I sense something is bothering you."

"Well, to be honest, I am finding the kids terribly hard work each day. I wish you could come home earlier to help me out."

"Jens, I know it's not easy. Let's talk about it over the weekend and see what I can do to help out more. You know you are the perfect mother and wife, don't you?"

"Well, I certainly don't feel perfect. I never seem to have a moment to myself; instead I am just running around for you boys. I just don't have a life anymore."

"Look, we talk about it this weekend. OK?"

"OK Have fun tonight at dinner with Sir James, and see you tomorrow, darling."

"Bye, Jens, will do. Cell phone: Call over."

As he continued towards the exit, he noticed a VCb uniformed security guard approaching him. His pulse started to rise again. This security guard looked more official and senior than the one that popped by his office a few minutes ago. He appeared to be around the same age as Richard. On his VCb badge, which he wore on his dark blue blazer, it read,

Paul Ruggiere
Head of Security, London

"Excuse me, sir, would you mind if I had a word with you? Please follow me into this room over here. It will be more private in there."

Richard initially smiled at the absurd reference to "more private." VCb staff, only a couple of years earlier, had moved into brand-new, award-winning premises. Similar to the Bloomberg and Google offices, the theme was open-plan spaces and glass-walled, see-through meeting rooms with different-coloured soft lighting. Richard raised his voice, leaned forward, and stared at the officer. "What, again? Why me? I'm in a rush to attend an important client dinner engagement for the bank."

"Sir, please, it should only take a moment."

"If this is a security check, why pick me? I was searched less than a month ago! I understood this process was meant to be totally random. This is quite ridiculous, officer."

How much do they really know? He wondered. He could feel his temperature rising as blood rushed to his face. His chest felt tight, and his hands moist. He walked slowly and took deep breaths. He prayed that he hadn't inadvertently left any incriminating documents in his briefcase, or that the V-Trax system had caught his presence that final second before he logged out.

"Follow me, sir. Yes, in here," said the officer as he motioned Richard through a yellow glass doorway. Richard stooped slightly to ensure his head cleared the top of the doorframe.

Inside the room was a row of CCTV cameras' images and stacks of multiple computer screens. There was also a security-screen machine on a long table with a conveyor belt.

"Can you take off your overcoat, please, and put it in this tray? Then remove any metal objects like your belt, mobile phone, car keys, coins—the usual stuff—and place them in this smaller tray here."

Richard bent down to place his treasured Coach Metropolitan calf-leather briefcase and old-school black overnight bag at the end of the table and then did as instructed.

"Please, now raise your arms out wide horizontally, sir, so I can scan you. It will only take a moment." Richard discreetly brushed the palms of his hands on his trouser legs to remove the surplus sweat. He looked to his left outside the meeting room, and noticed that no one was looking inside the room. Random searches happened almost every ten minutes or so and had become the norm, just like the security checks at airports.

The officer's hands swiftly patted Richard's clothing. He then waved his portable scanner methodically, covering Richard's entire body.

"Please place your briefcase under this screen so we can scan it next…Thank you."

The guard saw Richard reach out for a plastic container.

"No need to put the briefcase in the container, sir. You can put it straight on these rollers please."

"Actually, there is. It's a very expensive present, and I don't want it ruined by putting it on these rollers, which may be dirty, if that's OK?"

"As you wish, sir." The guard sighed. Terse people like Richard made his job unpleasant but caused him to be more diligent and thorough than he otherwise would have been. He went behind a computer screen and examined the image.

The guard said nothing. He's taking a long time, thought Richard. Then the guard placed the briefcase back on the table in front of Richard.

"Can you open your briefcase for me? Then step aside and allow me to check inside it, please."

"Sure, if you are quick," Richard snapped back a little too quickly. Then he softened his tone. "Like I said, I do have a client of the bank waiting for me." He stepped forward and unfastened the lock of the briefcase and stepped back.

The guard rifled through the contents. "Aha. What's this, then?" he said.

CHAPTER 11
MOORGATE

Richard tried to keep a blank look of being slightly bored. "Sorry, officer, what's the problem exactly?"

"This silver pen in one of the holders in your briefcase. Looks very familiar."

"Does it? It looks perfectly ordinary to me. It's my usual fountain pen, given to me as a present from my wife. Want me to call her up and waste her time and ask her where she bought it?" He hoped his changed mood of increasing irritation hid his nervousness.

"No need to be tetchy, sir. I am entitled to ask." He took it out of its holder and examined it. "Yes, thought so. Looks like a spy pen to me."

Richard laughed loudly and shook his head. "A what? You've been watching too many James Bond or Johnny English films, for Pete's sake, old chap!"

"Not at all. In my line of business, we see many gadgets. And this looks like a very sophisticated pen that is also used to record sound. And let me see…On the side near the top is what looks like a pinhead-sized camera to video record. I'm sure I've seen such a model before…Yes, I think it's a Segreto. Probably the P60X model, isn't it?" He started to examine it more closely.

Richard raised his voice. "Look here, that's a very expensive present. If you damage it, I will personally sue you and the bank, and make sure you will be collecting your own P60 redundancy form after you have been fired."

The security guard wasn't the slightest bit intimidated, and he thought Richard's change of tone might be due to him hiding something. The guard had an important job to do in protecting the bank's assets, and rich people like Richard, with their public school accents, would be treated like any other regular employee. He remained calm and continued, "Out of interest, sir, why would you keep your pen in your briefcase, instead of the inside pocket of your jacket like most other men?"

"It's my favorite fountain pen and one I use for special occasions like signing important documents or making notes when attending senior meetings. For regular stuff, I use my other pen, which happens to be in my inside jacket." He reached inside his jacket and pulled out his plastic Bic Biro.

The officer looked closer at the silver fountain pen. Inscribed on the side, it read, *To Richard, All my love, Jens*

He then held it in his hand. "I think I should take this into custody for examination, sir."

"OK, here's the deal," said Richard, stepping forward and invading the guard's personal space. "Your random program has now stopped me for a physical search three times in the last two months. Statistically, an employee would be searched randomly no more than once every two years. And now you wish to take my wife's anniversary present, which cost a small fortune, but more importantly, has great sentimental value to me. I think it's best that I file a complaint for harassment against the bank in general, and you in particular. I will make it my duty to have you fired, if I do nothing else. So think very carefully about your next action tonight, officer. I would like to have your name, title, and bank employee number, and to whom you report."

The security officer held the pen in his right hand and thought for a moment, deliberately taking his time. He had a much better idea.

"OK, sir. You win. There's nothing illegal about having such a toy in the public domain, but I am formally warning you that it is totally illegal to use it at VCb or while conducting business for the bank. It would be against the human resources code of conduct. So I'd be careful if I were you. That's all I will say for now."

Richard rolled his eyes. "You are mistaken, officer, it's an ordinary pen. That's all it is. But thank you for the advice, should I ever buy such an instrument."

The security guard pushed the briefcase towards Richard, allowing him to lock it up, and handed Richard back his fountain pen, which Richard promptly slid it into the outer breast pocket of his suit jacket.

"Happier now that it's in my jacket pocket, officer?"

"Whatever pleases you, sir. And now your overnight bag, please. Please unzip it for me."

Richard lifted the bag from the floor where he had left it. It was his old favorite black Fred Perry plastic holdall that he had had at boarding school. He placed it next to his briefcase and unzipped it, and then stepped back with a loud sigh.

The guard peered inside and then said, "OK, nothing out of the ordinary in there. You are free to leave. Mr. de L'Isle, please enjoy your client dinner and the rest of your evening."

"Out of interest, if this is a random check and I have no name badge on my lapel, how do you know my name?"

"When you go through the turnstiles, the system confirms your ID using various sources, including the data stored in the microchip implanted in the back of your neck. I noticed your identity only *after* the computer's random number generation system picked you out."

"How convenient. If I am searched again in the next six months, I will make a formal complaint, do you hear?"

"Absolutely. I will be happy to then give you the personal e-mail address of the bank's head of security, Mr. Udo Wasserman, to whom I report. Like I said, enjoy your evening."

Richard picked up his belongings and turned to leave. The security guard walked ahead of him and held open the glass door for him.

"Thank you, officer, that's *very* kind of you."

"No, thank *you*, sir."

Richard detected the sarcasm, and after he had exited the room, he smirked and said under his breath, "Faggot."

With a smile, the guard thought, Faggot, eh? Well, let's see we can have some fun. He reached into his pocket and took out his cell phone.

CHAPTER 12
MOORGATE

Richard left the security room frowning. He walked through one of the heavy bullet-and bombproof revolving doors, which opened automatically. He stepped outside into the darkening light: the sun would be setting in half an hour. For April, it was unseasonably cold, with below-freezing temperatures. He pulled his unbuttoned overcoat tightly across his chest and bent forward into the wind.

He spotted a cab about fifty yards away on the opposite side of the road and held out his right arm and waited. The driver saw him, flashed his headlights, made a sharp U-turn in the street and headed towards him. The cab stopped within a few feet of where he stood.

Richard glanced at his watch, 6:50 p.m. and cursed quietly to himself. *That jobsworth security guard delayed me twelve minutes. Now, I only have ten minutes to get to my club, a journey that will probably take about twenty minutes.*

His iPhone pinged. Richard glanced at the message from the travel app.

Cab Journey ETA RAC 19:07 hrs.

As the cabbie wound down his window, Richard stepped forward. "The Royal Automobile Club in Pall Mall, please, and as quick as you can, mate. I'm running a tad late. Appreciate it if you can see your way to getting there as near to seven as you can."

Richard opened the passenger door, bent down, and climbed in. He closed the door and slumped back into the rear seat. The warmth of the cab felt comforting. He briefly closed his eyes and gave out a loud long sigh.

"Sure, RAC, Pall Mall…I'll get you there pronto," replied the cabbie as he put the car into manual mode so that he could drive it quicker himself. They headed west towards London Wall.

Richard opened his eyes, took out his iPhone, and scanned the information contained within the first client file he had downloaded from V-Trax.

Richard's mouth opened slightly, and his head bent forward as he scrutinized the one-page summary about his boss, Chuck. The *financial wealth* section contained detailed information about his worldwide income and expenditure for the last five years, his global portfolio of stocks and bonds, the current value of his three houses, his investments in vineyards and hotels, and the amounts of his previous four divorce settlements.

Chuck's *medical record history* showed he had arrhythmias (an abnormal heart rhythm), some local-stage prostate cancer, and both dyslexia and dyscalculia. He drank to excess frequently, had a taste for expensive wines, and regularly smoked large, difficult-to-obtain Cuban cigars. He also occasionally smoked marijuana. His life expectancy was actuarially calculated at sixty-five, which meant he only had at most eight years left to live.

Amazing, thought Richard. How did someone with the reading disability of dyslexia, coupled with the more uncommon dyscalculia, which was a similar affliction for numbers, ever get so far up the ladder at VCb as a global chief operating officer? No doubt Chuck had something on his own boss, Celsius. Maybe some embarrassing secret that Celsius didn't want revealed. Interesting.

The *leverage* section listed Chuck's marital affairs, past and present. He was currently having an affair with his secretary in New York where he spent half his time, and also with a woman in London who worked as a stripper. It mentioned that Chuck had lied on his resume by embellishing his qualifications and achievements, and he had physically assaulted his current wife.

Chuck's file mentioned Richard's own name once in passing, simply as stating him as the most senior of five of Chuck's direct reports.

Christ Almighty! Richard thought. Clearly, VCb could use the personal information in the leverage section for its own financial gains.

Richard then opened the second file he had downloaded and scanned the one-page summary of Her Majesty Queen Elizabeth II, who had died unexpectedly the previous year.

Richard knew that it was fairly common knowledge that the royal family had German ancestry, but the revelations about the extent of their sympathizing with the Nazis and their relatives being members of the SS were astonishing to Richard. Not to mention that one previous high-ranking royal had, allegedly, written romantic letters to a senior member of the SS, the so-called "Vicky love letters."

Finally, Richard turned to the last client he had downloaded: US president John Fitzgerald Kennedy.

"Bloody hell!" he said aloud, as he read the endless list of women with whom JFK had had affairs, allegedly of course. How did he find time to run the country?

He then read the section in the file about the evening before JFK was assassinated. How Lyndon Baines Johnson met with Dallas tycoons, FBI moguls, and organized crime heads, and later that night apparently said to his mistress, Melanie Duncan Brown, "After tonight, those Kennedy sons of bitches will never embarrass me again!"

And as we all know, within a few hours after the assassination, LBJ was sworn in as the next president of the United States.

But how on earth could V-Trax know this? he wondered. Most of this

The Feather of Truth   Ian Campbell-Laing

was not in the public domain. V-Trax seemed to be as powerful as the FBI was to the US government. "Good God, what have I stumbled upon?" he said out loud.

The cabbie ignored his outburst, judging Richard to be a punter who liked privacy and didn't want to chat. But Richard admonished himself, realizing he'd better be careful about what he said in public about V-Trax.

Richard powered down his iPhone and put it back into his jacket. He had done enough work for one day. Now, he needed to think of the implications of what he had done.

He had seen within V-Trax, before he logged out, the size of the client file: over one gigabyte. That meant it contained the equivalent of around a million of these one-page-per-client summaries he had just read. With only fifty thousand employees, that left an awful lot of files on so-called "clients."

He knew VCb would do anything to keep this secret. If anyone in the public domain saw this information, VCb would face a crisis and lose all public confidence. That could bring the bank down very quickly. And given the size and importance of VCb, it would have a systemic effect on the financial system as a whole. And Richard of course had stock in the bank, so the last thing he wanted to do was cause the bank to fail and have his stock and pension assets rendered worthless.

Obviously, if anyone at the bank ever found out that he had hacked into the system, he would have his own crisis.

He then recalled JFK having one of the most demanding times of any presidency. JFK had observed during the Cuban missile crisis, at the height of the American-Russian Cold War in the 1960s, that when written in Chinese, the word "crisis" was composed of two characters, 危機, pronounced "wei" and "ji." Wei represented danger, and ji, opportunity.

While some employees and clients would view V-Trax actions as an intrusion into their civil liberties and as a crisis, Richard saw it as an opportunity. Sure, he knew of his own crisis and the danger he would face if he were caught hacking into the system, especially after seeing such personal data about his boss, the British monarchy and an ex-US president. But knowing this information existed was an immense opportunity for him, and with his expert IT knowledge, he planned on using this all to his advantage.

But, his first plan was to use the data he had already obtained about his annoying American boss, Chuck, and getting the revenge he bitterly sought.

Back in the taxi, Richard was glad that the cabbie was not the typical driver who wanted to ramble on and on and have a good chat or impart his political views on his passengers. He was also relieved to not be forced to listen to annoying music or to watch show idiotic TV programs in the back of the cab during the journey. He wanted the sound of silence to clear his mind after a very long day, albeit a successful one: the project he was working on for Chuck was taking shape nicely and would please Chuck.

What was also pleasing Richard was that tonight he would take a break from work and relax with Rebecca Falconer at his favorite venue, the Great Gallery restaurant, at his club, the RAC.

Rebecca was an American in her late thirties. She had shoulder-length, silk-to-the-touch, naturally fair hair. She wore it combed back and was always immaculately and appropriately dressed. She was five feet ten inches tall with a slim face, high cheekbones, and had just a hint of laughter lines around her mouth that gave a distinguished look to her natural beauty. She had a clever wit, a sensuous, tanned and toned body, and a sharp intellect. She was also, like Richard, very stubborn.

He smiled at the thought of spending quality time with her again: an intellectually stimulating dinner with exquisite food and fine wines, followed by the exhausting and adventurous intimacy that always flowed between them afterwards. But he frowned at what he needed to do tonight. He knew that by having this affair, he was risking a great deal.

Richard could not have predicted how events would unravel tonight, and that he would have to face his own crisis in a most brutal manner.

***

Teddington

Back in his cottage, Kofi was also facing his own crisis: last night's flashback was also a brutal affair—it was a recurring nightmare, where he was slumped sitting down on the floor with his back against two of the kitchen cabinets. He held a beautiful woman tightly in his arms. She had been shot point blank in the face. His white shirt and trousers felt cold and heavy, weighed down by her red blood. The police were on their way, but he knew it was too late.

He recognised her attacker, and he had failed completely in his promise to protect her.

CHAPTER 13
THE APOSTOLIC PALACE
VATICAN CITY STATE, ITALY

Nine hundred miles from Moorgate, VCb's CEO was patiently waiting for the finance cardinal to arrive. The tiny microphone implanted in his ear pinged quietly, alerting him to a message on his most private cell phone. Klaus frowned as he took his cell phone from the breast pocket of his expensive suit, and his lips tensed together; very few people had access to this phone, and it was only to be used in an emergency. The message read,

> Two boxes of Sigmund's eggshells appear cracked…trying to replace supplier.

He breathed in quickly, briefly held his breath, and then sighed loudly as he expelled the air. He understood the message and its implications, perfectly. Udo had given the nickname Sigmund to the V-Trax operating system because, in German, the Christian name Sigmund meant "victorious protector." Their precious system was designed to protect the bank and make it flourish financially. The reference to the eggshells related to the security system of firewalls around V-Trax, and "cracked" signified that part of the system's protocol had been breached. The reference to two boxes corresponded to a level two alert.

Klaus recalled that Udo had studied many government terrorist threat security systems, which typically had five levels of alert. The American Homeland Security Advisory System (HSAS) had used a colour-coded system of

green (low risk),
blue (guarded risk),
yellow (elevated risk),
orange (high risk), and
red (severe risk).

These were similar to the UK government's Secret Service MI5's Joint Terrorism Analysis Centre system of

low (unlikely any risk),
moderate (possible risk, but not likely),
substantial (strong possibility of a risk),
severe (a risk highly likely), and
critical (imminent risk danger).

Udo had designed the bank's own system of alertness for dealing with breaches of the V-Trax system. It was incredibly simple, and most effective. It had a base "noise" level, with only two higher levels. The base level was assigned the letter "D," which indicated that the system had detected a de minimus scratching at its surface: similar to when someone tries a four-digit PIN password, and after the third failed attempt, is locked out of the system. It was treated as only "irritating noise," but even this resulted in swift, harsh actions by V-Trax against the intruder.

The middle level, "E," was termed "elevated" and arose when the system's outer series of firewalls were breached and someone or something had gained access within the first key layer of the system. At this level, the hacker would not have seen anything highly confidential or been able to copy any files. This was a serious breach, but not critical.

The highest level, "I" or "imminent," indicated that the core layer had been breached and important data had been compromised, including copying, altering, or downloading of sensitive files. The system's barriers and firewalls were designed to ensure that a level "I" would never occur.

The three levels D, E, I spelled "DEI," which was the Latin for "of God." As Udo had remarked to Klaus, "If we have a level three, I, alert, then *Dei Manus*!" We were now in God's hands!

V-Trax reported each month a handful of level D alerts, as hackers used innovative methods to try and gain access to the system, mainly for fun and the intellectual thrill. But even at this relatively unimportant level, V-Trax was ruthless: it automatically created a mirror-virus code that swiftly caused the hacker's rogue virus to self-destruct. Then V-Trax unleashed its own newly created antimatter virus, Ares-X—named after the Greek god of war—back to the source, to wreak havoc on the user's operating system. It also anonymously alerted the authorities that they had been the target of hacking and serious money-laundering breaches and gave them the details of the hackers. So far, that had caused those hackers to never try and breach the system again.

V-Trax had only once before reported the middle level, E, elevated code status alert. That hacker was Jonathan James, an American who operated under the name "c0mrade," and then in 2000, as a bored teenager he managed to break into the American government's Defense Threat Reduction Agency (DTRA) computer system, for which he served a prison sentence.

Later, when he came out of prison, he hacked into VCb's V-Trax system, and in 2008, his clever virus appeared to have easily outsmarted V-Trax's levels D and E status alert both at the same time. He had breached the main firewall and was trying to download confidential client financial data, but V-Trax's sophisticated system was one step ahead of him: it cleverly diverted his virus to look at dummy data, and reported to Jonathan,

Downloading in progress
Time to completion: twenty-three minutes.

The Feather of Truth　　　　　　　　　　　Ian Campbell-Laing

A clock showed the countdown and gave Jonathan a false sense of security. V-Trax was not downloading any files to Jonathan's PC at all, but rapidly creating the antimatter virus that would in fifteen minutes cause his rogue virus to self-destruct and destroy everything on his PC. During this time, it also alerted Udo to the details of the computer Jonathan was using, including its real Internet protocol, or IP address. It then used its state-of-the-art, built-in satellite navigation system and algorithms that cross-referenced to data of known black hat criminal hackers. This had tracked the computer down to the physical address, and indeed the exact room, of the actual house where Jonathan was living in South Florida.

Udo's extensive global contacts were able to get to Jonathan's house thirteen minutes later, just as Jonathan realized that V-Trax's own Ares-X-created virus was perversely and silently attacking Jonathan's own computer system.

Later that morning, an unidentified call was made to the police, alerting them of a gunshot sound. When they arrived at Jonathan's home, it appeared that he had committed suicide from a self-inflicted gunshot wound earlier that morning.

From the start, Udo had adopted his own system of retributional justice for any elevated protocol breaches of V-Trax. The hacker would be found and eliminated swiftly.

Udo later read that more recently, the US National Terrorist Advisory System (NTAS) had replaced the five-level colour coding of the HSAS with two levels only: elevated and imminent. How satisfying, he thought.

Now, in the waiting room of the Apostolic Palace, Klaus thought to himself, For this level E status, Udo used the words "trying to replace supplier." Klaus was fully aware that the system was intended to automatically trace the supplier (the hacker), and within minutes or an hour at most, Udo would "replace" (i.e., assassinate), this intruder who had caused the elevated status. He also knew this had happened only once before. So, something was going wrong if Udo was reporting that he was *trying* to replace the supplier, instead of *have* replaced the supplier, which was what Klaus was expecting him to write.

***

Frankfurt

Udo went back to his high-back leather chair and ran some more tests on the V-Trax system. The report showed that an elevated level status had been triggered, but V-Trax could not yet identify which files the hacker had been looking at or had been trying to download. Nor could it detect any virus within its operating system. It simply couldn't identify the intruder. Instead, it displayed an error message:

Kann Eindringling Quelle zu identifizieren.

It's as if a ghost is moving within the system undetected while teasing us by leaving open the front door. There is either a major glitch in the report, or we have a computer-hacking genius on our hands, who may even have breached the inner-core imminent level without our knowing…Both are a grave cause for concern and obviously a major threat to our great bank. Either way, the hacker needs to be eliminated. We need to go to the next phase of this enquiry, immediately, Udo thought.

He scrutinized the information, and within a few minutes, he knew how he could get the answer. He conducted another test on the V-Trax system.

CHAPTER 14
MOORGATE

A few days ago, Richard also knew what he had to do: he felt compelled to end his clandestine affair with Rebecca. He reasoned that, in spite of his precautions and her discretion, there was still a risk of them being caught.

Rebecca's maiden name was Falconer. Her full married name was Rebecca Falconer Jelleners; she was Chuck's fifth, and current, trophy wife. Richard knew that if the affair were ever uncovered, Chuck would be merciless towards him.

Despite the freedom, privilege, and time that Chuck's wealth granted her, Rebecca was a deeply unhappy and depressed woman. Her arrogant, overbearing husband jolted her self-esteem by frequently belittling her. She had long ago realized that marrying him had been a mistake. She didn't love him anymore and now questioned whether she ever had. Worse, she felt she had no real purpose in her life: that is, until she met Richard.

His attentive and caring demeanor was evident inside and outside the bedroom. She also enjoyed their intellectual and controversial discussions, during which she often teased him, mimicking his British accent and use of non-American phrases. His acerbic, self-deprecating wit was so contrary to her husband's arrogance and coarse behavior. In bed, Richard was strong and adventurous. He had the stamina, willpower, and courtesy to ensure that she always climaxed before his ejaculation. Unlike for so many couples, their lovemaking had never become a chore.

She had found her kindred spirit, and they had often talked of divorcing their spouses and embarking on a new path together. She dismissed those friends who cautioned her that most married men who have affairs rarely leave the comfort of their wives and family.

Tonight, Richard planned on telling Rebecca that they should immediately end their physical relationship. He wasn't entirely sure how she would take the breakup with him. But, given her increasing attachment to him, and knowing how stubborn she could be, he imagined she would likely make a big, fat fuss. So, he thought it would be best to first simply enjoy a relaxing dinner with her. Then, when they were back in the seclusion of the bedroom that he had booked at the RAC, he would tell her it was over.

He sighed. He disliked confrontation and didn't like to hurt people's feelings. But he knew he should have the courage to do what was right and honorable, so he could be free of the persistent worry of being caught.

His thoughts turned to Chuck, or Jelly, as he preferred to call him behind his back, due to his flabby weeble-esque figure, moist handshake, and jellybean-sized brain. Jelly had blatantly lied to Richard about not being able to give him a higher bonus and instead had taken $8 million for himself—all due to Richard's hard work in uncovering a $200 million windfall gain for the bank, for which Chuck had taken all the credit.

Having the affair with Jelly's trophy wife had been just the first part of Richard's master plan—which he called Project Phoenix—the objective of which was to get even with his boss before the New Year's Eve celebrations. He wanted to destroy Chuck's career and engineer a series of events that allowed Richard to rise up from Jelly's smoldering ashes and triumphantly take over Jelly's role. He would, deservedly, then be earning Jelly's gargantuan salary, to boot.

Richard grinned in the back of the cab and recalled that in Roman times, when an emperor died, a phoenix would be placed in a wooden cage and hidden in the funeral pyre. When the pyre had burned through enough that the cage was sufficiently weakened, the phoenix would be able to break free and fly away. The fleeing bird was said to symbolize the emperor's spirit or soul arising from the ashes and flying free. Project Phoenix represented Richard's new career life arising from the liquidation of Jelly's.

***

Vatican City

Klaus also had death on his mind: that of the penetrator of V-Trax. It was one minute to the hour in Vatican City, and Klaus was about to turn off his private cell phone before the cardinal arrived, when he heard it ping again:

Source of cracked eggs, narrowing…likely our FTE.

The CEO considered this quick work. Udo had clearly tracked down the hacker to be a full-time employee of VCb. Well done, Udo, well done.

Well, well, now it's not a question of whether or not that employee will be in a job much longer, but rather, how long he or she will remain alive. Satisfied, Klaus powered down his cell phone in preparation for the cardinal's arrival.

CHAPTER 15
THE ROYAL AUTOMOBILE CLUB, PALL MALL, LONDON

Richard arrived at the RAC just a few minutes late. He needed to push hard with the palm of his hand to turn the heavy revolving door framed in dark oak, the same one installed when the club moved to its present site in 1911. Inside the entrance hall, he saw the familiar face of the head porter talking to a slim, African-looking man of a similar height to Richard, and who was wearing a light grey overcoat with a beige collar trim.

"Hi, Bill. How's it going?" Richard said.

"Ah, good evening, Mr. de L'Isle. How are you this cold April evening?"

The African turned to look at who had interrupted his conversation.

"Just fine, thanks. Heading up for a nice quiet dinner tonight," said Richard, stopping to shake Bill's hand. Bill had been with the club for over forty-five years and was part of the fabric of this one-and-a-quarter-century-old institution.

The club's rules dictated that all members must show their membership cards at the porter's desk on entering the premises. Bill always waved Richard through without interrupting his stride. Members were also requested to check all coats and briefcases into the cloakroom on the floor below. Richard took off his coat, and handed it and his overnight bag to Bill. "Mind if you just look after them for me whilst I check on my guest? I'm running a tad late."

"No problem, Mr. de L'Isle. I will leave it in the office here. Don't be too long though, please, or you could get me into trouble!"

"Sure, thanks. I'll collect it after we've ordered if that's OK?" said Richard without waiting for a reply.

Richard saw the African stare at him and mumble something. Richard smiled, greeted him with a simple "Hi," and then quickly ran up the central stairs, taking four steps at a time to reach the rotunda.

To his left was the Brooklands Room, an informal restaurant, and to his right, the stately Club Room, which boasted a ceiling and frieze modeled after the Old War Office that stood on this site before the club was built. There, club members could relax leisurely in plush, burgundy-coloured leather armchairs, read magazines, play cards or chess, and order drinks and snacks. They could also, bizarrely in this age of e-mail, hand-write letters on the club's embossed notepaper.

Bill returned his attention to the man standing in front of him. "Sorry, sir, what was the name again?"

The African replied, "Kofi Ghazini. I am speaking here tonight."

The porter opened his logbook. "Ah, yes. Please sign in here, Detective

The Feather of Truth   Ian Campbell-Laing

Chief Inspector, sir."

"Sure," Kofi said and turning around saw on the members' notice board what he had been looking for—his own name. "Hmm. It's OK, I know where to go now, thanks." His deep, resonating voice caused two ladies chatting in the nearby drawing room to look up and then smile flirtatiously at him.

Kofi then sighed, partly because he was tired as usual, but also in irritation. He wondered if he should voice his concern or just leave it be. He decided on the former. His voice remained calm, but it took on a more assertive tone. "Hmm. Whilst I am not a member of this club, there's one thing, please, for future reference which I would like to point out. If I or anyone else is talking to you, it is courteous to finish your conversation with that person first, before you assist another member or guest. It is impolite to be interrupted. Is that a fair point, and if so, understood?"

"Sir, of course it is, and apologies again," said the porter, bowing his head in shame, adding, "and whilst Mr. de L'Isle *is* a very important member, that doesn't excuse my behavior."

"Well, let's say no more about it, Bill."

"Thank you, sir. I see that you are giving a talk tonight in the Committee Room. Best of good luck with that. I am sure it will be a hit, just like the other one you did here about six months ago now I think it was?"

"Thank you. That's kind of you to say so."

"Chief Inspector, please allow me to take your coat to the cloakroom and check it in for you. I will then bring up the tag for you."

"Thanks. That's kind of you, Bill."

Kofi took off his coat, turned, and as he walked towards the steps, he glanced to his right and saw the two very attractive, elegant ladies in their midthirties still smiling at him and looking him up and down. He smiled back and bowed his head slightly in warm acknowledgment. As he headed to the sumptuous Committee Room, he thought about the presentation he was shortly due to give, entitled "Murderers: The Real Cost of Us Being Hidden from Plain Sight." He then thought, What an arrogant upper-class prat is that Mr. de L'Isle, whom I hope is not in the audience this evening. Or in fact, I do hope he is. I can ask him a question that will bring him down from his lofty, self-entitled height.

At the top of the stairs, standing in the oval rotunda underneath the high dome, Richard looked ahead. In front, parked on the carpet outside the Great Gallery restaurant, was a vintage car. Often, there was a special car on display, ranging from the first car to reach forty miles per hour, driven by Count Gaston de Chasseloup-Laubat of Paris in 1898; to *Thrust II*, which, driven by RAF fighter pilot Andy Green, broke the land speed record by exceeding Mach 1 with over 740 miles per hour; and modern-day luxury and F1 cars in between. This week, it was the infamous DeLorean.

In its day, it was meant to revolutionize the automobile industry with its radical gull-wing doors.

Richard glanced at the reception area and saw that Paul de Vere was on duty. Paul looked up and saw Richard approaching him, his right hand held out, and his boyish grin welcoming him.

"Paul, I see you have another failed relic of the past on display here waiting to be turned into the great scrap heap in the sky."

"Mr. de L'Isle," replied Paul quietly, "that's no way to speak of a few of our elderly members of this club, now!"

Richard always enjoyed Paul's quick and disrespectful wit.

"And to think our stupid British government gave that arrogant American with tight Farah trousers and coiffured silver hair sixty million of our Great British pounds to squander and produce such a useless piece of shite metal. Anyone with half a brain would know it would never sell at the price they were asking."

"Yes, indeed, sir. So, you dislike the DeLorean car then?"

"What? Don't get me started," said Richard quietly with a look of incredulity on his face. "Despite great styling by the Italian designer Gioretto Giugiaro, the DeLorean car was badly made, slow, and kept breaking down. Its only good use was in the film *Back to the Future*. No, Paul, I much prefer the Bugatti Veyron you had on display a few weeks ago. Now that *is* a real beauty with such amazing craftsmanship and technology by the Germans at Volkswagen, don't you think?"

"Quite so, sir," said Paul, adding, "and the owners of that million-pound car are unlikely to be concerned about such trifles as the recent hike in petrol prices!"

"Nope, not at all."

"Nor I guess whether their car had suppressed emission-cheating devices!"

"Yes indeed, Paul, very well said," said Richard, recalling the announcement on the news that morning of yet another car manufacturer falling foul of regulators some ten years after the 2015 scandal that hit Volkswagen. "And to be able to afford that car, of course their personal fortunes and future is probably secure," replied Richard.

"Yes, but who's to say what the future may hold for any of us mortals, in this depressed financial climate."

"Yep, Paul, who's to say indeed. We all have to keep our heads down below the parapet and not be detected by any business or government radar screen. It's the way of the world, I'm afraid."

"Yes, the world. Always, it's the way of the world," said Paul, nodding his head.

"But I am here tonight, away from the world of finance and stress."

"Right. You are dining with us tonight. If I recall, Mr. de L'Isle, you have a reservation in the Great Gallery."

"Yep, that's correct."

"You will be pleased to know that Chef Terry Guanosee has a new spring menu tonight. We will take care of you and your attractive guest, as always. Might I enquire if she is a relative or perhaps a work colleague?" said Paul with a smirk on his face.

"Um, let's just refer to her as a business colleague. But thanks, Paul, for your and your staff's discretion, as always. It is much appreciated."

"It's never in question, especially after all you have done for the club, and for me personally. I haven't forgotten the work you do, and the money you've raised for the Stroke Association, a cause close to my family's heart as you know. Have a pleasant evening, sir."

Richard strode into the Great Gallery. With its thirty-two-foot-high ceilings and a beautiful, magnificent Boulanger trompe l'oeil fresco on the ceiling, it always made him pause and look up in admiration of the craftsmen that created it.

He had reserved his favorite table on the raised floor on the right-hand side of the restaurant. It overlooked the other diners and allowed more privacy.

Richard saw Rebecca seated at the table looking down at her iPhone. Instinctively, she looked up when he came into her peripheral vision. She smiled and gave him a little wave with her right hand. He quickly raised his eyebrows to acknowledge her and smiled back.

He was well known at the club, and he acknowledged the many facial and hand gestures that greeted him. As he approached the table, she moved her chair back a little, as if to get up, but he stopped her and lightly placed his hands on her shoulders. She raised her head up to him, and he bent down and kissed her softly but quickly on the cheek, which was all they allowed each other in public. He immediately caught a whiff of her exquisite Baccarat perfume, which he had bought for her birthday. His nose filled with the scent of amber, jasmine, myrrh, and frankincense—the smell of ancient Egypt. He breathed it deeply into his lungs. A few wisps of her hair glanced his cheek. He shivered with a childish joy at the prize before him.

"Hello, darling. Don't get up," he whispered in her ear. "You look ravishing tonight, as always." He felt the gaze of other guests watching them.

He stood back absorbing her beauty, which she destined for him alone. She dressed elegantly, just like his mother had. Tonight, she wore a turquoise Chanel skirt that promoted magnificently her long, slender legs, a matching top, white blouse, and pearls around her tanned neck. Her long silky, naturally, fair hair was pinned up, just as he liked it, drawing his eyes to the light that reflected off her large diamond earrings. Her smile, like that

The Feather of Truth Ian Campbell-Laing

of many American women, was wide and inviting and revealed brilliantly white, perfectly shaped, healthy teeth: the product of expensive dentistry and wholly unnatural compared to many British women's off-yellow, chipped teeth. Her nails were polished and matched the colour of her suit. Her posture remained upright and regal.

Regarding her appearance, she once said to him, "You don't want me to look like an unmade bed for you, do you?"

Rebecca looked up at Richard, seeking the comforting reassurance in his piercing eyes. They had been the first things she had noticed when she had first met him. She was reminded of the famous young Afghan girl in 1985, pictured on the cover of the *National Geographic* magazine, with her haunting and haunted mint-green eyes: Richard's were the same colour and had the same effect on Rebecca—he had a haunting look that drew you to him.

She noticed that his height caused him to stoop his head and shoulders down when he talked to most men. He had been the captain of his school's rugby and tennis teams and kept in shape. His wavy, chestnut hair was cut short but always slightly unkempt and ruffled. Very stylish, she thought. His suits were expensive and tailor-made in England by Ozwald Boateng. His British Loake shoes were polished like those of someone in the military. And she simply adored his British accent, which—despite his expensive public school upbringing—was not at all painfully clipped like the British royalty: they seemed to have a problem correctly pronouncing some words, with their lips and mouths all screwed up as if they had sat on something uncomfortable or unpleasant. Richard's accent, whilst middle class, was soft, deep, and lyrical to her.

However, despite Richard's "soft yet rugged" appearance, as she had described him, he could be ruthless, and that, whilst not frightening her, did make her occasionally apprehensive. Rebecca had once heard him on the phone to a work colleague whom he suspected had lied to him, and he certainly had a vicious temper. Yet the next minute, he was soft and inviting.

She liked her men to be strong but also have a soft, sensitive, vulnerable side. Richard qualified on all counts: in fact, he was the complete antithesis of her husband, Chuck. She wondered how she had ended up with the squat, chubby, coarse husband of hers.

She also knew, of course, that Richard was married, with three adorable children and a great wife. She felt no sense of guilt in having the affair; she simply thought, if Richard was my husband, I'd take better care of him so that he wouldn't need or ever want to stray.

Richard smiled at his mistress. Her eyes were sea-blue wells inviting his gaze. Like a bell to Pavlov's salivating dog, her presence, her voice alone, her innocuous text messages even, involuntarily directed blood to his groin, which immediately stiffened in anticipation. Now, with her close to him, he sat down quickly before embarrassing himself.

Richard noticed that she was still looking at him—longer than usual, but he guessed it was probably because they hadn't met for over a week. However, he wondered if for some reason she still needed further reassurance of their long-term relationship.

With the distraction of the new menus presented to them in an elegant black leather folder with the RAC's monogram crest embossed on the front, and after laughing as they told their first stories of how their day and week had been, they soon relaxed.

Rebecca glanced at the menu, hunting for the relatively healthy option amongst a cornucopia of calorific indulgence—black truffle risotto; ravioli of pheasant and smoked pancetta; cappuccino of lentil; roast loin of Campbell Highland venison, with crispy potatoes, kohlrabi and parsley; slow-cooked Norfolk black chicken with black garlic emulsion and a sweet corn stuffing; loin of lamb with a goats-milk puree, grilled turnips, and long-stem broccoli.

"This new menu is so lovely. It all looks delicious, but the glycemic index on some of these dishes must be off the charts, hon!"

He smiled. "So, what takes your fancy, Rebecca? Will you be able to break that all-important goal of eating more than half of the dishes presented to you and consuming more than five hundred calories in one day?" Richard glanced his head towards her with his teasing smile. He knew that like many weight-obsessed American women, Rebecca ate sparingly. Rebecca had admitted to weighing herself daily. In fact, Richard thought, she probably did it at least twice a day. Instead, he believed in eating sensibly and in moderation, but with one still enjoying life—by having treats. All animals need treats. Rebecca is mine, he smirked as he saw numerous men at the club feasting their eyes on her beauty.

"Now, now, you incorrigible but gorgeous Brit, you!" said Rebecca, her cheeks turning slightly red. "I do eat, but it's just that I like to stay slim. You want me to look good for you at your club," she said, and then added, lowering her voice to a whisper, "and when we are alone, don't you, sweetie?" Her accent was an unusual confluence of her Texan father, New Yorker mother, and attending numerous private schools around the world, including the Dominican Academy Catholic school in New York, Saint Paul's Girls' School in London, and the College Alpine Beau Soleil in Switzerland. She had been a prefect at two of the schools, and the head girl at the third. She had gained a PhD in psychology, had a master's degree in archaeology, and was a subject matter expert on Egyptology.

But tonight, her New York twang appeared stronger. He had noticed that it emerged very prominently when she was either nervous or angry. She certainly didn't seem angry tonight, so perhaps she was nervous about something. He wondered if she had any idea of his plans for tonight.

CHAPTER 16
THE RAC

Robbin Sweeny, the club's sommelier, stepped forward to ensure that Richards usual drink in a wide-brimmed glass had been placed at the table just before he had arrived and was precisely to his liking – Jensen's Old Tom gin and Fever-Tree naturally light tonic water with three cubes of ice, two slices of lime, and a sprig of rosemary.

Richard picked up the glass, smelt the clean crisp aroma, took a swig, smiled, and nodded his head. "Perfectamundo Robbin, as always."

"Before I take the liberty to advise you on wines you might wish to have that would complement and pair with your food, would madam like another margarita?"

"No, thanks, Robbin. Not just yet."

Richard smiled and snorted softly. No wonder Rebecca ate so little: her one margarita was at least three hundred calories per glass, and that only left her with two hundred for the rest of the meal and probably the rest of the day. His wife didn't bother much with calories counting, especially after having had three children. Of course she wasn't as svelte as Rebecca, but even still, everyone said that she looked pretty good, despite the few extra pounds around her middle and the inevitable forces of gravity playing on her body that tended to move everything southwards.

"How are you and the missus, Robbin? Has 'er indoors had the hip-op yet? If so I hope the surgery went well."

"Yes, just great. Thanks, Mr. de L'Isle. The trouble's op went quite well, thank heavens, and touch wood." The sommelier gently tapped the top of Richard's chair.

Rebecca moved her head back and to the side, with her eyes squinting in confusion. He enlightened her. "'Er indoors' is East End London slang for 'her indoors,' or his wife. 'Trouble' also means wife. It was from the rhyming slang 'trouble and strife,' which rhymes with 'wife.'"

"OK, got it, you daft Brit!" Rebecca laughed.

Robbin stepped aside as Steve Grainnis, the head server who everyone called Hawker, on account of his passion for falconry in his spare time, came to take their order.

"Good evening, Mr. de L'Isle. Good evening, madam. We have a new menu tonight for the season, with some dishes that I think you will adore. Would you like me to go over any of them, or are you ready to order?"

Richard motioned his left hand towards Rebecca, to go first while he quickly scanned the menu, even though he rarely ventured away from his favorites.

"Good evening," said Rebecca. "Nice to see you both, as always. Yes, I think I'm ready to order. I will have the salad of quail to start, and as my entrée, I think…let's see. Yes, the line-caught sea bass with seasonal roasted vegetables would be nice, but no potatoes please."

"Sounds good, Rebecca," said Richard. "Hawker, I'll have the pan-seared scallops to start, and the roast loin of highland venison, medium-rare, with a small side of creamed spinach, as my main, please."

"Excellent choices, and Mr. de L'Isle, thank you so much for the legal contact you gave my mother. As you may know, she has received her settlement, and the op appears to have gone well."

"Excellent! I am so pleased. Please give Doris my best."

"I surely will. And also, the bill he charged me was minimal, and not the stiff amount I am sure I would have had to pay up if I had gone elsewhere, sir."

"I'm chuffed for you," Richard said, and then turning to Rebecca asked, "Do you know from where the word 'stiff' comes?"

"No. Enlighten me. I hope it's not crude—is it?" she said, putting her hand to her mouth in mock embarrassment.

"No, not at all. It comes from the Latin 'rigor mortis,' which literally means 'stiffness of death' and is due to the production of lactic acid not being able to escape from the cells, but hardening to form a stiff gel."

Rebecca raised her eyes, leaned forward, and whispered, "I am hoping that later I will witness a certain stiffness occurring in a member of this club, as it were!" She discreetly slipped her right hand under the tablecloth and rested it on his groin.

And with that, Hawker smiled at the two lovers and stepped back to allow Robbin to approach and, with great vigor as expected, recommend some appropriate wines.

Richard felt his own resolve waning and blood flowing down under. Maybe I shouldn't call off the affair tonight, after all? He knew this was dangerous, but what the heck. Like a compulsive gambler, he wasn't thinking rationally. Who cares? I am never going to get caught. Just one more throw tonight of this irresistible dice.

CHAPTER 17
THE RAC

Before Robbin stepped forward, Rebecca asked Richard, "What was the legal help you gave to Hawker's mother?"

"Oh, his mother was the vicar of her local parish in Kirkstall—which is a suburb of Leeds in Yorkshire, up in the north of England—and shortly before her retirement at aged seventy-five, she slipped on a pothole outside her church and fell down rather awkwardly. She needed to have a hip operation, which she could ill afford, and was in terrible pain. Her church advised her to sue the local council, but the council was resisting, saying she should have looked where she was going."

"Oh, how dreadful for the poor old dear."

"So, I gave Hawker the name of my friend and ace lawyer, Anthony Lea, QC, whom I bring in when I need to raise the ante when complaining about an intransigent service provider. He always uses a cunning private detective called Robin Daniels to help him on tricky cases. And, good old Daniels proved that the workman was drunk when he left the pothole exposed with no sign. Also, on the winter's late afternoon in question, Hawker's mother was walking in a light drizzle of rain, and this would have made the hole difficult to see, especially with her diminishing eyesight."

"So, what happened? Did the local council give in?"

"Well, it then got interesting. Even after a very cleverly worded letter from Anthony, who provided relevant case law showing they were guilty as hell, they still resisted, trying to avoid a big payout. Anthony was infuriated and took upon himself to fight this to the bitter end, pro bono. He said he would forgo his fees because to him it was simply a matter of principle that her employer, the church, should take her case on and fight the council to make them pay up. It was disgraceful that this old lady was in pain and had all the stress of legal action with no help from the church that she had served all her life!"

"So, how did it get resolved?"

"Well, Anthony had to be creative and, to be quite frank, was a bloody genius. He decided to sue her employer, the church, on the basis that they had a duty of care to their employees, and she was therefore subject to the usual employment protection rights, just as any other company employee."

"OK, so the church paid up. Doesn't sound that creative to me."

Richard rolled his eyes in slight irritation. "Now, now, hold your horses and have some patience! I was just about to explain the cool part, my dear. Did you know that the clergy under the Church of England's outdated laws cannot sue their employer?"

The Feather of Truth — Ian Campbell-Laing

"Why not? That's discrimination, isn't it? Surely the clergy has a staff or employee union to help them fight such an inalienable right?"

"Let me fast-forward a bit. The church's reply to Anthony's letter was incredible, but exactly what Anthony wanted. He had laid a trap for them. They replied, 'Under the Church of England's ancient ecclesiastical laws, all clergymen and women are office holders, and not employed by the Church, but by God.'"

"That's a cop-out, isn't it?"

"Absolutely right. So, Anthony brought a case on Hawker's mother's behalf to sue God himself, and made it plain that he would call the present monarch, the king of England, who holds the title as the supreme governor of the Church of England, as his de facto manager. This, of course, caused an absolute stink!"

"Aha, I got it, and now I think I remember reading about it in the press not that long ago in the *Daily Mail*. So, in addition to calling the monarch to the stand and cross-examining him, which has presumably never been done before, more importantly, it brought into question the very existence or not of God himself?"

"Precisely. Well concluded, Rebecca," said Richard, pleased that Rebecca's intellect as usual was quick to get to the key facts of the case.

"Because," as Rebecca's fast brain had already surmised, she then continued, "the church simply can't prove emphatically that God exists, and so Hawker's mother had to be, by definition, employed by the church, who must then pay up. And, presumably such bad publicity by such an uncaring, out-of-touch church would have caused Sunday's congregation attendance to plummet! So, then presumably, the church settled out of court to avoid any further embarrassment to it and the king of England?"

"Correctamundo! The church then sued the Leeds Council, who reimbursed the church for the considerable payout the church had given Hawker's mother. She then used part of her settlement for her operation, which was a week or so ago, kept some for her retirement needs, gave a nice lump sum to Hawker, and graciously donated the rest to charity. And I know what was Anthony's bill: five hundred notes—er, sorry, five hundred pounds. His chambers wrote off more than twenty thousand pounds in legal fees."

"You are a very kind and considerate person, Richard," said Rebecca, smiling at him, admiring the softer side of his nature.

Richard blushed. "Thank you. Yes, I suppose I help others every now and again. But, actually I have a big chip on my shoulder. When growing up whilst attending closeted boarding schools, I was conscious that my parents had very little money compared to my school friends' parents. I felt very inadequate most of the time, and still have the need to prove I am better than anyone else."

The Feather of Truth   Ian Campbell-Laing

Rebecca reached over and quickly, but briefly, touched his hand and whispered, "Inadequate you are most definitely not, dear lover."

Richard smiled but tried to concentrate his thoughts back to what he had agreed in his mind to say to Rebecca later tonight.

They saw Robbin move towards them and then cough, so they stopped talking and looked up at him, ready for the wine discussion. Rebecca had removed her hand from Richard's. She knew she had already shown far more public displays of affection tonight than what they both agreed was permitted, but she was so much in love with him, she just couldn't restrain herself.

"I know that you like the Sancerre region for your white wines, and we recently came across a rather nice Caillottes, from Francois Cotat's Chavignol vineyard. Formerly known as the Jeune Vignes, the Chavignol plot has now grown sufficiently to earn the title Caillottes, after its limestone-strewn soil. Compared to the leaner 2022s, the 2023s immediately dazzle one by the amount of sunshine radiating from the glass and of its beguiling *souplesse* and inviting demeanor. I think it will complement both your scallops and madam's sea bass." Robbin loved showing off his craft as a sommelier—especially to interested oenophiles like Richard—and his words were always accompanied by theatrical hand gesticulations.

Robbin continued, "Sancerre, as you know, sir, used to be the French person's average table wine that they drank daily. That's all changed now, especially with the American market snapping up the wines, and the vineyards improving the quality."

"The 2023 Caillottes it is, then," said Richard. "I only wish my mother was here to join us and have these new flavors of wines: she introduced me to the Sancerre."

"I think also one of the Chateau-neuf du Pape's would complement both your venison, sir, and indeed your quail, madam."

"Sounds perfect, Robbin. What producer and which year would you recommend for the Chateau-neuf? The 2025 Domaine des Saumades that I had a few weeks ago when I had the Mey Angus beef was absolutely excellent."

"Yes, I remember. We recommended the Saumades with its medium-bodied southern Rhone blend made from 100 percent Grenache: it's an elegant, almost feminine wine with a strong floral charm on the nose and a pleasing purity of musty hedgerow fruit on the palate that causes a tingling sensation down one's spine as the aromas erupt in unison. But let's have a different wine that better complements the gamier flavor of your venison. Also, I recall that madam prefers her red wines fuller bodied."

Richard looked at Rebecca, who was obviously trying to hide a smirk on her face. Respectfully, she put her hand to her mouth and looked away, trying not to giggle.

The Feather of Truth — Ian Campbell-Laing

Robbin, oblivious to a dissenter in the audience, continued his speech. "I tasted the 2025 Domaine de la Charnonnier this week, and it has a dark ruby, almost purple, colour and a classic nose of crème de cassis intermixed with a dusty, earthy fragrance topped with licorice, roasted bell peppers, and a hint of cayenne pepper. It's deep and full bodied, with ripe but noticeable tannin and decent acidity. I think this is what you will appreciate tonight. Feeling full bodied, sir and madam? Willing to give it a whirl?"

"Sure, Robbin, let's go for it," said Richard, not even asking the price of the wines. He handed back their menus and gazed at Rebecca's lips, the pink lipstick accenting their outline: her lower lip larger and full, her upper lip a thinner wave. He wanted to kiss her and bite and tug on her lower lip. My God, she's adorable, he thought. Driven by man's innate desires of sexual fulfillment, he concluded his thoughts, Yes, I definitely will continue the affair for just a tad longer.

After Robbin left their presence, Rebecca smiled as she looked at Richard and said, "What a load of old rubbish. What was he saying, 'pleasing purity of musty hedgerow fruit'? 'Almost feminine quality'? And 'dusty earthy fragrance of bell peppers and licorice'? Why can't wine experts speak in English and cut the wine snobbery crap? What did you say to me was the phrase you Brits use when someone is talking utter nonsense, cods and gallop? Tripe and beets?" She laughed.

"The two phrases are, my dear, a 'load of old codswallop' and 'tripe and onions,' and they are good British northern phrases. Although, I do totally agree that some of the wine language is utterly ridiculous and there is a certain arrogant snobbery about it all!" Richard said, nodding his head and laughing.

"But where on earth do these quaint British phrases ever come from, pray do tell me, as I am sure you know, given your classical English degree?"

"Actually, I do know a little about the phrases, and they are interesting."

"OK, come on, sweetie, intrigue me, as you always do with your encyclopedic knowledge."

"OK, sure."

"You have my full attention, Richard." Her shoulders leaned forward, and she brought the palms of her hands together, interlocking her fingers and resting them on the white tablecloth. Looking up at him, she slightly parted her lips. She saw his eyes search down into the top of her blouse and then revert back to her face.

"In 1876, Mr. Hirram Codd, a soft drink maker, designed and patented a glass bottle specifically for his fizzy drinks. Though his 'Codd-neck' bottle design was a success in the fizzy drink industry, alcohol drinkers disliked Codd's invention and said it was only good for 'wallop,' which is a nineteenth-century slang for beer. So, 'Codd's wallop' became a term for anything of low quality or rubbish."

"Oh, soooo jolly fascinating, old boy!" said Rebecca.

"In fact, there's another theory," continued Richard, smiling and knowing that Rebecca was actually interested, because she adored history and English as much as he did, "and it's to do with the codfish, which you had the last time we were here."

"Go on, let's hear theory number two for this literal rubbish!"

"After catching the cod out at sea, the fishermen put it into sheds for cleaning, preparation, and grading. The cold and wet waste trimmings would hit the ground with a distinctive sound, a 'wallop.' That began an association with 'cod's wallop' as any major spoken or written rubbish."

"I think either could be the answer. But I have a question for you. In the British Tudor times, didn't men used to wear a 'cod' piece around their groin, which was used to protect their male equipment?" Rebecca asked, raising her right eyebrow.

"Yes. What's your point?" Richard smiled, as he noticed that her New York accent had vanished. So she must now be relaxed, and whatever had been bothering her was probably unimportant. Good, he thought, that will make it easier should I decide to break off the relationship tonight.

"So, the third explanation could be that if a cod is the male genitals, then using the first definition you gave me, your three dangling appendages of your manhood are simply useless bits of rubbish!" Rebecca said, laughing rather too loudly, so that some of the nearby diners looked their way.

"Ha, ha, very funny and very perceptive, my dear," Richard admitted.

Rebecca leaned forward more, and said quietly, "Sweetie, as you know, your bits of cod equipment make me wild and satisfy me more than anyone else has ever done." And with that, she unlocked her fingers and discreetly again slid her right hand under the table to place the palm on his lap.

She waited. She leaned forward more and moved her shoulders slightly to one side, allowing his eyes to search out, in between the buttons of her blouse, her breasts. "And it seems, the old British codpiece has begun to stir and wake up and stand to attention!" He leaned forward, and she kissed him gently on the cheek.

He returned his focus back to his tutorial. "And tripe, I think, is the name for the stomach of a cow, and for many families in the north of England in the last century, I guess, tripe was roasted and served with onions. I suspect it tasted pretty disgusting, and hence was thought of as rubbish. But I'm not too sure of that explanation."

Rebecca smiled and withdrew her hand, thinking tonight's lovemaking would be amazing, as always. And besides, of course tonight she couldn't be happier. But, then later whilst they chatted away, she noted that Richard occasionally looked around the room, and there were more lulls in the conversation than usual. She wanted to know what was distracting him and

The Feather of Truth Ian Campbell-Laing

why he wasn't giving her his full attention.

"Richard, are you still smarting over your bonus that Chuck gave you last week? You seem at times miles away tonight, sweetie."

Richard sighed and nodded. "Yep, I'm still angry, but it's just been a long day trying to wrap up this ruddy London profitability project for Jelly. By the way, did he tell you how much bonus he got this year at the bank from Celsius?"

"Yes, he did. He got in total eight and a quarter million dollars, up from the year before when he got five and a quarter million dollars."

Richard, of course, knew that from V-Trax, but he pretended to be astonished. "Jeepers ruddy creepers. Oh, shit! That makes it even more unbearable, given what he gave me and considering its me that makes him look so damn good in front of Celsius."

"Well, I don't want to spoil it. It's actually worse than that, sweetie."

Richard stared at her and raised his eyebrows. He had a feeling he didn't want to hear what she was going to say.

At that moment, Hawker brought them their palate teasers, the amuse-bouche with the compliments of the chef. "May I present to you a little something on the house? It's a choux automobile—an airy, puff choux pastry shell, flavored with distinct northern England Wensleydale organic cheese, and filled with a Mornay sauce. Please enjoy."

Rebecca looked down at the little hors d'oeuvre delicacy served on a silver spoon, shaped like a ladies' high-heeled shoe. Her lips drew the contents into her mouth, and as she chewed, the combination of flavors and contrasting textures exploded in a hot sensation of delight. She put her hand to her mouth to stop the cheese oozing out of the sides of her mouth.

"How do you mean, 'It's worse than that'?" enquired Richard, trying to get her to focus again.

"He got a private call on his cell phone later that weekend from the CEO, who asked that the conversation be kept strictly confidential between just Chuck and him."

"Oh, really? What was the call about? Did our esteemed CEO give him some extra bank shares in his Christmas stocking as a thank you and say to keep it all quiet?" said Richard, cringing. He didn't want to know the answer but wasn't able to resist asking the question.

"Yes, pretty much. He thanked Chuck for his hard work in uncovering a gigantic windfall gain for the bank, and gave him an extra seven million dollars in VCb stock to vest over the next two years: four million dollars next year and three million the year after. He bought me these Graff earrings for 150,000 pounds the day he heard about it! Aren't they exquisite?"

Richard raised his voice, banged his fist on the table, and glared at her. Some nearby diners turned and stared at him. "Oh, shit. That's just so

The Feather of Truth — Ian Campbell-Laing

unfair, Rebecca. God, Jelly's an arsehole, a swindler, and a crook. And I'm a gullible moron to work so conscientiously for him and get so little in return. It was *me and my team* that uncovered the two hundred million dollars' windfall gain for the bank, not your ruddy husband! And I got squat diddly doo da as a bonus. Most of that seven million bucks is mine, dammit!"

"Richard, I know we've had this type of conversation before, but remember, with your base salary and bonus together, you told me your comp was in total around 900,000 pounds last year, which is, I guess, around one-point four million dollars. That's far more than what the UK prime minister and our US president earn, combined!"

"What are you going on about?" said Richard, who disliked being lectured, especially on this old chestnut of a topic.

Rebecca spelled it out for him, even though she had done so a few times before. "Look, Malcolm Quigley earns around 140,000 pounds, which is about"—she looked up whilst she did the calculation—"210,000 dollars. Your base alone is more than that, isn't it? Our president earns, I think, about 400,000 dollars and has a travel and expense account of an additional 150,000 dollars. Your bonus is double that! And just think what a fireman or ambulance crewman makes saving the lives of a family, or a teacher educating a child, or a nurse bringing carefully into the world a precious child. Probably less than 50,000 dollars. Come on, honey, you earn a huge salary and way more than you and I need."

Rebecca saw him roll his eyes and watched him look down and slowly take a deep breath in and then exhale loudly. "Oops…Sorry, Richard, I know you hate being called 'honey' or 'sweetie.' It's just a habit." She reached over to place her hand onto his.

He pulled his hand away. *She just doesn't get it, and she shouldn't treat me as a spoilt child.* Of course it was true that he was handsomely paid compared to others outside his industry, but relative to his peers within the industry, including his dimwitted boss, he felt hugely undervalued.

She noticed Richard wasn't listening to her.

"Richard, darling," she said, but rather too tersely and shrill, so she softened her voice and dropped it a tone lower. "Richard, darling," she said again and gently replaced her right hand on top of his left hand.

Richard turned his head, surprised. Normally when she wanted to persuade him to do something, her voice rose in tone and became baby-like.

"Let me cheer you up. I did a test this morning, and I have great news.

CHAPTER 18
THE RAC

"A test, sweetheart?" said Richard, trying to sound interested. He wasn't aware she was currently studying for any exams, so he wasn't sure what test she was going on about. His right hand moved to his mouth as he masked a yawn: he had been up since five, as always. He recalled that she had been thinking of taking some continuing professional educational exams to keep her psychology practicing certificate up to date in case she went back into that profession, so maybe that's what she was talking about. Whatever…He wasn't really interested, and her ramblings prevented him from thinking about more important matters. He needed to manipulate the secret information he had on Chuck to get back at him. But how?

"Yes, a test. You know, *the* test!"

"Your CPE practicing certificate exams—did you pass?"

"No, silly, I did those ages ago earlier this year…Don't you remember I told you? No, the only test that matters, a pregnancy test of course."

These words blocked out immediately all other sounds reaching his ear canal. "A *pregnancy* test?" His lips opened slightly and became flat as he spat out the words, forcing some of his amuse-bouche to spray out onto the table. He felt her hand pressing down on his. Nothing remotely amusing or enjoyable about this topic, he thought. His body became taut. His shoulders hunched over his chest. Fastidiously, and to allow himself more time to sift through and interpret the millions of chemical and electrical signals bombarding his brain, he used the palm of his other hand to wipe away the small splatters of food that had landed in front of him.

She whispered, "Yes, it was positive. I'm pregnant, Richard, and going to have a baby! I'm so excited!" She clasped her hands together and raised them to rest under her chin. Her mouth opened in a large smile, her brilliant white teeth shining at him. Her eyebrows appeared as raised arches above her wide-open eyes, inviting him to join in her exuberance.

Richard said nothing. He looked at the tablecloth and spotted a crumb that he had missed. He left it. He looked up and saw her elbows placed on the table but decided to not admonish her for this bad restaurant behavior.

"Hon, I wanted to tell you over the phone, but I know you don't like taking calls in the office, especially when you're so busy."

His Adam's apple moved up and then down as he swallowed.

"That's…" His voice came out high pitched and soft. He raised his right hand to his mouth and coughed into it, clearing his larynx. "That's great news, angel."

Then he realized something potentially wonderful. Thank God, he thought, Chuck is going to have a baby with her, and perhaps this is exactly the time to say our relationship is over. Now that she's pregnant, she'll need to devote her time to her marriage with Jelly and her new unborn baby. And I won't have to listen to her lecturing me any longer. But I may still need her to get back at my boss, so don't do anything hasty, Richard.

Richard sat back and took another large swig of his gin and tonic, finishing it. He smiled back at Rebecca, and then after squeezing the lips of his mouth, he quietly asked, "Does that mean our relationship is over, or can we still have some intimacy?"

Robbin suddenly appeared, bringing the Sancerre, and poured a small amount into Richard's glass. Richard lifted it up to his eyes and waved the glass in a circular pattern. He tilted it and watched the legs of the liquid fall down the inside of his glass. He inhaled its perfume and then tasted it. He nodded his head. Robbin poured their glasses to two-thirds full.

Richard waited for him to leave them. Rebecca looked confused by his comment. Richard added, "Chuck will be thrilled. I know that he wanted to have a baby with you."

"But—" she started, before Richard interrupted her.

"However, I thought you said that Chuck and you weren't having a physical relationship, apart from the odd time he forced himself on you when he was drunk. I didn't know that you and he were, how shall I put it…" Richard stalled in midsentence as another thought hit him. Had he missed her point completely? She was now staring at him with her eyebrows forced together and a bemused smile on her face, as if he had just said the most idiotic thing.

"Making love," interjected Rebecca flatly.

"Yes, quite. I did not know you and fat old Jelly Beano were doing it at all."

"He and I *aren't*, and *haven't* for ages, Richard." Her eyebrows narrowed further as she affirmed his point. Her eyes then widened, and she smiled, thinking, Men can be so dense sometimes.

"What are you saying, Rebecca?" he asked, panicking slightly. "Are you saying that Jelly is not the father?"

"Yes, you silly old thing," she said as she dropped her hands and lifted up both of his, pulling them together and enveloping them inside hers. "Yes, Richard, you are the father, obviously. I am only making love to you, you daft Brit. There's no one else it could be."

The sickness in his stomach was immediate and automatic as blood rushed to his brain, away from all unnecessary extremities, to help process this new information. His diaphragm rose, making it harder to breathe. His heart started racing. Don't panic. Don't say anything daft, or something you'll regret. Just keep a level head, old chap.

"I do so want this baby, our baby, hon. Isn't it such great news?" she said leaning forward, and squeezing his hands.

Richard now found it difficult to concentrate: the passage of time had halted, the large room felt small and claustrophobic, and the chatter of the diners, which before had been an unobtrusive background hum, now was irritatingly noisy and distracting. *How* could she be pregnant? She assured me she was always very careful. What on earth was he to do? How did this all happen? He wasn't sure who would want to kill him first, his annoying boss or his adoring wife. His career and his marriage were at stake, and probably now over. He had only just started to plan how to oust Jelly from being his manager and take over Jelly's role. All the information that he had secretly obtained on Jelly from V-Trax was potentially in vain. What a prat, what a moron he had been! And of course, financially, he was also likely to be ruined, given he had signed a prenup with his very wealthy wife before they had got married.

Initial conclusion, Richard, old chap, is this baby must never be born, and neither Jennifer nor Jelly must ever know or hear about Rebecca's pregnancy. His brain was trying to sift through his options while he was nodding his head and sycophantically smiling at his lover. He reluctantly pulled out his right hand from her clasp and placed it on top of hers.

He urgently needed to get away and start thinking of a plan.

***

Frankfurt, Germany

Udo was also formulating a strategy in his mind. He had just read an e-mail from the security guard on duty in the London office, who had copied in Nigel Longtone, the head of human resources for the region:

> Herr Udo, just to let you know that earlier this evening, as part of the computer-generated random search, a Richard de L'Isle was chosen, who works in the Asset and Private Wealth Management division here in London. Within his briefcase was a sophisticated pen that I know can only be purchased in spy shops, and which has the latest audio and video recording capability. I advised Mr. de L'Isle that it was perfectly legal to own such a device, but not permitted under the bank's code of conduct to use it on the premises, nor at client meetings.

Of course, Udo would have read about this tomorrow from the V-Trax report, which would have recorded and picked out the importance of the words used in the conversation being held and secretly recorded between the security officer and Mr. de L'Isle. But the officer would not, of course, have known of the existence of V-Trax, hence his e-mail alert.

Udo reached for his cell phone and dictated an e-mail to the CEO of

The Feather of Truth — Ian Campbell-Laing

that division, Chuck's own manager, Celsius Maysmith III:

Celsius, I would like to discuss one of your employee's actions, regarding a computer systems protocol breach. Will liaise with your secretary to find a suitable time today to discuss. Regards, Udo.

CHAPTER 19
THE RAC

Less than two minutes earlier, Richard had been dining with a woman with an almost flawless beauty and insatiable sexual desires and who was his peer intellectually. Despite her ramblings and her lecturing of him, he had still been looking forward to intimacy with her later upstairs in the suite he had booked.

She was now staring at him, awaiting his answer, to affirm the calibration of his excitement to her maternal joy.

But as he now looked at her, his angry brain transformed her image into an unappealing black widow spider, whose scheming had deliberately fooled and entrapped him in a deceitful maternal web. Her unnaturally large, white fangs were set on devouring his career and his marriage. Her American accent was grating on him, and her voice seemed shrill, unnecessarily loud, and indiscreet for a restaurant setting.

He replayed her last words to him. "I do so want this baby, our baby, hon. Isn't it such great news!"

He looked up to the ceiling, searching for divine help to glean some ethereal inspiration. He saw the clouds and cherubic figures on the enormous painted fresco. It was the trompe l'oeil, done by an unknown French painter. The style of painting literally meant "to fool the eye," he recalled. How appropriate.

He looked down and viewed Rebecca straight in the eye, and smiling again, raised his shoulders as he took in a deep breath and lowered them as he exhaled.

"*How* could you be pregnant?" he whispered. "I thought we were both being careful."

"I was surprised as well, given we usually are. As you know, my cycle is pretty regular, and I always check first using my little ovulation detector device that assesses the percentage probability of an impregnation, and if it's 1 percent or above, then as we agreed, we always improvise or have oral. I was trying to think when it must have happened. Do you remember three weeks ago, here at the club when we stayed over, and I said to you that the reading that morning showed 'one,' but we went ahead anyway, and you came inside me? I think then it must have happened. And it was, if I recall"—she beamed with delight at the memory—"one of our best sessions! Remember how you took me from behind and then, you placed your finger inside my—"

Richard interrupted her, saying quietly but tersely, "Hold on, hold on. I thought you said 'none,' as in no percentage, not 'one.'"

The Feather of Truth   Ian Campbell-Laing

"You must have misheard me. I definitely said one, sweetie!" As Rebecca smiled, twin grotesque laughter lines framed the sides of her mouth. They looked like those of the Joker played by Jack Nicholson in the Batman films, and it repulsed him. She squeezed her soft slender fingers onto his hands, not caring anymore if anyone noticed them being affectionate in this public setting.

He sighed quietly. No point going down this dead-end blame avenue of confusion, he thought. He lightened his tone, and smiled. "Well, anyway, this is all fantastic news, sweetheart, and yes, of course…what we ultimately wanted," he lied. "But not quite the timing you and I had planned for, Rebecca. I mean…I haven't even left my wife yet! What do you want to do? Do you want to have the baby? At this time, I mean?"

Rebecca frowned and looked anxious, needing that reassurance that she had partnered with the right man. "Richard, hon, of course I want to have our baby, and yes, I want him or her now. Don't *you*?" she said, laboring the last word in a long, babyish voice.

Richard knew the staff were getting impatient to clear the amuse-bouche and serve their starters. He briefly raised his eyebrows and nodded his head, motioning to Hawker to come over, hoping it would give him more time to think. He took a large swig of his white wine, wishing the cold alcohol would numb his brain.

The starters were placed before them with great fanfare and a long description of what the ingredients were and how the dish had been prepared. But Richard could not even acknowledge their existence. He just nodded in obedience of his predicament, barely hearing the waiter's enthusiastic voice saying, "The salad of quail egg for madam: an exquisite quail egg from Campbelltown's superb organic farm in the north western Highlands of Scotland, lightly poached with organic, pan-roasted, honey-coated seasonal vegetables on a crisp salad with a truffle foam. And for you, sir, the pan-seared scallops…with a fennel and mushroom duxelles…shallot puree and a vanilla and licorice foam. Bon appetite."

Rebecca saw that Richard was distracted and clearly not listening to her, so she repeated her question. "Richard, hon, of course I want to have our baby, and yes, I want it now. Don't you?"

Richard just sat there, consumed by his own thoughts. His right index finger gently circled the rim of his wine glass, going around and around in a rhythmical, almost trancelike manner.

Rebecca added more food to his already overburdened thoughts. "And you know that I am a devout Catholic, and in God's eyes, abortion is out of the question. It's clearly murdering an innocent precious life. The fifth commandment says 'Thou shalt not kill.' You know that life begins at conception, and any Catholic who supports abortion should not receive the Communion but instead must confess their sins and face permanent damnation."

Richard hated being lectured to, especially by the God Squad, and it seemed to him, unless he was completely mistaken, so hypocritical that in the Catholic Church, one could commit a crime—murder, even—and then if you confess your sins to a priest who claims to have a direct line to God and say a few Hail Mary's for penance, you would then be forgiven and saved from hell. Why couldn't Rebecca simply have the abortion, confess her sin to the priest, do a bit of penance, and let it be, so we can all move on? He knew that this wasn't the appropriate time to have a long debate with his intelligent and stubborn mistress about the Catholic Church's apparently—well, to him at least—paradoxical rules.

"Well, er, yes, of course. It's just all a bit of a shock to the system. You've got to admit it's a tad sudden, Rebecca. What and when are we going to tell Jelly…sorry, er, Chuck? He'll go apeshit, that's for sure."

"I don't know what I, or rather *we*, will tell him. That's why, hon, I want to talk it through with you first and agree on a plan. But let's eat, sweetie. I'm starving. Bon appetite, darling. My salad looks great. And your scallops look scrummy yummy."

When Richard had arrived at the club, he was famished, having skipped lunch. Now, less than two handfuls of words spoken in less than a couple of seconds: *I'm pregnant and of course you are the father*, had replaced his appetite with questions and had changed his calm, confident demeanor for the emotions of regret, fear, and anger. He didn't understand how Rebecca could be taking this all so matter-of-factly. So much was at stake for him. And he needed more time to regroup his thoughts. Now he knew why he had detected earlier on a hint of her New York nasal accent; she had been nervous about telling him her news.

He continued his act of the concerned but happy lover. "So how are you feeling? Any morning sickness?"

"Nope, not yet. I do feel on top of the world. I'm having a baby with the man of my dreams, and I can now leave my moronic, abusive husband."

"Are you sure about the results? You've done the test properly?"

"Yes. It's in my handbag and clearly says the word 'pregnant' in a blue box. I won't bring it out here, but I'll show you later. I'm so proud, and I was hoping you would be, too."

Oh well, it was worth asking, he thought. "Yes, of course I am proud, but you've just caught me off guard, Rebecca. It's obviously great news, and what we ultimately wanted, but the timing is just sudden, that's all. Look, Jelly gets back from New York next week, doesn't he?"

"Yes, that's what he said originally, but he left a message on our voice mail at home this afternoon saying he hoped to be back this weekend, probably on Sunday morning on the red eye."

"When do you plan on telling him the news?" asked Richard.

"I'd like you to be with me when I do. Hey, why not come for lunch on Sunday at our house? He mentioned to me on the phone that he wants to talk to you about that project you're working on, so maybe you could use that as an excuse to come over. Or do you want to just tell him over the phone tomorrow when you're in the office?"

"No, I wouldn't tell him just yet and so soon, and it's not fair to convey such shocking news on the phone. Let's think about it and decide tomorrow. We can coordinate when to tell Chuck, Jennifer, and my kids in the best way to minimize the pain to everyone. How's that sound?"

Her voice suddenly went up an octave. "So…you do still"—she lowered her voice back to its natural tone—"so, you do still want me, Richard, as your wife? You do want to raise a family together with me, don't you?" She needed solace that he meant what he had said before so many times, and that he was committed to the plans they had made about a future together. Losing her soul mate, especially now, carrying his child, was inconceivable. She had trusted his word. They had no secrets. He would never lie to her. They believed in the Feather of Truth, as they referred to their pact.

"Of course I do, sweetheart, but actually, to be honest, I'm dying for a pee. I'll be back in a moment. You start eating, or it will get cold."

Richard got up, lightly patted her on the shoulder, and left the room in search of the sanctuary of the toilets. He glanced at his watch. It was only 7:45 p.m. He had spent less than forty minutes with Rebecca, and in the last four minutes, his misstep had caused his perception of his life's favorable future path to completely change direction.

As he left the restaurant, he heard laughter and clapping from one flight upstairs. Must be from the Committee Room, he thought. Well, some folk are clearly having a better day than I. He trod heavy footed down the two flights of stairs, past a view of the enormous indoor swimming pool, and entered the gentlemen's. He saw that all of the dark-oak-paneled cubicles were open, and no one was at the urinals or the washbasins. He locked himself in the corner cubicle and then took off and hung up his jacket, undid his belt, unzipped his flies, and dropped his trousers. He sat on the toilet with his forehead in his hands and gave out a large sigh.

The cubicle's walls gave him solace: they were a fortress, protecting him from his mistress's ambush on his way of life. He needed to formulate a plan expeditiously, given Jelly arrived back in Britain in just over two days. What had he done? How in the world was he going to survive this? What could he do?

Well, it can't get any worse, surely? he consoled himself.

The Feather of Truth   Ian Campbell-Laing

***

New York City, United States of America

Celsius rubbed his temples and sighed. He hated these dreary internal audit meetings. He had been going through the latest monthly report of violations and errors for his division—all innocent mistakes that his doggedly persistent head of audit, Hans Talisman, would surely rectify to ensure they didn't occur again. He discreetly checked his cell phone under the table and saw an e-mail from the head of corporate security for the bank.

Mmm. Why would Udo be contacting me? Wondered Celsius. He scanned the key points of the message and was intrigued.

Discuss…employee's actions…systems protocol breach…Today.

There was no mention of which employee, which office had been breached, or which security system, but Celsius knew that for the mighty Udo to be involved, it had to be serious. The culprit was done for. Poor bastard; he or she will never work in this industry again, he thought.

Excellent. Things are livening up my otherwise rather dull day. I wonder which idiot it is? Probably that moron, Gunter Schwarzkopf, my less than esteemed head of IT and ops. Celsius smiled. If so, good. We've been trying to find a way around the rigid Germanic labor laws to get rid of that serial philanderer for ages!

CHAPTER 20
THE RAC

Richard sat on the toilet, his forehead still bent forward and resting on his hands. He breathed slowly and deeply. His thoughts pounding his brain.

Shit, shit, shit! This is an effing nightmare of a day. How on earth am I going to get out of this one, Houdini? I should have kept my zipper done up and never, ever had sex with her, or at least had the nouse to persuade her to let him use a ruddy condom. Christ Almighty, what a numpty I am, what a right Herbert.

His mistress was clearly far more besotted and madly in love with him than he had appreciated, and was now determined to have his baby. Richard did not love Rebecca; he was very fond of her, of course, and was very attracted to her. She was a gorgeous woman. And yes, she was intelligent and fun to be with, but so was his long-suffering wife, Jennifer, or rather, she had been in the good old days. Rebecca was never meant to be "the one"; instead it was always just a bit of fun for him, let off some steam, satisfy his inherent male need for passion, and a secret way to get back at his annoying thief of a boss. Richard should have known she was getting more serious about him. She had intimated as much, often, but like the fool he now knew he was, he had ignored it. And when she had talked about ultimately starting a family, he had said whatever she had wanted to hear, and after saying it, he blocked it from his mind and focused on arousing her for more intimacy. God, he was a prize prat.

One thought came to the front of his mind. Maybe Rebecca had deliberately got pregnant to trap him into marriage? Suddenly he loathed her deceit.

No matter. Start thinking straight, he thought. I better come up with a plan, and ruddy sharpish, and before Jelly Bean gets back on Sunday morning. But what if the silly cow spills the beans to her husband in a moment of weakness during Sunday lunch, or before?

What was absolutely certain was that if Jelly found out, Richard's career—created during fifteen years of hard work, networking, and long hours—would end abruptly. Jelly would make Richard's life an utter misery. Richard had witnessed Chuck's ruthlessness many times before: once when one of Richard's colleagues made disparaging remarks about Chuck's lack of intellect, behind Chuck's back, that person was fired the next day.

Today was Thursday evening, and in a few days, maybe tomorrow, Richard's world could collapse, and all because, like so many men before him, he had thought with his balls and not his brains. He tried to calmly weigh the pros and cons of his newfound predicament. He started thinking and occasionally speaking softly to himself, even though he hadn't heard anyone come into the men's room.

Let's start with the bad news: the cons, the demons I have to fight.

"Fact one," he whispered and then thought, Rebecca is a devout Catholic and madly in love with me. She is clearly determined to have my child and settle down with me, very soon. Whether or not she deliberately got herself pregnant isn't relevant immediately. I have to trust her for the moment that the baby is mine, and there seems to be no point in fighting or questioning any of these facts. She would probably have the baby with or without me. "Yes, to abort the baby is murder in her eyes. Damn it."

"Fact two." The birth of that baby, or even the announcement of the pregnancy, would ruin my career and my marriage and eliminate most of the time I would have with my precious children. "Not to mention my ruddy finances, which would be decimated," He said softly. "Similarly, for the same reasons, leaving Jennifer to start a new life with Rebecca was out of the question."

"Fact three." Rebecca was so keen to announce her "great news" to Jelly, it was all Richard could do to get her to delay it until Jelly's return on Sunday. Given it is my birthday this weekend on Saturday, in practice that only left tonight and all day tomorrow to figure out a plan. Just over a day. Time has drawn me a lousy hand. I have to make a decision very soon. "*Tempus fugit*, no question. Time flies, especially in a crisis, Richard old chap," He said rather too loudly.

He paused to stretch his arms, and then placing them back on his forehead, he continued in his part thought, part sporadic soliloquy.

"OK, so now let's turn to the good news, the pros." Initially, Richard couldn't think of any at all. "Come on, think, man. There must be something good to emerge from this sad episode?" Then they came to him.

"Fact one." It seems that only Rebecca and I know of the situation.

"Fact two." Today, I have nearly finalized the London office profitability project I've been working on for Jelly, and it is a masterpiece. I could, in less than an hour, finish it completely and not be distracted further by it.

"Fact three." Jelly's boss, Celsius, will yet again be reminded of my abilities, this time for the work I have done on that project. Perhaps I could use it to undermine Celsius's confidence in Jelly and get Celsius to start appreciating me more. "But that doesn't help me in the immediate short term, of course."

"So let's see, fact four." I am a pretty smart guy, and surely someone else has been in a similar predicament and found a perfect solution. He racked his brains and recalled some pompous Cambridge doctor who had an affair with someone way back, maybe twenty years ago now, and then tried mildly poisoning her to force a natural abortion. *Of course!* He mumbled to himself, "That's what I need to do—by stealth induce an abortion!" He tried to remember the guy's name and the consequences of his actions. It had been all over the press, so something must have gone wrong, but at least Richard could then learn from the doctor's mistakes. He now remembered. His name was Dr. Edward Pervin, or Ervin or Evert, or Pervert more likely, or something like that. And he had had an affair with his secretary, Bella somebody or other. The philandering quack could not persuade her to have an abortion, so he allegedly spiked her Starbucks latte with a miscarriage-inducing drug. Was he acquitted? Richard could not recall. Worth checking this out though, he thought.

Richard went online on his iPhone and searched "Doctor Ervin abortion Starbucks spiked drinks."

"Erin" came up as the likely answer. One click downloaded it:

2009…Doctor Edward…not first affair…with secretary Bella…at office party…bombarded her with texts to try and get her to abort…refused…spiked her drink…she detected funny taste in latte and orange juice…told her best friend with whom she always confided…they went to police…analyzed latte…found miscarriage-inducing drug…doctor had access to prescription…Bella gave birth to healthy boy…trial…Doctor got six years…career ruined…Baby would grow up eventually knowing his father was this demented doctor who had wanted to kill him before he was even born.

"Shit, shit, shit!" he swore in frustration. This was not going to be easy. And Bella had confided the whole saga with her best friend. "Good point," he mumbled. What about Rebecca's best friend, Dawn? My God, I've completely forgotten about her. I wonder if she knows about Rebecca's pregnancy? Christ, those two are thick as thieves, and don't women share all secrets like that between themselves? OMG! Add fact four, "Dim Dawn" to the cons and demons list, he thought.

Sighing, he exhaled and then spoke, softly, "Fact five." I already have a file of very useful incriminating information on Jelly to make Jelly's professional life uncomfortable, with questions raising doubt about his integrity. Unique knowledge is often powerful, and this could be a very useful bargaining tool at the right time.

Richard quietly concluded his assessment. "Yes, I will devote more time tomorrow to getting more information from VCb's V-Trax system. Maybe I could find an angle to get Jelly fired for cause by revealing some of this information I have and the additional info I am going to obtain. But can I do all that before I see Jelly on Sunday, which is only in a couple of days?"

Richard sighed knowing that that kind of information would take time to accumulate and then plant in the correct manner, and before then, long before then, Jelly would hear of his wife's and his so-called loyal manager's tryst. Oh God, what an unholy mess!

The Feather of Truth   Ian Campbell-Laing

"I have to take very swift and measured action," he said, softly. His conclusion was, *extremis malis, extrema remedia.* Desperate times call for desperate measures.

He checked his watch and saw that he had been gone for about eight minutes. That's too long, he thought. Rebecca would wonder what he'd been doing. He got dressed, left the cubicle, and as he was washing his hands, in came a tall, well-dressed African-looking man who went to the urinal to relieve himself. Kofi had been sitting with the other guests at the top table and decided to nip into the restroom after he had given his presentation, before returning for the after-speech Q&A, drinks and socializing.

Kofi and Richard now both stood at the marble basins without speaking, looking down at their own hands as they washed them under the taps. As they then dried their hands on the embossed linen towels, each looked up at their own reflection in the mirror. One of them, with his mind racing, was concentrating on the predicament in which he had landed himself due to his selfish act, and the other man, breathing measuredly and slowly, was delighted that his speech had been well received and he could now relax.

Kofi glanced to the right in the mirror and recognized the man instantly, even though he had only seen him for a few seconds, and he had since been in a room of fifty people. It was a skill he had used extensively during his career: being able to recognize and immediately put a name to a face.

"We meet again, Mr. de L'Isle," said Kofi, smiling warmly.

Richard's shoulders rose up quickly in slight shock at the sound of this man's unusually deep voice. Each looked across in the mirror at the other man's eyes, which were in line with his own. Richard noticed a long scar down the right hand side of the man's face.

"We do?" Richard sighed, and raised his head back in surprise, his eyebrows narrowing. He thought it was the first time he had met the man, and had no idea how he knew Richard's name. He snorted through his nose at this irritating person who had interrupted his thoughts.

Richard waited for the man to finish drying his hands and turned to his left to face the man and held out his hand to him. "You apparently know of me sir, but I have no idea who you are."

Kofi turned also and saw Richard smiling somewhat nervously at him. They both noticed how firm a handshake the other had, and as each was sizing the other up, they both noticed that the other was slim, fit, muscular, and wearing an expensive suit, almost identical in colour to his own. Richard thought however, that Kofi's tie somehow didn't seem to go with the suit.

"I'm Kofi Ghazini, Mr. de L'Isle."

"Pleased to meet you, Kofi, and please call me Richard. I've been a member for around ten years, I guess. How about you?"

"I'm not a member; I am an invited guest. I've just finished giving a presentation tonight."

"Oh, good for you. I'm in banking. What's your line of work?" Richard said, hoping the conversation would be brief.

"Crime, Richard, crime—I catch criminals."

Unsure how to respond, all Richard could muster was, "Happy hunting then, Inspector!"

"It's *Detective chief* inspector, actually."

"Good for you. Bye, Chief Inspector."

"Goodbye Richard," Kofi said, and he didn't know why he added instinctively, "until we meet again, then."

Richard walked slowly back up the stairs to the restaurant, his mind searching for a way out of his mess, but each time ending up with a similar unhelpful conclusion.

He arrived back to the table to see Rebecca tapping away on her iPhone.

"Sorry, sweetheart, I was chatting with Ivano about his wedding plans: he cornered me in the men's room. And then some DCI introduced himself to me, and we chatted briefly." Richard found it effortless to supplement a lie with the truth, seamlessly creating credibility. "Anything going on?"

"Nope, just e-mailing my baby sister; she's going to be in London in a month. As you know, she's based in New York, and we don't get to see each other as much as we'd like. I've always looked out for her."

"That's Mia, right? She's in HR or something like that, I think you said?"

"Yes, she works for a firm of headhunters. You should meet her—you'd like her. She's a couple of inches taller than me, a brunette, and very athletic. I've always thought she is a bit skinny, but she has no trouble attracting men. Unfortunately, she's just going through a rather messy divorce with a very rich guy. The three of us should all go out for dinner together."

"Great idea." He then kissed Rebecca's forehead lightly and whispered in her ear, "I love you, darling, and we are going to be so very happy."

"Oh, Richard, you are so right, and I am so lucky to have such a great guy like you. I was just talking about you to Dawn in the bookstore this morning, and—"

"Hold on, Rebecca, you haven't told anyone of our very personal news, have you? Not even your best friend, Dawn?" He grabbed her arm, rather too roughly.

"Ouch, you are hurting me."

"Oh, sorry." He relaxed his fingers. "Please don't tell me you have already told Dawn, darling?"

"Well, not exactly…"

PART TWO

Here's to the feeling of being trapped!

Thomas Crown (Pierce Brosnan) speaking to
Catherine Banning (Rene Russo)

The Cipriani restaurant, Manhattan, New York,
in the film *The Thomas Crown Affair*, 1999

CHAPTER 21
PARK AVENUE, NEW YORK CITY

Celsius Maysmith III was sitting at his desk in his corner office. A blend of traditional maple, mahogany, and old masters paintings contrasted the ultra-high-definition screens of four computers and two TVs. Outside on the streets of Manhattan, an early surge of weary humans dressed heterogeneously would start filling the sidewalks and become the army of commuters scurrying to subway and railroad stations, with a shared mission to carry them home, quickly and without incident.

His phone intercom buzzed, and the shrill voice of his secretary, Amy Doerringer, came through. "I have Udo Wassermann on the line for your five p.m. call, Celsius, if you're ready."

"Thanks, Amy. Yes, put Udo through, please," said Celsius, amazed at her sudden professionalism but knowing that tomorrow was his secretary's last day: her slapdash approach, frequent mistakes in setting up meetings, and constant errors on his expense claim forms had been too much for him to tolerate.

"Mr. Wassermann, Mr. Maysmith will take your call now, thank you. Just putting you through."

"Udo, how nice to hear from you. It's been a while since we met and spoke. It's quite late your time in Frankfurt, isn't it?"

"Yes, Celsius, it is. I'm sorry to trouble you, but an incident has come up, and I wanted to get your help in resolving it," replied Udo in perfect English but with a hint of a German accent.

"With pleasure, of course. You mentioned in your e-mail an employee breaching a system. May I ask what VCb system, which employee, what damage did they do, and when was this, precisely?"

"All good questions, Celsius. However, I am not at liberty to divulge which system, precisely, but it's one that contains confidential client data and personnel records of employees at VCb."

"Did this person download such data? If so, that is theft, surely?"

"Precisely, it is. However, this employee only managed to *see* the data and not download anything, as far as we can tell."

"Well, that's a relief. By personnel records, do you mean those files including compensation information of my division, Udo?"

"Yes, Celsius, this employee appears to have had access to the entire compensation file of your division, so, all 3,500 employees."

"Can I assume that this employee isn't part of and didn't see my own senior management committee's compensation? It's presumably on a separate file, as is my own compensation, which is on the highly confidential file for the bank's Global Operating Committee's eight members."

Udo smiled, thinking that Celsius is cunning. He is quietly pulling rank by mentioning that he's in the inner circle of the top eight employees at the bank, and therefore, more senior than me—and also trying to ascertain the extent of the hacker's probing and hence, the possible culprit. Udo suspected that Celsius's logic was that there would be few employees that would dare search for Celsius's compensation—only a disgruntled person. No *sane* person would go into a system and search for the CEO's compensation file. If discovered, that CEO would fire him or her immediately, and they would never work in the industry again.

"Celsius, you are of course correct that your compensation is on a separate file. Incidentally, there are other senior managers on that file, including myself."

It was Celsius's turn to have respect. So, Udo had seen his thought process and recognized that he, Udo, was high up in the ranks and also reported directly to Dr. Klaus. We are playing an interesting game of one-upmanship here, he thought.

"But the main reason that I am calling is that I have to say, your employee *did* access the bank's GOC compensation file, and hence saw your, and indeed my, salary. Therefore, we need to consider how best to treat this delicate systems protocol breach."

"I see," Celsius said and then paused while contemplating the implications. "We have some very smart people with extensive IT knowledge that would be needed to breach a complex system like that..." He paused, wishing Udo would name the system but suspected Udo would not. "But to be frank," Celsius said, "that IT knowledge would probably not be available to my most very senior managers, apart from the head of IT, as you can appreciate."

"Celsius, I can inform you that our system alerted us that the hacker *appeared* to be using a PC from his New York office, in your building."

Celsius missed the emphasis of the word *appeared*. "Oh, really? Well, that narrows it down. Why don't you tell me the name of this male employee? I need the name if you wish me to take further action."

"Yes, certainly. It's your global chief operating officer, Chuck Jelleners."

"What? I don't believe it! He is my most senior manager, the number two in my department, but I doubt he has the IT skills to hack into a complex system, whatever its name is. Are you sure, Udo?" He knew that Chuck—that little weasel of a man—was certainly brash enough to try and find out Celsius's salary; he was fully aware that Chuck had been angling after his CEO role of the division for years.

"Yes, at this stage we believe that it's his PC, Celsius. We located it from the IP address and confirmed that he was at his desk working on his PC throughout the systems breach."

"I would like to see the evidence of his or his accomplice's hacking before we take any action, naturally."

Udo smiled again. *Of course you would. That way you can learn more about the V-Trax system itself.*

"Of course, Celsius, but in the meantime, please do not do anything further. Obviously, do not notify Mr. Jelleners. We need to play this very carefully. We plan on trapping Mr. Jelleners before we dismiss him."

"Before *I* dismiss him, Udo, I presume you mean?"

"Yes, Celsius, that is what I meant, of course."

"Good, Udo. Then I await your further instructions."

"Thank you, Celsius, and have a good day."

"You too, Udo."

***

Frankfurt, Germany

Udo continued to sit behind his desk, into the late hours of the evening, staring out at a streetlamp from his office window. Some moths were attracted to its warm light. He reflected on the call. Celsius had reinforced Udo's own thoughts about Chuck Jelleners's IT skills, or lack thereof.

Udo had researched Chuck's human resources file, and there was no evidence of any extensive IT skills at all. Which is why Udo had already asked the V-Trax system to list the top five employees within Celsius's division with the highest IT skills on their resume, or those who had demonstrated exemplary technology aptitude when performing their role. Of course he couldn't be sure it was definitely someone within Celsius's division, but he had to start the search somewhere.

He looked at that V-Trax report again. At the top of the list was Richard de L'Isle, the employee with the fancy spy pen. He was ex Oxford University, England, earning an MA, but more importantly, had come first in his electrical engineering and computer science class at MIT. Interesting. There were four other names, none of which he recognized.

Perhaps Chuck was working in collusion with one, or several, of these five? Or perhaps the hacker was simply using Chuck's PC as a smokescreen to blame Chuck? So who has a grudge against Chuck – any of these five?

The plot thickens. The net is closing in on our perpetrator or perpetrators.

I wonder how many employees are involved here, and how many need to be eliminated? Like the inviting streetlight, I need to seduce the hacking moths into making a mistake.

***

Teddington

Kofi sat in his cottage reminiscing. He was also thinking of seduction: how this beautiful woman had captured his heart. He thought when he first met her that she was far too good for him. She was beautiful, intelligent, and very witty. She had just qualified as a doctor and was now studying for her psychiatry exams. Her family was also very wealthy, and she was white.

They had met ten years ago at a mutual friend's Christmas party and had started going out soon afterwards. Kofi, who was usually methodical and liked to piece together the mosaic of evidence before concluding, proposed to her a month later. He couldn't believe it when she accepted.

She said that when she first met him, she had never before seen a man so handsome, gentle, strong, and powerful. With his intellect and dry sense of self-deprecating humour, she knew he would be her soul mate. She just had one lifetime request of him. "Always protect me, please."

Then, in his memory, the gunman burst into Kofi's cottage, and the nightmare flashback began again, and Kofi screamed out loud, "No, no, don't do that! Not my Francesca, please. We can work this out!"

Now, as he sat in his favorite armchair, his heart rate racing from the memory, he wiped the sweat that had appeared on his forehead. Yes, I should take the chief constable's advice and seek help in coping with my PTSD, he thought.

CHAPTER 22
THE RAC

"Rebecca darling, what do you mean by 'Well, not exactly'? What did you *say* to Dawn?" said Richard, calmly, but forcibly, adding, "I want to keep this little secret between ourselves, just for now, so that we can manage it properly. After all, we don't want Dawn spilling the beans too early, do we?"

She noticed him tapping the table with his index fingers, which she knew he did only when he was anxious.

"No, of course not, and anyway, Dawn wouldn't say a thing," Rebecca replied softly, and shrugging her shoulders.

"So, what *exactly* did you tell Dawn, sweetheart?" Richard viewed Dawn as a serial blabbermouth who couldn't keep anything to herself.

"All I said was that I was seeing you tonight for dinner and that of course I was really looking forward to it, but also I had some good news for you."

Richard fired questions at her, unconvinced. "OK, but what do you think she understood by 'good news'? Will she guess you might be pregnant? I mean, has she any idea? Have you been giving her any hints about ultimately wanting a baby?"

"Hey, sweetie, calm down. Of *course* not. Look, Dawn obviously knows about our affair; she is, after all, my best friend. She knows your name and who you are and where you work. She also knows how much I enjoy being with you, and how deeply we feel for each other. I suspect she assumes we could at some stage become a pretty serious item. But all I said was I had a little surprise for you."

It was worse than he thought. Even dim Dawn could probably easily guess what was the surprise. It was looking increasingly like he would have to not just worry about what to do with Rebecca and her unborn baby and her husband, Jelly, but also her best friend, Dawn. Christ in heaven, what an unholy trinity of a mess, he concluded.

"Don't fret, hon. Dawn spotted me in the local bookstore, and so we had a coffee there and a chat. And I only said I had a present for your birthday on Saturday. So she just thinks I have a birthday pressie, that's all. And she didn't even ask what it was. So, no, I don't think Dawn suspects the real news. Obviously I will tell her soon, but not yet. She thinks our affair is still in its early days and so far just a bit of a fling, and nothing too serious, yet."

"OK, that's good, so Dawn probably just assumes you bought me a book for my birthday?"

"Absolutely, Richard. There's just no need to worry about Dawn."

The Feather of Truth   Ian Campbell-Laing

He wanted to believe Rebecca, but the more he thought about it, the more he found it hard to believe that a woman would not tell her best friend such matters like how serious was their affair or that she was pregnant or that they intended to marry. So, Dawn probably knew. Damn.

Rebecca smiled and patted his hand, as if calming an anxious pet.

Richard sighed and tried to put Dawn out of his mind. One thing at a time, Richard, he thought.

"So, Rebecca, let's talk about the weekend. What time does Chuck usually land when flying from New York?"

"He always gets the same flight when coming back on the weekend: takes off from JFK at a quarter of nine at night and lands at Heathrow at a quarter of nine in the morning."

"OK. So that's a busy time, especially at the weekend. So he'll clear passport control and customs, by about half nine, and should be at your gaff by no later than ten thirty. So, why don't I come by around half nine-ish, so we can gather our thoughts and plan how we're going to tell him the news? I'll set him up by e-mailing him now, asking him if he's free over the weekend to discuss the London project."

"OK, perfect, hon."

Richard took out his iPhone and, looking down, quickly punched out an e-mail to his boss. "And you, Rebecca, suggest that I pop over on Sunday morning. When you speak with him, you can hint to him that I should stay for lunch."

During the rest of the evening, Richard chased his food around his plate, taking small bites every now and again. He was only partially absorbing Rebecca's babblings on and on about where they should live, baby things, cots, and nursery wallpaper colours. It was constantly distracting his thoughts. He had so little time to come up with a plan.

As an English literature honors graduate, he had a memory bank of Shakespearian phrases and quotes. He often referred to them for comfort, guidance, or humour. He thought about one of the Bard's most famous ones:

To be or not to be—that is the question:
Whether 'tis nobler in the mind to suffer
The slings and arrows of outrageous fortune,
Or to take arms against a sea of troubles
And, by opposing, end them.

He continued his thoughts: in the play, Hamlet, just like Richard, was reminiscing about the unfairness of life and avenging a wrong. But unlike Hamlet, Richard wasn't considering his own death or suicide.

Yes, I must end all my troubles, end them all. So far, as a law-abiding citizen, Richard previously had only a disputed parking fine to his name.

The Feather of Truth Ian Campbell-Laing

Well, apart from one other incident, which he would prefer to forget.

A lady in the dining room had just started getting a few diners' attention when she couldn't stop coughing and then started choking, her face flush with anxiety. Her husband slapped her on the back a few times, and after a glass of water, she seemed to be fine. Richard had heard of some folk dying of choking if help didn't arrive quickly. A natural but unfortunate death, thought Richard. It happened to many people. Even Rebecca had choked in front of Richard a month ago. He smiled to himself and said, "Shall we take the remaining grapes to our room, darling?"

"Richard, yes, why not. They look delicious—large and such a bright-green colour."

"Oh, by the way, I thought we would try the Kent double bedroom suite tonight: it's on the third floor, Rebecca."

They left the restaurant, and after thanking Robbin, Hawker, and Ivano, made their separate ways to the lifts. Richard grabbed his coat and overnight bag from the front lobby and decided to walk up the stairs instead of using the lift, in order to give him more time to think. As he strode up to the first floor, he heard more loud laughter and clapping from the audience in the Committee Room. Lucky them, he thought.

Richard arrived first at the suite. He opened the door, and inside was a double bed, with an en suite bathroom and separate living area with a sofa and two armchairs. Rebecca deliberately dawdled and then used the ladies' room to freshen up. She then searched for the bedroom on what she thought was the third floor, until a chambermaid reminded her that she was actually on the second floor. She then remembered that in England what Americans refer to as the first floor, Brits call the ground floor. Carrying her overnight bag and shoulder bag, she hurried up one more flight of stairs. Out of breath, she knocked quietly twice on the door. Richard let her in. He put the Do Not Disturb sign on the outside doorknob and double-locked the door from inside the room.

Finally, they were alone.

CHAPTER 23
THE KENT SUITE, RAC

Rebecca entered the suite and put down her overnight bag and handbag. She turned around and shook her head when she saw Richard was now slumped back on the sofa, staring at the blank screen of the TV. His tie was undone, and his jacket hung over the armchair. He had kicked off his shoes and socks, and unusually for him, had left them sprawled on the carpet.

"Thinking about work, hon, still?"

"Yep, a little bit, and other things. The presentation I am working on is rather complicated," replied Richard.

"I know that Chuck is a demanding so-and-so."

"That he is."

"Once you've told Jennifer, and she's got used to us being together, she will be fine. You'll see."

"Yep. Not ready to tell her yet, obviously." He sighed loudly, desperately trying to concentrate on formulating his master plan.

"I know, and I am here to help you."

His vulnerability aroused her. Rebecca kissed him lightly on the lips, and she pulled herself away, saying, "Let me fix us both a drink. You've had a long day, and this American girl who adores you is here to help you relax and take your mind off things, sweetie."

Rebecca made them both a gin and tonic. Into each glass, she scooped a handful of ice, poured a large measure of Bombay Sapphire. and filled it up with Slimline tonic. She used the small toothpick on the silver tray to add a slice of lemon.

Then, she slipped off her silk jacket and undid the second button of her blouse, revealing the top of her black lace bra and sumptuous cleavage that she knew he loved to hold, caress, and kiss. She turned around to see Richard slumped even further back on the sofa. She needed to bring him back to his normal self. She knew precisely what to do. She grabbed their drinks and walked provocatively towards him, her hips swaying. She kicked off her shoes on the way. She leant forward and handed him his drink.

"Thanks." He sighed. He took a large gulp, and immediately spat it out, narrowly missing her face. He examined the glass and shouted at her, "For Christ's *sake*, it's the wrong make of gin and the wrong tonic. And, it's got too much ice, and lemon instead of lime! How ruddy difficult can it be?" He then rolled his eyes, shook his head and exhaled loudly.

Rebecca jolted her head back and froze. He had never before raised his voice at her. For a moment she felt nervous, but then she quickly reasoned that he simply was tense and uptight with work and the pregnancy news.

The Feather of Truth   Ian Campbell-Laing

Richard saw the effect his words had and said in a soft tone, "Darling, I'm sorry. It's not *your* fault. I have a lot on my mind and I'm a tad fussy about my drinks. Please forgive me for shouting. That was unacceptable."

"It's OK. I understand, sweetie," she said and sat down astride his powerful thighs. She took his drink, and placed it and hers on the side table. As she leaned forward to kiss him, she unclipped the clasp out of her hair and let the silky strands gently fall, caressing his face.

His mouth didn't open or respond.

Rebecca tried the ploys that usually excited him. Breathing gently near his face and kissing and nibbling at his lips and ears, pressing her chest against his, cupping his face with her hands and moving his head towards her breasts.

He just sat there, motionless, his eyes now closed.

She leant over and took a swig of her drink and the ice, and without swallowing it, she got off his legs and knelt down in front of him. She started to undo his belt. She knew that the coldness of the ice on the warm skin of his member, coupled with her hot, moist mouth clamped around this most sensitive part of his body, would quickly surge blood to his expanding vessels, springing it upwards and desiring more frictional action. She started to feel slightly moist just thinking about it. But now he turned his face away, opened his eyes, and gently placing his hand on hers, he started to pull her hands away from his belt. "Not now, darling," he said. "Let's just relax first awhile, OK? In fact let me open the bottle of wine I brought with me. Chuck's boss, Celsius owns Chateau Maris, an organic vineyard in the Languedoc region, which produces some amazing wines."

Richard got up and retrieved the 94 point stunner, Les Amandier Syrah 2022 from his overnight bag. He uncorked it, poured two generous glasses and walked back to the sofa. He handed Rebecca her glass and took a large swig of his.

"Now *that's* a very good wine." He sat down on the sofa, closed his eyes, and said softly, "Yes, let's just relax here first, Rebecca."

Oh, well, she thought. He and I have a lifetime together and plenty of opportunities for me to keep him interested in me, so there's no rush. I am so lucky to have found such a great person like Richard, who adores me and wants to start a family with me—unlike my deceitful, arrogant, abusive husband. I couldn't be happier. I need to just be patient with Richard and let him rest.

"Would you like any of the grapes?" asked Richard as he opened his eyes again.

"I thought you were feeling too tired for some fun, sweetie!" She smiled and raised her eyebrows.

The Feather of Truth   Ian Campbell-Laing

"Uh? Oh, sorry, no. I didn't mean doing *that* to you with the grapes. I just meant that I fancy some of those large, juicy, dark grapes to eat, along with my drink. That's all. Do you want some as well?"

"I will get them for you, sweetie, but none for me, thanks. I'm completely full, and I find them difficult to swallow. You may have forgotten that I choked on them as a child and nearly died. I certainly don't want to end up choking like that woman in the restaurant tonight!"

Worth a try. Pity, he thought. Then his eyes opened wider, in recognition of his folly. Think, Richard, think of consequences. Your mistress chokes on a grape in your hotel room of your club and dies? You will be front-page news and soon receiving divorce papers together with your redundancy letter.

They watched the predictable schoolboy humour of a rerun of an old episode of *Top Gear* on the TV, talking very little. Later, they undressed and went to bed. He said good night to her, briefly pecked her on her forehead, and turned away from her. She nuzzled her breasts into his arched back, with her mouth gently breathing onto the back of his neck. She reached her left hand over his hips, to feel between his legs for any sign of him being aroused—he was just flaccid and warm. She sighed—she was moist with anticipation. She considered whether or not she should relieve the pressure of her desires by herself, but decided it would disturb him. So she just pecked him on his neck and soon fell into a deep sleep.

Richard couldn't sleep, his mind weighing up his options. He winced as he heard her snoring and elbowed her in her stomach. She grunted, turned over facing away from him, and the noise stopped. Maybe she got pregnant deliberately. She wouldn't be the first woman to trap a man into marriage—but was she capable of that? Yes, he concluded.

After awhile, he thought he had the guts of a plan to extricate him from his predicament. He still couldn't get to sleep, but he had two methods for calming himself in such situations: reciting Shakespeare to himself and doing anagram puzzles in his head. Tonight he decided to think of anagrams of the names of the four staff at the restaurant.

The first to tackle was Robbin Sweeny, the sommelier. After just a minute, he smiled and came up with *Wine Snobbery*.

Then the chef, Terry Guanosee, who was Italian born but raised in the United Kingdom. It took him ten minutes, until he remembered how the restaurant had taken an age to introduce a vegetarian option on their menu, after he had first raised it with the Food and Beverage Subcommittee. The letters fitted perfectly—*Eat your green*s! Perfectamundo, he mused.

Hawker Grainnis was next. He thought about his job as the main server and how Richard would not be able to cope with having to be so nice to guests all the time: especially to people who obviously had so much more wealth than the staff. It must grate on them at times, surely? After fifteen minutes, he came up with what Hawker must often think when a restaurateur calls him over, or when a butler is summoned to help his master: *A wanker rings. Hi.*

Finally the last person, the Swiss-Italian born maître'd, his old friend Ivano Gerdellms. After nearly twenty minutes, he was no closer. He was getting tired and knew he must sleep soon. Finally he cracked the code: *Smile and grovel.*

***

Frankfurt

At that precise time, seven hundred miles from London, Udo put down the updated V-Trax report and glanced at his watch: 2:30 a.m., Frankfurt time. He was now tired and needed to be getting some sleep. It was too early to wake his master and inform him that he believed it could now be a team of up to six employees—and not just one person—who had accessed their highly confidential security system.

"So," Udo said aloud to himself, "let's just recap where we are. V-Trax had identified the unique Internet protocol digital address of the hacker's PC in New York that had made the penetration: it was Chuck Jelleners's PC. At the time of the penetration, only Chuck was at his desk in New York, with no one else present in Chuck's office.

"However, given Chuck's apparent, but not confirmed, lack of hacking knowledge, that meant someone must have accessed Chuck's PC remotely. To accomplish that, these hackers would have had to access Chuck's PC knowing his user ID and password, obtain a copy of his fingerprint, pass a retinal scan, and create a voice copy of him saying his name into the microphone on his PC. Then, their keystrokes would have had to mimic those used by Chuck's fingers, and finally they had to mask their own computer's IP address and replace it with Chuck's PC's to lead the trail away from the hackers and back to Chuck."

Udo paused and then added, "Clearly, it's either Chuck accessing V-Trax with help from an IT geek, or not Chuck at all, but one or more highly sophisticated and determined hackers, who remotely accessed Chuck's PC and deliberately made it look like Chuck was the culprit. And that someone presumably had a grudge against Chuck. Interesting."

First, Udo needed to get V-Trax to run some more enquiries on these six employees' PCs, personal laptops, and cell phones, to establish who exactly was involved and then decide on how to deal with the traitor or traitors; a final solution, if you will.

Udo had known the CEO since they had served in the Swiss army together, and he would not break his honor code towards him. He would protect the bank against these cyber terrorist attacks. Whatever it took.

***

Pall Mall, London

Richard was now feeling weary and ready for sleep, but he reached for his iPhone and clicked on the BBC news app, which he always did last thing at night and first thing when he awoke. His face froze when he read the headlines of the first story:

Online criminal suspected of insider knowledge hacks into top European bank.

CHAPTER 24
THE RAC

Richard started sweating and clicked to read more. Then he said quietly to himself, "Thank God—it was a British, not a German bank."

Although it was early days yet, but so far he appeared to have gotten away with breaking into the V-Trax system without anyone knowing. He had accessed confidential data, and more importantly and rather cleverly, left a deliberate trail back to his boss's PC. Hopefully, soon, the head of security would be knocking on Jelly Bean's door and asking him some awkward questions. Jelly would, of course, deny everything—but the seeds of doubt about Chuck Jelleners's integrity would be irrevocably planted in the minds of Celsius Maysmith III and Mr. Udo Wassermann. Finally Richard got to sleep at just after 2:00 a.m.

Four hours later on Friday morning, Richard quietly got up, and slipped out from under the thick feather-down duvet, trying to not wake his mistress. He checked his cellphone and saw that last night he hadn't spotted the text message from his wife, sent at 20:30.

Hi, it's me. I know I don't text often, just wanted to ask how your dinner with Sir James was going? Call me before you go to bed, I will stay up late for you. Love Jens xx

"Damn," he chastised himself quietly. I should have called Jens. She hasn't been herself recently. Seems a bit depressed. I must call her this morning. He tapped in a reminder into his calendar to do so and then quickly texted her back.

Jens, sorry for late reply. Mtg with Sir James went well. Ended up being a late night and didn't see your text until just now. Hope you didn't stay up too late. Will call this morning and be back for you and the boys early tonight. Love R xxx

He silently put on his swimming togs, grabbed his goggles, and wrapped a towel around his shoulders. As often happens, even though he quietly opened the bedroom door, the clunking sound of the lock closing shut after he had left always seems to be too loud. He strolled down the flights of stairs to the basement and entered the club's twenty-six-meter pool. He was alone and swam fifty laps very hard. He then went back to the bedroom, showered, and got dressed for work. The club rules were strictly a suit and tie on weekdays.

The morning swim had been exhausting, and he was still tired from it and the lack of sleep. He looked at his watch: a quarter to seven. The key to today, he reminded himself, was to leave only those additional tracks and clues that he wished to be found—just like those he had left in the V-Trax system yesterday. He was sure that by now, Udo Wassermann had been alerted of the bank being hacked by Chuck's PC. The only question was whether or not Richard's G-H0st had exited V-Trax before detection, and if not, there was the possibility of him having inadvertently left a trail back to himself and his spy pen.

***

Frankfurt

Udo had just finished briefing Klaus at their weekly meeting.

"That's very interesting, Udo, but troublesome. You were quite right to bring this to my attention." Klaus knew that he could trust Udo in keeping him informed; after all, they had known each other and remained close for over forty years.

"Yes, indeed, Herr Doktor, and thank you. At first, we considered that the report by V-Trax was incorrect and had a glitch, but we now know that not to be the case. The perpetrator who broke through the firewalls in V-Trax is clearly an elite hacker expert enough to leave virtually no trace of their presence."

"But *you* are more of an expert in being able to detect them breaking through the sophisticated firewalls and accessing confidential compensation and important client data, surely?"

"Well, yes, thank you. The system we developed was set up to do precisely that. Initially, V-Trax's security protocol couldn't ascertain which files the hacker had been viewing. The hacker created a dummy file, which temporarily stored data before transferring it to their own computer, after which the dummy file automatically self-destructed, leaving no track of its presence. Ordinarily, any other system not as sophisticated as ours would have not seen any presence of the hacker. But we had inbuilt a subprogram that created a slightly higher magnetic field around any new file created. This remained there, unseen by the hacker after his or her self-destruct program deleted the dummy file.

"We then ran a report on the magnetic densities of the files that V-Trax itself created and compared them to the original total densities of files within the system. The density program then alerted us to any slightly higher than normal intensities, reflecting those new files set up by the hacker. That showed up for the compensation file, the biometric data files, and some key client files, all of which had intensities one-thousandths of a percentage point higher than normal," said Udo, relishing discussing high-tech security issues with this CEO who, unlike many other senior bankers, actually liked to understand the details.

"So spotting this hacker was like finding a needle in a proverbial haystack but rather cleverly with the use of the V-Trax metal detector!"

"A good analogy—precisely! V-Trax was able to identify the PC's IP address and then also replicate the computer screen seen by the hacker and trace his computer strokes and where he placed the mouse over the data at which he was looking within V-Trax. Together, these identified that the computer was in the New York office and the individual was Celsius's right-hand man, Chuck Jelleners, and it listed what data he saw."

"And Chuck was looking at the compensation of whom in particular—since you could tell by his keystrokes, whose package did he look at?"

"He looked at his own first, and then not surprisingly, he went into files of the salaries of the bank's Global Operating Committee and saw your compensation, Celsius's, and the other members of the committee."

"Why would Chuck look at his own compensation?"

"That is slightly odd, agreed, but maybe he wanted to see that his own salary was correctly recorded, perhaps."

"I'm not so sure, Udo. Surely such an employee who's number two in the division would be more interested in seeing his peers' salaries across other parts of the bank?"

"Yes, indeed, Herr Doktor. So it's strange that just before logging out, he looked at the compensation of Celsius's own Senior Management Committee."

"Yes, those are his peers, Udo, and I suspect your point is that as global COO to Celsius, he would already know this information because he and Celsius are the ones who determine this committee's salaries and total compensation package. So that does seem rather odd."

"But perhaps he didn't trust Celsius to pay correctly other members of his senior management team, and so he went into the system to check?"

"Mm, perhaps. But why is he then looking at important client files?"

"Maybe to get leverage of some sort against Celsius. Some folk believe that Chuck and Celsius don't get on that well," Udo suggested.

"OK. But given that Chuck is not an IT genius, and V-Trax is saying his computer's IP address was used to access the data, that implies either an expert accomplice was in on the hacking with him, or the penetrator is not Chuck at all and he is being set up, doesn't it, Udo?"

"Yes, I agree. The perpetrator could have hacked the file remotely, and then left a trail that pointed to Chuck, throwing everyone off the trail of the identity of the real hacker."

"I don't think Chuck would use an accomplice from the bank for so delicate a task, so perhaps he employed an IT consultant to help him, or more likely in my view, Chuck is being set up. But by whom? One or more on that list you mentioned of the five IT geeks working at the bank?"

"Maybe, Herr Doktor. We don't know yet. I need to do more work, run some more queries on the files, see if Chuck ever researched hacking or has an IT geek friend whom he sees outside the bank. And I will also thoroughly investigate the five. What is clear is that a very clever IT brain is involved, and I want to know what game he or she is playing and why."

"If you had to place a bet, who do you personally think is the mastermind behind all of this, Udo?"

"It's a bit early to say. I could go with any of them, so far, for different reasons. Let's take Richard de L'Isle, for example. He's Chuck's right-hand manager; maybe Richard doesn't like Chuck and is harboring a grudge. But what my enquiries reveal so far is that it seems he and Chuck get on very well. Richard has been promoted many times, is now a managing director, and earns a very good salary. Not one disparaging remark or e-mail by Richard against his boss has been picked up by V-Trax. However, there are many such remarks by Chuck against Richard and Richard's direct reports. If Richard knew about these, then that would give him a motive to get back at Chuck.

"And regarding the next four names. It could be John Witley, who wasn't promoted last year. Allegedly, Chuck blocked the promotion, so John could be angry with Chuck, if he found out about this.

"Then, there's Anna Lo. My sources tell me that Chuck made a pass at her at last year's Christmas party, saying some lewd comments. She told a colleague that she was disgusted by his behavior. Or the Russian girl, Olga, could be in collusion with Andrew, her fiancé."

"Interesting. Having read the file you gave me on Chuck, he seems a particularly nasty individual who might anyway be putting our bank at risk of a lawsuit given his sexist comments and behaviour."

"But what's more important and more immediately frightening is that this hacker now knows we use biometric screening without employees' knowledge or approval, and also has seen some very important data of some high-profile clients, including presidents of countries. This information must not be allowed to get out in the public domain, of course. So ascertaining who is or are the hackers is my top priority. The hacking took place only yesterday and hasn't been used by the hacker to extort money or any leverage yet, but clearly, this is a ticking time bomb for us."

"Yes indeed, Udo. Unravel this mystery quickly, please. I may use this as leverage in another matter I am currently working on regarding Celsius."

CHAPTER 25
THE RAC

While waiting for room service, which Richard had ordered before going to bed, through the quaint RAC custom of writing your order with a white chalk pencil on a small blackboard attached to the outside of the room's door, he watched the BBC 1 morning news. With the sound on mute, he scanned the captions scrolling across the bottom of the screen, so as not to disturb his mistress from her contented maternal slumber.

But soon, Rebecca's own body clock awakened her, and she tilted her head on the pillow to her right in search of Richard. In the large, king-size bed, her tanned, silky-smooth, toned body was cocooned between the sheets, with her right leg draped seductively over the top. Ordinarily, it would have excited Richard into diving back into bed and arousing each other into deep and passionate lovemaking, but certainly not today.

There was a knock on the door. "Room service, please." Richard glanced at his watch: 7:00 a.m., precisely.

Rebecca slid her warm body from under the sheets and walked naked to the bathroom, briefly turning her head to see Richard staring at her with his mouth slightly open. She smiled and quietly closed the door.

Richard opened the suite door. "Good morning, Hawker," he said.

"Good morning to you, sir," said Hawker. "I hope you had a comfortable night."

"Yes, it was very relaxing, thanks," he lied.

"Where shall I put your breakfast?"

"Please put the tray on the table there in front of the sofa," said Richard, pointing his outstretched right hand.

Hawker set the tray down and lifted the silver domed lid so Richard could inspect it. "It looks perfect." He had ordered the Full Monty, which was allegedly named after British field marshal Bernard Montgomery, hero of El Alamein in North Africa, and the D-Day commander of the Allied forces in World War II. Montgomery, whom everyone called Monty, had insisted that his soldiers, like him, have a proper "full English" cooked breakfast each morning when in the barracks: bacon, sausage, eggs, baked beans, toast, and a strong mug of tea.

Richard always enjoyed the RAC's Full Monty, with the exception of the black pudding, which he thought was just too much of an acquired taste: he just couldn't face the thought of eating a concoction of onions, pork fat, and pig's blood first thing of a morning. As for Rebecca, she always ordered the healthy option of muesli, dried figs, soymilk, fruit, and chamomile tea.

Hawker said, "If there's anything else you need, please call down."

"I'm fine, thanks," said Richard. "Have a good day, Hawker."

"You, too, sir," said Hawker as he glanced at the bed, said nothing, and just turned and left the room.

Rebecca came out of the bathroom in her white silk dressing gown. "Oh, wonderful! Breakfast! I'm simply famished."

"Good morning, darling," said Richard. "I hope you slept well."

"Yes, I did, thank you very much, hon. Did you?"

"Yes, very well indeed, thanks."

They sat down at the table and consumed their breakfast whilst watching and listening to the BBC news. Seeing that Richard's appetite had returned and he was quite chatty, Rebecca decided to try and entice him back into bed. She stood up and leant over him. She then pulled at the tie of her gown, allowing gravity to reveal her firm, pendulous breasts, which she positioned just below Richard's face. She gently took hold of Richard's right hand and placed his palm to her right breast. She shivered with anticipation and, closing her eyes, waited for him to stroke her and then place his lips on and suck at her nipple. But Richard resisted and pulled his hand away.

Oddly, he viewed her as desirable again. Tempting though it was to consume her body, he simply couldn't dawdle, even for a quickie with her. It was now 7:30, and he knew he must skedaddle.

"Sweetheart, I'd love to stay and make love to you, but I have to get going. I have a lot to do today."

"Oh, you are no fun!" she said, pretending to be heartbroken and retying her gown.

"I know, but look, I promise to call later, OK?" he said.

"OK," she said. "But I hope you're feeling better about the baby and our future."

"Oh, I most certainly am, having slept on it. Let's talk about the details later," he said. "Now, you make yourself comfortable, use the club's facilities: spa, gym, pool, massage. You know they have everything here, so stay as long as you want, darling."

Despite his upbeat tone, she sensed that he still hadn't quite come to terms with her news. Also, she hadn't forgotten the way he had angrily snapped back at her the previous evening—all for getting his silly gin-and-tonic drink wrong. She had never seen that side of him aimed at her. Yes, she desired him, but also, she was now slightly apprehensive of what he was capable of doing when he didn't get his way.

He pecked her on the lips briefly and headed out the door while she just sat there with a feigned frustrated look on her face. She had never remembered a night together with him without having sex. She knew she had to be patient. His anger and lack of intimacy last night, she now reasoned, was simply—and quite understandably—because Richard was under a lot of stress at work, and the timing of her unexpected personal news had hit him hard. She only hoped he'd come to realize how wonderful this was for them. After all, she reminded herself, he had said many times how much he adored her, was in love with her, and wanted to spend the rest of his life with her. To her, it simply wasn't in Richard's nature to lie. No question in her mind, the Feather of Truth, again.

Carrying a cup of latte and his shoulder briefcase, within which was his laptop and the documents for the London office Turnaround project, Richard hurried down the stairs and into the library on the first floor of the club. He was surprised, given the hour, but relieved that he was the first person in there.

He plopped down into a comfy, dark-tan leather, high-back armchair by the tall window overlooking the street of Pall Mall below. His saw that his spy pen was still in his breast jacket pocket, but he didn't check it. He powered up his laptop and e-mailed Sam to remind him that, as planned, given he hadn't any meetings today in the office until his scheduled 3:30 call with Celsius, he would be working from the RAC today on the project for Chuck. Sam should call him on his iPhone if anyone needed him urgently; otherwise he was not to be disturbed.

Now, thought Richard, I need to finalize this ruddy project straightaway, just in case Celsius surprises me and asks for me earlier than the planned call later this afternoon. Always plan for the unexpected, which often arrives at the most inconvenient and inappropriate time, he mused.

Celsius was of course immensely busy but always seemed to have time for Richard. Someone once told Richard, "Celsius thinks highly of you and knows how much of the work that Chuck presents to him is actually work you've done. Celsius said to me once, 'Richard is someone I would always have on my team, no matter what.'"

Once the PowerPoint is out of the way, I can concentrate on the matter at hand: Rebecca's pregnancy, Jelly, and now of course, ruddy Dawn as well. A triple whammy of challenges.

Richard spoke into the tiny microphone on his laptop, activating the voice command, which recognized him through its Iris, Retinal, and Voice Recognition System, or IRVRS.

He scanned the library briefly again and noticed that he was still the only one there. Good. He sipped his latte and placed it between the window and his chair so that the strict librarian wouldn't see it when he arrived. No drinks were allowed in the library, even though he was sure he had seen the librarian at his desk with a cup of tea and a sandwich more than once.

Richard requested that the computer perform specific tasks for him.

"OK, computer, bring up the EQ-P5 project PowerPoint version CMIII.3 on the left-hand half of the screen and the European Equities' industry market data from McKinsey and last year's strategic planning file for Global Equities, on the bottom segment, on the right-hand side of the screen, with the strategic planning on the top."

Within a second, the files he had asked for appeared, arranged correctly on the laptop screen. He smiled briefly, marveling at the computer's efficiency. Then, over the next hour, he issued commands to the computer, rearranging data in the slides of the PowerPoint presentation, until he felt they conveyed the right message and he couldn't improve on them.

"Computer, verbal commands complete. Remove all documents discussed from screen. Keep laptop open."

He sat back and relaxed in the comfort of the chair, took another sip of his now luke-warm latte, and moved his wrist to see the time—it was only 8:30 in the morning and the PowerPoint was done. Perfect, he thought. I now have all day until my meeting with Celsius. He stretched out his arms but was interrupted when his iPhone pinged in his ear.

"Cellphone, please advise," he whispered.

Voice message from Celsius's PA:

"Richard, Your video conference today has to be postponed until Monday next week 09:00 a.m. EST, 2:00 p.m. BST. Apologies for the short notice."

Oh great, just spent nearly a ruddy hour on it for nothing! Although, to be fair, it means I am now free to divert all my time for the rest of the day to resolve this mess with Rebecca and I won't have to worry about running through the presentation. He looked at the time of the voicemail—11:00 p.m. EST, 4:00 a.m. BST last night—he had turned off his iPhone, so he hadn't noticed it.

Then, out of the corner of his eye, he spotted George Lewis, the head librarian, in his tweed jacket, grey flannels, plaid shirt, and RAC tie. His brown brogues had been polished and shined to an inch of their lives: clearly the ex-military find solace in such fastidiousness. Although Richard knew that he himself did as well.

Mr. Lewis spotted Richard and made his way towards him.

Oh, crumbs, thought Richard, Here comes the headmaster to give me a bollocking if he's seen my ruddy latte.

Richard hurriedly slid the latte under the chair, but it slipped out of his hands and spilled onto his fingers and the carpet. Richard stood up, hid his left hand that was dripping with coffee, and with his right hand shook Mr. Lewis's outstretched hand.

"Mr. Lewis, it's very good to see you again. How are you? It seems very quiet in here this morning, doesn't it?"

"Mr. de L'Isle, always a pleasure to see you, and I am glad you always use our facilities so extensively. I believe that the Club Room is open if you require your hourly latte, as you seem to have not fully enjoyed the one you have presently."

"Ah, is it? Then I must go and get one right now, after I have shut down my laptop. May I leave my briefcase with my papers and laptop with you, for safekeeping? I know that laptops aren't allowed in the Club Room, and I can't be bothered to trog down and leave them in the cloakroom, to then have to fish them out again," asked Richard.

"Of course you may. May I also take this opportunity to thank you for your donation to the library of the five brand-new PCs for use by members? It would be a pity to ruin them, or indeed these precious, fragile books around us, by the careless spillage of drinks, don't you think?" He smiled and gestured with his hands at the books all around the long room. Richard knew that many of them were very old and extremely valuable.

"Point well taken, Mr. Lewis," said Richard, smiling. He gathered his things and turned off his laptop. He walked over to Mr. Lewis's desk and handed over his briefcase with the laptop inside it.

Relaxed, Richard strolled downstairs.

***

Teddington

Kofi answered his phone and frantically ran out of his cottage to the crime scene, a narrow-boat pleasure barge berthed near Teddington Lock: whilst he had been relieved of his caseload in preparation for his sabbatical and wouldn't be assigned this case, he was the closest officer on call that morning. As the first responder, he would stay there until his colleagues arrived.

Instinct told him to gingerly open the unlocked door, just an inch. He smelt diesel oil. Even after fourteen years on the force, during which he'd seen all manner of depraved acts, he still felt sick upon seeing the scene of the main living area. As he peered in, he could see the doorknob was attached to a piece of string. At the other end, it was tied to the bottom of a lit candle that stood on a small plate resting precariously on the edge of a high shelf. Sitting bound in a chair under the shelf was a girl aged around eight or ten years old. She was naked, doused in liquid, alive but petrified. The string was taut and attached to a pulley—opening the door more than another half an inch would pull the saucer off the edge of the shelf, and the candle would land on and ignite the girl.

Add this to my recurring nightmares, he thought.

CHAPTER 26
THE RAC

Richard's mood started to improve a few hours after the physical exertions of the swim. His tired body had begun to be reinvigorated as the post-warm-down chemical endorphins swept through him, and once in his brain gave him a heightened alertness and feeling of increased confidence in his ability to be in control of his predicament.

He ambled down the two flights of stairs to the ground floor and entered the Club Room. He spotted to the right in the corner, by the large windows overlooking Pall Mall, an empty basil-green-coloured sofa.

As Richard settled into the deep seat, Svetlana, one of the Russian waitresses whom he recognized, walked over to ask for his order.

"Just a large, skimmed-milk decaf, extra hot latte, please. And can you get me a piece of paper, because like a twit, I left my notepad in my briefcase upstairs in the library."

"Well, Mr. de L'Isle, you not allowed do to business here, so must be pleasure?" said the petite girl with a thick Russian accent and a cheeky, flirtatious smile.

"But, of course. I wanted to start planning my family holiday and make some notes, that's all."

"Where, I ask, you think you will going?"

Richard gave it a brief thought, and then remembered the importance of the room, the sofa upon which he was sitting, and the nationality of Svetlana. "I've always fancied exploring Russia, with its beautiful architecture, rolling hills, and deep history. Svetlana, where would you recommend I explore, being a novice to your country?" said Richard, who had thought of saying the word "virgin," but decided "novice" would be in better taste.

She enjoyed his innuendo. "Of course, you must see Moscow and Saint Petersburg, but depends on how long have to explore our beautiful country. Nearer time, I give you personal details more of sights you would like."

"That would be great. Tell me, does your name, Svetlana, mean anything special, and in which city did you grow up?"

"Svetlana means 'shining star,' and I grew up Kaliningrad, which is small town that was one of most beautiful cities in world, until flattened and destroyed in world wars and our beautiful paintings and artwork taken by Germans. However, it now has beautiful cathedral built to commemorate our city, and those that died in fighting. I will get latte now. Here's pen and notepad, I always keep spare one here in pocket," Svetlana said, reaching for them in the side pocket of her tight waistcoat and then handing them to

Richard.

"Thanks, smart idea," replied Richard.

Richard sank his back into the deep, soft sofa and crossed his right leg over his left. So here he was, sitting on the sofa where the British spies Harold "Kim" Adrian Russell Philby and Donald McLean had sat during a lunchtime meeting at the RAC, plotting their escape from British justice as the net around them closed in during 1951. Soon after their meeting, McLean, with fellow spy Guy Burgess, defected to their masters in Moscow to begin a new life. These spies, recruited at the infamous Cambridge University, were a perverse product of their period.

Richard knew that final scene had been set in motion much earlier. After the Wall Street crash in 1929, when the world plunged into an economic crisis causing mass unemployment, socialist groups formed at the British universities to have a political voice and find an "alternative anticapitalism" way.

Some went to fight for Franco and the Nationalist cause in the Spanish Civil War, and others went to start a new life in Russia. Four, and possibly five, of these Cambridge students chose the more sinister and treacherous route of espionage and betrayed their great country of England.

The first to enter Cambridge was Anthony Blunt, who studied history of art. The son of a vicar, he joined the secret Marxist society the Apostles, and when he was visiting Russia, the KGB recruited him. At the outbreak of war, despite his known communist sympathies, on the recommendation of a friend using the "old schoolboy network," the geniuses at the British Foreign Office employed him into the British Secret Service's Military Intelligence Section 5, more commonly known as MI5. There, he started spying for the Russians almost immediately.

Guy Francis de Moncey Burgess was the eccentric son of a naval officer, a hard drinker and openly homosexual. Burgess also joined the Apostles Club, where he met, and allegedly had an affair with, Blunt. Burgess also then went on to spy for Russia. He joined MI6, where, given the shortages in the British Secret Service, he was given the task of recruiting more like-minded souls.

Two other Cambridge students, Donald McLean and Kim Philby, joined the espionage game. Philby probably did the most damage of all the spies in terms of the number of secret service personnel who lost their lives through his treachery. The so-called fifth man at Cambridge was believed to be John Cairncross, but apparently couldn't be named as such until after his death. How ridiculous, thought Richard. If you have proof that he's a spy, then name and shame him. If you don't have it, then leave the bugger alone, surely?

Richard was deep in thought, staring into the distance across the long room to the patio window at the end, and didn't notice that Svetlana had

The Feather of Truth   Ian Campbell-Laing

discreetly put down on the table in front of him a tall glass of latte with a long silver spoon in it and a small plate of enticing biscuits. He then noticed her walking away from him. He guessed that she was about five feet two inches tall, and she had slim hips, a small backside, and very shapely legs. He reached forward and took a large slurp of the latte and popped into his mouth one of the delicious almond biscotti biscuits. He continued to look at her, and just before she reached the pantry, she turned around and smiled when she saw him spying on her.

Spies had always fascinated Richard from a young age, and his thoughts returned to the Cambridge Apostles and how the net of British Intelligence—or rather, Unintelligence, given the spectacular cock-ups in these traitors' recruitment and the time it took to work out that they were spies—had closed in on them.

The net is closing in on me as well, he thought. And now, I have to plan my own escape from the jaws of financial, professional, and domestic disaster if Rebecca's pregnancy is made public. But I don't have the comfort of having a handler to turn to. I'm totally on my own.

At the end of the war in 1945, Anthony Blunt left MI5 with the permission of his Russian handlers but didn't leave the service of the KGB. Using his extensive contacts and knowledge of art, he became the surveyor of the king's pictures, a prestigious role at Buckingham Palace, and one that would create a barrier to the secret service and also eliminate suspicions of him being a spy and courier for passing sensitive information.

It seemed to work, and Blunt was knighted in 1956. But eventually, in 1964, after further interrogations, and amazingly securing immunity from prosecution for fifteen years, he finally confessed to being a spy. The British authorities were deeply embarrassed and wanted to hush it all up. But in 1979, when the immunity had expired, the prime minister at that time, Margaret Thatcher, "the Iron Lady," went public in the House of Commons and denounced Blunt as a spy; in that same year, Queen Elizabeth II removed his knighthood.

But there was something about this whole episode that continued to intrigue Richard. Why was Blunt allowed for so long to be on the previous king's and then the queen's payroll, as the keeper of the royal pictures, when both royals must have known, or surely at least heavily suspected, Blunt's sinister and nefarious past? Was the royal family in collusion with this treacherous spy?

Both majesties not only gave him the premier position of the art world, but Queen Elizabeth even knighted him! So what had he done to not only secure protection but also earn such an exalted prize?

Richard now knew—after accessing the information on the previous monarch in V-Trax—that the answer appeared to go back to 1945 when

The Feather of Truth   Ian Campbell-Laing

Her Majesty's father, King George VI, sent Blunt to Hamburg, Germany, on a top-secret mission: to retrieve and bring back highly embarrassing letters held in the vaults of a bank with which the British royal family had had dealings for centuries. These letters contained secrets that, if entered into the public domain, could damage the monarchy, the church, and Parliament. Allegedly, they included letters written by the monarch to the German High Command sympathizing with the Nazi cause, which would obviously embarrass the monarch if shown to the public.

The public had a short memory, given it was relatively well known that the British royal family was descended from the German Saxe-Coburg-Gotha family; hence, why Parliament permitted the monarchy to quickly change its surname to the more British-sounding Windsor, after the castle with the same name. Also allegedly, in the vault were romantic letters from Queen Victoria to some of her German admirers, the so-called "Vicky love letters."

If all of this was true, then Blunt was on a very important mission. If successful in retrieving those damaging letters, he would presumably earn the silence of, and protection from, his paymasters. Given he obtained the latter, one could assume he did retrieve that damning documentation.

What Richard had uncovered from the V-Trax system was that the German bank with which the British royal family had had links for centuries was none other than the bank at which he toiled, VCb. And the vaults in which these letters were now housed were in a mysterious castle in Hamburg, Germany, called Burg Heiligtum. Coincidentally, this was none other than the weekend retreat of the current CEO of VCb, namely Dr. Klaus Becker.

Interesting, thought Richard. Everything is connected. That information I secretly obtained just might be useful as a bargaining tool later in my career. That was the opportunity within his crisis. But Richard had no illusions. There was great danger here. If V-Trax suspected him of accessing this information, he was in trouble. Deep trouble.

But Richard, for heaven's sake, stay focused on one problem at a time. Until Udo or Celsius summons you in connection with V-Trax, you have more immediate challenges to solve today, and you don't have the luxury of a royal benevolent protector like Blunt had. *No one* will protect you if Rebecca has her baby. And you will have nowhere to hide.

He finished the latte and biscotti and left the Club Room to jog up the two flights of stairs to the library. He had originally planned on taking the next three months to delicately frame Jelly using the information he had been gathering. But Rebecca's pregnancy had now become an urgent priority.

He needed to get back on his laptop and access Jelly's e-mail system without V-Trax's detection

CHAPTER 27
THE RAC

Richard was back in his window seat in the library, refreshed. He looked through the electronic encrypted dossier he had compiled on his boss. He had started retrieving the incriminating evidence against Jelly last year, the day after a colleague had told him that Jelly had belittled Richard and Richard's team behind his back. Then recently, on the day Jelly had given Richard his relatively disappointing bonus, he accelerated the secret data collection on him.

Using the G-H0st software, Richard was able to access Jelly's e-mails, amend the contents of those Jelly had written and received, and then delete the original e-mails without leaving any trace of the original on either Jelly's PC or the PC of whomever Jelly had sent the e-mail to. It was recreating a historic trail, an act some previously thought was impossible.

Using his secret fountain pen-recorder, the one that the clever jobsworth security guard had recognized, Richard also had recorded Jelly's conversations with him on numerous occasions, including when Jelly had spoken his user ID.

A month ago, he had put the recording through a voice synthesizer that created Jelly's voice based on the hundreds of words spoken by Jelly. Then, as if by magic, whatever Richard typed into his computer would be converted into a simulated voice of Jelly, as if Jelly had said those exact words. It was so realistic, the words spoken sounded exactly like Jelly's own voice, with his own intonation, pauses, and inflexions. Then Richard downloaded those created recordings and integrated them into V-Trax's secret voice recording system back to the date Richard had predetermined: it was as if Chuck had actually spoken those words at that time.

Richard had secretly left his fountain pen in Jelly's office the morning of the day bonuses were announced, during which Jelly had back-to-back meetings. He then retrieved it when Jelly popped out in the afternoon. He recorded the conversation Jelly had with Rebecca and during the meeting Jelly had with Richard.

Richard knew that at Jelly's level of seniority, he would be very careful about what he said in public or what he wrote in his company e-mails. But he had witnessed Jelly occasionally having a loose tongue during one-on-one meetings in his office, and he wouldn't have known that V-Trax monitored his personal cell phone traffic, e-mails, and text messages on his personal phone. Richard surmised that probably just a few carefully crafted pieces of incriminating evidence against his boss would be enough for Richard's nefarious purposes.

Richard surveyed his creation of data on his boss, which included potential insider dealing of confidential information, discrimination against women, drinking to excess, and derogatory remarks against his staff, his boss, and the CEO of the bank. He then printed off the e-mail that Jelly wrote to Gunter. Richard thought, Just that e-mail, in the right hands, will help the plan that's coming together in my mind. The rest I will save for another day.

Richard surveyed his handiwork and knew he had enough to get Jelly suspended, and hopefully, after a successful investigation fired with the loss of all his stock in the company. If so, it was unlikely that Jelly would ever be able to work in the industry again.

But, Richard needed to think how he could get this evidence into the hands of Celsius or HR—and of course, it could not come from Richard. However, that was for the medium term. In less than two days, on Sunday, he had to go to Rebecca's house and face the music of his affair with his boss's wife and getting her pregnant. To prepare, he now needed to remotely log into Rebecca's home PC and take control of it.

Richard called Rebecca on her cell phone, as he had promised to do, later that morning.

"Hey, darling. How's it going?"

"Hi, sweetie. It's fine. How's your morning going? How's the presentation?"

"It's getting there, but I'll need all day today and this evening to polish it off. What are your plans for today?"

"Well, I took a shower after breakfast, read the *Daily Mail* on my iPad, and now I'm in a cab on my way to go to my weekly reading club, where we also take turns to prepare a light lunch and discuss the book we are reading. I'll probably go to the shops afterwards to get food for the Sunday meal. I may then tidy up the house. Hey, I miss you, you know that?"

"I miss you, too. Look, I better go, as this presentation is stressing me out. I'll call you tomorrow."

"OK. Bye, sweetie. And remember, hon, everything is going to be OK, concerning our news."

"I know," Richard said, adding, "Things have a way of working out. Bye."

Richard's calendar pinged, reminding him he had another important call to make. "Dial home," he said quietly. The phone rang, but no one picked up.

"Hi, Jens. It's me. Sorry I missed your text last night. Was tied up with Sir James and felt obliged to stick with him obviously. Hope you didn't stay up too late. I am working on a presentation today at the club to get some peace and quiet and not be disturbed by office calls. Will not be late tonight—back around sevenish, so will be able to say good night to the little monkeys. See you later, sweetheart."

Richard adjusted the cushion to give his back more support from the armchair and tapped instructions onto the keyboard of his own laptop to log into and disable Rebecca's PC. If then, for any reason, she logged on at the same time he was accessing her PC, she wouldn't be able to see what he was doing. He was getting ready to alter history and change his destiny.

Twenty minutes later, in the corner of his eye, he saw some text messages flash up on his iPhone—he checked and saw six text messages from Rebecca. She is so clingy, it's suffocating me.

He then spent the next few hours logged into Rebecca's PC remotely, researching various alternative ways to commit the perfect murder. Whilst it was exhilarating work, it was also frustrating because he saw a flaw in each one. He knew from watching TV detective series, that it was extremely rare to pull off the perfect crime because the murderer inadvertently nearly always leaves at least one clue to his or her identity.

In order to outwit the law, Richard concluded that he needed to approach his nefarious task as viewed from the eyes of a detective. Yes, he thought, it was all about the clues that were left behind.

He wasn't unduly concerned, because he believed he was smarter than anyone else. But that said, time wasn't on his side, and of course he wasn't exactly an expert in this area.

An hour later he smiled, remembering a previous dinner he had had at Chuck's house. In his mind he started to weave together the first few strands of an optimal solution that might just work. It would be very painful for his victim, and rather drawn out, but 'needs must'.

He glanced at the lens of his reading glasses and noticed his heart rate and blood pressure were only slightly elevated. He was rather enjoying himself, but decided to get up and take another break by having a drink in the Club Room. He continued to smile.

CHAPTER 28
THE RAC

Richard's preferred seat in the corner of the Club Room near the window overlooking Pall Mall was again free, so he went over and pressed the switch on the wall. A waitress soon came over.

"Hello. Can I have a vodka and tonic with ice and a slice of lime?"

"Sure. What vodka would you prefer? We have a very good Russian one, if you like, called Stoli Elit?" she said, in a southern English accent.

"Sounds good. Thanks."

"Right away, Mr. de L'Isle."

He smiled. It seems all the staff know me. She wore dark fitted trousers, a white blouse, and a dark grey fitted waistcoat, with a blue badge with her name on it: Suzy. He liked the way the staff dressed at the club, always very professional.

Richard got out the RAC notepad and pencil that Svetlana had given him earlier this morning. He thought about his favorite film, made in 1973, *The Day of the Jackal*, where Edward Fox, the Jackal, planned the assassination of President Charles de Gaulle. The Jackal had written down just three words, as now did Richard.

Richard started to write "Where," when the lead snapped as he was forming the letter "W."

"Damn," he said out loud. He turned over the sheet to start on a new page. He pulled out his silver fountain pen from his jacket, unscrewed the cap, and then wrote *"Where?"* in beautiful italic letters in green ink—his favorite colour for signing important documents. Beneath it, he wrote *"When?"* Then, under that, *"How?"*

"Well," he said quietly to himself, amidst the chatter in the room, "the *where* has been decided already—in Jelly's house." He placed a tick against it. "The *when* has also been predetermined—Sunday, during lunch," he said, still talking aloud to himself. He placed a tick against that word also.

But, he thought, whilst in his mind the *how* had been thought through, it was more tricky. The timing had to be perfect, because both Rebecca and Jelly would be near him. He asked himself why he seemed so calm, given what he was intending to do. "I have no alternative solution," he whispered, "but I also do not intend to get caught, and instead, if my plan works, Chuck will be in for an unpleasant surprise."

He looked around to ensure he wasn't being heard and saw that other members were talking amongst themselves and not paying any attention to him.

The Feather of Truth   Ian Campbell-Laing

Suzy returned, and as she leaned down to put his drink on the table in front of him, it slipped out of her hand. Some of the drink spilled on Richard's crisp white shirt and onto his notepad, smearing the ink. She gasped and apologized repeatedly: "I'm so sorry, I'm so sorry." She grabbed a tissue from her pocket and held it out for him to dry some of the moisture on his shirt.

She rushed her words and was soon out of breath. "Oh, crumbs, sir, what a clot I am. It just fell out of my hands. I think there was water on the side of the glass. Please, please, forgive me. I think it's mainly ice, and I don't think vodka stains, does it? Do you want me to get you a new shirt from housekeeping?"

"Suzy, it's OK. No need—it's nothing," he said, dabbing the wet patch on his chest. "And as you say, it's just ice, and I'm sure vodka doesn't stain at all. It's absolutely fine. Honestly, no harm done now. Just forget it ever happened. I am perfectly fine, seriously," said Richard, trying to concentrate on the task in hand and not have his thoughts continuously interrupted.

Richard then, still holding the notepad, turned over the top few pages so he could write on a page further underneath that wasn't wet. He then placed the wet notepad on the middle of the table and looked around the room, distracted by some of the other members who were looking his way.

Suzy took out a new notepad from her waistcoat side pocket and put it on the edge of the table for Richard. She felt she had been such a klutz. Then, seeing the wet notepad lying there, she picked it up and put it in her pocket. She left quickly before the volatile member got upset with her.

Richard continued musing over his Sunday plans. He reached for the notepad, assuming it was the old, wet one. Without thinking, he folded over the top few pages and then rewrote the three words again. He then placed a tick against the *where* and *when*. He stared off into the distance, hoping for further inspiration on the precise details of the *how*.

Suzy hurried back. She was out of breath, flushed, and armed with a small kitchen towel, a fresh vodka tonic ice and lime, and a large glass of red wine.

"Mr. de L'Isle, thanks for being so understanding. I've taken the liberty of getting you a glass of one of your favorite clarets—a Chateau Margaux, 2008, Premier Grand Cru Classé—as an apology and to warm you up on this cold spring afternoon. Also, some crisps and nibbles and some freshly made sandwiches."

"Oh, thanks. You really didn't need to, but much appreciated, Suzy," said Richard, raising his eyebrows, impressed with her knowledge of one of his favorite wines and knowing that this French Bordeaux would probably be over seven hundred pounds if he had ordered a bottle at the Great Gallery restaurant.

"It's our pleasure, sir. We all know how much you've done for the club,

The Feather of Truth   Ian Campbell-Laing

promoting it and all. Also, you forgot to take your bill for this morning's latte. It's now on the house, of course, along with this afternoon's fare. So, I'll just leave you with a copy of this morning's bill." She placed it on the table.

Richard reached first for the fresh vodka drink and said, "Thanks very much, indeed."

And as the waitress walked away, he sipped his drink, and then picked up the bill, wondering why she would leave him with a bill for something that was now free of charge and on the house. Didn't make sense. He turned it over, and on it was written an eleven-digit number decorated with hearts. Presumably, it was a mobile number. Next to it was the words, in a girlie handwriting, "From Russia, S" with a little heart above the letter "i" and a smiley face above the capital letter "S."

Richard smiled, guessing that was Svetlana's mobile number. He was flattered, but thought, Tempting though that would be, that's a distraction I do not need before Sunday. But certainly *after* Sunday, most definitely.

Suzy went back into the pantry and said to the other server, "I just can't believe Mr. de L'Isle was so calm, charming, and polite."

Many of the staff at the RAC had been there when Richard became livid a year earlier when his dinner guest, who was a vegetarian, was served a very bland and boring meal, clearly with no thought or attention. And then later, his guest was served one dish that had contained some chicken. Richard had jumped up from his table and shouted for the first time at Ivano, the maître'd and his close friend, saying, "What sort of club is this that you can't do an effing vegetarian meal? Why is there no vegetarian option on the menu, for heaven's sake? This is outrageous! You have totally embarrassed my guest and me here tonight. How difficult is it to drum up an interesting salad and some crisp, boiled or sautéed vegetables with organic rice and mushrooms or whatever, for heaven's bloody sake? Or would it be too much to ask for some asparagus on a plate with hollandaise sauce?"

Ivano was taken aback by Richard's sharp tone. Within a week, the chef had created an excellent separate vegetarian menu.

Suzy unfolded the notepad and was about to throw it into the bin but noticed Richard's writing and the three words "where," "when," and "how" with ticks next to the first two. Now I wonder what that is? she thought. Maybe it's his thoughts on Svetlana and where he wants to meet her! Svetlana had been bragging earlier that Richard was precisely the type of man she wanted to get into bed with and had predicted that before the end of the month, she would have slept with him. Suzy giggled and decided to keep it and give it to Svetlana when she was back on duty again. She had told Suzy boastfully, "If I not succeed, then I will shave head."

An hour later, Richard smiled, as he realized he now had in his mind the

The Feather of Truth   Ian Campbell-Laing

perfect *bow*, and so he then drew an elegant tick by it on his notepad. He placed it in his breast pocket, deciding he would destroy it later. There was no going back now.

He scanned his iPhone for any important emails. There were a couple which he quickly replied to. Then he spotted one from Sam, asking if he would like to sponsor some work colleagues who were raising money to go to Turkey on a humanitarian mission and build a school. They had raised 30,000 pounds. He replied to Sam.

> Excellent cause, but very dangerous location so near to the Iranian border. Tell the four to be very careful. Put me down for £20,000 so that they achieve their goal of £50,000.

He got up, strolled down one flight of stairs to retrieve his overcoat from the coatroom and then sprinted back up the stairs to the exit of the club. He pulled out his woolly hat from inside his overcoat and put them both on. He left through the circular doors, turned right and walked the short distance to Jermyn street. There he browsed the windows of the clothes shops waiting for the right moment.

Through the reflection of the window he saw a young man in a white chef's tunic and blue scarf around his neck, appear from the tradesman's entrance to Fortnum and Mason, and light up a cigarette.

Richard turned around, pulled his woolly hat down further to cover more of his face and walked across the road towards the smoker.

"Excuse me," Richard asked in a Scottish accent, "Sorry to bother you during your well-earned break, but do you mind me asking – do you by any chance work in the Wine Bar at Fortnum's?"

"Yep, I do. I'm a line chef. Just needed to get out for five mins." He drew on his cigarette, exhaled and continued, "Why do you ask?"

"Oh I'm in the restaurant business myself, but I'm in a bit of a jam. Our sushi bar has nearly run out of the puffer fish delicacy, and our next order doesn't arrive until tomorrow. I know Fortnum's serves it and in fact I've been at your bar and enjoyed it many times. I had it as part of your chef's tasting menu."

The young man briefly smiled at the compliment, but then looked suspicious.

"If you want some, why don't you just go in and order it and take it out and use in your restaurant, then?"

"Well, I could, but you would remove the liver before serving or selling it wouldn't you?"

"Of course we would. The liver is very toxic and we have strict rules about how we prepare that fish. You know that people have died from eating the liver, right? In fact, I saw on the news only last week in Japan five businessmen died from eating the fish because it had been poorly prepared.

The Feather of Truth   Ian Campbell-Laing

It's a thousand times more powerful than cyanide, but not as quick acting. It's a slow painful death that's for sure. You can't mess around with that fish."

"Ach, I know. Our chefs have to be specially licensed. And we have the same strict procedures. But *we* like to prepare the fish tableside in front of the punters. It adds to the allure and mystique of the danger."

"Oh I get it." He nodded. Then shook his head. "But as I said, I can't get you the whole fish with the liver intact, that's against our rules."

"Oh come on. As one chef to another? All I need for tonight's service is a couple of puffers. What do they sell for at your bar, one hundred quid each?"

"Yes just under that I think. As you said it's part of our tasting menu. Of course we buy it for much less than that. But there's another problem. We have to account for all our inventory. So it won't be easy."

Richard noticed the threadbare cuffs on the chef's tunic, unwashed scarf and scuffed trainers. He had researched the wages of a sous-chef and they were pretty low; probably taking home less than four-hundred quid a week. And the hours notoriously long.

Richard pursued his prey further.

"Look in our game there's always some wastage. Tell you what, you nip inside and get me two puffers, and I'll give you two hundred quid, cash, and no questions. We'll be doing each other a favour."

The man thought about it, and drew heavily on his cigarette.

"Two-fifty, and I'll do it."

Richard paused and then said, "Aye. Deal."

CHAPTER 29
BLACKDOWN CLOSE, HASLEMERE, SURREY, ENGLAND

Richard slept in the guest bedroom, as he had done for ages. He had had a restless night. At five o'clock on this Sunday morning, he decided to forget trying to get back to sleep and instead get up, take off of his sweat-ridden T-shirt, make a mug of tea, and face the day.

The day before, he had spent his birthday at home with his family. After each time he spent with his family, he vowed to see them more. He relished being with them, and it allowed him to unwind from the pressures of his job.

Jennifer, with the help of the boys, had baked him his favorite dessert, tiramisu, and they had given him thoughtful presents including, from their eldest, some adorable cufflinks with a union jack flag motif he'd made in his silversmith class at school. Each of his sons had created their own "Happy Birthday, Dad" cards, and Jennifer had brought him a rare, 1723 first edition, six-volume set of Shakespeare's plays, that he'd hinted he would love to read, together with some fine wines for his small cellar. In the evening, they had dined at their favorite restaurant, in the tree house of the grounds of Undershaws, in nearby Hindhead. The restaurant was where the notorious writer of Sherlock Holmes, Arthur Conan Doyle, wrote *The Hound of the Baskervilles*. It had fallen into disrepair but recently had been expensively renovated back to its former elegance.

Seeing her husband being distracted throughout the day, Jennifer kept asking him what was wrong. She was beginning to wonder if Richard had something else apart from work on his mind. He continued to still be a workaholic and even tomorrow, on a Sunday, he was going to his boss's house for a meeting to discuss a PowerPoint presentation upon which he was working—time when he should have been at home with her and the boys. She was miffed to say the least.

She saw the e-mail on his laptop from Chuck confirming the lunch meeting and knew it was genuine, but she still wondered, was it just the pressure of work, or something else that was bothering him? She didn't think that Richard was having an affair but decided that when she saw her friend Isabelle for coffee next week, she might ask her for her opinion, again.

Preparing for the ordeal ahead, Richard sat for a moment in his car, parked in the driveway of his large house in the leafy suburb of Southern England. His eyes were closed, and his hands gripped the steering wheel. It was a neighborhood populated with clones of middle-class, affluent

The Feather of Truth — Ian Campbell-Laing

families, most of whom today would be spending time together relaxing or indulging in predictable pastimes. However, Richard, who had just said good-bye to Jennifer and the boys, faced an uncertain day—no, more an uncertain future. He knew there would be no turning back after this. *The die is cast.* Like the Roman emperor Julius Caesar, who, having exhausted all political compromises by which he might have returned to Rome without risk, decided that his only safety lay in civil war but, realizing the perils and the ruin that this would bring, he paused at the border of Italy and Gaul, his assigned province, before taking the fatal step. When finally he had made up his mind to enter Italy with his army and cross the Rubicon River, a movement that would be treated as an act of war, he so declared, "Jacta alea est"—*The die is cast.* Richard was crossing his own Rubicon and was approaching his own point of no return.

The consequences of his actions would live with him forever. But, to him, the consequences of no action and allowing the pregnancy to proceed were far worse. He had never contemplated such a heinous act before, and previously wouldn't have thought himself capable.

Richard spoke. "Ignition, on." Recognizing his voice and touch on the steering wheel, the six-liter, V12 engine of his Aston Martin DB13 GTX growled in response. He opened his eyes when he heard through the loudspeakers one of the episodes of the hilarious BBC radio show *I'm Sorry, I Haven't a Clue*, starring Humphrey Littleton. Sir Humphrey was signing off with his usual reference to Samantha, the fictional administrator. He said, in his typical deadpan voice, 'Our researcher Samantha has gotten up from sitting on my left hand, and made her customary trip to the gramophone library, where she often helps out running errands for the elderly archivists. She sometimes pops out to get their sandwiches. Their favorite is ham and cheese with chutney, but they never mind when she palms them off with relish…and so, as the delicate mayfly of time collides with the speeding windscreen of fate…"

Richard smiled. He usually ended up in stitches of laughter when he listened to those old radio programs, but today, he said, "Music off." Instantly it went quiet again, and all he could hear was the sound of the throbbing engine.

He said out loud to himself, shaking his head, "Today is too important for any distractions."

After another pause, he said, wearily, "Auto drive on. Location, Copse Hall, Wentworth, Surrey." The car's satnav glowed, confirming the address.

"Commence drive."

The car released its parking brake, the accelerator started to smoothly press down, and the steering wheel turned in the driveway. The car would now drive itself to Copse Hall, Rebecca and Jelly's eight-thousand-square-foot mansion, at 8:40 a.m. on a frosty, cold, but sunny Sunday morning in

The Feather of Truth   Ian Campbell-Laing

April.

    Richard rarely used the auto drive system because it ruined the fun of driving his 540 break-horse-power sports car. But today, the journey would be hands free so that he could go through his mental checklist one more time during the drive—totally uninterrupted. He had made no notes: it was all in his mind—he had created a mnemonic, "Switch Fear KGB," to remember the tasks he needed to carry out, in a precise order.

    Slowly, he now went through in his mind, without saying anything out loud, what each letter meant for each action and in the order he would perform the task. Over the next fifteen minutes, he had remembered them exactly. Then he thought of the week that had passed and considered that he had planned for today as best he could, and he was about to commit the perfect crime, with two added beneficial outcomes.

    Fifty minutes and thirty-three miles later, his car entered into the gravel driveway of Copse Hall. He saw Rebecca standing in the doorway to greet him. Looking at his watch, he checked the time. "Damn. I'm wearing the wrong watch," he exclaimed, and punched his fist on the steering wheel.

    He was wearing the watch his grandfather Ben had given him years ago on the fifth of April, for his twenty-first birthday. Out of respect to him, he wore it on the fifth of each month and on the thirteenth, the day Grandpa was born. Richard had worn it yesterday on his birthday, but in all the planning for today's events, he put the same watch on this morning, the sixth of April, in haste. He briefly wondered if it was a bad omen—then dismissed such superstitious claptrap from his mind.

    She stood in the entrance wearing tight denim jeans, a white blouse, casual flat shoes, and a loose pink sweater. Her fair hair nestled gently over her shoulders, and her wide, blue eyes were framed by a touch of mascara. He saw that she was wearing her favorite pearl necklace and earrings—Excellent, that's perfect, and was planned for.

    Richard approached grinning, and Rebecca ushered him into the house. Once she closed the door, she reached up to pull his face down towards her and kissed him full on the lips, feeling her tongue for his. As he continued to stoop down, she nestled her head between his neck and shoulder, and wrapping her arms around him, gave him a long hug before he could even put down his briefcase. She wouldn't let go.

    "I'm so glad you're here and that the day has finally come. But, God, I'm nervous. Chuck has a foul temper—as you know—and God knows what he'll do. Are you sure that we should announce our news to Chuck today over lunch, Richard?"

    "Yes, most definitely, but let me do all the talking, and only I will mention it, and only when I'm ready, please. You leave it all to me. No hints of anything until I bring up the topic. And anyway, he won't lay a finger on you if I am in the house. So, don't worry," said Richard as he finally had a chance to put down his briefcase next to the wall in the hallway.

"OK, sweetie, you do all the talking, and we'll be fine," she said with her New Yorker accent coming through.

"It's terribly important that he's relaxed, has had a few drinks, and that I have had a chance to go through the project with him first. So, we can't say anything before that, please. You just be the beautiful hostess you always are. Be yourself, like you were when I was last here for dinner with my family, a few months ago."

"OK. Jolly good," she said in her mock British accent, then eagerly added, "Hon, I know you said you didn't want a birthday present, but I had to get you *something*. I've got you two small things. Here is the first." She leaned over to the side table and pulled out from inside the drawer a small, elegantly wrapped box. She handed it to him. "Go on, open it!"

"You are naughty, Rebecca, but thanks." Richard tore the wrapping from the package, eager to get it hidden before Jelly turned up. Inside was a pale blue box from Tiffany & Company, the London jewelers. He opened it, and inside was a pair of gold cufflinks. "My God, Rebecca, they are beautiful. Thanks." He examined them and, raising his eyebrows, smiled. "Aha, is that your family crest on them?"

"Yes, the Falconer crest. Our Latin motto is *Vive ut vivas*, which translated means 'Live life to the fullest'—which I intend to do with you, hon. Also, you can see there," she said, as she pointed with her index finger, "below the words is our crest, which is that of a falcon's head, fashioned around a heart with three stars. Welcome to the Falconer family, hon!"

"Thanks, but let's sort out things with Jelly Bean first, darling." With that, Richard placed the little box, wrapping paper, and ribbon into one of his jacket's pockets.

God, just another thing to worry about, he thought. I must now remember to get rid of these cufflinks, for my sins. As if today I don't have enough to worry about. Note to self, checklist is now "Switch Fear KGB C." But chill out, Richard, you knew the unexpected would happen, so just stay calm.

"And now for the second present. I want you to have it for safekeeping. Promise me you won't ever throw it out, but cherish it, OK?"

"I promise," he replied, intrigued what it could be, but thinking it was probably a locket of her hair inside a small but expensive crystal box.

Rebecca reached into the front pocket of her jeans.

"At your club, I forgot to show you this." She handed him the pregnancy test chemical strip. "See the little blue lines with the word 'pregnant' typed on it? Isn't it cute? Why don't you keep it for us both, because I don't want my pain-in-the-ass husband to get his hands on it."

He breathed in loudly, and quickly amended his mental checklist to be

The Feather of Truth Ian Campbell-Laing

"Switch Fear KGB PC" and banked the new mnemonic in his short-term memory section of his brain for later retrieval.

He sighed quietly and said, "Thanks. Yes, it's cute, and of course we will cherish it," adding, "Excellent idea, darling." Instead he thought, Oh, gross, a urine-encrusted confirmation of the mess that I am in! He kissed her on the lips. She then nibbled his lips and put her hands on his face again. They held hands and chatted in the front hall. He then saw the control panel on the wall.

"Didn't you say that this control panel monitors the curtains?"

"Yes, hon, it does. At sunrise and sunset, the curtains open and close automatically and silently. Or if you want, you can open or close any of the rooms individually or all of them. See, here is L for 'library,' and H for 'hallway.'"

"Ingenious. So M is 'morning room,' and K is 'kitchen'?"

"Yes, hon, that's it. It's pretty simple."

Perfectamundo. He smiled.

Rebecca left the hallway to go and check on the food. Richard excused himself to go to the toilet. Once she was gone, he whispered to himself his checklist, sprinted upstairs to the master bedroom, and took out some latex gloves from his jacket pocket. He always kept a spare pair in the glove compartment of his car to avoid getting his hands dirty if he needed to top up the engine with oil or mess around with the dirty tyre caps when inflating the tyres with air.

In the closet next to their bedroom, where Jelly had his suits hung neatly in row, was a cabinet. On the top stacked neatly were Jelly's trademark white handkerchiefs, which he always had ironed and folded into a W shape. Each day he placed a fresh one into the top left-hand pocket of his suit jacket. Richard counted them. Good, exactly the number Rebecca told me he would have.

Richard took the top handkerchief and went into their en suite bathroom and locked the door. He lifted out the cellophane jiffy bag from his jacket pocket. Inside the bag were two dozen light grey grains of powder. He unzipped the bag, opened up Jelly's handkerchief, and sprinkled half of the grains into the center. He then refolded the handkerchief and put it back into the neat, crisp shape that Jelly obsessed over. Richard placed the handkerchief into his own jacket's small inside left-hand side pocket and zipped up the cellophane bag, putting it in his right-hand pocket.

Richard briefly thought about the cufflinks Rebecca had just given him. He could not have something so personal from Rebecca in his possession. Chuck was obviously oblivious to their affair, and it would be odd for Richard to get such a present from his boss's wife without his knowledge. He decided to put them in Rebecca's bedroom with her other cufflinks and

The Feather of Truth   Ian Campbell-Laing

later get rid of the box and wrappings, along with the pregnancy test kit. He swiftly wiped the cufflinks free of his fingerprints and took a minute to find her jewelry drawer. He then placed them amongst the other cufflinks. He kept the wrapping paper, ribbon, and small box, and put them in the pocket inside his jacket.

As he went downstairs, he pulled off his latex gloves inside out and put them in the remaining unoccupied pocket of his jacket.

Rebecca stood there at the bottom of the stairs holding a drink in her hand. She looked at him curiously and said, "Oh—what are you doing upstairs, sweetie?"

"Er, I had forgotten where the downstairs loo was and didn't want to disturb you in the kitchen because I remembered where the one upstairs was…and, to be honest, I wanted to see your bedroom again."

"Come here, you sentimental, romantic old fool. I adore you, Richard de L'Isle. Let me give you a hug." She put the drink down on the side table.

They embraced for what seemed to Richard to be ages. And he had so much to do before her husband arrived. Eventually she released him and stood back and looked at him. "I like the combination of your jeans and a smart suit jacket, but if you keep your jacket on, you're going to look a bit formal for a Sunday lunch, hon."

"I think I will for a while, if you don't mind; I feel a slight cold coming on and a bit of a chill in the air. Shall I get a nice claret from Jelly's cellar?"

"OK, yes, get a good bottle or two of wine, and bring them into the dining room, and then to warm us all up, can you draw the fires for me in the living room and the dining room. You're right, it's getting chilly, sweetie, and a log fire is more welcoming than just putting the central heating on higher."

"Sure, no probs."

"And I poured you a drink to start – Jensen's gin with tonic, ice, and a slice of lime. Just the way you like it, hon. I think I got it right this time!" she said as her fingers fidgeted with her apron.

"Thanks." He sipped at it. "It's perfect," he lied. She had completely ruined the drink by using an inferior tonic which masked the taste of the gin, and forgetting the sprig of rosemary.

He went into the cellar and looked around the room. Jelly had boasted that it cost £100,000 to install with its beautiful woods and temperature-controlled environment. According to Jelly who kept meticulous stock record, there were over three thousand bottles of wine, costing a million and a half pounds.

He looked around and selected two reds that Richard judged would go well with the beef: a nice expensive Pomerol and an exquisite, reasonably priced Chateau Maris Oeuf Neuf 2023. He took them into the library.

CHAPTER 30
COPSE HALL, WENTWORTH, SURREY

Richard drew the fires as Rebecca had instructed and went into the kitchen. He was ready for the day's proceedings to play out. "Anything I can do to help?" said Richard as he spotted Rebecca cleaning wine glasses.

"No, thanks, hon. The lunch is under control, and I won't be putting in the beef to roast until eleven. I've taken it out of the fridge to let it come up to room temperature."

She gave him another long hug and didn't want to let him go: he was her comforter today. Over a glass of iced Moroccan mint tea—he didn't want to raise his body temperature with a hot drink—he described to her his birthday with his family the day before. Then they heard the tyres of a car on the gravel driveway. "Oh, that must be the airport limo," said Rebecca, fidgeting with the corners of her apron.

Rebecca checked Richard's face for lipstick and, with a wet finger, touched his lips to remove any telltale marks. She also checked that none of her blond hairs were visible on his dark blue jacket. She spotted one near his collar and removed the incriminating dead object. She straightened the handkerchief in his breast pocket, and said, "Oh, you've brought your fancy fountain pen with you, then?"

He looked down and saw it clipped inside his outer breast pocket.

"Oh, that's right. I must have left it there the last time I wore this jacket for work, I guess."

Shortly, a key turned in the lock. Richard checked his watch: Just a quarter past ten and right on schedule. His glasses displayed a number showing his heartbeat up 40 percent and blood pressure up 20 percent. He walked into the hallway to greet Jelly, while Rebecca remained in the kitchen.

"Game on, then," said Richard under his breath.

"Hey, Richard, old buddy, how the devil are you? Been looking after my wife for me, have you, you little scoundrel? Is that her lipstick on your collar?" Jelly laughed with his booming New York accent echoing around the hallway.

Richard's cheeks turned crimson as they shook hands.

Jelly set down his carry-on case and briefcase in the hallway.

"Hey, Ricardo, just joking!" Jelly said and slapped him on the back.

Richard feigned a smile at his boss's piss-poor humour, which Richard rarely enjoyed.

Richard cleared his throat and, speaking in his usual soft, firm voice without a hint of apprehension, said, "Chuck, it's good to see you. How was the flight? Get any sleep? You must be knackered."

The Feather of Truth   Ian Campbell-Laing

"As usual, British Air first class is pretty good. Those nice fluffy pillows and a sumptuous duvet is just my style. But recently, you never know if the flight's going to take off, with their unions always on strike."

Richard nodded, trying to balance blocking out such mindless, distracting drivel with remaining alert and feigning interest.

Jelly continued and boasted, "Oh, but you can't fly British Air, because you're not on Celsius's Operating Committee! You can only fly Virgin, right? Although I hear it's pretty good in upper class, eh?"

Richard thought, This guy is such a wanker. "Actually Jel…er…Chuck, it's British Airways, not British Air, and yes, I much prefer Virgin. They have wider, longer, and flatter beds, a better lounge than BA, especially at Heathrow, with a great Full Monty breakfast, and either a free massage, haircut, or manicure. I also tend to think they have a more cosmopolitan range of passengers. And their unions don't seem to go on strike."

"But, Ricardo, my man, there are so many riffraff on board Virgin's flights. The only time I went on it, when British Air was on strike, I hated it. It was infiltrated with trailer trash. What is it you Brits call them, East End Barrow boys? Them and also overpaid footballers and their Gucci-wearing tarty wives."

Richard shrugged his shoulders and pulled an unapproving face. My boss is so self-entitled and embarrassing, he thought.

"I suspect they also give too many free upgrades for the young staff. It's not like the more civilized British Air's first class at all!"

"To each their own, Chuck."

Richard hated being called "Ricardo" by Jelly, which gave the wrong impression that he and Jelly were friends, almost as much as he detested being referred to as "hon," or even worse, "sweetie," by Rebecca, which made him feel trapped.

"Let's go into the living room, shall we?"

"Sure, Chuck. Why not."

As they walked, Chuck said, "You know, I did meet a very interesting young man from UBS. Ashley Carpenter, a very likable Aussie guy who heads up their asset management arm of the Swiss bank. We compared notes, and I think he and I can do some business together on the shared services infrastructural side—even though we are competitors. Would be very innovative, for sure. I'm only pissed off that I wasn't allowed to use the corporate jet. Dr. Klaus and his Gestapo seem to be clamping down on its usage, more and more. Seems like only the Iceman is now allowed to use it, and very infrequently at that."

Richard discreetly shook his head in despair at his boss, thinking, Ever the businessman was old Napoleonic Jelly Beanie. He could never just relax on a flight and be quiet, or just read a classic book. He was always looking for an angle and any networking that would bolster his career and paycheck.

The Feather of Truth — Ian Campbell-Laing

The guy was an unbearable, arrogant social and business climber.

"Are you still afraid of flying, Chuck? I know that it used to make you nervous even after all the travel you do," asked Richard. He looked at his watch and wished Rebecca would join them.

"Yes, I am still wary of it, although I went on a course run by British Air to help me control my irrational aerophobia. It helped a little. They explained why the engines sound different at various stages of the flight, the whining noises made when they move the flaps and ailerons, and the loud bang when the wheels are put in position for landing. They even talked about the black box, in case you crash in a faraway place, and how it's so sturdy it will survive any impact, so that you'll be discovered due to it sending out a signal. I thought they should have left that discussion out, as it then caused some of us to panic about why the black box was so sturdy and more resilient than the plane itself or the seats we sat in, and hence more likely to survive a crash than us, the human cargo!" Chuck boomed with what he thought was a good joke.

"Interesting," said Richard, seemingly acting normal and polite. "And did you know that the black box is, in fact, not black at all. It's yellow, for easier identification."

"Well, heck, no, I didn't!" said Chuck. "Aren't you the know-it-all!"

Rebecca had heard them talking in the hallway, pleased that they sounded like they were getting along all right. She was very anxious, though. What would Chuck do when they told him the news? The last time Chuck hadn't got his way with Rebecca, he had hit her. Oh well, Richard's here to defend me now. Best we just get this over with as soon as possible. She left the kitchen to greet her husband.

"You're home, then." She smiled, fidgeting with her hands.

"Yes, dear, I'm home," said Chuck, giving her a peck on the cheek.

Richard felt calm and not nervous. However, he had to keep his wits about him, so he alternated between small sips of his gin and tonic and taking gulps of his iced tea.

They all sat in the living room, listening to stories recounted by Chuck. Rebecca popped in and out to check on the food. At 1:00 p.m., after consuming two strong gin and tonics and most of the bottle of wine that Chuck had separately brought up from his cellar soon after arriving, Chuck was feeling very relaxed. Rebecca announced that lunch was soon to be served. "Please, go and sit down in the dining room, you guys."

Rebecca had already laid out the starter in bowls on the plates in front of them: butternut squash soup of a delicate consistency, not too watery and not too thick and heavy. The light cream in it had a sprinkle of chopped chives and a delicate seasoning with freshly ground pepper. And it was piping hot, just the way Richard liked his food.

The Feather of Truth   Ian Campbell-Laing

Chuck noisily slurped at the soup, invoking the constant disapproving eye of his wife. Richard delicately wiped the underside of his spoon on the side of bowl before each mouthful, and despite not being hungry, in order to line his stomach for any wine he consumed, he slowly finished the entire contents of his bowl. Richard stood up and offered to clear the plates away and then go and get another bottle of wine so it could have time to breathe.

"OK, thanks, and I'll bring in the beef for you to start carving, Chuck," said Rebecca.

"Excellent idea, Becks," replied Chuck as he chugged down the remaining half a glass of his wine.

Before getting the next bottle, Richard joined Rebecca in the kitchen as she was about to spoon out the roast potatoes and veggies onto the three warm plates in front of her.

"Rebecca, has the beef been resting long enough before carving?" Richard always thought he might have been a chef in another life: he liked the creativity and using the different side of his brain—the right-hand, arty side, which typically most people only use a small portion of the time.

"Yes, it has, for about ten minutes, hon," she whispered, and smiled at his fastidiousness.

"OK, perfect." He knew that meant the moisture, which during the heating process was driven to the center of the beef, would be partially reversed whilst resting and be redistributed through the joint. Richard took off the aluminum foil that Rebecca had placed on the joint to prevent the surface from cooling off too fast and placed the meat onto the ornate, antique silver dish set, with accompanying carving knife and fork.

"Richard, why don't you take the beef in to Chuck for me whilst I finish with the servings?"

"No way! I think, given you cooked it, you should proudly bring it out. So why don't you go ahead and take the beef out to Chuck for him to carve, and I'll finish dishing up for you. And just two small potatoes for you then, as always?" recalled Richard.

"Yes, never any more than that!" said Rebecca, pleased that he had remembered. She then said, "OK, yes, you go ahead and finish up serving. Anyway my annoying husband is already quite sozzled. I can then have a quiet word with him to slow down his drinking."

She walked into the dining room carrying the silver tray of beef. Richard knew he had no more twenty seconds, maybe a tad longer if she admonished her husband for embarrassing her.

"Thanks, Becks. Looks delicious, as always. As do you," said Chuck. He grabbed her arm playfully and started to pull her towards him hoping for a kiss.

"Chuck, let go of my wrist, please. We have a guest."

He squeezed her wrist.

"Chuck, you are hurting me, stop now."

"OK, then, later," he said, smiling and licking his lips. His drunken eyes, which were mentally undressing her, repulsed her.

"Chuck, let's talk about it later when Richard is gone, please!"

"OK, OK! I surrender." Chuck snorted and made a big gesture of removing his grip and hand from hers.

"Don't make a scene, Chuck. Let's just enjoy the lunch with Richard, OK? Please, carve the roast. You always do that so well." Chuck, surprised at his wife complimenting him, mistakenly wondered if this was a sign that perhaps tonight there would be a thawing in their long period of celibacy.

Meanwhile, Richard had spooned out the veggies and potatoes onto the three plates and then taken Jelly's handkerchief with the grains in it from his left-hand jacket pocket. He leant over with his back to the door and sprinkled them over the vegetables on the plate with the smallest serving of potatoes. The grey, translucent colour wasn't noticeable amongst the vegetables' honey-glazed sauce. He lightly dabbed a corner of the handkerchief onto the vegetables and was about to put it back into his jacket, when he realized that he had not stuck to his plan. Instead, he should have done Rebecca's plate completely, hidden the handkerchief, and only then spooned out his and Chuck's plates, and thus, should he run out of time, he would have already completed the crucial part.

"Damn!" he said quietly, and added, "You effing idiot, de L'Isle."

"What's that, Richard—who's an idiot?" asked Rebecca as she came back into the kitchen.

Her voice behind him made his shoulders jump, and in his haste, he nearly dropped the handkerchief onto the plate as he tried to cram it back quickly into his pocket. He turned around slowly to the right, giving his left hand time to conceal the action of putting away the handkerchief out of sight. He straightened up and said, "Oh, sorry, just talking to myself. I just realized that I think I messed up one of the slides in the presentation for Chuck. No matter," he said, shrugging his shoulders.

As she stared at him, he added, "So the plates are all done. Here on the right is Chuck's plate with the most veggies and tatties, yours here on the left with just two tatties, and mine here in the center. I'll go fetch the other bottle of wine, too. I think I left it in the library."

"Oh I thought you took them into the dining room, like I said?"

"You did? Oh sorry. For some reason I took them into the library, by mistake I guess."

"Oh, OK. But you look flustered, Richard, as if I startled you. Is everything OK?"

"Yep. I guess I am a bit jittery—just want to get on with the day."

"Oh, you poor love, of course you are. I am too." Rebecca smiled. "See you back in the dining room then, in a moment. I'll take the plates in now."

The Feather of Truth Ian Campbell-Laing

Richard went into the library, closed the large double doors, and drew a small fire. He waited for it to take hold whilst he put on his latex gloves. He reached into his jacket for the cellophane bag with the remainder of the grains and placed the bag onto the middle-burning log. The flames crackled and engulfed the bag. Richard smiled. He was delighted with his planning, so far. One more item on his checklist done and dusted, but his heart was beating hard after his close encounter with Rebecca in the kitchen.

He took off his gloves, put them back in his jacket, grabbed the bottles of Pomerol and Chateau Maris, and headed back into the dining room. He slapped Chuck on his back in a jovial manner and placed the wines on the table. He uncorked the Pomerol, and seeing Rebecca wasn't yet back in the room, said, calmly "Let's not pour it until Rebecca has returned." But he wondered why Rebecca was taking so long to just bring in the plates that were already served up.

"Sure," said Chuck. "I've still got a few more pieces to slice." Chuck stood at the head of the table, carving the beef into rather inelegant, thick slices. Swaying slightly, he rocked forwards and sideways on his feet.

Rebecca came in with the first two warmed plates of vegetables and roasted potatoes and put one in front of Richard and the other in front of her husband. She then went back to the kitchen to fetch her own plate. Richard glanced down and saw that his plate had four potatoes, and Chuck's had eight. Just as he had spooned them out. Good.

Rebecca brought her plate in and put it on her place setting. Richard glanced briefly at it, and did a double take. To his horror he saw that it also had four potatoes. He stared back between his plate and hers, but couldn't tell whether he had his own plate or the one he had prepared for her, to which she must have added two more potatoes—he had instinctively given her and himself the same amount of veggies. The plates looked identical. He wondered, Has she picked up my plate instead, and I now have hers?

"Rebecca, thanks," he said, and then turned to her and whispered, "*Four* potatoes?"

"Yes, I added two more. I thought I would be a bit naughty today!" She giggled, not registering the look of concern on Richard's face. Instead, she looked sternly at her husband, after noticing that he had piled a huge mound of beef onto his own plate and had just sat back down to quaff yet more wine.

She remained calm. "Chuck, please offer the beef around to our guest, if you have finished carving."

Chuck said, "Oh, sure!" He pushed the silver tray of sliced beef just a few inches on the table towards Richard. Richard sighed, stood up, took it, and walked to Rebecca. He bent down and offered the tray to her. She took one small piece and then said, "What the heck—I shouldn't be always watching my figure now, should I?" and glanced up at Richard, cheekily.

The Feather of Truth — Ian Campbell-Laing

Richard looked away from Chuck and raised his eyebrows at Rebecca's untimely, dangerous remark. Rebecca smiled at him and mouthed the word "sorry." She looked at the mound of beef presented to her and picked a slice that was slim at one end but that, when she unraveled it, was rather chunky at the other, but she nevertheless put it on her plate. Richard then placed the tray near his plate and sat down. He reached over and took two of the thinner slices of beef for himself.

Rebecca looked at the second slice of beef on her plate and said, "Oh dear, that piece is a little larger than I thought. Here, one of you two boys have it!"

Chuck boomed, "I am fine, thanks, Becks. Have more than enough for me here!"

"I am fine also, Rebecca. You have it, or if you can't finish it, just leave it, perhaps," said Richard, turning his head to look at her and smiling.

"Nonsense, Richard. Here, you have it—you only have two slivers of beef—not enough for a strong, young man with a hearty appetite to have for sure! Here, pass me your plate," she said, motioning with her outstretched right hand.

As Richard hesitated, Rebecca looked confused at his dawdling. "Come on, Richard, or your plate will get cold!" she said.

He looked at her plate as she took her fork and pronged the offending piece of beef. Her plate looked like she hadn't started to eat her veggies yet, and the beef was placed an inch or so away from them. But could he be sure the fork or the beef wasn't already contaminated? He couldn't. But he couldn't also appear to act suspiciously either.

He still couldn't tell if she had picked up his plate by mistake, so that he now had the one he had carefully prepared for her. He knew the deadly consequences of ingesting just one grain of the ground up liver of the puffer fish.

He had only just started carrying out the initial steps of his master plan, and already the unexpected was wrong-footing him. What should he do?

CHAPTER 31
COPSE HALL

Richard knew he couldn't appear hesitant any longer.

"It's OK. That piece looks a bit too well done for me, as I think it's from the edge of the joint, which tends to cook slightly more. Here, I have spotted two pieces that are perfectly medium rare." And with that he pierced two pieces from the silver tray, one on top of the other, and placed them to the side of his plate.

Rebecca gave him a look that he didn't understand. Was she in some way either suspicious, or perhaps offended that he hadn't taken the piece she had lovingly offered him? He had to think quickly.

Suddenly it was obvious what he should do—placate her, before she got pissed off any further and risk her blurting out something indiscreet at any moment.

"OK, Rebecca, sure. I will have that piece from your plate, as well. After all, it looks delicious also."

She placed the piece between her fork and knife and reached over to pass it over to Richard. He offered one side of his plate to her where there was no food, but her fork slipped, releasing the slice of beef onto the middle of his veggies.

"Perfect, Rebecca, thanks!"

"There's horseradish sauce and mustard in the silver servers and a wine-reduced gravy in the server over here, Richard. Please, help yourself, and dig in before it gets cold." She smiled at him and looked down at her plate trying to decide what to eat first.

"Great, thanks. This looks a magnificent spread." Richard smiled. He selected a roast potato and bit into its warm, crisp texture to release the hotter inner softness onto the sides of his mouth and his tongue. He tried some of the vegetables that were away from the center of his plate. He knew that if this was Rebecca's plate, he had only sprinkled the grains near the middle of the veggies. Alternatively, if this was his own plate, he couldn't be certain whether or not her fork had already been contaminated by touching the veggies on her plate. But he also couldn't just leave the veggies uneaten.

He started to feel hot and wiped the sweat from his clammy fingers onto the napkin that rested on his lap. That was the first sign of ingesting the poison, but he knew that he shouldn't feel any impact so soon. His stomach tightened.

The beef was from an organic farm in Ayrshire, Scotland. He discreetly and very carefully moved his knife under the mounds of beef to get at the bottom of the two original pieces that he knew couldn't be contaminated. It

The Feather of Truth   Ian Campbell-Laing

was done and tasted just how he liked it: medium rare with a pink tinge, succulent, and with an herb-and-mustard-crusted coating. He then separated some of the vegetables from the edge of the portion and tried them. They were "done to a turn," as they called it in England—steamed, still firm and crunchy. The carrots and parsnips were fresh that morning from their organic garden, and the honey in the glaze was from a local specialty apiarist. The horseradish sauce and mustard were clearly not bought from a supermarket, either. The mustard was not like the usually harsh, bitter taste that British schoolboys grew up on; the small grains' subtle flavors complemented the beef instead of destroying it.

There was a small salad on their side plates. The hydroponic lettuce was grown in their special greenhouse, using no soil but with their roots in water.

Richard had eaten the soup starter and the rolls that accompanied it. He looked at the two plates in front of him; the small side plate of salad was clean, but he had only eaten about a third of his main—probably contaminated—plate. And soon, Rebecca would nag him to eat it all up.

Then he had a stroke of luck. Rebecca got up and excused herself to go to the restroom. Richard glanced down at her plate. Immediately she was out of the room, he said to Chuck, "Mind if I grab some more veggies and potatoes, old chap?"

"Sure, go ahead." Chuck didn't even look up but continued to examine the label of the Chateau Maris Oeuf Neuf 2023.

Richard shot up, grabbed his plate in his right hand and Rebecca's in his left hand, and strode into the kitchen. He put them down on the countertop. He cleared a space in the dustbin and forked into it from her plate all of the veggies she had not eaten and the top slice of the two pieces of beef she had left. He then forked the veggies and top slice of beef from his plate and rearranged them onto Rebecca's roughly as she had left them. Then he got rid of the rest of the contents of his plate into the bin and put some other trash on top of it. He placed his plate in the dishwasher and grabbed a new plate from the cupboard. He then placed onto his plate some potatoes and veggies from the pans on the stove and nipped back into the dining room with the two plates. He sat down and took some beef from the bottom of the carving tray and started to eat just as Rebecca came back into the room.

"Oh, good, you're eating again. I wondered if you had lost your appetite, Richard," she said, smiling at him.

"Nope. Feeling great, and this food is delicious. I am going to eat it all, you'll see!" He exhaled loudly. He knew that his new plate was uncontaminated. And he was confident that either Rebecca's first plate where she had eaten most of her veggies contained the poisonous grains, or that his original plate which he had just given her now was contaminated

The Feather of Truth   Ian Campbell-Laing

with them.

Rebecca stared at Richard and smiled. But she didn't start eating again.

"Sssuch a pity your wife wasn't able to join us today, Richard. The meal is delishhious." Said Chuck starting to slur his words.

"Yes, indeed. Unfortunately she and the boys had other commitments. Another time though. Most definitely."

Richard now feeling relaxed again, continued, "Yes, you are right, once you've had vegetables grown this way, you never want to eat another vegetable grown in the soil, even if it's organic."

"Quite sho…soooo, Ricardo."

Rebecca had included in the fare her own version of Yorkshire pudding, a clever mix between the traditional southern English, small-sized ones and the larger ones from Yorkshire in northern England that took up the whole plate and were a meal in themselves. Her pudding was cut into triangular shapes stacked up into a small mound; they were crispy on the outside and smoothly soft on the inside. It was packed with delicious herbs, which emitted a pungent aroma. Rebecca had accented it by adding some wine-reduced gravy to the pudding mix.

Heavenly! thought Richard, remembering the overcooked, brittle Yorkshires that his boarding school dished up for him in his youth.

This was all washed down with the nice bottle of Pomerol. The meal was exquisite. Richard wasn't hungry, but he forced the food down.

Chuck opened two other bottles—one called Old Bastard 2020, from a vineyard owned by the bank's head of Asia, and Oeuf Neuf 2023 from Celsius's 79 acre biodynamic and organic French vineyard, Chateau Maris.

Half an hour later, this prompted a debate about which was the better of the two. Richard and Rebecca thought the Maris won hands down, and was even better than the far more expensive Pomerol.

Chuck was perspiring heavily and looking tired, due to the weight of the heavy cocktail, of being near obese, the vast quantity of alcohol in his bloodstream, and the effect of jet lag.

Richard moved to fill up Chuck's glass, just as he saw Chuck start to undo his tie. Richard deliberately knocked the bottle against Chuck's waving hands, spilling wine on Richard's jacket.

Chuck apologized. "It's no problem, Chuck. It's due to be dry cleaned tomorrow anyway," said Richard.

Rebecca said, "Hey, relax, you two." Her comments were mainly aimed at her husband. This for some reason prompted Rebecca to start eating again, and she dived into the remaining veggies.

Chuck finally took out his monogrammed white handkerchief and was about to wipe his sweaty, flushed forehead, when Richard remarked, "Hey, that's an elegant-looking handkerchief. Mind if I see it, Chuck?"

Chuffed at the compliment, Chuck lobbed it towards Richard. Richard

The Feather of Truth   Ian Campbell-Laing

picked it up from the floor and then examined it.

"How elegant, Chuck. Recently I've also been putting a handkerchief in my top pocket, as well. Here, let me show you mine. Tell me what you think of it." Richard got up and placed his own handkerchief on the tablecloth in front of Chuck.

"Uh-huh, sure, but yours is all colours. I think white makes a bigger sshtatement, don't you think, Becks?"

Richard sat back down and, while keeping his eyes on Chuck, discreetly put Chuck's handkerchief on his lap. With his left hand, he deftly pulled out the identical handkerchief with the tiny amount of grains in it and swapped it for the one on his lap. He placed the one in his lap back into the side pocket of his jacket.

Rebecca watched Chuck, and, shaking her head from side to side, she let out a large sigh. "I think both you men have nice handkerchiefs."

After Chuck scrutinized Richard's handkerchief, he tossed it back to him and said, "It's very good quality silk, but linen is just a personal preference I have for *ultimate* luxury, Richard."

Rebecca rolled her eyes thinking, How could I have fallen for such a pompous ass? She desperately wanted to shout to the rooftops, "I'm having Richard's baby, you idiot!" But, she didn't because she had promised Richard she wouldn't. As she got up to go to the kitchen to retrieve and serve dessert, she bent down and invaded her husband's face space. "Chuck, you're embarrassing me. You are, as usual, wasted."

Richard glanced at her plate and saw that it was clean. Finally, we are back on track. He still felt hot, but he judged no more so than before. And through his reading glasses, he could see that his heartbeat and blood pressure were only slightly above his normal level.

"Ungrateful bitch," Chuck murmured to himself as Rebecca left the room.

"If I had your salary, perhaps I could enjoy such *ultimate* luxury myself," Richard said. He carefully handed the grain-laced handkerchief back to Jelly, who inelegantly stuffed it back into the breast pocket of his jacket.

"When you have my experriensch, my intellect, my contacts, and my asshhertiveness, then maybe you will," Chuck loudly announced.

Richard was also tiring of Chuck, and as he reached for a sip of water, he didn't notice his boss pull out his handkerchief and shake it open over the table, and then wipe some beads of sweat from his brow. He scrumpled it up and stuffed it back into his jacket pocket.

Rebecca came back in with dessert just as Richard replied, "Something for me to aspire to, Chuck. Here's to you, Chuck."

Rebecca sat down and looked at Richard with questioning eyes. What were these two talking about? she wondered. She hated the way Chuck treated Richard at times.

"So I would like to make two toasts. Firstly, to the chef, who has surpassed her own unbelievably high water mark of culinary excellence," said Richard, "for that main course was absolutely the best Sunday roast I've ever tasted. So, a toast to you, Rebecca."

He couldn't help but wonder how long it would in practice take for the grains to take effect. He knew that it depended on so many factors: the higher the victim's physical fitness, and the more food and alcohol they had eaten, the longer the poison would take to act. The die had been cast. It was now just a matter of time. He just prayed that he hadn't ingested by mistake one small grain of it himself. He knew the deadly effect it would have, and there was no antidote. There was a knot in his lower stomach starting to ache, but he had had that feeling before. It didn't seem a new feeling, just one he got when he was anxious. But there was nothing he could do now.

Chuck and Richard raised their glasses and Chuck said loudly, "Hear, hear, to Re-becca!"

Rebecca blushed and briefly looked down. She raised her head and lifted her own glass and turning only to Richard, said, "Thank you. You're welcome!"

Chuck had difficulty focusing. He closed one eye in an attempt to get rid of his double vision, and squinting, stood up and pushed his chair behind him. He swayed slightly, saying, "I have a toasssht to make, to successsshful men…to…ME!"

Richard wasn't sure what to do, but he went along with the charade and said, "Fine, Chuck, to you. Well done in all that you have achieved at a relatively young age."

"Shhhank you, Ricc-hardo, you are most welcome." And with that he flopped back into his chair, spilling some of his wine onto the linen tablecloth and the Persian rug below.

Rebecca was beyond being embarrassed. She knew her lover hated her husband, and she did now too. It confirmed to her that she must leave Chuck and be with Richard, as soon as possible. She gave her husband another long glare and said quietly but firmly, "You are drunk and embarrassing our guest. No more wine for you. Drink some water right now, and I'll make us some coffee."

"Wha-tt-ever you shayyyyy," Chuck slobbered.

Rebecca turned to her lover, nodded her head in despair of her husband's actions, and saw the antithesis of her husband: tall, good looking, polished, courteous, and calm. "Richard, what was your second toast?"

"It was simply a toast to good friends. I believe that friends are the salt of the earth, one of the most important things in our lives. To me, one's family, friends, and health are the keys to life."

Rebecca nodded and smiled. Chuck would never say or believe anything like that.

The Feather of Truth   Ian Campbell-Laing

Richard turned to Chuck and said, "Chuck, wealth is one thing, but it can't buy you true friends, an adoring family, or health. So, here's a toast to good friends and our health."

Rebecca clapped her hands in delight, saying, "Eloquently put, Richard, and yes family, friends, and health is all the wealth you need." She wished that she could take Richard upstairs, right now, and make love to him. She thought how different Richard and her husband were. Ying and yang, black and white. Richard's soothing, articulate words; Chuck's drunken ramblings. Her lover's powerful, muscular frame and long, slender, manicured fingers; her husband's potbelly, sweaty face, and dirty, chipped nails. She desperately wanted to say, 'I am ready for you to take care of me, Richard, my lover.' She reached for her wine. She briefly closed her eyes, thinking about the next amorous time with Richard, planned for two days' time at the RAC. She shifted in her chair as she felt moisture dampen her panties.

After a dessert of mixed fruits sorbet, Richard looked at his watch and saw that it was just after four o'clock in the afternoon. He had observed that Rebecca had started drinking more wine, which was unlike her. She usually just had a couple of small glasses, max. Already, she had consumed four large glasses and was halfway through her fifth. She was also starting to make a few unsubtle comments.

Jelly was very drunk and now looked like all he wanted to do was sleep. He was glaring at his wife and muttering obscenities under his breath. With Rebecca getting a little sozzled, Richard knew she might blurt out something inappropriate, or Chuck might order him out of the house before he could complete his plans.

Rebecca scowled at her husband, her fingers firmly arched and pressing down on the table, her knuckles taut and white. "Richard, I do apologize. But, Chuck, I can't bear it any longer, there's something I have to say."

Richard turned his head and stared at her in disbelief.

CHAPTER 32
COPSE HALL

Richard's heart was pounding. Oh my God! She's going to confess about the affair and pregnancy to her husband right now! Her few words will light a powder trail with a short fuse, culminating in Chuck likely to blow up in anger and physically attack me.

He glanced up at the upper section of the right hand lens of his glasses and saw his heart rate was double its resting level.

"Your behavior is so embarrassing to me and our guest," Rebecca said and paused. As Richard quickly turned to her, facing away from her husband, he shook his head and mouthed the words, "No, no, not yet! Wait!"

He then looked at his watch; it was 4:10 p.m., right on schedule for the next phase. He needed Rebecca in the morning room and Jelly in the library within thirty minutes, he estimated.

Richard quickly interrupted her. "Rebecca, please don't be embarrassed on my account. Chuck just has jet lag and probably is a little tipsy, that's all. More importantly, that was a superb meal. Thank you. You are one of the best chefs and hostesses I have ever known. It's a privilege to be with you here today, er, with you both, I meant." He rambled.

He then turned to Chuck. "Listen, I came to show you the presentation I've been working on, so why don't we retire to the library and let me whiz through it, so I can make any changes you recommend before your presentation tomorrow afternoon to Celsius. How's that sound?" With his eyes, and moving his head slightly to the right, Richard signaled to Rebecca to leave the room.

Chuck replied, "Sure, good idea."

"Richard, will you help me clear the plates first?"

"Sure thing, Rebecca."

Rebecca's face was red. She marched over to Chuck, her right index finger held out in front of her. She bent down and whispered, rather too loudly, whilst jabbing her finger in his face. "You are too worse for wear, dear pathetic husband, to be able to do anything useful. You are a total embarrassment to me, and after your arrogant behavior today, you *will* continue to stay away from my bedroom."

Chuck just shrugged his shoulders and took solace by reaching for the bottle nearby to refill his glass with wine.

Rebecca announced that she would make coffee for everyone and would go to her morning room to read while they tended to business.

Richard joined her in the kitchen and whispering said, "Rebecca, don't come into the library. At the end of my presentation, in about twenty minutes, I'm planning to mention to Chuck that you and I are madly in love, and you're going to have our baby."

"Oh, thank heavens," Rebecca said, adding, "I can't bear to wait any longer. You may have suspected that I was bursting to tell him of our news!"

"Yes, I did, and thanks for holding back. It's going to be OK. I'll come and get you in the morning room, but *only* when I am ready."

"Do be careful, Richard. In his drunken state, he is a brute and very strong like an ox. I know you are much taller than him and very fit, but he used to box at school and may take his anger out on you physically. He's a violent man, as you well know. He has slapped me a couple of times in a fit of rage."

"Yes, I remember you said—he's certainly a drunk, a bully, and an oaf. It will all be over soon. Trust me." He smiled.

She started to sway a little—from the alcohol, she assumed. She pulled Richard around the corner, out of sight, and held him. "God, I want you, Richard de L'Isle, and if I hadn't had so much to drink, or hadn't gotten this dreadful stomach and throbbing headache, I would make love to you on this kitchen floor right now, and show you how much you mean to me."

"Me too, sweetheart, and it's all going to be fine, and very soon. But tell me. When did you get a stomach pain? Is it the pregnancy?" Richard asked, knowing full well what it was, and feeling much better in himself: his body had now cooled down, and his stomach cramp had also gone. He suspected that if he still felt the same in no more than an hour, then he would be in the clear.

He estimated that the tiny powerful grains had been in Rebecca's body for between two and three hours, just the time needed for the stomach cramps to start getting quite painful. Then, within the hour, the pains would be intense.

"Nope. I don't think so," replied Rebecca. "It's too early for any morning sickness feeling. But I've had the pain for an hour or so now, and it's like the feeling I get just before having a bad period, with a cramping in the bottom of my stomach. Bloated, headache, some heart palpitations." She then lowered her voice and said, "But it can't be a period, obviously, given I am pregnant! Maybe it's the alcohol. I drank more than I usually do: I was and still am so nervous!"

She smiled and grabbed Richard's hand, pressing his palm against her tummy. Then she grimaced and she let out a little cry, like an injured child.

"Hon, anyway, the coffee cups are all laid out, and the coffee machine is all set to brew in about ten minutes, so I don't need to do anything more. But I think I'll sit down. Will you get me a glass of water with some ice? I'm having hot flushes, as well."

"Sure. Do you want a pain killer or something, or do you think it will simply pass after a good rest and maybe a light snooze?"

"It will pass, hon." She caressed his face gently with her hand. "I am so lucky to have you, Richard, so very lucky. We are soul mates, aren't we?" His presence and soothing words comforted her and gave her the strength to bear the pain.

Richard got her a glass of iced water and she took a sip of it. He walked with her to the morning room. He opened the door for her, and she took the glass and walked over to her favorite overstuffed armchair by the window. She awkwardly put the water on the glass coffee table next to her, turned on the tall reading light, and slumped back in her chair. She smiled, gave him a little wave, and said, in a whisper, "I think a little snooze is in order, hon. See you later when you have good news for me, darling! Good luck!" She winced again in pain and held her stomach in an attempt to quash the intense throbbing.

"See you later. Get some rest. We won't disturb you. Just stay in here and rest."

Richard closed the door and as he walked back into the dining room, he mentally went through his checklist and then said to Jelly, "Why don't you help me clear up in here—why not take in the silver carving tray, whilst I start making the coffee?"

Richard watched Jelly get up and grab with both hands the plate and stagger into the kitchen. Richard followed Jelly, not clearing up any of the plates and leaving the wine bottles on the table.

"Thanks, Chuck. You look tired. Why don't I meet you in the library directly—I can finish up here for you."

"Thanks, Risshhard."

Richard collected his briefcase that he had left in the hallway and went into the library. Chuck sat there, his body awkwardly slumped back in an armchair.

Chuck glanced up at Richard without moving his head as he entered the room. He watched him as Richard took out his laptop and placed it on the antique table in front of Chuck.

"Her morning room is her little sanctuary, and I am absolutely forbidden to enter it. It all ssshtarted after a shhtupid row a few months ago, when she retreated into it one morning and refused to come out and talk to me. When she wants some peesssh and quiet, she goes in there. Pro'lly gets on her cell phone and has a natter with her girlie friends and tells them how mean I am," said Chuck, trying to account for what he genuinely believed were Rebecca's unreasonable actions.

"Well, all women need a sanctuary, it seems," said Richard. "It's probably good for her."

"Yeah, pro'lly," said Chuck, slobbering on his shirt a little. He lifted his head up and tried to think clearly.

Richard then showed Chuck his presentation. Not the version Richard had for Chuck's boss, Celsius, but a tamer one that was nonetheless very impressive. It showed a ten-million-euro profit for this year (compared to the twenty-five million he would privately show Celsius) and a fifty-million profit for next year (compared to the 105 million that Richard would show Celsius).

Chuck beamed a sly smile and thought this presentation would continue to make him look good in Celsius's eyes, not realizing that Richard had set him up for a fall with Celsius. After about thirty minutes, Richard got up to get the brewed coffee. He looked at Chuck, who could hardly focus. Chuck said, "Yes, Richard, you get the coffee—I might just have a little snooze, if that's OK with you. We are, I think, pretty much done with the PowerPoint, yes? Why don't you wake me up in, say, half an hour? Can you also go and check on Becks for me?"

Richard said, "Roger, WilCo," and knew that Rebecca hated being called Becks by her husband, even though Richard called her that from time to time.

"Roger will go? What are you talking about, Ric-arrrr-doh?"

"Not will *go*, but will *co*. In the British forces, 'roger' means 'message received,' and 'WilCo' is an abbreviation for 'will comply.'"

Richard then added, "Chuck, I'll close the door and leave you be. While you're napping, I'll tidy up the PowerPoint and put through the suggestions and recommendations you asked for. I'll go into the living room, if that's OK, so I don't disturb you."

Richard gathered his kit and then looked up and saw Chuck's head lying back on its side in the armchair, his mouth open, and his shoes kicked off nearby. He was already fast asleep and snoring very loudly. Perfect, back on plan, he smiled. And apart from the beef slice and potential wrong plates, which briefly threw a spanner in the works, all relatively easy, and now tickety-boo.

Richard hadn't even needed to give Chuck a sleeping pill he had brought with him, just in case he took too long to fall into a deep asleep. The two very generous gin and tonics, and probably at least three bottles of wine, along with jet lag, had finally taken their toll. He was fairly sure that Chuck should not wake up until the early hours of the morning. Also, Richard was certain that Chuck would not dare check on Rebecca and disturb her sanctuary. So far, so good. Glancing at his watch, he saw that it was 4:45 p.m.—he was bang on his plan's target.

As he walked towards the kitchen, he went through his mental checklist again to ensure he hadn't missed anything. He poured out three cups of coffee. He took two of them with him and quietly placed one cup and saucer on the table near where Chuck was snoring away loudly.

Richard took his coffee cup and saucer and set up his laptop in the

The Feather of Truth   Ian Campbell-Laing

living room. He put his fingers on the coffee table near the laptop and coffee cup and sipped the coffee. He updated the presentation and then sat back and pondered whether he had forgotten anything. He went through his mental checklist again, Switch Fear KGB PC.

He put on his latex gloves and went back into the kitchen. He picked up the silver tray and took it back into the dining room. He closed the doors, and, standing where Chuck had stood when he had been carving, he whacked the side of the plate onto the table to leave a small dent. He then took it back into the kitchen and put it on the worktop precisely where Jelly had previously left it. He then left open the dining room doors. He stood in the hallway and waited in case he heard either of them stir from the noise. Nothing. Excellent. Before the top of the hour, I will be out of here, thank God, he thought.

At 5:30 p.m., he checked on Chuck, who was still fast asleep and snoring loudly. Richard looked at Chuck's discarded slip-on shoes. He thought about his plan, and even though he had promised himself to not deviate from it, he then decided this opportunity was too good to be ignored, and he couldn't think of any downside. He nipped upstairs to Chuck's bedroom and selected one of Chuck's pair of black socks, and walked back downstairs.

He undid the laces of his own shoes and put his shoes down behind the sofa, out of sight. He then put on Chuck's socks over his own, and then Chuck's shoes. The slip-ons were too tight a fit, but by pushing down the back heel of the shoe, he could just force his large feet into them. It helped that Chuck clearly wore very thick socks and had unusually wide and long feet for his short size.

He shut the library doors after him as he left. He saw Chuck's overcoat hung up in the hallway and reached into the pockets and pulled out Chuck's tan-coloured gloves, which Chuck always had with him. He stuffed them into his trouser pocket. He opened up the central console keypad, and pressed *M* to close the morning room blinds.

He went into the kitchen and grabbed the remaining coffee cup and saucer. He gingerly opened the door to the morning room and peered in. "Christ!" he gasped as his head jolted back, and the coffee cup rattled on the saucer in his left hand—Rebecca was staring straight at him, her mouth slightly open. It was if she was about to say something to him. The curtains were closed, and the room was quite dark, with only Rebecca slumped back in her armchair illuminated by the lamp from the stand behind it. The scene reminded Richard of when, just before a play on stage commences, the audience sometimes only sees a spotlight in the darkness focusing on the first actor.

He stepped inside, closed the door, and locked it from the inside.

"Rebecca?" he whispered. "Rebecca?" She stared at him, motionless, her right hand remaining on her lap. Her eyes didn't move or blink. Her mouth remained slightly open. He approached her chair slowly, almost tiptoeing towards her.

He put the cup and saucer down on the side table. As he walked up to her, he heard an eerie sound: her shallow breathing made a rasping sound—like that in the paranormal films that depict haunting noises. Then he remembered his research—that in the final moments before death, there is what's called the death rattle: a chilling sound after one loses the cough reflex and the ability to swallow, resulting in an accumulation of saliva in the throat and lungs.

He put on Chuck's gloves and was about to complete his final, unpleasant task—when the front doorbell rang.

CHAPTER 33
COPSE HALL

"Oh, shit, shit, shit!" Richard cursed, loudly. "Who can that be at the ruddy door? What bloody timing!" That wasn't part of the plan. Do I answer the door or not? He knew that the doorbell would not affect Rebecca, but it could wake up Chuck.

Richard decided to ensure that Chuck was still asleep, because he could not afford to have him wandering around the house at this time. He unlocked and left the morning room, closing the door behind him, and went back into the library.

Chuck was still completely out cold and snoring loudly with his mouth wide open.

The front doorbell rang again.

Shit. They will bloody wake up Chuck if they do that once more.

He stepped out of the library and quietly closed the doors. With his heart pounding an alarm hurting his chest, he went to the front door and turned the key in the lock twice, and started to open it. *Cripes!* He spotted that he still had on Chuck's gloves. He didn't have time to take them off, so he quickly hid his hands behind the door when he opened it halfway.

In front of him stood a somber-looking, middle-aged lady, a young girl—probably her daughter—and a man who could have been the woman's husband. They were all smartly dressed in black. The daughter was holding a Bible to her chest. Christ, he sighed in despair. What a day to have a visit from the God Squad.

"I'm so sorry, we are terribly busy today. Thank you," said Richard quietly, and closed the door on them.

He went back into the library and peered anxiously through the window from behind the net curtains to make sure they had gone. They were making their way back to their car, which was parked about twenty yards away in the driveway. He waited until he saw them get in the car and drive off. A few beads of sweat popped out on his forehead. Stay cool. Just stay cool. Get this done.

He checked his watch again. That whole episode had taken three minutes but seemed much longer. Always know that the perfect plan can take an unexpected turn.

And that was his fifth glitch. With the slice of potentially contaminated beef passed to him by Rebecca; uncertainty about whether or not Rebecca by mistake had given him the plate he had reserved for her; the God Squad at the door; and the cufflinks box and pregnancy kit, both of which he still had to get rid of…Let's hope we don't have any more interferences.

He checked that Chuck was still out for the count. He was. Richard left and closed the door of the library, and went back into the morning room, and for the second time, he locked that door behind him.

He approached Rebecca and placed his ear near her mouth again. This time, he couldn't hear her breathing or feel her warm breath. Then suddenly, she started to hyperventilate, and her breathing became rapid and noisy—which gave him a start and made his head jolt back.

He watched Rebecca for a few minutes. She was experiencing what the medics called Cheynes-Stokes respiration: her heart was now very weak and overworked, and this made her body want to breathe abnormally fast, and as a consequence, she then had no more energy to breathe for a period of time, which is called apnea.

He gently called her name. No reply.

Her eyes, still staring straight ahead at him, unnerved him. When he moved to the side of the room, her eyes didn't follow him but continued their stare that seemed to be aimed towards the door.

He walked back to her, took off Chuck's glove from his right hand, and through his thin latex glove, felt her pulse with his index fingers—it was very weak—probably about twenty-five beats per minute: less than a third of her resting heartbeat. "Good," he said quietly to himself.

Her face was slightly contorted, and her right hand hadn't moved from resting on her stomach. He knew she was, and had been, in great pain. "Yet, you still look beautiful, Rebecca," he said, smiling at her.

Richard turned his wrist and checked his watch. It was now at least over four hours after she must have eaten her contaminated veggies, and the full force of the poison, whichever plate she had been given, would be in her body searching to control the last few critical-for-life organs. According to his research, given her wheezing, her lungs must now be heavily affected. And within the hour, her heart would fail, by which time he would have left the house. He knew that Rebecca would not be able to cry out because her nervous system had seized up. In fact, she was likely to already be in a coma and not sense anything. He hoped so. He had wanted her to be spared of as much pain as possible.

He undid her belt and unfastened the top buttons on her jeans, leaving them open. He pulled at the top of her black lace panties until they tore apart, about two inches. He put back on Jelly's glove and slapped her face very hard with the back of his right hand. She didn't flinch, blink, or wake up. Her left cheek started to redden.

He slapped her again in the face and then with his fist. He pummeled her stomach several times. He remembered Rebecca telling him that Chuck had done precisely that to her after an argument a month ago. She had showed Richard precisely where he had hit her. His target was the same spot. Then, he put both of his hands around her neck and squeezed. He counted to thirty and then let go.

Yes. Good. Perfect. Red marks precisely where I wanted them to be.

He then gently tugged at her left earring to ensure that some of the fabric of the glove was left snared on it. He stood to the side of her and pulled her pearl necklace and ripped it off her neck. Pearls scattered everywhere, some into the crevices of her chair; some landing noisily on the glass tabletop and bouncing off onto the floor and into a silent embrace of the thick threads of the woolen carpet; and others continuing their energetic momentum, rolling and finally resting on the glass top of the side table.

Taking off the glove on his right hand, but still wearing the latex glove underneath, he removed her watch. He changed the time forward to 8:05 p.m. and scraped some fibers off the glove onto the gold clasp on the watch strap. He then put it back on her wrist exactly as she had previously worn it, remembering to ensure that it was the correct way up, as she would look at it. That was on his checklist—a rookie mistake to get that wrong had helped convict other murderers. He slipped the glove back on his right hand.

Richard looked at his victim with no remorse and no emotion. He was detached from her, as he knew he had to be in order to complete his task efficiently and effectively. She was just a thing—no more, no less. Strange. Only a week or so ago, he had expressed his undying love for her and had adored her. Now, he felt nothing for her.

He quietly said to her, "You *forced* me to behave like this. It wasn't my fault at all. If only you had agreed to not have the baby, instead of putting me and my family's own future at risk and ruining what I had worked for all my life, none of this would have had to happen." He also knew that she would have never agreed to break off the affair. She was infatuated with him; after the evening at the RAC, only three days ago, she had sent him thirty-five texts. He really had no choice but to end it all. She had trapped him, and then suffocated him, and would have ended his future plans.

He leaned her forward, and grabbing tightly her left wrist, he smacked her watch hard on the glass table. The coffee in the cup spilled over slightly into the saucer. He placed her back in the chair and repositioned her right hand back onto her stomach as he had found her. She still didn't move; she was like a ragdoll—limp and unresponsive.

He checked her watch. The face was cracked, and her wrist was red. His gloved hand took it and squeezed it hard one more time.

Originally, he had planned on taking Chuck's shoes and smashing them on the pearls, but even though he had been careful to tear the pearls away from himself, he knew in his original plan that he still ran the risk of his own shoes doing the same by accidentally treading on one of them. But now, of course, he didn't mind standing on any of the pearls and crushing some of them under his feet, because he was wearing Chuck's shoes. He had promised himself to not deviate from the plan, but this late adjustment seemed to be a win-win.

He made one last check of the morning room. He surveyed the scene: all seemed in place and as he had envisioned. Giving Rebecca one last look, he said softly to her, "Good-bye, Rebecca, my dear. I did love you, but your pregnancy left me with no choice. I am so very sorry. Hopefully, your pain will end soon. Forgive me for lying to you and for what I have now done. I know we will never meet again, and I have failed our pact of the Feather of Truth and will go to eternal oblivion for this. So be it. That's in another lifetime. I have to concentrate on this one."

He felt calm, and noticed from his glasses that his heart rate and blood pressure were at normal resting levels.

He unlocked the door and left the room, closing the door after him.

He was correct that the effect of the poison was shutting down her vital organs one by one, and that her heart would be the last to go. Rebecca's nervous system had completely collapsed, so she was unable to move any muscles. She could not move even her eyelids to close her eyes. However, she was not yet in a coma, but instead still fully conscious.

Rebecca had indeed experienced the horror around her. She had heard everything, including all that Richard had said to her. She smelled his breath when he leaned close. She smelt his distinctive Tom Ford Noir aftershave. *God, please don't desert me. Please help me!* she screamed silently. No words came out of her open mouth, nor was there any change in expression from her bruised face. She wanted to fight back, but she was helpless, locked in her paralyzed body. She couldn't believe it. *How could you kill our baby? Who really are you, Richard?*

She thought she must be having a nightmare and couldn't wake up. She felt the full force of his palm slapping her face, and his fists pummeling her stomach. Her love, her one and only love, her soul mate, had lied and betrayed her. In dying, she realized she had loved a monster. One far more ruthless than Chuck or anyone she had ever known before.

Had Richard gone back into the morning room again and now looked at her face, he would have seen that tears were slowly making their final journey down Rebecca's bruised, red-blotched cheeks. Ordinarily, the poison might have taken another hour or two to finally kill someone as healthy as Rebecca who had a full stomach, but instead, she had a fatal heart attack ten minutes later, at 5:55 p.m.

More than anything, she literally had died of a broken heart.

CHAPTER 34
COPSE HALL

Richard went into the hallway and pressed *M* on the control panel, reopening the blinds in the morning room. He then went into the dining room, restoked the fire, and tossed Chuck's leather gloves into the flames, leaving the surgical latex gloves on his hands.

He then went back into the library for the last time and took off Chuck's shoes and placed them where Chuck had discarded them. He pulled back up the squashed heel of Chuck's shoes to their original position. He took off the socks he had taken from Chuck's closet drawer, placed them inside the wrapping paper of the cufflink box, and stuffed them back into his own jacket pocket. He slipped into his own shoes and tied up the laces.

He restoked the fire, and added more logs. He reached into his jacket, and took out the last cellophane jiffy bag which contained a joint. He tossed it into the flames. He then checked on Chuck who looked like he was still oblivious to the world, not having moved. Richard left the library and closed the doors.

Perfectamundo!

He grabbed his laptop and copy of the presentation and placed it into his briefcase. He took a swig of his cold coffee and then retrieved the incriminating documents he had created from V-Trax and placed them at the bottom of a pile of documents inside Chuck's briefcase.

That's pretty much it, I think, he concluded. He resisted the urge to go back and check on Rebecca one last time. He knew that was not in his carefully thought-out plan, and he could not improvise at this stage of the game. He didn't want to tempt any more forces of evil.

He ran through each of the first ten of his fifteen acts within Switch Fear KGB PC and ticked them off in his brain, leaving just the last five letters of his plan to complete after he left the house.

What the heck, let's get a souvenir from Chuck, as well, he thought. After all, he won't need it where he's going! He went to the wine cellar and scanned the bottles. He spotted an ornate case of Italian wine, Brunello di Montalcino, 2015, in the special reserve section in the corner. He remembered that Chuck had boasted that it was his most expensive wine, at £20,000 a bottle. He picked up the case from the shelf and carried it to the front door. Resting the wooden box on his left knee, he unlocked the front door. After opening it, he placed the box on the front door mat. He smiled, thinking "Finally, a little bonus from Chuck for all my hard work – and I didn't even bring a bottle as a gift!"

The Feather of Truth   Ian Campbell-Laing

Richard grabbed his briefcase and checked the time. It was 6:05 p.m. when he stepped out the door of their house. He double-locked it from the outside, using the key that Rebecca had given him at the start of their affair.

He put the wine in the boot of his car and sat behind the wheel. After taking off his latex gloves and placing them on his lap, he said, "Command. Engine on."

He drove the car himself, enjoying the control and feel of the steering wheel. He called his wife using the hands-free system at 6:20 p.m. before stopping at the local petrol station. He told her about the lunch and how well the presentation was received by Chuck, and that Chuck had given him a nice case of wine as a thank you. He mentioned also that he had left Chuck and Rebecca alone so they could enjoy the rest of their Sunday together even though the two had argued.

Richard stopped at the petrol station on the pretext that his tyres looked low. There, he checked each of the tyres with a new pair of latex gloves on. He then wiped them on the dirty tyres and on the ground. Afterwards, he put them and the pair he had used at Rebecca's house deep into the dustbin, which he had previously checked would be collected overnight. He then filled up the car with petrol and collected the Visa card timed receipt and put it in his wallet. He went into the men's toilets and locked the door.

He turned on the taps to mask any noise. He took out the small cufflink box and ripped it into small pieces, then flushed it down the toilet—along with the socks inside the wrapping paper, and ribbon. He took the pregnancy test kit out of his jacket pocket and snapped it into two pieces. The blue fluid trickled out into the toilet. He then took the front-door key that Rebecca had given him and flushed that down the toilet, as well. He flushed the toilet again and checked to make sure nothing came back up. He did it one more time. It was 6:45 p.m. He had completed his mission. He was exhausted but exhilarated.

Nothing would be the same ever again. He knew that. But surprisingly, he didn't feel any fear. Only relief. He felt no remorse.

He said to himself out loud amidst the noise of the flushing of the toilet, "In the face of adversity and fear, I had the courage to do what was right, what needed to be done, and persevere. I am truly a de L'Isle."

CHAPTER 35
BLACKDOWN CLOSE

Richard arrived home just before 7:00 p.m. He chatted with Jennifer, describing the afternoon where Chuck had made an arse of himself, the arguments he had with his wife, and how he had got drunk and spilled wine on the carpet and onto Richard's jacket and shoes.

Whilst Jennifer prepared dinner, Richard went upstairs and checked that none of his pockets had anything left inside them. Afterwards he read his youngest a bedtime story from the Gruffalo's Child, and put him to bed. Then he went downstairs and helped his eldest son with his maths homework.

Later that evening, Jennifer took his jacket with the red wine stains on it and placed it in the dry cleaning bag that would be collected first thing tomorrow morning, on Monday. She put his shoes into her car to take to the cobblers for cleaning.

Richard appeared calm, relaxed, and his usual self to Jennifer. As always, each Sunday he made a call on the landline to his mother, to see how she was faring. He spent the remainder of the evening at home with his family, making the occasional work related call, e-mailing colleagues, and watching TV—the same things he always did on a Sunday evening with his family. Richard was surprised that he felt so relaxed, given what he had just done.

***

Copse Hall

Chuck awoke from his deep sleep in the library around ten that evening. He had a headache and a parched, dry throat. After drinking two glasses of water, he went to the toilet, and while relieving himself, called Richard to thank him for the presentation that afternoon and asked him to send it to him so that he could show it to Celsius the next day.

"Chuck, I already sent it to you when I was in your living room updating it. I sent it, oh, probably just before I left at around sixish. You then kindly gave me a case of wine from your cellar as a thank you, and then you showed me out. Don't you remember?"

"Oh, you did? Did I? Can't remember, but OK, thanks. Enjoy the wine. You deserve it, after all your hard work, Richard."

Even though Richard knew the answer, he said, "Would you like me to present the deck with you to Celsius?"

"No, it's OK, I can handle it. Best I do it alone. I need to talk with the Iceman on some other topics, as well," Chuck replied.

"What's that whooshing sound, Chuck?" asked Richard.

"Oh, I'm on the throne, as you call it. You know me, always multitasking, Ricardo!"

"How's Rebecca? I popped my head into her morning room before I left as you had asked me, at around sixish, and when I noticed that she looked like she was snoozing, I thought best to not disturb her."

"Very sensible. I'll leave her snoozing, as well. I daren't go in there, especially tonight, as she will bite my head off after the bickering we had all afternoon. I will see her in the morning, instead, and try and patch things up with her then."

"Your voice sounds different, Chuck. Is everything all right? You've not had another row with Rebecca, have you? God, you were at each other's throats all afternoon!"

"Nope, but I will stay well clear of her. She drives me nuts as it is," said Chuck, not even thinking of apologizing to his guest for his bad behavior over lunch.

"Sounds like a plan. Enjoy the rest of your evening, Chuck, and see you tomorrow in the office."

"Bye, Ricardo. Many thanks. I think I'll head up to bed now. I'm exhausted." Instead, Chuck went back into the library to watch some golf on TV. He had another drink and fell asleep in his armchair. He was relieved that his wife was being quiet in the morning room and leaving him alone.

It was midnight, and Rebecca had been dead for six hours. Her tears on her cheeks were now dry, and her right hand was still resting on her stomach.

CHAPTER 36
COPSE HALL

The next day, on Monday morning, Chuck's alarm woke him in the library at 6:00 a.m. He couldn't remember much of the evening after Richard had shown him the presentation. He didn't even remember calling Richard or later watching TV.

He went upstairs, took a shower, and dressed for work. He looked at his slip-on loafers that he had worn yesterday and noticed that they looked dirty. So he put on another pair that were clean and polished.

He then thought he better check on Rebecca even though she was unlikely to be up for a few more hours. He quietly went to the master bedroom and saw the door ajar, which was odd to him: she always kept it closed, even when she wasn't in it. He looked inside, and not finding her there, he checked the bathroom. She wasn't there either. He thought maybe she was in the kitchen having a coffee. He went downstairs. She wasn't there. He then went into the forbidden morning room and hesitantly and slowly opened the door.

"Becks, darling, are you in there? Just checking you are all OK," said Chuck quietly and nervously.

The curtains had just opened automatically at sunrise a few minutes earlier. The floor reading light was on, and he could see clearly into the room.

"Oh my God!" he screamed as he saw her eyes staring right ahead, directly at him. She was slumped back in her armchair.

What he saw shocked him. Apart from the clothes that she wore, he hardly recognized her. Her face was pale, her mouth was open and seemed to have some red fluid in it, and her right hand lay across her lap. She was motionless, and her fingers were bent into an arch shape. His beautiful wife, in her mid-thirties, now looked like an old woman. Her pearls were lying on the glass table, and there was a dreadful smell in the room.

CHAPTER 37
HASLEMERE STATION, SURREY

Richard's cell phone rang at six-thirty in the morning, as he was standing on the platform with other commuters at Haslemere station, waiting for his SouthWestern train to take him to Waterloo. There he would take the Waterloo and City Line, commonly called the Drain, to get to Bank station, and then he had a short walk to the office. It was cold, exposed to the wind, and as usual the electronic signboard said Normal Service, which usually signaled that the train was running late by at least ten minutes.

He saw that it was Chuck calling from his cell phone. Richard nodded his head. Finally, he calls, he thought. So, now the fun begins. Stay calm, Richard, and only reply to what you can or should know, not to what you really know. Caution. Take your time before answering any question.

Richard turned to one of the commuters he recognized but whose name he couldn't recall. "Keep my place in the queue, will you, mate? I just need to take this call."

"Sure."

Richard stepped aside and walked towards an alcove in the wall outside of the station waiting room. "Hi. Richard here."

"Richard, it's Chuck. Something dreadful has happened. I...I...I think Becks is dead!"

Before Richard could respond, Chuck continued, "I woke up this morning and went to check on her, and she was still in the morning room sitting in her favorite armchair. She wasn't breathing and had no pulse. Her body was cold, and her face a dreadful grey colour. I tried to resuscitate her, but couldn't, and so I rang 911, then realized it's 999 in your country, and the ambulance is on their way now. She looks like she slipped or something, because the coffee table is cracked, and her pearls are all over the floor."

Aware that the police would probably check Chuck's cell phone records and could get transcripts of conversations, Richard went through his rehearsed script. "Oh my God! Chuck, are you sure? She seemed fine yesterday afternoon when I took coffee to her in the morning room. Must have been around four, just before you and I started on the presentation. You even called me in the evening about the presentation, and said you looked in on her and you saw her in her favorite chair and thought she was asleep. Did you and she have another row after I left? You said you were also going to check on her before you went to bed but would try and not disturb her, if memory serves."

"I remember some of the evening, but not all of it. I must have had far too much to drink, even for me. I don't remember much after the presentation you showed me, quite frankly."

"Don't you remember calling me at around ten to ask me to send you the PowerPoint deck?"

"No, not really. It's all a bit of a blur. I ended up sleeping in the library."

"Did you have another row with Rebecca after I left around sixish?"

"No. Er, well, no, I don't think so."

"Chuck, I'm so sorry. Rebecca is, sorry, was, a lovely woman. Do you want me to come over to your home right now?"

"No, it's OK. Oh...there's the doorbell," said Chuck, and as he looked through the net curtain, he added, "I see the ambulance is here. I'll call you back." The line went dead.

***

Copse Hall

Chuck put his cell phone down and went to answer the doorbell.

"Sir, are you Mr. Chuck Jelleners, who called about his wife, Rebecca?" asked Bob Rolland, the consultant paramedic with over twenty years' experience in emergency care with the South Western Ambulance Service.

"Yes, I did. Come in—be quick."

"Thank you. Please show us where your wife is."

"In here at the end of the hallway, in the morning room. But please get on with it," said Chuck impatiently and turning around as he walked ahead of them. They entered the room.

"OK, stand back to the side please, sir, and let me and my colleague examine her," said Bob.

Chuck didn't move, but kept staring at his wife.

"Just stand over there, please," said Bob more forcefully. Chuck shrugged his shoulders and moved to the side. "Thank you, sir, that will allow us to do our job properly. And your wife's name is Rebecca?"

"Yes, yes, that's her name. Goddamit, just hurry up and resuscitate her, will you, man?"

Bob and his new recruit, Emma Oldershaw, ignored the terse remark.

"Emma, remember, let's try not to disturb the scene. Go behind the chair here where there are no pearls on the floor, and access Mrs. Jelleners from the right-hand side of her chair."

Bob knew immediately, by just looking at Mrs. Jelleners, that she had been dead for some time, but partly for the education of Emma, who had only just joined the force from university, and also given the anxious husband was standing nearby, he guided Emma through some of the standard protocol, in a calm, quiet voice.

"Emma, first let's check vitals...Airways: no breathing...no pulse…Eyes: no dilation…no reaction to torchlight, and in fact "tache noire"—see the dark, reddish-brown strip that has formed horizontally across her eye, here."

"Yes, sir, I see the tache noire, or black spot," Emma said, waiting for the right moment to add an additional observation.

"Rebecca, Mrs. Jelleners! Can you hear us?" said Bob, raising his voice and then quietly talking to his assistant. "Note, Emma, that there's no reaction. Body is not warm. Algor mortis, the reduction in body temperature to the ambient surrounding, has taken place, given this room is quite chilly. No colour in her cheeks, and her mouth and eyes are open. Slight reddish-purple colour on her lower extremities, the fingers, and see here on her ankles where livor mortis has set in—the draining of blood to the lowest point, once the heart had stopped working. Note also, rigor mortis has taken over and started to set in; her limbs are stiff to the touch. Obviously no point in resuscitation now, I'm afraid."

"And the eyes must have been open, at death, sir," Emma now said, also quietly.

"Correct, Emma. If they had been closed, then the eyeball would have been moist through blinking."

Chuck moved forward, not liking all the whispering and being told to stand back. "She's dead, right, Doctor?" he asked.

"Yes, sir, I'm afraid she is. And I think has been for some time. Probably, er, let's see, twelve hours or so, is my initial guess. I'm very sorry for your loss, Mr. Jelleners, sir."

"Oh my God! For Christ's sake, what on earth did she die of?" screamed Chuck. "I thought she was healthy, and—"

"Sir, we are trying to find that out, but we need to get her to the hospital to run some tests. Please just stand aside for a few more minutes, sir."

Bob continued to speak quietly, given Chuck's presence. "Emma, notice that her watch face is broken, and showing a time of 8:05, and also that the coffee table is cracked. There are some lesions on her neck, and wrist, and face."

Emma added, "And, sir, the buttons on her jeans are undone, and her panties ripped at the top." Emma lifted up Rebecca's blouse from her waist. "I can see some bruising on her stomach, as well."

"Indeed. So yes, perhaps, an eightish death seems about right given the state of rigor mortis, which is now"—he glanced at his watch—"er, ten hours or so later."

"And the pearls all over the floor, sir," observed Emma.

Bob lowered his voice again, saying, "Looks like to me that there's been a struggle, attempted sexual assault, then probably strangulation, possibly followed by a massive heart attack, I suspect. We should treat this as a crime scene. We can't disturb anything. I'll make some notes."

Chuck was pacing around the room and overheard part of Bob's remarks. "Did you say she had a heart attack?"

"Sir, as I said, she is dead, and has been for some time—probably earlier last night. She'll be taken to the mortuary after the police and forensics have been here and signed off. It's standard practice to call the police in such cases. Please just be patient."

"The police? Be patient? I don't have time for them—I have to get to work. I have an important video call with my CEO this afternoon, that I can't miss."

"That meeting will probably have to wait, sir. As I said, be patient."

Bob took Rebecca's temperature. It showed 83.5 degrees Fahrenheit. He nodded as he did the calculation. That stacks up to be around ten hours since death, given the cold room, and it's between one and one and a half degrees of temperature loss per hour, from a typical temperature of around 98.4 when alive, he thought. He did one further thing. He lifted up her foot and took off her slip-on shoe and observed that the sole of her foot was also a blueish tinge, indicating that since death her feet had remained resting on the floor, with blood slowly draining under the force of gravity. She had died in the chair and hadn't been moved since her death. He made some more notes and sent the form he was filling out electronically to the ambulance centre, who would log it and then automatically forward it to the local police.

Just before seven o'clock, Chuck heard the doorbell and opened the door.

"Mr. Chuck Jelleners?"

"Yes," said Chuck, wiping his sweating forehead with his handkerchief.

The man held up his badge to Chuck. "I am Detective Chief Inspector Kofi Ghazini of the Surrey Police, and this is my colleague, Detective Inspector Harriet Gilmore. We understand that your wife has died. May we come in, please?"

Chuck was taken aback by the incredibly low, deep voice of Ghazini. He stared at the young, black, slim, muscular detective, probably in his thirties, standing on the doorstop and towering over him, and next to him, a pretty woman whom he guessed was in her midtwenties. Neither was in uniform. The DCI wore a tailored, fitted dark blue suit and white open-neck shirt. Chuck had expected the policeman to be white and dressed rather shabbily, and any assistant also to be male. He reminded himself to not stare at either of them or appear to be prejudging them.

"Yes, yes, of course, but why isn't she being taken to the hospital? And how come she had a heart attack? She was extremely fit. Christ only knows how many times she went to the gym and worked out—she was fanatical, and ate very healthfully. Doesn't make sense to me." Chuck saw them still standing in the doorway, and added, "Let's go into the library, shall we?"

"Thank you, sir. DI Gilmore, why don't you join Mr. Jelleners while I take a quick look at his wife, whom I understand is in the Morning Room down this hallway. I'll join you both shortly."

Chuck noticed the chief inspector spoke in a measured and unhurried manner. Chuck took an instant dislike to him and his sidekick policewoman. "OK, but I need to get to work soon, Detective, so please, just hurry up."

Harriet followed Chuck as he walked into the library. She immediately noticed the lingering smell of cigar smoke. Chuck sat down in the same armchair as the previous day. Harriet examined Chuck's face and body language. He wasn't crying and didn't look distraught in any way. A little flummoxed, maybe, but that was all. Also, he was sweating profusely—often that was a sign of nervousness, and hence, possible guilt. However, given he was so overweight, she knew that he would tend to sweat easily, due to his fat acting like an insulator and raising his core temperature. So he would generally feel hotter and need to sweat more than a fit person in order to cool down.

And interesting to her was that one of his first statements was about insisting on getting to work. She would expect most husbands to be distraught if they had just learned their wife had died—unless they had had something to do with the death, or the passing away of their spouse was not a surprise, or was something they had wished for.

Harriet sat down opposite Chuck. She wore a dark blue pinstriped suit and white blouse. She noticed that he glanced at her chest and then at her legs as she crossed them whilst getting herself settled in the chair. She cringed slightly as she guessed what sexist thoughts he was having about her. She sat upright, and in her hand was her iPad. She accessed the ID app.

She then leaned forward and placed it on the table in front of Chuck, and said, "Mind if we get some ID sorted before we start?"

"Sure." Chuck reached into his wallet and passed his driving license to Harriet.

Harriet examined and took a photo of it, and moved it pushed it across the table towards Chuck. She then passed her iPad to him. "Let's do your fingerprints first. Please place your right hand here on the tablet."

Chuck did so. "And now your left hand…Good."

"All done then?"

"Now just a quick DNA sample please."

"I thought you only took fingerprints and DNA for suspects in murder cases, Detective?"

"No, sir, we take them for everyone we meet involved in a case, including witnesses. Standard procedure now. Nothing to be concerned about."

"Oh, OK."

The Feather of Truth   Ian Campbell-Laing

Harriet took back her iPad and passed Chuck a small vial. "Now can you please spit into this container for me now, and then push down the cap, place it in this cellophane bag, and pass it back to me."

Chuck made a loud coughing sound and then did as instructed.

"Good, one final thing. Do you mind if we record our conversation sir, using this tablet? And I should also warn you it also has an inbuilt voice stress analyzer. It saves me taking notes all the time and speeds things up."

"Go ahead. I have nothing to hide, Detective. But yes, do get on with the proceedings, please," said Chuck, frowning at being a prisoner in his own home.

Harriet said, "I'm very sorry about your wife, sir."

"Yes, it's a bit of a shock, to be honest, Detective. Thought she was pretty darn healthy."

She noticed that his voice was firm, assertive, and unwavering, with little emotion. He looked at her directly whilst speaking to her and then glanced around the room, appearing distracted. Harriet glanced down at her iPad to see that Chuck's fingerprints had been analyzed and compared with the records of millions of others in numerous national and international databases. It confirmed his ID—his name, address, date of birth, place of work, social security number, and driving license details. It also showed that he didn't have a criminal record, but he had numerous speeding tickets.

"I loved her dearly, you know," he added, rubbing his eyes with his hands.

Harriet had earned a degree in psychology and was married to a psychiatrist. She thought that Chuck's comment seemed more of an afterthought than one of sincerity from a distraught husband.

"Sir, do you mind me asking how was your relationship with your wife?"

"What do you mean by that? Seems an impertinent question to me!" said Chuck in his booming New York nasal accent. He then softened it, realizing he should appear helpful and not annoyed. "But if you must know, my wife and I were happily married, Detective." He then reached for his coffee cup with his right hand and slurped at it.

She noticed that as he spoke, he now looked down to his right, which for a right-handed person some experts suggest meant that he was accessing the right hemisphere of his brain, where his creative thoughts are stored, and indicating that he was constructing his answer, and therefore probably lying. When accessing the left hemisphere, by looking to his left, he would be recalling an event and more likely telling the truth. But, Harriet was also aware that some experts didn't think there was any correlation. She knew to not rely on any one indicator, but instead to observe all of the many facets of a potential liar and create a holistic view.

She then glanced at her iPad screen and tapped on the computer voice stress analysis app—Chuck's last comment indicated potential deception and not truth. The app compared micro tremor changes in Chuck's voice pattern caused by the emotional stress of trying to conceal something or deceive. She knew that the app was just a tool in her armoury, and one that she usually ignored during interviewing—preferring to use her own observations—and only afterwards review the voice analysis. Also, by frequently glancing at the screen, she might miss an important gesture made by the interviewee.

At that moment, Kofi joined them so he could observe the interaction between Harriet and Chuck. Kofi sat down in an armchair next to Harriet and opposite Chuck. He said nothing, crossed his legs, and took out his own iPad tablet. Kofi saw Chuck stare and then frown at his odd-coloured socks: today being Monday, Kofi had deliberately chosen one red sock and one orange. He smiled at this typical response.

"I mean, did you and she get on well as a couple? Did you fight?" said Harriet.

"She was my fifth wife. We've been married for two years. Like all couples, we have our ups and downs, but I think we were a good couple who loved each other very much." Chuck crossed his arms and sat back in his chair, staring at her.

Harriet noticed the hint of annoyance and guilt in his voice. The crossing of the arms was a classic defensive action. She decided to pursue her gut feeling.

"Did you and your wife have an argument yesterday, sir?"

Chuck sighed, partly annoyed at having to answer so many questions, but also in acknowledgment. "In fact, we did, yes, when Richard de L'Isle—who is my senior manager, was here with us for lunch. I'm afraid I got rather drunk. She was beginning to irritate me by telling me off and patronizing me, as she often does, to be quite frank."

Harriet thought the surname de L'Isle was distinctive and familiar. Ah yes, she remembered. The woman who had discovered Mr. Joachim Goldschmidt dead in a pond of ice a month ago was a Mrs. Jennifer de L'Isle, she was sure. Not a very common surname, she recalled, so they were probably related. Kofi smiled. His excellent memory for names immediately recalled that Richard de L'Isle was the annoying man at the RAC that evening the previous week, when Kofi was there speaking for charity. Interesting coincidence, he thought. Kofi continued to observe, silently.

"A Mr. de L'Isle, you say, Mr. Jelleners? Does he have a wife named Jennifer, and do they live in Haslemere, here in Surrey?"

"Er, yes, Richard's wife is called Jennifer…well, I think so. Haslemere? Don't know precisely. Just know they live in Surrey. Why, is it important or relevant?" Chuck raised his eyebrows, wondering how long this was all going to take.

"Oh, it's nothing," Harriet said. "So what time did Mr. de L'Isle arrive for lunch, sir?"

"I don't know, but he was here when I arrived from the airport. I just got in that morning from New York. I guess he'd probably just arrived, as he was still in the hallway with his jacket on and his briefcase nearby. It was around ten thirty when I arrived home. Why on earth does it matter when he arrived?" Chuck said, screwing up his face in irritation.

Kofi, who had seen enough, decided to join the conversation. "Hmm," he said slowly. "And when did Mr. de L'Isle leave, Mr. Jelleners?"

"I don't know. Probably around six, I guess. As I just told you, I was drunk, and so I don't remember all that much after he and I went through a presentation he was preparing for me, late in the afternoon."

"And what time approximately would that be—when you had finished reviewing the presentation?" asked Harriet.

Chuck shrugged his shoulders. "Oh God, I don't know, probably around five o'clock maybe."

"Do you recall if you or Mrs. Jelleners showed Mr. de L'Isle out of your house when he left to go home?" enquired Kofi.

"I don't know; I can't remember. Christ, all these annoying questions. Yes, I would think one of us must have done. Would have been rude not to, don't you think? Actually, no, to be precise, I do recall that Richard said to me this morning when I called him that *I* showed him out of the house and that he heard me lock the door. So assuming Richard isn't a liar, and we can hardly ask my wife that question now, can we, Inspector, given she's dead, for Christ's sake, there's your answer." Chuck shook his head in frustration.

Kofi's ignored this American's belligerent manner—the chief inspector's calm demeanor remained. "It seems there was a struggle in the breakfast room yesterday. Do you recall any of that, sir?"

"Meaning what, young man? That *I* had a struggle with my wife, for heaven's sake? Of course not. And it's not a *breakfast* room; it's her *morning* room."

Kofi briefly smiled at the expected reaction to his deliberate misnaming of the room and quickly pressed Chuck. "When you say 'of course not,' how do you know for certain if you did or didn't have a struggle with your wife, when you said earlier that you got rather drunk, and after the presentation at around five, you couldn't remember much, sir?"

Chuck laughed, understanding the policeman's logic. "I mean both."

Kofi and Harriet didn't have a clue what he meant. They both frowned and looked confused.

Chuck saw this and explained. "Look, one, of course I can't remember because, as I said, I was rather drunk, Inspector. I had had a very long week in a very demanding job as a global COO. But, two, of course I didn't have a struggle with my wife, because I am not in the habit of attacking or abusing my wife, Detective. Got it now?" Chuck sat back and crossed his arms again.

"So you have never hit your wife or abused her, Mr. Jelleners?" said Harriet. Kofi smiled at the question.

"No, not that I recall," Chuck said defensively and looked down to his right.

Kofi smiled in amazement and said, "Hmm, what? You can't remember whether you have or haven't? Surely, you would remember something like that, sir?"

Chuck disliked this African man pummeling him with quick questions. Raising his voice, nodding his head back and forwards, and jabbing his index finger at Kofi, Chuck said, "No, I haven't, Inspector. Satisfied? Now, let's not waste any more of my valuable time, and get on with finding out how and why she died, shall we, Detectives?" He then rolled his eyes and looked down at his iPhone to retrieve an e-mail.

Both detectives always enjoyed trying to unravel what was fact and what was fiction in someone's story. It was one pleasurable part of an otherwise often distasteful job. An intellectual game of chess, where the detectives manoeuvred their pieces in response to the suspect's moves to firstly gain control of the board and then ultimately secure a confessional checkmate.

Kofi changed the topic. "Do you know if your wife had any enemies, or anyone who would want to harm her?"

Chuck uncrossed his arms and relaxed in his chair. "No, she didn't. She had loads of friends, worked out each day, saw her circle of girlfriends all the time, especially her best friend, Dawn." He laughed loudly, adding, "And, like all women married to successful men like me, she spent her day spending my money!"

"What's Dawn's surname – would you know sir?"

"Peabody, I think, madam."

"Hmm. Sir, can I get you a drink—some water, tea, or coffee, perhaps?"

"No, I'm fine, thank you, Inspector."

"Do you mind if *I* have a glass of water, sir?"

"Not at all, Inspector."

"DI Gilmore, could you get me some water, and then make a quick search of the house to see if there's any evidence of a break-in."

His words "quick search" were their code that he wanted her to search inside anything personal of Chuck's—like his briefcase—for anything that might be useful or incriminating. To give her time, he would continue questioning Chuck for another five minutes or so.

Within a few moments, Harriet returned with a glass of water for her boss. She had seen all she needed to see of the body. She grabbed her satchel and then left to find Chuck's briefcase, which she recalled had been

The Feather of Truth   Ian Campbell-Laing

left in the hallway.

"Sir, did you have many fights with your wife?" asked Kofi.

"I've answered that question, Inspector. I already told Detective Gilmaw, but to tell you again, well, yes, we argued occasionally, but I suspect no more than any other couple. She did have a habit of nagging me, but no more than any woman would nag her husband, I suspect."

"Hmm. I meant physically and recently. Were you aware that your wife has marks on her neck, her stomach, and wrist?"

"What marks? God no, of course not!" Chuck shouted. He crossed his arms again and scowled at Kofi.

"So when you went to bed, you didn't notice any marks on her?"

"Detective, we have been sleeping in separate rooms for a few months after a silly squabble, and I have been in New York for a week on business. I only just returned yesterday morning on the red-eye. I slept in the library, on this chair here, after watching some golf on the TV."

"Sir. Can you describe to me what you did after you arrived from the airport?" asked Kofi.

Chuck sighed loudly. "The *whole* day?"

"Yes, in as much detail as you can, please," insisted the inspector.

Chuck sighed again, shook his head, and rolled his eyes.

Kofi leant forward and calmly said, "Hmm, sir. Let's just be clear about a few things, before you roll your eyes again at me and continue to take on your belligerent tone. I am very sorry for your loss, but my job now is to find out why and how your wife died. I really couldn't give a toss, if you pardon my language, what meetings you have and may miss this morning. And I will continue to ask you questions for as long as I feel it's necessary. You've been very generous with your time so far, and your answers have been very helpful. If you just let me get on with my job, the sooner you can go and get back to your office. I would think within half an hour or so, we should be done. But please be thorough, and don't skip any detail, however unimportant it may seem to you. Does that seem fair, Mr. Jelleners?"

Chuck smiled back at him. He knew he should just let the DCI get on with it and stop interrupting him or complaining. Harping on about the office wasn't helping in any way. He accepted that. "Detective Chief Inspector, my apologies. I am not myself this morning. My wife was very precious to me. Ask whatever you need to ask."

Chuck then went through from the midmorning to the current morning in as much detail as he could remember.

"So, you were all a bit tipsy after Sunday lunch with some wine?" said Kofi.

"Yes."

"And what about Mr. de L'Isle, who went home after the lunch?"

"Now come on, officer, I know what you're getting at. You must speak to Richard, but I think he's a pretty sensible person and wouldn't drink and drive. Yes, he had a glass or two over a long period, but no, I don't think Richard was drunk, but I don't remember much of the evening, to be honest. As I keep mentioning, I was quite drunk and tired. And before you waste your time asking me, no, I didn't leave the house, and no, I didn't drive." Chuck sighed again, but this time less loudly, and was horrified to see that the time was now eight thirty. He had been questioned for an hour and a half.

"So what time did you check on your wife last night, before you went back into the library to watch some golf?"

"I'm not sure whether or not I checked on her, Inspector, to be honest, but if I did, it must have been around ten p.m., when I woke up after a snooze and called Richard."

"Hmm. But you said earlier that she was asleep at the time in her favorite chair. So you must have checked in on her, surely?"

"Oh, did I? I am confused. I can't recall if I did or not."

Kofi paused to type in some notes on his tablet. Creating periods of silence usually unsettled the guilty.

"And you didn't have a fight with her that evening, as far as you recall?"

"Not that I remember. Er, we did have a row at lunchtime and during the earlier part of the afternoon, but I'm pretty sure we didn't row again in the evening. I'm not really allowed in the morning room and didn't want to disturb her, so I think I just peeked inside to check on her. Richard said that I called him at around ten p.m. to ask him for the presentation, and I must have gone back to the library soon after that and watched some golf, then fell asleep. Next thing I know, I woke up this morning to find her still in the armchair, and that's when I called the ambulance."

"So, to be clear, you can't recall whether or not you went in to check on your wife last night before going to sleep, but you can recall precisely that you didn't have another row? It seems very inconsistent, Mr. Jelleners." Kofi paused, but there was no response from Chuck. Kofi made another note to check Chuck's and Richard's phone records to confirm timings.

"Hmm. Sir, have you ever hit your wife?"

"Absolutely not, Inspector. I am not a violent person," said Chuck, screwing up his face after hearing another long-drawn-out deep, "Hmm."

Kofi made another note on his iPad, again deliberately taking his time. Chuck's body posture and the tone of his voice conveyed more annoyance than being flustered. Chuck was clearly wanting to get back to his precious job. But Kofi wasn't to be hurried in any way. The first interview was crucial.

"Let's talk about the curtains, shall we?"

"What about the curtains, Inspector?" said Chuck frowning, not knowing where this was leading but trying to not sound irritated, given the

The Feather of Truth Ian Campbell-Laing

lecture he had received from the policeman.

"So, Mr. Jelleners, who closed the curtains last night and then opened them this morning? Looks like a lot of rooms with a lot of curtains."

"They're automatic. When it's dark outside, they close. When it's light, they open. It's how my wife liked it. Something about her being in touch with nature, or some such nonsense."

"So last night they would automatically shut—say about half past seven, which is roughly when it gets dark, right?"

"Yeah, I guess so. But you can override it and close them when you like, or not have them open until after daybreak. But it's usually set automatically, to open at sunrise and close at sunset, like I said."

Kofi doodled a picture of some curtains on his iPad.

"You don't recall the conversation with Mr. de L'Isle later that evening, then?"

"No. As I said before, I don't."

"Did you try and resuscitate your wife this morning, sir?"

"Yes, of course."

"Was that before or after you called 999?"

"Both before and after."

Harriet, who was listening in from the hallway, sent Kofi a message from her iPad, which flashed up on the screen of his tablet, not seen by Chuck:

Mr. Jelleners had said to the ambulance driver that he had only tried to resuscitate his wife <u>after</u> he had called the ambulance.

"Sir, did you notice any marks on her neck during lunch yesterday?"

"None at all. Well…er…I didn't exactly examine her, for Christ's sake! We had a guest for lunch, but as far as I can remember, no marks."

"And no marks on her neck when you went in to see her at ten p.m.?"

"No marks then, as I'm sure I would have noticed them. But I only glanced at her. Look, it was dark in the room for Christ's sake and as I said, the curtains were drawn, with just her floor-stand light on very low."

"Could your wife have drawn the curtains herself?"

"Yes, if she wanted them closed earlier than when they automatically close. She is fastidious about the house, keeping it spotless and having the curtains closed at night and open in the morning. But she can override that by simply pressing a few buttons. They're all electrically drawn. Very expensive to install, by the way. But as I said, they were usually on automatic mode governed by the light outside. But I don't know whether she did or not. Quite frankly, what the hell does it matter who drew the bloody curtains and when, Inspector?" Chuck was now at the stage where he couldn't take much more.

Harriet flashed another message to her boss.

Interesting docs in briefcase, and something's just occurred to me about his shoes.

Kofi read it and replied to Chuck. "I don't know, Mr. Jelleners, how relevant it is, but allow me to do my job, please. I'm trying to get to the bottom of why and how your wife died—that's all."

"OK, OK…Sorry. But you said she has marks on her neck, so who did them or how did they get there, Inspector?"

Kofi sighed loudly. *"Precisely*, sir. *That's* what we're trying to find out. Would you mind if we search the house again, in case there's evidence of someone entering without your knowledge?"

"Sure, but I thought you said you had already asked your assistant to do that? But hey, if you need to look again, sure, good idea. Mind if I stay in here and check my e-mails?"

"By all means. DI Gilmore will be outside the room if you need us."

Kofi left the room, leaving the door open. He went to the front door and noticed that the lock had a double mortise. The ambulance crew had said earlier that it took Mr. Jelleners some time to unlock the door. So, thought Kofi, Unless Mr. de L'Isle had a key, then Mr. Jelleners probably saw Mr. de L'Isle out and then locked the door, assuming this happened around 6:00 p.m. *Or* perhaps Mrs. Jelleners let Mr. de L'Isle out before she died at 8:05 p.m.?

Harriet had rummaged inside Chuck's briefcase and removed some printed e-mails. She noticed one in particular. She copied it using the app on her iPad.

Kofi approached her and quietly asked, "What's up?"

"Sir, see the bottom of this e-mail? I guess it's to a work colleague, Gunter Schwarzkopf. Looks like they were discussing IT issues. If you look at the bottom, Mr. Jelleners talks about how depressed his wife was, and if only someone would get rid of her! I've highlighted in yellow the interesting parts for you to read."

Kofi scanned the e-mail:

> Becks and I are always having rows. You know that she's even forced me to sleep in the spare room for the last few weeks, which is a clear breach of the marriage contract, isn't it? She can be so very moody, it's really getting on my nerves. She says she's depressed—well I'm bloody depressed living with her nagging.
>
> Problem is, I can't divorce her because it will cost me too much. A lawyer I met last week confirmed that I would lose at least half my hard earned assets, for sure.
>
> You're so lucky that you and Sylvia have such a good marriage. I wonder if I did the right thing marrying Becks?
>
> Well, hopefully when this weekend I get back to my pain in the ass wife, who God, I wish I hadn't married, she won't make a fuss about me taking

The Feather of Truth   Ian Campbell-Laing

another trip to Asia and won't nag me and go on and on about it, like always.

Women just don't understand what we men have to do and go through each day to make a living. There must be something I can do…Will no one rid me of this troublesome wife?

"Why would anyone so senior be stupid enough to write this stuff? Let's see, it seems to be from an AOL account, so it's probably not his work e-mail address, Harriet. Still, stupid and potentially incriminating evidence."

They walked towards the kitchen to remain out of Chuck's range of hearing. Kofi said, "I had a look around, and there's no sign of a forced entry or break-in. And given the strangulation marks on her neck, that rules out suicide. So that just leaves Mr. Jelleners and Mr. de L'Isle, or as a long shot, someone who knew the Jelleners and had a key and entered the house whilst Mr. Jelleners was asleep."

Harriet said, "So, let's say Mr. de Lisle leaves at around six p.m. Then around eight p.m., there are signs of a struggle in the morning room—no blood, however. My immediate guess is that the husband had another argument with her and then attempted to have sex with her and started to rip open the buttons on her jeans, then tore her panties. When she refuses his drunken advances, he goes to grab her neck, rips off her pearls, and maybe didn't initially intend to kill her, but more to force her to have sex with him. But, with his strength and being drunk, he strangled her and she fell backwards, hitting her watch on the table, and maybe her head on the chair. Time of death, 8:05 p.m., per her smashed watch face. Post mortem will confirm this, of course. And rigor mortis, which would have set in well some ten hours after death, seems to concur with that time of death."

"Hmm. Yes, indeed. But, one thing's odd—the way she was lying on the chair, she seemed quite comfortable in her pose, and not as if having fallen backwards and collapsing after being strangled."

"Unless, sir, her husband then moved her to look like she was comfortable."

"But why would he do that? Did you check what beverage was in the tumbler on the table next to her chair?" asked Kofi.

"Smells like nothing more than water with some lemon. Can't smell any alcohol, but I will let the labs examine it, sir."

"Let's get the forensic boys in sharpish, and then once they are done going over the evidence, get the coroner to do an autopsy on her. We'll take her husband down to the station for more questioning. Let's hold him for the maximum forty-eight hours and figure out if we should apply to a judge for an extension—which of course in the case of murder, we'll get while we gather more evidence."

"Yes, sir. So do you also think he murdered his wife by strangulation after a drunken argument, an attempted sexual assault, then a further struggle, in view of the evidence so far?"

"So far, the clues all lead that way, don't they, Harriet? Not to mention how cold and detached the husband seems about everything. But we need to interview Mr. de L'Isle, obviously, to get his story and the exact timings of his coming and going, along with anything her friend Dawn Peabody can shed light on."

"Yes, sir."

Kofi paused in thought. "Hmm. I'm wondering why was she lying with her right hand holding her stomach? I wonder if she was in some sort of pain, Harriet."

"Yes, I did also. I can think of three explanations. She had been physically hit there, or she may have had stomach cramps from her period, or from being pregnant. The autopsy will confirm more of what she was suffering from, of course."

"Indeed."

"And also, I noticed one other thing. Her cheeks and eyelids."

"Oh yes, Harriet?"

"Beneath her left eye, below the eyelid, the mascara was slightly smudged. And there were very tiny streaks down her cheek. Looks like she had been crying."

Kofi stifled a yawn: as usual, he hadn't slept well the previous night. "Good observation—but not surprising if she and her husband were having a major row—worth noting in our preliminary report. Also, ensure that the forensic boys examine each fireplace's residue in case someone tried to destroy something interesting. We should examine Mr. Jelleners's clothes that he had on yesterday, including his shoes and jacket. This case is far from an open-and-shut case until we have done some more digging, in spite of the arrogant husband who is obviously capable of murdering his long-suffering wife."

"I will check with her doctor of any reported physical assaults on his wife. Oh, and my hunch about the shoes, sir. Do you mind if I go upstairs and check on something? I might need to ask him one more question before we take him in."

"Sure, go ahead. I'll see you back in the library."

Kofi went back into the library and, standing in the doorway, spoke to Chuck as he sat in his armchair looking at his e-mails on his iPhone. "Hmm. Mr. Jelleners, I think we are about done here, but would you mind waiting just one more moment, please?"

Chuck continued to peer at his iPhone. "Sure, and then I can go?"

"Perhaps."

Chuck now looked up at the detective. "What does 'perhaps' mean?"

Kofi remained standing and looked around the room. He said nothing. A few minutes later, Harriet came back into the study with her left hand behind her back.

"Mr. Jelleners, are the shoes you're wearing now the ones that you put on this morning when you discovered your wife?"

"Obviously, Detective. I don't change shoes once I have gotten dressed for work. Why are you asking?"

"Do you mind taking them off and handing them to DCI Ghazini, please?"

"OK, but I don't know where this is leading. I mean, why would you care about my shoes?" Chuck shook his head and bent down. He breathed heavily as he reached over his large belly, struggling to take off his tight-fitting shoes. When he finally did so, he handed his shoes to Kofi, who had already slipped on some latex gloves.

"And of course, your shoes will have residues of crushed pearls on their soles, from when you stepped on them this morning, upon discovering your wife?"

"Huh? Well, of course they will. I couldn't help stepping on them. They were strewn all over the carpet, and I had to get to my wife to see what was wrong with her."

Kofi examined the soles and nodded to Harriet. There were crushed pearls indented within the soles.

"But I'm guessing these aren't the shoes that you wore yesterday when you had lunch, or last night?"

"Correct. They're similar, but not the same. These are black slip-ons. The ones I wore yesterday were slip-ons identical in design, but brown, and when I saw that they were dirty, I changed my shoes this morning and left them upstairs. Why do you ask?" asked Chuck.

Harriet removed her latex-gloved hand from behind her back and showed Chuck the shoes she was holding.

"Are these the slip-on loafers you traveled in yesterday and wore in the afternoon and evening, sir?"

Chuck looked at them without touching them. "Yes, they are. See, they look dirty. What of it? I wore those shoes yesterday, and these shoes this morning. So bloody what?"

Harriet turned over the shoes to reveal their soles. There were fragments of pearls in the treads.

Kofi smiled at the young detective. "It seems, Mr. Jelleners, that you may indeed have entered your wife's morning room yesterday, then stepped on the pearls that were strewn on the floor. Yet, you said to us, more than once, that you opened the door, peeked in, and didn't enter the room until this morning."

"But…"

"No buts, Mr. Jelleners. You need to come down to the station with us, please, for further questioning."

The Feather of Truth   Ian Campbell-Laing

"Inspector, do I have any choice in the matter?" enquired Chuck.

"Let me be quite frank. In theory, yes, but in practice, Mr. Jelleners, you don't. Here's how it goes. You voluntarily accept our request that you come with me, and we ask some more questions and then get a written statement from you. If you refuse to cooperate, then I will arrest you on suspicion of the murder of your wife, read you your rights, and then you *have* to come with me. The latter, should this all proceed to a court of law, would not look as good as voluntarily cooperating with me now," Kofi explained.

Chuck sighed loudly in resignation. "Are you going to handcuff me, Inspector?"

"Hmm. No, not if you come willingly."

Kofi motioned by tilting his head to the right in the direction of Chuck and raising his eyebrows to one of the officers who was standing in the hallway near the front door. After allowing Chuck to fetch and change into another pair of shoes, the officer escorted him to the police car.

Kofi's thoughts turned to the Goldschmidt case that he was under pressure to close. And coincidentally, it seemed that it was Richard de Lisle's wife who had discovered Mr. Goldschmidt dead in the pond. Small world. The de L'Isle family had cropped up in two murder enquiries in just over a month. A coincidence or not?

"Harriet, the story does seem to have one logical explanation, but as I said, let's see what Mr. de L'Isle and the Peabody lady have to say for themselves. Let's also go back into the morning room again, shall we, and check to ensure we're not being set up here."

"You think we might be?"

"You never know," said Kofi. "You just never know. I know that I shouldn't complain, but sometimes I don't like it when it seems so simple."

Kofi started to hum the last act and the moral tale of his favorite opera, Mozart's *Don Giovanni*–and then sing the words in perfect Italian—"—Questo è il fin di chi fa mal, e de' perfidi la morte alla vita è sempre ugual." *Such is the end of the evildoer: the death of a sinner always reflects his life.*

CHAPTER 38
VCb's LONDON OFFICES

When Richard arrived at his office, he proceeded to work on projects that he had planned for the day and tackled the blizzard of e-mails he received. Anyone who saw him would have said he was his usual confident and charming self and engrossed in his work.

It was now just after 2:30 p.m., and he had just finished giving his presentation to Chuck's boss, Celsius, who was suitably impressed with Richard's work. Richard leaned forward to turn off the audio and video settings on his PC. He then sat back in his chair, exhausted but relieved and thrilled with how the presentation had gone. However, he knew he had played a dangerous game by whining on about how Chuck was a difficult and unappreciative boss, and dared to even suggest to Celsius that he could do Chuck's job in his sleep. Celsius could easily have fired him on the spot for insubordination. But, Richard figured that nothing risked, nothing gained.

Sam popped in to check all had gone well.

"It was brilliant. I played a risky strategy that may just succeed. Now we're cooking."

"Good! I am glad for you, Richard. And there's..."

Richard looked up at Sam from his desk. He was a young chap who wanted to travel and experience life, and in a few weeks would go on a six-month sabbatical with his partner. Richard would miss him. He was so efficient at what he did.

"Sorry. Yes, Sam... What were you saying?"

"Oh, there's a detective sitting in the reception area who wants to see you. Can you meet him now? He said it was quite important."

CHAPTER 39
VCb's LONDON OFFICES

"The police? Yes, of course. Must be about Chuck, since I was at his house yesterday for lunch with him and his wife. Sure. Just let me take a leak, and I'll be back in a few minutes. Can you offer him a water or coffee, and keep him there until I get back?"

"Already done that, and he said he was fine. Will do."

"OK, good. See you in a few moments then." Richard could feel his heart beating stronger and quicker against his chest cavity as he made his way to the toilets down the hallway. Once there, he locked himself in a cubicle and sat with his head in his hands. He slowly took deep breaths.

So, this is it, then. Time for me to start the play-acting and behave naturally and calmly, he thought.

Of course he knew he'd be a suspect, along with Chuck, but with the evidence he had planted on Chuck, he was sure Chuck would soon—if not already—be the number one suspect, and Richard should fade away from being a person of interest to one of unimportance. But he knew his whole life could change based on the next thirty minutes or hour of questioning. As he reminded himself, you don't get a second chance to make a first impression. He had to be very cautious and not incriminate himself inadvertently. The first few minutes would be crucial, as the inspector sized him up.

Richard said quietly to himself, "You have never been in this situation before. Play it cool and stick to only what you *should* know, not what you *really* know. Better to not know something, and then remember it, rather than show you know something that you could not possibly know. Also, you won't know anything until the inspector tells you of a new fact. So you don't know about the pearls or the watch, and be very, very careful about what you say. Don't rush your answers: you need to take your time. Remember your army training at school."

After the pep talk to himself, he was composed. He looked at himself in the mirror. He straightened his tie and saw that his face was not flushed. He slowly walked back to his office, and Sam went to retrieve the catcher of criminals.

"Richard, this is Detective Chief Inspector Kofi Ghazini of the Surrey Police."

Richard thought he recognized the detective, but couldn't place where. He guessed he was probably a similar age to him. The detective was slim and broad-shouldered, and his dark head was shaved. His outstretched right hand looked large, and his palm very pink. His suit looked more expensive than Richard would have expected. No doubt about it, Ghazini is a strikingly good-looking man, acknowledged Richard. He stood eye to eye with Richard, and as Richard reached out his own hand to shake the detective's, Ghazini gave him a welcoming, disarming smile, showing a full mouth of brilliantly white teeth set against his black complexion. The detective seemed a pleasant sort of chap, which made Richard even more cautious.

"Detective Chief Inspector, pleased to meet you," Richard said, shaking the inspector's hand firmly. "Do please come into my office. Why don't you take a seat over here? Would you like a cup of tea or coffee, or some water?" Richard deliberately spoke more than just one sentence of pleasantries to allow his voice to settle.

"No, thank you, Mr. de L'Isle. I'm quite fine for the moment." Kofi's well-educated British accent resonated around the office—as if one was listening to a bass speaker that had been turned up a few notches too high for a concert. Kofi's words had the effect more of a command than of a pleasantry. Richard noticed that the detective also didn't hurry his words.

Kofi remained standing and interrupted Richard's thoughts. "Mr. de L'Isle, do you mind if I record our conversation on my tablet, here? I find it tends to speed up the meeting through not having to continuously make notes as we go along."

"Not at all," Richard said, appearing outwardly confident but feeling this detective was to be feared.

"And it has an inbuilt voice stress analysis tool, if that's OK with you?"

"Is that just a fancy name for a voice lie detector, Chief Inspector?"

"In essence, yes. But it's just one of many tools we use. Nothing to be concerned about."

Richard didn't convey his slight apprehension. "I've heard about them and am not concerned at all; just pleased how very modern is our police force."

"Let's also get the ID out of the way first, shall we, Mr. de L'Isle?" Richard knew the procedure, having seen it on many TV documentaries. He placed his hands on the tablet and spat into the vial given to him by Kofi. Kofi then checked that his tablet had sync'd with and downloaded the data contained in Richard's microchip implanted at the bottom of his neck. It had.

Kofi saw that Richard was tall, good looking, fit, and exuded confidence and professionalism. Mr. de L'Isle had a firm handshake, stood erect, and looked Kofi straight in the eye when he introduced himself. He liked that about a man. He almost appeared as if he'd been in the military, considering his well-polished shoes, his crisply starched blue shirt, and a Windsor knot on his university tie. Kofi thought you could tell a lot about a man by the way he kept his shoes and overall appearance. It showed a certain minimum standard and attention to detail. Of course, this was not always the case.

Richard waited for the detective to sit down first and then took a seat himself. He spoke first again. He now wanted to take things slow in order to keep his voice clear of any nervousness, just in case the inspector tried to trip him up with difficult questions early on. He had read that often was a tactic detectives used. Then he realized where he had heard of the name.

"Chief Inspector, your name seems familiar. Didn't we meet at the RAC last week, and also didn't you recently interview my wife, Jennifer, in connection with the Goldschmidt death a month or so ago? I understand from watching the news that it is still being investigated."

"Yes, Mr. de L'Isle, both are true. I did interview her, but we have eliminated her from our enquiries."

Richard smiled. "Oh, jolly good, and quite rightly so." He then noticed that Kofi didn't have a tie on today, unlike at the RAC, and that when he crossed his legs, they revealed that he was wearing odd-coloured socks. How odd, mused Richard. I wonder what statement the detective is making with that?

"Eliminated her from our enquiries, *for now*."

"Oh, OK," said Richard as he just shrugged his shoulders and didn't alter his nonplussed expression, not being sure what to say.

"There are still some matters that are of concern to me. But they are not the reason I am here today, as I am sure you must have guessed."

"Of course. Chuck phoned me earlier this morning and said he thought his wife, Rebecca, was dead. Is that true, Inspector? He cut the call short, saying the ambulance had just arrived."

"Yes, sir, it is true. She is dead."

"Oh my God! That's awful. She was a nice lady. Where's Chuck now? I should go and see him. I report to Chuck. I don't know if you know, but he's my manager," said Richard, feigning concern for Chuck, and delighted that so far his voice had remained firm and not hurried.

"You can see him later, but first, would you mind answering a few questions for me? Some things just don't stack up presently."

"Not at all. And of course, Chief Inspector, I will help you in any way I can. In fact, as I am sure you know, I was with Chuck and Rebecca only yesterday afternoon for lunch, to present a PowerPoint presentation he and I were working on for our boss and CEO, Celsius Maysmith III. Chuck seemed very pleased with it and believed it would be well received by Celsius."

Kofi didn't immediately respond. He let the silence hang between them like dull, stagnant, oppressive air. He just sat there and watched Richard. He knew that often the guilty would embellish their answers to give them more time to think. Sometimes, the guilty would panic and ramble on nervously, generally saying something they would later regret.

He waited. Richard said nothing and continued to look relaxed. He crossed his right leg over his left, and his hands remained resting on his lap. Kofi thought that Richard appeared calm, with his voice firm, but perhaps he was adding just a little too much detail to his answers so far.

Richard felt uneasy with the silence but didn't show it. After what seemed like a long time, he broke the silence and asked, "So, how can I help you, Chief Inspector, *specifically*?"

"Hmm. Mr. de L'Isle, why don't we start by you telling me about your movements yesterday, including the lunch with Mr. and Mrs. Jelleners."

Richard spoke calmly, recalling the events as he had rehearsed. He looked directly at the inspector and only occasionally let his eyes dart around the room, when he paused appearing to be thinking of an exact time of an action or event.

Kofi noted that Richard gesticulated with his arms when making a point, blinked in a normal manner, and occasionally crossed and uncrossed his legs. Liars often move their body much less than normal, due to the extra effort required when trying to stick to a story or remembering what they had previously said. His speech was calm, and he didn't mispronounce any words, implying he was not nervous. But Kofi knew that sociopaths were often skilled liars and differed from psychopaths by being calm and calculating, not acting on impulse, and appearing to their family and friends to be outwardly normal. Not that he so far particularly thought Mr. de L'Isle was a sociopath, but he had been surprised before. After twenty minutes of Richard's story, Kofi thought either this guy had nothing to do with the murder or was a seasoned professional, a sociopath, and had absolutely everything to do with it. It was a binary situation, and Kofi wanted to quickly find out into which category Richard fell.

Richard was now talking about opening the door to the God Squad. Kofi interrupted him. "And so you were in the living room at the time the doorbell rang? Updating the presentation, is that correct?"

"Yes, Chuck was feeling sleepy, and I didn't want to disturb him with all the noise of my tapping away on the computer, so I went to another room after I brought him his coffee and left him be."

Kofi paused and tapped out a note on his tablet:

#1 Check for RDL fingerprints on own coffee cup in living room and on Jelleners' cup in library.

"Hmm, and why do you think Mrs. Jelleners didn't answer the doorbell?" Kofi asked.

"I am not sure. I waited for her to do that, but when the doorbell rang a second time, I got up and answered it because I was in the room just off the hallway near the front door. I assumed that Mrs. Jelleners was either preoccupied or napping."

"Why did you think she was napping?"

"When I took her some coffee, soon after we had finished lunch, she mentioned she might take a little nap, because she was tired."

Another note:

#2 Check for RDL prints on RFJ coffee cup in morning room.

"Hmm, so, both of your hosts were sleeping in the afternoon, having invited you around for lunch. That's kind of odd, isn't it? Was the conversation so dreadfully boring that they were forced into slumber, or are they just not very attentive hosts?" said Kofi with a deadpan voice.

Richard smiled at the detective's quick wit. "Neither. But I just assumed that they were clearly both very tired, Chuck from jet lag and too much wine, and Mrs. Jelleners from preparing the meal—and to be quite honest, she had also drunk quite a lot. But I assumed that Mrs. Jelleners would wake up in an hour or so, as would Chuck, around the time I would have finished the presentation. And sure enough, Chuck did wake up. He showed me out once I had finished updating the presentation."

"So, Mr. de L'Isle, Mr. Jelleners, according to you, had consumed a lot of alcohol, and he and his wife had two arguments during lunch that you recall."

Richard knew the detective had a sharp brain and spotted the deliberate misquote to see if Richard corrected him. "Actually, Inspector, I don't recall saying they only had *two* arguments. I believe what I said to you earlier was that they were bickering most of the afternoon. But, yes, as a general statement, it seemed Mrs. Jelleners was very irritated with him for being drunk and for belittling her. He was often quite pompous with her. And if I recall, she told him that if he entered her sanctuary—which is what she called her morning room—that she would kill him."

"And do you think she meant it—that she was capable of killing her husband?"

"Absolutely not, Chief Inspector. I think it was a figure of speech, but a warning that she wanted to be left alone, and she would be very angry if her husband didn't heed to her threat."

Kofi, looked down at his tablet and mentally counted to ten, allowing more silence to permeate the room's atmosphere, in search of the truth.

"Hmm, how do you get on with your boss, Mr. Jelleners?" said Kofi, now looking up.

Richard was beginning to find the frequent very deep "hmms" preceding certain questions rather off-putting, but he carried on. "Pretty well, actually. He's generally very supportive of my efforts, pays me pretty well, promoted me to managing director two years ago, and we've been working together fine for three years."

"No arguments or disagreements with him, then?"

"Not really. However, and this is just between you and me, I sometimes find his attitude to women rather old fashioned and at times derogatory. But I guess he's a typical alpha male. One of those assertive Yanks, if you know what I mean."

"No, I don't know what you mean. What sort of things does he say about women?"

"Well, and again, this is just between you and me, he called three women bitches in front of me and another colleague in his office, and on a separate occasion, referred to two other women as 'the two witches from hell.' I don't know about you, but I think that's hardly acceptable in modern society."

"Did you report your boss for making these remarks?"

Richard was ready for this one and smiled briefly.

"Chief Inspector, internal procedures are confidential. I can't relay any information like that to you. If you have an issue with this, please see our regional head of human resources, Nigel Longtone. But let me say this, Chuck and I get on pretty well, and overall, as his most senior manager and right-hand man, I have no real issues with him. And the evidence for that is he gives me excellent annual appraisals, and says I'm his number one producer and chief lieutenant. So I'm pretty happy with my lot, if that answers your question?"

"Hmm, I see." The chief inspector let fifteen seconds go by in total silence to see if Richard maintained his composure. He did.

"What was your relationship with his wife, Rebecca?"

Richard guessed that this would be asked, of course. Again, he was prepared. He knew he couldn't lie about the affair—that was too risky. He was sure that the detective would interview Dawn, being Rebecca's best friend, who would certainly say Rebecca and Richard were having an affair. He needed to maintain credibility and an appearance of honesty. Instinctively, he maintained his natural mannerisms and looked Kofi straight in the eye.

"Chief Inspector, Rebecca Jelleners and I were just friends, although a few months ago, we did have a *very brief* affair."

"You did?" The chief inspector's eyes opened wider, and he leaned forward in his seat like a stalking panther who was now ready to spring onto his prey. "So when did this affair start and end, exactly, Mr. de L'Isle, and who ended it?"

"It started later last year in December at the annual Christmas party, like I suspect many office flings. And it ended a few weeks ago."

"But *who* ended it and *where* and *how?*" The detective's voice was more assertive, and he fixed his gaze on Richard.

"It was mutual. Neither one of us felt comfortable about it, to be

The Feather of Truth   Ian Campbell-Laing

honest. We met at Starbucks near the office a few weeks ago now and had a discussion about it. It seemed the right thing to do. Oh, we've also had a few conversations in the last few weeks, and in fact, we had dinner last week at my club, the RAC, on Thursday evening. And it went well, with no animosity, which pleased us both. Rebecca and I were both glad that we could remain friends. You are at liberty to ask any of the staff there that saw us, and I am sure they would confirm we had a very pleasant and cordial meal together."

"Mrs. Jelleners, whom you said earlier did not like being belittled by her husband, was happy to end the affair with you, Mr. de L'Isle, and stay with her husband? That seems rather odd, doesn't it?" Kofi's eyes narrowed and he pursed his lips in disbelief at what he had heard.

"Not at all. She hadn't left her husband. Yes, they had their differences, but she said to me that he had provided a good life for her, and she wanted to make a go of it with her husband. And we both realized that the affair was wrong—that it was just a fling—and that our partners could be hurt, and we should end it. Seems entirely logical and morally defensible to me, Inspector."

As Kofi tapped out some more notes, he said quietly, but deliberately loud enough for Richard to hear, "Logical and morally defensible affair."

"Are you right or left handed, Mr. de L'Isle?"

"Right. Why, Inspector?"

Kofi said nothing, just noting that during this last period of more personal questioning, Richard didn't look down at all: often a telltale sign that a person was embarrassed or making something up. He also didn't look to the right. Instead, when he looked away from his gaze at Kofi, it was always to the left, suggesting he was recalling a detail from his visual memory. Pity, he thought.

"You have evidence of the meeting at your club with Mrs. Jelleners last week?"

"Of course. I booked a table for dinner in my name. We spent the evening together, stayed in a suite there, but as I said, there was no intimacy, just friendship."

Kofi laughed out loud. "Oh, come on, Mr. de L'Isle. You must take me for a fool. After dinner, you stayed in the same bedroom, but you had no intimacy with the very attractive Mrs. Jelleners, whom you had been having an affair with for three months, and abruptly ended it with no recourse from her? Come on, Mr. de L'Isle. Are you seriously telling me that after your mistress dressed in her seductive negligee brought you a cup of cocoa, you fell asleep alone on the couch, sucking your thumb and gripping your favorite teddy bear?"

Richard smiled at the acerbic wit. This detective is thorough and simply won't let go! But now, oddly, Richard was beginning to enjoy himself, battling against the wits of this policeman. He had remained calm and knew he had given a good account of himself, so far. He replied, "It was out of respect. We had in effect previously broken up. I wasn't going to take advantage of her after we decided to call it quits."

Kofi didn't say anything, but there was one thing for sure - Richard was very good. But perhaps, too polished?

CHAPTER 40
VCb's LONDON OFFICES

"Mr. de L'Isle, you haven't entirely answered my question. So, instead of sleeping alone on the couch, you and Mrs. Jelleners slept in the same bed?"

"Correct. We slept in the same bed, but as I said, we had *no* intimacy: we treated each other as friends only."

Kofi paused again, chastising himself. Set the trap, Kofi! Stop dawdling!

"So when was the last time you did cheat on your wife by having physical intimacy with your boss's wife?"

Ouch, thought Richard. "As I thought I mentioned, roughly a few weeks ago."

"Hmm. Actually I don't recall you mentioning it at all. More importantly, you usually don't remember the exact date of when you last had sex with a woman, Mr. de L'Isle? Somewhat cavalier, isn't it?"

Richard paused. He didn't like it that this relatively young detective was trying to fluster him with rapid-fire questions followed by long pauses, which allowed the policeman to stay in control. Richard knew this was a mind game, and he wanted to gain control himself.

"I don't recall immediately when I last saw Rebecca Jelleners in an intimate manner, no. But as I said, it would have been no longer than three weeks ago, I presume. Is the exact date important, Inspector?" asked Richard. He remained calm despite the policeman's tactics. He wished he could ask the inspector if he could remember when he had sex with his own wife or girlfriend.

Kofi paused again and then said, "And does your wife know about this liaison?"

"No, she does not know about my *fling*, Chief Inspector."

"And does your boss, Mr. Jelleners, know about it?"

"I don't think so. I guess he would have mentioned it to me if he was aware of it, don't you, Inspector?" said Richard, now realizing the policeman had a double hold over him.

Kofi had spotted the reference to "Inspector" for some answers and "Chief Inspector" for others, and started to wonder if Richard was playing some kind of game with him, or if it was unintentional. He made a mental note to later highlight on the transcript which questions evoked the less respectful "Inspector" responses.

Silence, again.

Kofi cleared his throat and said, "Do you respect your boss, Mr. de L'Isle?"

"Yes, I do, professionally. However, I don't really socialize with him much outside the office, so that's all I can really comment on."

"Were you aware that for many months now, he and his wife were arguing a great deal and having marital problems?"

"Yes, of course. He was sometimes rather derogatory about his wife, and when Rebecca and I had our *very brief* fling, she mentioned that he wasn't the easiest of husbands to live with and had, on occasions, hit her, and that she had gone to her doctor more than once, afterwards."

"I'm not sure I consider a fling of nearly three months as brief, Mr. de L'Isle. Do you?"

Richard wanted to say, "I wouldn't know, not ever having conducted a scientific survey or poll on the area." Instead, he didn't answer, and just shrugged his shoulders. He then said, "It seems brief to me, in the grand scheme of things."

"What's perhaps more interesting, is that you *were* aware of your boss's violence towards his wife." Kofi quickly tapped on his tablet,

#3 RDL knew of CJ violence to RFJ—probably aware of <u>precise</u> area she had been hit?

Again, Richard said nothing. He wasn't going to be baited into saying anything stupid.

"Hmm. You do know how Rebecca Falconer Jelleners died, Mr. de L'Isle, don't you?"

At the mention of "Falconer", Richard thought back to the cufflinks she had given him and how she had beamed to him, "Welcome to the Falconer family."

He admonished himself for not keeping control. He refocused.

Kofi noticed Richard was briefly distracted and wondered why.

"No idea. How would I know? I haven't spoken to Chuck since this morning before the ambulance arrived. He just said his wife looked dead. The rumor mill in this office is working overtime, and I heard that he is in police custody. But I have no idea where he is, and he's not answering his mobile. So, I was getting concerned, actually."

Kofi noticed how effortlessly Richard answered questions and deflected them with additional facts. Careless or controlled rambling?

"It seems she was strangled," said the inspector, matter-of-factly.

"Oh, how awful, Chief Inspector." Richard feigned a look of disgust.

"Do you know why Mrs. Jelleners was holding her stomach when she was found this morning?"

That question was the first one Richard had not rehearsed. It threw him initially, but he had practiced looking straight ahead if asked a question he hadn't anticipated. He would immediately think about his reply, perhaps looking to his left but never to his right, and then only respond calmly and without fidgeting or moving his arms. He had positioned his chair such that it was easier to look left, and be a strain to look to his right.

"No idea, Inspector. Perhaps she had a stomach ache? What's your view on this, Inspector? To be honest, you would know this better than I, given it is more your domain than mine."

"It's not for me to say, Mr. de L'Isle. I am not the one being questioned. It appears that she was also crying. Any idea what that would be about?"

"No idea. Perhaps she had just had another row with her husband and was upset again?" suggested Richard.

Kofi paused and started to doodle a guillotine on his tablet.

"So, Mrs. Jelleners let you out of the house when you left, correct?"

"No, *Mr.* Jelleners let me out of the house, Chief Inspector, as I think I previously mentioned."

"But, Mr. Jelleners doesn't recall letting you out or double-mortise-locking the door afterwards."

"I thought, Inspector, that we had already established that Chuck was very tired, very drunk, and had jetlag that afternoon. He slept a great deal, so may not have been able to remember everything."

"Mr. Jelleners thinks perhaps he only woke up much later, after you had gone."

"Chuck is mistaken. He definitely let me out of the house around six, Inspector. I recall that."

"If you are mistaken, and both Mr. and Mrs. Jelleners were asleep at that time, then perhaps you let yourself out with your key?"

Careful here, Richard, he thought to himself. You cannot admit to having a key.

"Chief Inspector, we are going to be here a very long time if you continually question and re-question the same facts over and over again. I didn't have a key, and I didn't let myself out. Chuck let me out. Is that clear enough?" Richard raised his voice slightly, but without appearing angry.

"So, your mistress never gave you a key to her house? I find that rather surprising, given her husband was traveling outside the country quite a lot, and I assume you had *some* dangerous liaisons at their home?"

"You assume incorrectly, Inspector."

"Sorry? I am incorrect in my assumption that she gave you a key, or that you and she had liaisons at her home—which is it precisely, Mr. de L'Isle?"

"That she gave me a key."

"So you *did* meet at her house for liaisons?"

"Yes, and at my club. Nowhere else."

Kofi paused again and noted down,

#4 Trysts at RAC and RFJ home. RDL says no house key. Ask Dawn if

The Feather of Truth Ian Campbell-Laing

RDL <u>was</u> given a key.

#5 RDL appeared unusually momentarily distracted when mentioning for the first time, RFL's middle name, 'Falconer' - significant or not?

Then, he stared at Richard, with his elbow on the arm of the chair and his left index finger resting on his mouth. He didn't move or say anything. It felt like an eternity to Richard.

Kofi put his hand over his mouth to conceal a large yawn and then broke the silence. "Do you regard yourself as a trustworthy person, Mr. de L'Isle?"

"Yes, Inspector, I do."

"Hmm, yet you had your sexual encounters at your boss's house behind his back? Not a very trustworthy person in Mr. Jelleners's eyes, I would think."

"On a business level with my boss, I am very trustworthy, yes."

Kofi paused again then continued. "Are you a violent man, Mr. de L'Isle?"

Richard inhaled and then calmly breathed out. "No, Inspector, I am not," and then smiling added, "Are you?" Richard couldn't resist baiting the chief inspector and then regretted it. He sensed, given he had been interviewed for nearly an hour, and the repetitive nature of questions to try and catch him making a mistake, that the interview would soon be over, and he would be free of this irritating, intelligent man.

Kofi noticed Richard did not appear irritated by his questions, which slightly surprised him. Richard was being forceful, but not flustered. Kofi doodled on his iPad, a picture of Richard's head on the block of the guillotine.

"As I said, it's not *me* who is being interviewed, Mr. de L'Isle, but *you*. Mrs. Jelleners was recently punched, probably that afternoon—very hard and in many places. Did *you* ever punch her?"

"As I said, Inspector, I am not a violent man. So that I am very clear, and that you don't waste our time asking me again—I have never, ever hit or struck any woman: that's simply not in my nature."

"But having an affair that would hurt your wife and potentially ruin your family, and probably decimate your career, *is* clearly in your nature."

"As I said, I regret having the affair, as did Rebecca. I can't force back the hands of a clock, but instead, I can try going forward to be a better husband for my wife and father to my children. Men, and indeed, women, make mistakes. I made one, and I am not proud of what I did."

"Not your finest hour then, Mr. de L'Isle," said Kofi, enjoying laboring the point.

"No, Inspector, it wasn't. But I hope you and others can judge me on my overall actions in my life, which I believe are good for society. No one is perfect, Inspector." He paused and couldn't resist adding, "Maybe not *even* you."

Kofi thought he needed to scare the arrogant and increasingly cocky Richard with a curveball question to get an unexpected reaction from him. Richard's baiting was starting to annoy the detective. But he just couldn't work out, so far, how this calm young man could have committed murder less than a day before, unless he was an incredible actor and had been rehearsing for this meeting very thoroughly. He also reminded himself that Mr. Jelleners was clearly the main suspect here, not Mr. de L'Isle. Whilst it seemed all too easy to just assume it was Mr. Jelleners, something just didn't stack up. But he was damned if he knew what that was.

He looked down at his tablet, and whilst completing the guillotine doodle with Richard's chopped head in a basket, tried to think of a question that could upset Richard. He paused for another count of ten and waited.

Richard remained perfectly calm. He wasn't sweating or fidgeting.

"Hmm. Will you be telling your wife about the affair?"

"Inspector, I wasn't planning on doing so at this stage. What would it achieve except to upset my wife? Isn't it better that I deeply regret my actions and realize it was a stupid thing to do and spare my wife's feelings? As I mentioned, I'm trying to be a better father and husband. Anyway, Rebecca is dead, and I think it would be best to leave things be. Unless you plan on betraying our confidence and telling Jennifer or indeed Chuck?"

"That information may have to come out during our further investigations, Mr. de L'Isle."

"Well, let's cross that bridge when we come to it—if it does, Chief Inspector, shall we?"

Kofi decided to try a long shot, but the timing had to be perfect. And if that didn't work, well, perhaps this cocky banker was, in fact, innocent after all.

"OK then, I think that will be all, *for now*."

Kofi stood up and went over to Richard to shake his hand. He needed for Richard to be out of his comfort zone.

"Do you mind coming down to the station, Mr. de L'Isle?"

"For what purpose, Inspector? I have a rather busy afternoon and have told you all I know. I was hoping to see Chuck later today on my way home, but I don't know where he is. Presumably, he is at home, right? Although I tried that number as well, but there's no answer."

Kofi didn't detect Richard flinching on Kofi's request. Maybe he had rehearsed that question.

"He is being held in the cells at the Ascot Police Station, Mr. de L'Isle," informed Kofi.

The Feather of Truth — Ian Campbell-Laing

"So, why do you need me to come to the station also, Inspector?"

"I would like you to make and sign a written statement."

"OK, sure, I would be happy to do that, but can it wait until after work when I'm on my way home, given my workload today? I'm obviously having to cover for my boss somewhat unexpectedly, Chief Inspector."

Kofi smiled and suddenly thought, Yes, it would be convenient if you got your boss's job through this whole murderous affair. That's more than motive enough for some.

Kofi gave Richard's request some further thought and considered it was a good idea because it would allow him and Harriet some extra prep time.

"Sure, it can wait. Be at the station no later than eight o'clock tonight. Would that be convenient for you, sir?"

"Yes, that's perfect. I'll be there at exactly eight. Thank you, Inspector. And may I see my boss when I am there?"

Kofi considered this. He hadn't ruled out that Chuck and Richard could be in collusion, and letting them meet each other before either was formally charged would be against protocol. But he thought the benefit of seeing how they reacted together under strictly controlled circumstances would outweigh the risks.

"You may, but only briefly."

Kofi walked towards the closed door, and in a Columbo-esque manner, turned around and said, "Oh, one more thing. Earlier this afternoon, we impounded your flashy car from your home for examination, by the way."

"Will that be all, Chief Inspector?" said Richard, annoyed by the inconvenience at not having his toy.

"Yes, for now. Oh, and you aren't planning on any holidays in the near future, are you?"

"No, not until the end of May with my family. We're going to Zimbabwe on a safari for ten days during the Trinity half-term break. Why?"

"Then I won't need to ask you to surrender your passport immediately. Good day, Mr. de L'Isle. I'll see my own way out, thank you."

Again, no flinching by Richard, but the inspector had one more area he wanted to cover. As Kofi reached the door, which Richard had now opened for him, he asked quietly, for the second time in the same manner of the American TV-hit detective, "Oh, Mr. de L'Isle, one final thing."

"What now, Inspector?" Richard wondered how long it was going to take to get rid of him.

"May I ask you a very personal question?"

"By all means, Chief Inspector, fire away," said Richard as his stomach muscles tightened.

"Are you planning on having any more children?" asked the inspector, deliberately a little too loudly. He was sure that everyone sitting at their desks outside Richard's office would be straining to hear any conversation with the police.

Richard of course hadn't rehearsed this specific question, and didn't immediately see its relevance, but he didn't flinch. Instead, he just moved his head back and looked confused. "That's an odd question, Inspector. Of what relevance is this to the case, may I ask?"

"I understand that Mrs. Rebecca Falconer Jelleners was pregnant, Mr. de L'Isle, and I just wondered if you were the father of the baby, given what you said about the timing of your last intimacy with her."

Kofi smiled at the immediate effect it had on Richard, who swiftly closed the door and stepped forward glaring at the Inspector.

Richard was furious and thought that this inspector had a bloody nerve, asking that question to bait him. Richard paused. He acknowledged the question was clever, but, thought Richard, I'll outwit him if it's the last thing I do. He composed himself first.

"Chief Inspector, I had no idea that she was pregnant, but of course, if that is the case, then that is a double blow to me, given I have lost Rebecca, who was a good friend." Then he raised his right hand and pointed his index finger in front of the policeman's face and stepped forward, deliberately invading his personal space. "But to ask me such a question deliberately with my office door open, in earshot of people who work with me, is tactless, and quite frankly, a breach of the trust and confidentiality between us. Such an approach is somewhat underhand, deliberate, and deplorable."

Kofi laughed and then looked serious. "Mr. de L'Isle, it was you who opened the door for me, as I was in the middle of asking the question."

"Not so, Inspector. You are well aware that you were leaving and I had opened the door for you, and only then, deliberately in earshot of my staff, did you start to ask your question in a raised tone," said Richard.

He is being assertive, but starting to look a little flustered, the chief inspector thought. Good.

"Whatever. But I'm conducting an enquiry over a *deplorable* and *deliberate* murder of both a woman with whom you have admitted having a very recent affair, and her unborn child," said the inspector. "So it is a double-murder enquiry, and I will ask whatever questions I see fit to get to the bottom of this and to find out what went on yesterday and which person or persons were responsible."

"Of course you must, Inspector, and you have my full support in any line of enquiry you choose. But I must ask you to respect my privacy and not blurt out such tactless questions in public. Or I shall report you to your superiors. Is that clear?"

"Yes, Mr. de L'Isle, your position is quite clear to me, and I am beginning to understand what happened yesterday. Good day to you. I'll be in touch, as they say."

The chief inspector left the office, humming opera to himself. Richard quickly closed the door. He walked back to his chair and briefly slumped back in it, exhausted. Then he quickly sat up straight and recomposed himself.

Richard saw that the chief inspector had left his tablet stylus pen on the table, probably deliberately. He had heard of that tactic, whereby the detective would then return, unannounced, to catch the suspect's actions in private. Richard wasn't going to let the policeman see him exhausted and anxious. He sat at his desk, updating the notes of the presentation he had given to Celsius for his comments.

Ninety seconds after he'd left, the door opened, and in walked Kofi again.

"Apologies for disturbing you again, Mr. de L'Isle."

"Yes, Inspector, what is it now? I believe you left your stylus pen on my table."

"Yes, I did. How observant of you. Nothing gets past you, does it?"

"Inspector, I had just noticed it. But next time you enter my office, have the courtesy to go through my secretary, and then knock first, please. As I would when seeing you in your office."

"But of course." Kofi retrieved his pen and walked back to the door. He turned and said, "Oh, just one last thing. I don't suppose that the clothes you are wearing today are those that you wore yesterday at the Jelleners' house?"

"No, they are not. I wear casual clothes at the weekend, Inspector."

"Yes, we thought so too. When we collected your car, your wife confirmed that earlier the dry cleaners had collected your suit jacket and she had dropped off your shoes at the cobblers. So we intercepted them and handed them over to the forensics team for analysis. Good day. We will be in touch, as they say."

These last few minutes flustered Richard more than he thought they would. He was unable to do any more work that day. He now realized that his murderous act would stay with him forever, and he would always be looking over his shoulder. How on earth had the inspector found out so quickly that Rebecca was pregnant? The autopsy would not have been performed already, would it? He had been ready for the question, of course, and thought he had deflected it quite well, considering how angry he became when the inspector opened his office door, letting the staff hear the conversation.

Richard desperately wanted to know what the inspector thought and whether Chuck was still the prime suspect, given the information he had planted on Chuck. Richard knew that he had successfully established multiple motives for Chuck murdering his wife, and Richard was fairly certain that there was nothing incriminating in his own jacket, but he wasn't a hundred percent sure of course.

While heading to the ground floor in the lifts, the inspector considered Richard's reactions to his questions. He kicked himself for allowing Richard to ramble on about his privacy. It was a trick people used to give themselves time to regain their composure. Especially con artists and murderers. This murder enquiry was proving most intriguing, he thought.

The chief inspector couldn't wait to interview Mrs. Jelleners' friend Dawn, and of course, Chuck, again. He knew that Chuck had plenty of motives because he seemed to detest his wife, had physically assaulted her before according to Richard, and he had the opportunity and the means to personally strangle her. But if Mrs. Jelleners was pregnant, then Richard also had motive in not wanting the pregnancy to proceed. Richard also had the opportunity and perhaps the means. But of course, the inspector had no idea if Rebecca was or wasn't pregnant, it was just a guess by him to try and trap Richard. The inspector also had no idea, even if she was pregnant, whether or not she would have wanted to have the baby, or what she actually had died from. All of this was speculation, so far. One thing for was sure, though—he would make sure that both Mr. Jelleners and Mr. de L'Isle took a polygraph test to have another gauge of their true posture under pressure. They were always interesting to watch.

PART THREE

Oh, Sinnerman, where are you going to run to?

Song track "Sinnerman," *The Thomas Crown Affair*, 1999
By Nina Simone, from the album *Pastel Blues*, 1965

CHAPTER 41
ASCOT POLICE STATION, SURREY

At just before 8:00 p.m. that evening, Richard's cab from Ascot railway station arrived at the police station. He had gathered his thoughts during the train journey. Before he got out of the cab, he looked inside his briefcase for his spy fountain pen but could not see it. Then he realized that after the security guard incident, he had put it back in his jacket. He reached inside his jacket but couldn't find it in any of the pockets.

How odd. I wonder where it's gone? He wondered. Then he realized it was in the jacket he wore at the Jelleners's house yesterday for lunch. He hoped that Jennifer had the sense to retrieve it before the police had intercepted the jacket. He sent her a quick text.

He got out of the cab, paid the driver, and casually strode up the steps and into the hallway. He stood patiently in front of the reception desk.

After no one appeared, he coughed slightly, and, noticing a bell to ring for attention, he pressed it with the palm of his right hand. It made no sound, so Richard knocked his knuckles twice onto the counter, saying, "Hello, any one here?" A man in uniform walked into view.

"Hi. I'm Richard de L'Isle. I have an appointment to see Chuck Jelleners, whom I understand you're holding here, and I need to provide you with a statement for DCI Ghazini."

The desk sergeant looked slightly bored and, without looking up, scanned a list on a note pad near him and said, "C. Jelleners, ah, yes. Do you have ID, Mr. de L'Isle?"

"Er, you need to see one?" Richard was confused: in this new age, the microchip embedded in his back above his shoulder blades had all the information any government official would surely need. But maybe the Ascot police force weren't yet on the system due to the inevitable government cutbacks, he concluded.

The desk sergeant looked up at Richard, wondering if he needed to repeat the request.

"Sorry. Sure, here's my driving licence, officer."

After scanning the license for the name and with a brief look at Richard's face to check that the picture vaguely resembled him, the desk sergeant passed back the licence. He said, "OK, seems in order. Please sign the register here with the time and then follow me. My name is Sergeant Yarrow."

"Thank you, Sergeant," said Richard.

"It says here you should also hand over the keys to your car, Mr. de L'Isle."

"Nope, no need, because the car was collected from my home earlier today. Please recheck your records."

"Er, OK, I will."

Richard casually followed him through the double doors and then down the stairs to the cells below.

Sergeant Yarrow went past rows of cells, each with a name written on a blackboard attached to the door:

J. Rowen, 20th Mar, Securities Fraud
M. Ferron, 28th Mar, I/Trading
F. Watt, 23rd Mar, Rape
R. Weatherstone, 25th Mar, Arson
J. Sayle, 2nd Apr, M/S 2nd deg
S. Nastro, 18th Feb, Harassment/GBH
S. Mills, 1st April, Embez
T. Blair, 30th Mar, Property Title Fraud

Richard thought, This is a real den of thieves who have committed crimes ranging from financial and real estate fraud, grievous bodily harm, insider trading, embezzlement, to rape and manslaughter. How quaint that they use a board and chalk; nothing electronic here to save their life!

Richard stopped at the board of the end door:

C. Jelleners 8th Apr, NYC/SOM

"Sergeant, what are 'NYC' and 'SOM'?" enquired Richard.

"Oh, sir, that's just our own peculiar shorthand meaning that Mr. Jelleners has not yet been charged but is under suspicion of murder."

Richard smiled. Jolly good.

Sergeant Yarrow continued walking and then looked back towards Richard, who had stopped at the cell.

"Yes, that is his cell, sir, but you will find him in the interview room just along here."

The sergeant opened the peephole, looked inside, and with one of what looked like dozens of keys on a massive chain, unlocked the door and threw it open.

Richard noticed the sergeant did not let go of the door handle, and his view was fixed on the occupant inside. Richard was amazed that in this climate of advanced technology, the police still had physical keys to open and lock a door.

"Sir, you may now enter. You have twenty minutes exactly, but if any time beforehand you wish to leave, either press the bell near the door here, or call for an officer who will be nearby and can hear you at all times. Please now go on in."

Richard entered the cold, whitewashed room, which was no bigger than

The Feather of Truth   Ian Campbell-Laing

the mudroom in Jelly's palatial Surrey home. Jelly sat behind a wooden table and, following instructions, only stood up after the door had shut.

Richard watched his boss walk over towards him. His eyes looked tired, his face haggard, and his cheekbones, despite him being a chubby man, were somehow gaunt. His hands were handcuffed.

"Richard, I am so glad you could come. It means so much to me."

"Chuck, I'm your friend and colleague. Of course I would come. I just want to help you get out of here."

Richard hugged Chuck, who then said, "Thanks, Ricardo."

"How are they treating you? I heard that they took you straight to the police station this morning. They told me that, despite the alleged crime, you are not in the high-risk category, and at this stage, you could get certain privileges, like newspapers, books, and cigarettes. So is there anything I can get you—are you allowed wine and cigars?"

Richard then stepped back and tried to make more small talk, but suddenly the old Jelly was back in control. He started to outline an action plan for his release and what he would do if formally charged with his wife's murder.

"It goes without saying, Richard, that you have been a real rock for me in this ridiculous farce about the death of Rebecca. You know that I did not, or could not, kill her. Heaven knows that she drove me up the wall, yes! She spent all my money, certainly! She denied me my marital rights, yes! But as God is my witness, I did not have any need to kill her. Divorce her, yes. Kill her, no!" Chuck sighed and then said quietly, "But, there's only two scenarios I can think of, assuming there's no break-in. Either she committed suicide, which I doubt, or you or I must have killed her, Richard."

Richard's heart started pounding. He stared at Chuck, uncertain how to reply.

"But, given you obviously had no reason to kill her, then maybe I *did* kill her. God only knows. I remember so little of that afternoon and early evening. I had rather a lot to drink, but I do remember falling asleep."

Richard thought to himself, Damn! Wish I had my pen with me, that admission by Jelly would be very good as evidence. Although he reminded himself, it probably was not admissible because it hadn't been approved beforehand. This process of having to warn a person before he incriminates himself, Richard thought, was slightly ridiculous.

"But don't you remember waking up and talking to me? You said that you went discreetly into the morning room to check on her. I think you said something about going in with some magazines for her, as an excuse to see her, but her telling you to leave her be? Don't you remember? I then left shortly afterwards, when you said you wanted to watch some TV. You asked me to go and take a case of wine as a thank you for the hard work on the presentation, and then we shook hands, and you showed me out. Don't you remember that?"

"I don't remember that, er, but maybe I do. It's all fuzzy, and I'm confused about what I do and don't remember. I don't want to spend another minute in this den of iniquity. I've got work to do, and I've already missed giving the presentation to the Iceman this afternoon. He must be furious."

"It's OK. Celsius asked me to give it to him, but he only had five minutes due to a fire drill from Dr. Becker, so I guess he was too busy. Celsius liked what we had prepared and said when you are out of here to give him the full deck when he will have more time. So, Chuck, it's all under control."

"It is? Oh, good. But I can't stand it here. I have only been here since this morning, and it's utter hell. It's so noisy and there's nothing to do."

"I know, Chuck. Let's not talk about it. Let's think about how to get you free. I think I read somewhere that they can hold you here for only forty-eight hours, after which they must either charge you or release you or apply to the judge to get an extension. Have they interviewed you again after meeting you at your home?"

Chuck replied initially calmly, but eventually raising his voice slightly after each sentence. "Yes, they came in to see me again this afternoon, after the black detective had a chat with you in your office. They were pretty aggressive, especially that bitch of a lady detective, Gulliver or Gillmare, or whatever her name is. They kept going on about the arguments that Becks and I had, and that they knew I had a temper. I then admitted to having slapped her just once, when I was very angry with her. I regretted it as soon as I did. That's when Becks permanently banished me from her bed and used her morning room as a sanctuary." Chuck threw up his arms in despair of his mistreatment and then continued. "And of course they said that I had denied this when they had a chat with me in the morning, and so what else was I lying about?" Chuck's face was now red, and he was sweating heavily.

Richard thought Chuck seemed more frustrated with the mess he was in than with the distress of losing his wife.

Chuck, now pleased that he had someone at whom he could vent his anger and obtain sympathy, kept picking out pieces of his second interview with the police. "They said that she had bruising on her face and stomach similar to those her doctor had witnessed, and he said Rebecca had told him that I had hit her more than once. The police then mentioned that they had searched my PC and had evidence of rude and incriminating e-mails—that I was a womanizer and evidently belittled women, and I must have some kind of psychological problem with women or some such rubbish. They also saw that I had crushed pearls on my shoes, so that I must have gone into her morning room, yet I initially said I hadn't. They kept going on and on about there being so many inconsistencies. Seems they are trying to build a case against me, alleging I strangled my wife. It's utter nonsense, of course." Chuck was now literally spitting and had to use a piece of tissue paper that Richard had passed to him to wipe his mouth. The soliloquy had caused him to be out of breath and become exhausted. He slumped back down into his chair.

"Of course it is," sympathized Richard. "I think you need to get a good criminal lawyer, and he may need to also hire a private detective. I can get you the name of a lawyer, if you want."

"It's OK. I have got one," said Chuck, sighing. "Tell me, Richard, how is the office? It's very odd not being there today."

"Well, as you would expect, everyone is talking about you, but mainly of course, as the guy who always knew what to do to fix things. In fact, people keep saying to me, 'You know Chuck well. What would he have done on this or that issue?' So, I've been doing my best to keep you alive in the minds of the people who worked, er…work for you," Richard lied.—Most of the people Richard had talked to were delighted that Chuck,—the annoying, unreasonable, booming boss, was in custody, and that Richard,—the gentleman who had time for everyone, had taken over.

"I knew you would, and when I get out of this mess, you have my word of honor that I will reward you handsomely for your unquestioned loyalty. I know that you were disappointed with last year's bonus, but unfortunately, I wasn't given much to play with on that front from the Iceman," Chuck said, staring directly into Richard's eyes.

Richard thought, What an utter lie! Richard knew from V-Trax what Celsius's—the Iceman's—bonus pool was, and there was plenty of wiggle room to reward Richard properly. At worst, Richard reasoned, one could simply take some from Chuck's own gargantuan bonus. Also, Rebecca would not have invented the additional secret bonus of shares that Jelly got from the CEO. Even when I am here with this Jellybean, pretending to try to help him out, he has the balls to lie to my face. The guy's a deceitful liar, and I will take great pleasure ruining him.

Chuck added, lowering his voice to a near whisper, "You would not be aware of this, but before this nonsense, I was about to make a bid for the top slot, for Celsius's job, and was going to oust him out. Of course, I would need someone to take my old role of global chief operating officer, and I think you should have that role if I move up the ladder. What do you think, Ricardo?"

"Well, of course, I'm flattered, and I'm sure I could step up to the global COO role in time, but how on earth could you get Celsius's job? I thought he is well liked and trusted by Dr. Becker. Isn't he?" enquired Richard, amazed at Chuck revealing his hand to him.

"Celsius is not as well liked as you might imagine, and he has made some serious mistakes, which I mentioned in total confidence to Dr. Becker when I sat next to him at dinner at the MD conference in Paris in February last year. I also know a little secret about Celsius's private life that could be very, very valuable in the right hands."

"Well, Chuck, I don't really want to know about those things. You know that I'm very loyal to you and also to Celsius, who has been very good to me, supporting my promotion over the years from VP, then director, to managing director. So I haven't forgotten that. As far as I can see—well, at my humble level, anyway—he's a great leader and has done some great things for asset and private wealth management. I don't want to get into any of the politics at the bank, nor comment on the behavior of others, so for now, let's just concentrate on your defense."

Interesting, Richard mused. So Chuck is the Brutus to Celsius's Caesar and wants to oust him. I can report this back to Celsius and score some valuable brownie points.

This is all working out perfectly, thought Richard. He was calm. In fact, he was beginning to even enjoy himself. Maybe committing and getting away with murder was not that hard, after all. Especially if you have as a scapegoat such a buffoon like Jelly who deserves to be taken down.

CHAPTER 42
ASCOT POLICE STATION

"Let's deal with one problem at a time, Chuck," Richard said. "Judging by the type of questions the police are asking you, it seems likely that within the next thirty-six hours, they will formally charge you for murder. So let's get your defense team and strategy in place, and if it goes to trial, we can then get you acquitted with no blemish on your good name and have you restored as the division's global COO. Then we can decide what role you or Celsius want me to do."

Richard thought to himself, I simply can't stand you, you pathetic, stodgy worm of a man, who only got promoted by Celsius due to you sucking up to him and claiming the credit for everything your subordinates do for you, especially me. I despise you and cannot wait for you to get your just rewards. And, if that means you spend the rest of your miserable life in a rat's hole of a prison under the custody of His Majesty's pleasure for a murder that you did not commit, but which I planned to perfection, then who is the better and more clever a man: you or me, Jelly? Yes, I am smarter than you, and a better tactician. And now, after shafting me on my bonus, you need me more than ever, because, in fact, there is no one else who can save you, with the knowledge I possess. And I plan to use this to my advantage and crucify you once and for all.

Richard said good-bye to Chuck and promised to return in a few days.

He was then escorted upstairs and was shown into a private room to write his statement. It didn't take him long: he had rehearsed that afternoon in his office what it would say. He made it brief. Less is more, as they say.

He left the police station in an unmarked police car. As he sat in the car at the traffic lights, the police constable giving him a lift to the railway station tried to make conversation. Richard was polite but focused on reading and responding to his e-mails on his iPhone. Even on the train, he didn't let down his guard. He was suspicious that Ghazini might have put someone on the train to watch him. Only when he arrived home, after the front door was locked and he was in his study alone, with a glass of wine from one of the very expensive bottles he stole from Chuck, did he then allow himself the luxury of a huge sigh of exhausted relief.

Little did Richard know that the Surrey Police at Ascot were more au fait with technology than Richard had believed. Kofi and Harriet had watched and listened to the meeting Richard had with Chuck from hidden cameras and microphones, which relayed their conversation and actions to a separate room on a different floor. They were also video-recording everything.

The Feather of Truth   Ian Campbell-Laing

Kofi yawned rather too loudly and then saw her laugh. "Sorry, Harriet. Still not getting enough kip! It's this ruddy job as usual."

"Yes, I know. It gets to one, especially the more horrific cases we deal with. I thought you were about to go on your sabbatical?"

"Yep, I was, or rather I am—just trying to wrap up the Goldschmidt drowning, which on the one hand still appears a straightforward accidental death, but a couple of things don't stack up in my mind. But the chief said I should take this Jelleners case on, and then I can take my three-months leave."

"Lucky you sir, in being able to get away from all this nonsense!"

"Hmm. So, Harriet, how did your discussion today go with Mrs. Jelleners's best friend, Dawn Peabody?"

"I didn't get much out of her, unfortunately. She was so distraught, we left an officer in her house to keep an eye on her. It appears that Rebecca didn't mention too many details about Richard to her best friend, which is surprising, given how women sometimes love to gossip."

"Oh dear. Didn't she mention *anything* that could help us?"

"Dawn knew that Rebecca was having an affair with Richard a few months ago but wasn't certain if it was still ongoing, which is a real pain and stacks up with what Richard told us. She did say that when they were going out, Rebecca was infatuated with Richard though, which is interesting. Dawn thought, in fact, that they could have broken up, but that Rebecca was hoping to get back together with Richard when they met last week for dinner at his club. But Dawn said she was only guessing. Dawn also made it clear that Rebecca hated her husband and wanted a divorce, especially after he had hit her."

Kofi sighed. "Not much to go on, is it?"

"But there was one other thing she mentioned which may be useful, and that was that Rebecca had mentioned to her on Thursday morning last week that she had received some very good news to tell Richard, but Dawn didn't know what that news was."

"But hardly a witness that we could use in court. She would be savaged by a good QC defending Richard." Kofi paused in thought and then added, "So what do we think, Harriet? Who's your money on for killing Mrs. Rebecca Falconer Jelleners? The acknowledged assertive, fifth-time-married Yank, who seems more concerned about getting back to work than the death of his trophy wife, who has a reputation for demeaning women, and has written e-mails saying he can't stand his wife? Or, is the murderer the ex or maybe very current suave British boyfriend who works for him, and whom I suspect actually doesn't like his boss at all? We must remember, however, at the alleged time of Rebecca's death, the smooth-talking Richard was already at home with his family and had—conveniently or perhaps deliberately—stopped at the petrol station afterwards to ensure the time was noted when he filled up his car."

"Sir, I'm still going with the husband, assuming it was a drunken, attempted sexual assault and then a struggle ending in strangulation. Maybe her husband didn't initially mean to kill her, so murder at worst, and manslaughter at best for him."

"Yes, so far, Chuck is the leading suspect. But let's see what the path-lab boys say is the cause and provide a more precise time of death, and also what forensics turn up in his house. This may be a simple husband battering case, or it may be far more cunning."

"And, sir, have we ruled out collusion between Richard and Chuck?"

"Not entirely, but what would be their motive? Whilst I can't see them as accomplices with the aim of killing Rebecca, let's dig some more to see if there's any evidence of collusion."

"Just a thought but since we've just heard Chuck admit he wants his boss, Celsius 'the Iceman's' job. Could he have said to Richard, 'If you murder my annoying wife, then when I get Celsius's job, I will promote you to my existing position'."

"Hmm. Harriet, what a devious mind you have! No, Richard wouldn't be so stupid to make such a gamble."

"It's a pity, sir, that our department is so stretched with the other cases we have open, as well. Isn't it?" said Harriet, sighing and frowning.

"Yes, that doesn't help, but that can't mean we have to come to an incorrect conclusion. As you know, if we want to keep Chuck longer than forty-eight hours, we need to either charge him or apply to the court for an extension, and then when that runs out, a warrant for further detention. Chop chop, so as usual, we are really up against it. Tempus fugit—time flies and all that."

"We can always charge Chuck with murder, go to the judge for a court order and hope the judge doesn't grant bail due to the flight risk, so that we can interrogate him further. And then at the same time, keep an eye on Richard to see how he reacts, or if he lets his guard down with further questioning," Harriet suggested.

"Precisely. It's obviously either Chuck or Richard who did this murder, given there is no one else in the picture because there's no evidence of any breaking and entering in their house. But I think Richard may *not* be telling us all he knows. I have a gut feeling that the affair he had with Rebecca may not have ended a month ago. But I may be wrong. As I mentioned, I tried to trick Richard with questions, but he certainly didn't act like a man who had committed murder less than twenty-four hours beforehand. Mind you, under questioning, neither did the serial killer Peter Sutcliffe in 1981, who was cool as a cucumber initially, and the police released him."

Kofi paused and then added, "Let's go and see her friend, Dawn, again tomorrow and press her a bit more about Jennifer's relationship with

Richard."

"Sure, sir."

"But, Harriet, let me ask you this question: As a woman, let's say you are a very attractive and intelligent woman."

"You're saying I'm not, sir?!" smiled Harriet, teasing and interrupting him.

"Of course you are. Let me rephrase it. Let's say you are a very attractive and intelligent *American* woman, in her midthirties, living what outwardly appears to be a charmed life with money and time no object. But you are probably a bored housewife and have been mistreated by your arrogant arsehole of a husband, Chuck. And you seize at the opportunity to have an affair with the dashing, rich Brit who wines, dines and lavishes attention on you at his exclusive club. So, tell me, why would Chuck murder his trophy wife of only two years, if he didn't know of the affair his wife was having?" asked Kofi, raising his eyebrows.

"Well, sir, in a drunken rage, the assertive, entitled Yank snapped and throttled her after an argument where she was telling him what to do or nagging him, or refusing to have sex with him. He would hardly be the first henpecked or deprived husband that murdered his wife. Or…"

"Or what, Harriet?"

"Or Rebecca did tell Chuck about her affair, and he murdered her out of jealousy, sir."

"Nope, I don't think Chuck knows about Richard's affair. We have seen them together in the cells, and I think so far it's a secret. Well, a secret for as long as we want it to be, of course," Kofi said, smiling and pleased he had some leverage over Richard.

"But let's remember that Chuck has openly stated that he would like to divorce his wife, but it would be too expensive to do so," countered Harriet.

"Yes, that is motive, Harriet. Let's check if Chuck had any life assurance policies out on his wife that pay out a large sum on her death, will you?"

"Sure."

"And also into the mix, we have no idea if Rebecca was pregnant. It was only something I decided to ask Richard in an attempt to trip him up when I was questioning him. He didn't appear flustered by the nature of the question; he seemed more concerned that his reputation was being tarnished in public."

"Hold on, sir, you may have hit on the real reason for the murder…"

"Hmm. What reason, Harriet?"

"Perhaps the good news that Dawn mentioned Rebecca was giving Richard, was that she was pregnant with Richard's baby. Good news for Rebecca, who was besotted with Richard and could start a new life with her lover, but bad news for Richard, who knew his boss, Chuck, and his own wife, Jennifer, would be furious. So the clever Richard decided to end her and their baby's life and put the blame on his boss. Now that would be very neat, wouldn't it, sir?"

"Yep, that's a very smart hypothesis. But if Rebecca only told Richard about her pregnancy on Thursday evening while at his club, then he didn't have much time to plan this very clever murder. Conversely, with the incriminating documents going back many months showing Chuck hating his wife and wanting to be rid of her, together with the knowledge that he previously slapped her around, the court on balance would surely convict Chuck," reasoned Kofi, opening his hands and revealing his pink palms.

"All very convenient for Richard, if he is the murderer, that all these documents exist," Harriet said.

"Yes, the one in Chuck's briefcase was very convenient. But for the others, the tech guys had to search quite hard on Chuck's laptop to find them. What's Richard's background, Harriet? Can you find out if he's a computer geek and if there's a way for someone to plant this kind of evidence on Chuck's laptop? If there isn't, I agree, we are back to the husband as the likely murderer."

"Certainly, sir, and may I also say, given his very likely conviction, your 100 percent homicide conviction rate would remain intact!"

Kofi smiled. "But you know what, young lady, I would happily drop that success rate if I knew I had convicted the wrong man. No question."

"Of course you would and should, sir." Harriet smiled back at her boss. She felt privileged to have been singled out by Kofi and assigned to the brilliant detective so early on in her career.

Kofi turned around to see the sergeant motion to him. "Yes, Yarrow. What is it, old chap?"

"The preliminary forensics report has come in, sir, by fax, like you asked. They did a rush job for you, and I have the coroner holding for you on the phone. They have partially completed the autopsy, as a matter of urgency as you requested, but given you may want to charge Mr. Jelleners tomorrow, they wanted to give you a quick heads-up."

"Perfect, thanks. Let me just scan the forensics report, and then I will take the call in a few secs."

Kofi read the front-page summary and conclusions section from the forensic boys who had visited Chuck's house earlier that day.

Attendance at Copse Hall, Wentworth, Surrey—Home of Mr. and Mrs. Jelleners—at the request of DCI GHAZINI.

Visit 10:00 a.m. to 12:00 a.m., Monday 7th April 2025

The results of our examination strongly support the following hypotheses:

1. That the questioned burnt fibers (threads) found in the fireplace ash of the dining room (item 1), match those fibers (threads) found in the morning room on the victim's left earring (item 2), watch strap clasp (item 3), jeans' zip (item 4), and fabric of her panties (item 5), and matched the type of fibers of the suspect's gloves found in the pockets of his overcoat (item 9).

2. That the questioned crushed pearls (item 6) came from the victim's necklace and found in the fibers of the carpet of the morning room, matched those on the suspect's shoes: both the black ones the suspect was wearing (item 7) and the pair of brown slip-ons found in his closet upstairs (item 8).

3. That the questioned fireplace ash in the library contained a burnt cellophane bag (item 10) and a protein substance residue (item 11)—which is still being analyzed—but matched the same compound found in the suspect's pocket-handkerchief (item 12) within the front pocket of his jacket left in the dining room.

4. That the questioned fireplace ash in the library contained a substance (item 13) whose compound resembles marijuana.

5. That the questioned sock fibres (item 14) found inside the suspect's brown slip-on shoes matched the socks found in his closet upstairs.

"Hmm. Not only does Chuck smoke cigars, but someone has had a joint recently."

Kofi then scanned the last four sections—crime scene, processing, evidence collected, and pending—and noticed that it was very comprehensive, with percentage probabilities to the conclusions of their hypotheses of at least 98 percent.

Interesting, thought Kofi. All of this was somewhat pointing to Chuck again as the leading candidate here. I wonder, what exactly is the protein substance?

Kofi then took the call from the head coroner, his dear friend of many years. "Ghazini here. What have you got for me so far, please, Mr. Coroner, sir?" he smiled.

Sebastian Granier at the Royal Surrey Pathology always liked talking to the detective and helping him unravel the perpetrators of heinous crimes. "Hi, Kofi, old chap. How's it going?"

"Thanks. Very well, Sebastian. What's the story on our Rebecca Falconer Jelleners, please?" Kofi put the phone on speaker so that his assistant could hear, as well.

"Well, it's preliminary, but she died of a neurotoxin protein-based poison, which shut down her nervous system, resulting in a heart attack."

"Oh, really? Poison and not strangulation?"

"Yes, there was strangulation, but that did not kill her; the poison started the whole death sequence much earlier than the strangulation."

Kofi looked at Harriet and said, "This adds a new dimension. Clearly, Rebecca could not have strangled herself with her husband's gloves, given the marks on her neck, and especially after the poison took effect. But could Rebecca have poisoned herself from the start, and if so, why?"

Harriet spoke to Kofi, offering her thoughts. "Well, maybe she was so depressed—being with her abusive husband, and the ending of her affair with Richard—she felt there was no purpose in her life."

"But Dawn said she had some very good news and was in high spirits, which doesn't sound like a depressive considering suicide," replied Kofi.

"Sir, with all due respect, suicide candidates often appear fine on the outside to friends and relatives, but inside, their minds are going through turmoil. Perhaps for the time being, we shouldn't rule out suicide by her administering the poison to herself, until matters become clearer," suggested the young detective.

"Quite so, Harriet. Sebastian, when was the time of death and the time the poison was administered? Can you estimate that?" asked Kofi.

"The time of death, based on what the ambulance officer reported as the temperature of the victim's body, and various rigor mortis and other corneal tests we carried out, was probably between eleven and thirteen hours before she was examined by the ambulance crew at oh-seven hundred. So TOD was between six p.m. and eight p.m. on the Sunday evening. But our further tests should be able to narrow that down more for you, Kofi."

So, thought Kofi, if Richard—by his own admission—left at 6:00 p.m., that still puts him clearly in the timeframe…although Rebecca's watch showed it was smashed at five past eight. Mmmm, something's not right here, but I know one thing—Richard is still definitely a person of considerable interest.

"OK, thanks, Sebastian. I appreciate you doing this so quickly. Any thoughts as to which poison was used?"

"It's difficult to say. It's not a poison we have come across much in the UK."

"So not cyanide or ricin, Doctor?" asked Harriet.

"No. Those are very easy to detect, and there were no traces of them. But whatever it was, was extremely deadly. We need more time in the lab. We should know by early tomorrow morning precisely what it was, and we can then assign a more narrow time frame during which it was likely to have been administered."

"OK, thanks. Hmm. Oh, I've just thought of something. Forensics analyzed a residue of marijuana in the library fireplace. Any such substances present in Mrs. Jelleners's bloodstream?"

"Nope. No drugs whatsoever, Kofi."

"Well, this is very helpful, Sebastian, and as you know, this is an urgent rush job. Please call me tomorrow or my assistant, DI Harriet Gilmore, when you know more."

"Sure, Kofi."

"Oh, sorry, one other thing, Sebastian," remembered Kofi. "We are guessing that Mrs. Jelleners was recently sexually active, and we have a hunch that she may have been pregnant. If so, how many months was she, and was there any evidence of recent sexual activity?"

"Oh, yes, we checked both those questions for you as you requested, given her hand resting on her stomach. I should have mentioned that earlier—my mistake, Kofi. In connection with the second question, there was no evidence of any sperm in Mrs. Jelleners's nutrient-rich, fertile cervical fluid, suggesting that she had not had sexual activity for the last three to five days—so from Wednesday evening last week."

Harriet said, "So, Richard might have been telling the truth—that he had finished the affair a while ago and did not have any sexual relations with her on the Thursday night they spent together at his club. Damn."

"Hmm. Unless he did but just used a condom. Anyway, he could have had plenty of other sexual activity with her, of course. Doctor, sorry, we digress, and interrupted you."

"No problem, Kofi. It's always interesting for us in this gloomy lab to have such discussions and feel part of the investigation team. The pain in her stomach from the poison's neurotoxins would have been quite severe, however, and perhaps the most probable reason she put her hand on her stomach. But in answer to your first question as to whether or not the deceased was pregnant, I can categorically answer that for you. She had heightened levels of the human chorionic gonadotrophic, or hCG, hormone in her body, typical of women who are pregnant…"

***

Frankfurt, Germany

Udo called his CEO on his private, secure cellphone.

"Herr Doktor, were you aware that the Surrey Police have earlier today arrested Celsius Maysmith's global COO, Chuck Jelleners, in connection with the sudden death of Jelleners' wife?"

"Yes, I was, Udo. Celsius advised me that obviously Jelleners has been suspended from his duties, pending the police enquiry, and in the interim, Jelleners's chief lieutenant, Richard de L'Isle, has been promoted."

"Indeed he has."

"Any further news about Sigmund's cracked shells?"

"There's been no contact from our list of potential suppliers, one of which who may recall is coincidentally the same Mr. de L'Isle, and who incidentally was present yesterday for Sunday lunch in Jelleners's house, the day his bosses' wife was killed."

"Mr. de L'Isle seems to be popping up rather too often. But *he* hasn't been arrested?"

"No he hasn't, but if Jelleners is formally charged, then Mr. de L'Isle would likely be called as a witness at a future trial. And, my sources at Interpol mentioned that Mr. de L'Isle is also 'a person of interest' to the Surrey Police."

"Meaning that Mr. de L'Isle could *also* be involved in his bosses' wife's murder?"

"Perhaps, but far too early to say, sir."

"Udo, if you conclude that our cracked eggs' supplier *is* Mr. de L'Isle, let's hold fire and see first how this murder enquiry pans out. We may not have to take any action ourselves, if you get my meaning."

"Indeed so. Understood. The law may well for once be on our side and protect our bank's systems."

CHAPTER 43
VCb's LONDON OFFICES

The next day, Kofi turned up unannounced outside Richard's office. Sam knocked on his door.

"Yes, come in."

"Richard, sorry to interrupt, but DCI Ghazini is here to see you—if you have a minute?"

"What, again?" Richard sighed.

"Yes, 'fraid so."

"OK. Show him in." Richard glanced at his watch: it was 10:55. "I can give him five minutes before my next meeting, I guess."

Kofi was ushered into Richard's office.

"Inspector, I am surprised to see you again, *so soon*. You interviewed me at length yesterday, and later that evening I provided you with a detailed statement," said Richard, shaking his head in annoyance, adding, "I've so much work to do."

"It shouldn't take long, Mr. de L'Isle."

"Well, OK, but make it quick as I due to leave for my next appointment, in less than five minutes."

"That's *most* generous, but all I need," said Kofi sarcastically. "Hmm, so here's the thing, Mr. de L'Isle—it's English literature," Kofi continued, taking a seat on the couch and crossing his legs, revealing today's sock combination, one orange, and one yellow.

Richard stared at Kofi's socks thinking them literally rather odd. Perhaps he's colour blind? He wondered.

"Well, what is?" enquired Richard, intrigued.

"We have read many e-mails left in Mr. Jelleners's briefcase and allegedly written by him, incriminating himself in so many ways, but one of which stood out."

"What on earth are you going on about, Inspector?"

"The words he wrote were, 'will no one rid me of my troublesome wife?'"

"Well, that's just a figure of speech, isn't it? Unless of course he really meant it, and then I could understand how that might look a tad damning. I knew that he and his wife were having marital problems, as I mentioned before," Richard replied quickly and tried to not appear to be blaming Chuck outright.

"I agree it's pretty damning," said Kofi.

"Good."

"But not for the reasons you may think, Mr. de L'Isle."

Richard looked confused.

Kofi tempted Richard into showing his superior knowledge. "And which phrase is that sentence closely aligned to—would you know?"

"I'm not sure what relevance that has, but it's a very common phrase most educated people should know about, and refers to King Henry II in around 1170, getting fed up with his archbishop of Canterbury, Thomas à Becket, and saying, 'Will no one rid me of this troublesome priest?'"

"Precisely it is, and as an English literature honors graduate, of course you will know of it, as did DI Gilmore and I—although not in as much detail as you have just explained, *obviously*."

"So what, Inspector? I still don't see the relevance of the point you are making," said Richard.

"When interviewing Mr. Jelleners earlier this morning, in a lighter moment, DI Gilmore asked him if he ever went to any literary plays, like Shakespeare. He said he didn't, preferring action films. She then asked him to name one king of England or one archbishop of Canterbury before the present century. He couldn't. She even tried to help him by giving him five names, one of which was Becket, and asked him to pick out the archbishop. After he got it wrong three times, do you know what he said?"

"How could I, Inspector?" queried Richard.

"Mr. Jelleners sighed and said, 'Look, I don't have a clue about British priests or kings, or what relevance it is to finding my wife's killer, but I wish I had Richard here to help me answer your questions—after all, he's the bloody English literature major, not me!'"

Richard said nothing. He hadn't rehearsed this question. What a clever policeman you are, he thought.

"Hmm, it raises some doubt about whether Mr. Jelleners, or someone smarter than him, and more au fait with literature, wrote that e-mail, wouldn't you agree, Mr. de L'Isle?"

"Not necessarily. Perhaps Chuck heard that phrase being used and simply repeated it, Inspector?" Richard smiled at his own clever quick response.

"Perhaps, indeed. That's all for now. I will see my own way out. Good day to you, sir."

Kofi walked to the door, smiling and humming to himself the opening scene of *Don Giovanni*, where Leporello, Don Giovanni's long-suffering servant, sings in his deep bass voice, "Notte e giorno faticar" *Night and day I slave away.*

CHAPTER 44
VCb's LONDON OFFICES

Later that week, Kofi paid Richard yet another visit.

"Mr. de L'Isle, thank you for seeing me again. It won't take a minute, just like last time."

"It's my pleasure, Inspector. I know you are only doing your job and need to be thorough." Richard knew he should appear willing to help, and had regretted his rather terse behaviour the last time the inspector had called on him.

"Thank you for being so understanding, especially given you have a demanding role covering for Mr. Jelleners."

"So, how can I help you this time?"

"Hmm. Today's discussion is about wine."

"As usual, I am intrigued to learn about how this new topic is of any relevance to the death of Mrs. Jelleners."

"You mentioned that Mr. Jelleners was so pleased with the PowerPoint presentation you showed him that he generously gave you a case of wine."

"That's correct."

"And in your statement, you said that you went to his cellar alone and picked out the wine."

"Indeed I did."

"Why didn't he join you to select the wine himself?"

Richard was cautious. He hadn't rehearsed this question either. In reality, of course, Chuck at the time was sound asleep in his library, but in Richard's statement and answers, he reported that Chuck showed Richard out of the house at around that time, 6:00 p.m.

"He seemed very tired at the time and simply told me to go into the cellar and select anything I liked."

"Do you recall what wine that was?"

"Yes, it was an Italian wine, Brunello di Montalcino, 2015, if I recall."

"And you are a connoisseur of wine, I believe?"

"No, I'm not, but I appreciate a good wine."

"When we questioned Mr. Jelleners, he didn't recall what case of wine you took."

"I didn't 'take it,' I was given it, Inspector."

"Hmm. Either way, it's odd he didn't know. Surely he would have asked you which wine you had chosen—if nothing else so that he could update his meticulous stock records?"

"Inspector, I can't answer for Chuck's actions, but as I mentioned, he was getting very tired from jet lag and too much to drink."

"But not so tired, he couldn't get up and see you out, though?"
"Correct."
Kofi smiled and shook Richard's hand.
"That's all for now, Mr. de L'Isle. I know where to find you if I have any more questions."
Kofi turned and walked to the door, humming quietly to himself from his usual opera, this time from the "Champagne Aria": "Fin ch'han dal vino calda la testa". *Till they are tipsy.*

He then stopped before the door and, turning around, looked down at Richard's shoes.
"Hmm. I see like me, you only appear to wear smart, highly polished, black lace-up shoes at work, Mr. de L'Isle."
"Yes, that's correct."
"And at the weekend, you stated you only wear the same style, but brown lace-up shoes, never slip-ons. Correct?"
Richard was on his guard again. "Yes, I believe so. Why?"
"Hmm. Interesting."
Richard, you are still a person of considerable interest, Kofi thought.

***

Ascot Police Station

Later that afternoon, Kofi was paid a visit by a Miss Mia Falconer, the ex-wife of a successful hedge fund manager and younger sister of Rebecca. She had arrived in London that morning, having flown in from New York where she was based. They had an hour-long discussion and were wrapping up the meeting.

"Miss Falconer, this has been extremely helpful. It confirms much of my understanding about your sister's difficult relationship with her husband and some of my suspicions about her lover, Richard. But please keep our conversation confidential. We will keep you posted as this case unfolds. And again, my sincere condolences about your loss."

CHAPTER 45
BLACKDOWN CLOSE

Two months later

The policeman arrived unannounced at 11:00 a.m. and rang the doorbell. The lady inside opened the door, recognized him but didn't look pleased by his presence.

"Hmm. Mrs. de L'Isle, may I have a quick word?"

Jennifer held up her arms in dismay. "Chief Inspector, what is it *now*? You have asked me so many questions about the Goldschmidt case, I simply don't know what more I can tell you!" She sighed loudly and held the door half open.

"That's not why I am here," said Kofi, shaking his head and smiling warmly at her.

"It isn't? Then what on earth do you want *this* time?" she said tersely.

"It is the death of Mrs. Rebecca Jelleners, the wife of your husband's boss. There are just a few questions I would like to ask you to clear up a couple of matters. Is it OK if I come in just for a quick chat? I shouldn't take up too much of your time." Kofi moved forward towards the door.

His deep voice had the power of instructing her to do what he had requested and making her fearful of not complying. "Er, well, yes, come in, but please make it quick. I have so much to do today—I have to be at the school by lunchtime for a parents' meeting, you see."

"That's fine, it won't take long. Thank you."

Kofi entered the hallway, and Jennifer guided him into the kitchen. She showed him a seat but didn't offer him a cup of tea or coffee.

"So, Chief Inspector, what can I tell you? I hardly know Mr. Jelleners and barely knew his wife, having only met them probably two or three times—at social events, the last one of which was in their house for dinner with some of their other friends. I had assumed that Mr. Jelleners was the only suspect because I understand that he alone has been charged. His trial is set for a few months' time, isn't it? So, I am not sure how I can really help with your enquiries."

"Yes, he has been charged with his wife's murder, and the trial is set for early September." He then waited, deliberately.

Jennifer broke the silence. "So, why on earth would you like to talk with me then?"

"Some things still don't quite stack up in my mind, and I wondered if you can help me order them into a better perspective."

"But I have no idea why *I* can help you, Chief Inspector."

"Can you go over the day your husband went for lunch at their house that Sunday in early April?"

"Inspector, I came to the station the very next week and made a detailed statement, as has Richard, separately. You have been to my house once after that, so I am not sure what else there is to say. Nothing has changed in what I said or what I can recall."

"Just once more, please. Often, we find it's the smallest of details, when one has had time to digest matters, that reveal themselves and help us put the pieces of the jigsaw together. As I have said before, you are not under suspicion in any way. But your further insight into Mr. and Mrs. Jelleners, and perhaps your husband, may help us tie up some loose ends, as it were," suggested Kofi, trying to put her at ease.

"Well, I don't know where to start to help you…Er…"

"Hmm. Well, perhaps start with the day before, the Saturday, which I understand was your husband's birthday. Incidentally, it was my birthday that day also. How uncanny! How was he that day?"

"Oh, really? Yes, a coincidence. Well, he liked the presents we got him, and we all enjoyed a walk through Blackdown in the afternoon. And in the evening, we had a nice early dinner together as a family in a local restaurant. He seemed his usual self…well, no, to be honest perhaps he seemed more preoccupied with work than usual—he was on his iPhone quite often."

"How do you know he was preoccupied with work, precisely?"

"As I mentioned, he was on his iPhone, Chief Inspector," said Jennifer, thinking he must have misheard her comment.

"Could he have been on his iPhone for non-work-related matters—for example, e-mailing or texting or twittering friends, or going on Facebook?"

"I doubt it, he hates Twitter and is one of the few folk who don't use Facebook. No, he receives so many e-mails a day, I am sure it was business e-mails that took up his time, as they always do, Inspector," she said, sighing, and then added proudly, "My husband is a very senior person and has a very responsible role at the bank."

"I have no doubt he is, Mrs. de L'Isle, but you presumably can't be absolutely sure he is always e-mailing work colleagues unless you are monitoring all his e-mails?"

"Well, that's true, but why on earth should I be monitoring his boring work-related e-mails, for heaven's sake, and why indeed does it matter who he is e-mailing?"

Kofi shook his head, saying, "As you rightly say, Mrs. de L'Isle, why indeed?" He let that first thought sink in before proceeding. "But let's turn to the next day, the Sunday, the morning your husband left for their house. What—was his mood? How was he feeling then?"

"Well, gosh, I can't remember really, it seems a long time ago now. He seemed to be himself, as far as I could tell. He is a workaholic, as I am sure you know, and always wants to do a good job in the eyes of his boss and other senior folk. He seemed to get good reviews and enjoy his role. He was working on some project for Mr. Jelleners and was keen for him to see the fruits of his hard endeavors, if I recall. So, perhaps he was anxious it would go well, but confident that he had done a good job. Does that help?"

"Yes, it does. So he was, as far as you could tell that weekend, his normal 'in work mode' self, slightly anxious about the project but perhaps determined to enjoy their hospitality over lunch?"

"I think that summarizes it perfectly, Chief Inspector," said Jennifer, still not understanding where this was all going but hoping that if she agreed with whatever he said, he would quickly go away and let her get on with her chores.

"And his mood, when he called you to say he was on his way back home?"

"He only called for less than a minute, saying when he would be back, but I just remember him sounding quite his usual self and joking about how the Jelleners had argued—but he was pleased that the presentation had gone well, so much so that he had been given some nice wine from them."

Kofi made a few notes on his tablet and continued. "And when he arrived home, did he appear any different in his mood?"

"Nope, not at all. He seemed relaxed, just sitting at the kitchen table where you are sitting now and where he always sits, watching TV with us all. He read a bedtime story to our youngest, and helped our eldest do some homework, I think. Then as usual, he was monitoring and responding to the plethora of e-mails he gets each day on his iPhone."

"Hmm. So he didn't seem concerned in any way, for example about Mrs. Jelleners?"

"No. Why should he have been?" asked Jennifer, thinking what an odd question.

"Well, your husband mentioned to us that the Jelleners that afternoon had been arguing quite strongly, and it was embarrassing your husband, and later that day Mrs. Jelleners is murdered allegedly by your, er sorry, by her husband," said Kofi, trying not to smile at his deliberate misspeak, but which unfortunately Jennifer didn't seem to notice.

"Inspector, Richard that evening also mentioned to me about their arguing, but he had said that to me before. So I got the impression that the Jelleners often argued, and hence I thought nothing of it, to be quite honest."

"Oh, I see. Well, then, as you say, your husband shouldn't have been concerned for Mrs. Jelleners's health at all."

"And especially also because he didn't really know her, Inspector. I got the impression that he, like me, had only met her a few times, and each one with her husband in tow. I had only met her once or maybe twice, at dinner, and she was a quite charming hostess."

"Hmm. On that one occasion that you met her, did she and her husband argue?"

"Yes, they did, a little, but it seemed more mildly amusing to me than irritating, to be honest."

"And going back to the fateful Sunday lunch that Richard attended. Later that evening, your husband was himself when you went to bed to retire for the evening?"

Jennifer's mouth opened wide. "My, what a bloody nerve you have asking such an impertinent question! I am not sure what ruddy relevance that is to the court case of my husband's murderous boss!"

"Forgive me. You misunderstood my question completely, and I certainly didn't mean to pry or ask any insensitive questions. It is often the case that one shows one's feelings—especially anxiety—either last thing at night or first thing in the morning after a restless sleep. So, all I am trying to establish was whether or not everything to you seemed normal about your husband's demeanor. Was he, for example, easily getting off to sleep and then sleeping as soundly as he usually did? He was, after all, the last of two people to see Mrs. Jelleners alive, and any additional information you know or that he may have told you could help us piece together why Mrs. Jelleners was murdered."

"Chief Inspector, this is getting tiring, and I don't know what relevance is my husband's frame of mind, or demeanor. The next day when Richard got a call from his boss in the morning saying that his wife was dead was the first time we realized that perhaps the arguing between the Jelleners was more serious, and obviously they had had some very personal problems between them."

"Hmm, did your husband seem surprised by Mrs. Jelleners's death?"

"Yes, he did. We both did. When he got home that evening, he said to me that he hadn't realized his boss was capable of murder and how much he must have hated his wife."

"He said that to you?"

"Yes, I just said that he did. Inspector, we will be here a very long time if you ask me to confirm everything I say to you, won't we?" Jennifer said, raising her voice and adding, "Perhaps it's time for you to leave, Inspector."

"Mrs. de L'Isle, yes, indeed, I have taken up too much of your time already, but this has been helpful. I don't think we will need to bother you again. We may have to ask your husband a few more questions, because of course he will be a witness at the Jelleners trial."

Jennifer's calm voice returned. Confused, she pursed her lips and shrugged her shoulders and then said, "Not sure what help I have been, Chief Inspector. All I have confirmed is that my husband seemed to be in the same work mode all weekend before this unfortunate incident and afterwards."

"Well, as I say, this *was* useful. Let me also just say that in my line of work, as you will appreciate, one sees a very different side of humanity. I am sure, Mrs. de L'Isle, that you are the very model of a supportive wife to your husband, and an adoring, caring, devoted mother of your children. But during my career, I have seen reprehensible acts carried out by despicable people."

"Yes, Chief Inspector, I am sure you have, and it's not a job I would relish," Jennifer said and started walking towards her front door, hoping the policeman would quickly follow.

"Oddly, I have also at other times seen atrocious acts by folk who on the outside appeared quite ordinary."

"I can well understand the difficulty of your job, Chief Inspector," said Jennifer, not really sure what the detective was driving at. She turned and looked at her watch, hoping that the inspector would see this and hurry along the proceedings.

"You may not be fully aware, but Mrs. Jelleners died a most horrifying death that was not quick at all."

"Yes, I understand that she was strangled, Chief Inspector. Most dreadful."

"She was indeed, but that wasn't what killed her. She was first poisoned, by use of the deadliest of poisons, a few grains from the liver of the puffer fish, we believe. It caused her body to become paralyzed, and it would have taken her over three or four hours to die, as each organ, one by one, slowly gave in."

"On my God, I had no idea! That's simply awful for her, and her family."

"Yes, it was—excruciatingly painful: she would have felt as if she was drowning, struggling for breath," said Kofi, shaking his head.

"So, what was the motive, do you think, Chief Inspector, for Mr. Jelleners to kill his wife in what you are saying was a premeditated act of poisoning? They simply didn't get along, and he wanted to be rid of her?"

"Spouses have killed for far less, Mrs. de L'Isle, as you may have read. You probably aren't aware that Mr. Jelleners was having an affair."

"Given what I have heard about him, I am not surprised. But isn't that more a motive for her to kill him, rather than the other way around?"

"Hmm, not necessarily. Husbands have killed their wives so that they can be free to live with their mistresses. Happens all the time. But equally, if his wife had learned of his affair, they may have had an argument with matters turning ugly, or…"

"Or what, Chief Inspector?" said Jennifer, suddenly deciding that she would at least like to know more about what had happened, despite being in a rush.

"Unless she was also having an affair, and the husband found out, and

The Feather of Truth   Ian Campbell-Laing

in a fit of rage he poisoned and then strangled her for good measure? Anyway, as I have said, I have taken up too much of your time already. I will see myself out. Good day, Mrs. de L'Isle," said Kofi, nearing the front door, which Jennifer had now opened for him.

"Out of interest, Chief Inspector, how do you know that Mr. and Mrs. Jelleners were both having affairs?"

Kofi smiled. Finally she was taking the bait! "Oh, that's easy. We talked to Mrs. Jelleners's best friend, Dawn Peabody, who confided in us that she once spotted Mr. Jelleners at his Wentworth Golf Club on the evening he had told his wife he was seeing an important client from Scotland—whereas he was in fact seeing a very attractive woman twenty years his junior. Miss Peabody also informed us that Mrs. Jelleners told her that she was having an affair with a very handsome man about the same age as her."

"Oh, really?"

The inspector was about to leave, hoping he had said enough to start raising questions in her mind, when he spotted on the antique side table in the hallway a book entitled *Understanding Your Ancestry*.

"Mrs. de L'Isle, I see you are into ancestry. It's fascinating uncovering the past, isn't it?"

"Oh, er, yes, Inspector, it is. I did some research on my side of the family last year and made a start on Richard's. But there never seems the time," she said, looking at her watch again and thinking that this policeman, whilst being very intelligent and quick-witted, certainly was slow to take a hint.

"Indeed. I did my own family's a few years ago and discovered something very interesting but rather perplexing." Kofi smiled.

"Oh yes?" said Jennifer, trying to not sound too bored or in a rush, out of respect to Kofi, but wishing she had booted him out earlier. Then, suddenly she started to think, rather oddly—given how much he had been irritating her—that the detective was rather handsome, and his voice deep somewhat reassuring. She had to stop herself looking at him in that manner and remind herself how annoyed she had been over his incessant questions when they last met and during this twenty-minute visit today.

"I uncovered that my distant ancestors were thieves and murderers, Mrs. de L'Isle—not exactly a desirable quality in a policeman who is meant to be catching such lawless citizens!" Kofi proclaimed and smiled, showing his large, brilliant-white, neatly aligned teeth against the dark background of his Nigerian face. She glimpsed at his pink tongue, which seemed rather large for his mouth. She feared him but was drawn towards him.

"Oh my God, really? But then again, I am sure we all have some ancestors with a chequered past, Inspector. I know that I have," said Jennifer, feeling rather foolish and rude to be still holding open the door, when they hadn't finished their conversation.

"No, mine are quite unusual. We Ghazini's have what has recently been identified as the so-called 'warrior gene,' which, coupled with adverse environmental upbringing conditions, apparently predisposes us to commit violent acts when provoked."

She felt compelled to keep him in her house and learn more about him. The chores can wait, she thought. She was rather enjoying his company suddenly; she rarely had any intellectually stimulating conversation as a mum.

"Inspector, how does this warrior gene work, exactly?" She closed the door and strained her neck to look up at his face. He stooped down, making it easier for her.

He clasped his hands together and said, "Well, it's quite complicated, but in essence, within the brain there are various enzymes that control our whole being through releasing chemicals—called neurotransmitters—to the separate parts of the brain that regulate our mood, our coordination, our memory, our behavior, our desires, and so on. There are four basic neurotransmitters in the brain, and they tend to be either inhibitors"—he then opened up the palm on his left hand—"which calm down the brain, or excitors"—he gestured the same with his right hand—"that stimulate it. They work together to create a balance and harmony within the brain. You don't want to be too calm and laid back, nor too aggressive and on edge."

Kofi paused and saw that Jennifer was listening attentively, with her eyes widening.

"Goldilocks, Chief Inspector," said Jennifer.

"Sorry?"

"You want your porridge neither too hot or too cold, but just right!"

"Hmm. Precisely!" said Kofi, thinking the analogy rather good. He continued gesticulating with his large hands. "So take serotonin, which controls one's mood and makes one feel calm and relaxed. Some folk have a defective gene that causes too little serotonin to be released, and they end up feeling irritable, anxious, can't sleep, and are often depressed. They then take, say, Prozac, which causes more serotonin to be released, correcting their imbalance by making them feel calmer."

"Fascinating, so how about the warrior gene that you inherited. How does that work?"

"Well, I was getting to that!" said Kofi, thinking she was a little impatient. "One of the excitors in the brain is dopamine, which controls our ability to focus and remember information, coordinates our actions, and determines how aggressive we are. In most folk, there is a gene that controls the release of dopamine. In patients with too little dopamine, they lack coordination and often shake uncontrollably. They take a drug like L-dopa that increases the amount of dopamine in the brain and tries to ameliorate their symptoms."

"But, Chief Inspector, the warrior gene—I am dying to learn about that. You—can't keep a lady waiting this long!"

He ignored her and wouldn't be rushed. "Those with the so-called warrior gene have too low levels of the enzyme MAOA, whose function is to break down and reduce levels of serotonin and dopamine in the brain, resulting in excessive levels of these chemicals in their brains and causing these folk to be potentially aggressive, and under certain circumstances, violent."

"Aha. So for these people, it not their fault that they are aggressive; it's just the way they were born, because they inherited this trait from their ancestors?"

"*Precisely*, Mrs. de L'Isle."

"Fascinating, Chief Inspector. I have always wondered about how much the human race is driven by instinct, by our surroundings, and by peer pressure. The age-old nature vs. nurture debate, if you will."

"Indeed. Our childhood upbringing and our current environment influence us all. Interestingly though, 90 percent of violent crimes are committed by men—as opposed to by women—and of these men, 90 percent of the time the man knows their victim."

"And some of these male murderers presumably have this warrior gene?"

"Yes—some do, some don't. But for those that have this gene, typically for them to be violent, they tend to also have had a bad upbringing—for example experiencing poverty, witnessing or being a victim of aggressive behavior by their parents towards them, and so on. And even then, they may not commit murder. It's generally only when something upsets them, and they snap and commit an act they ordinarily wouldn't have considered. So, a confluence of the forces of nature and nurture, if you will, and an interaction of these three factors: the warrior gene, a poor upbringing, and feeling trapped."

"But you don't need to have the gene to commit a violent crime?" asked Jennifer.

"No, you don't. All psychologists are saying is that, for example, a young black boy brought up in a harsh environment is more likely, on the basis of past probabilities, to commit a crime—than, say, a rich white kid brought up in a nurturing and well-educated environment."

"But of course the black kid, like the rapper Jay-Z, lived crime free and the white one, like Ted Bundy, ended up being violent, Chief Inspector."

"Correct." Kofi was amazed that she had even heard of the rapper.

"But I think you are also saying that any ordinary person, whether or not they have the warrior gene—like the white kid in your example—could, in certain circumstances where they perhaps feel trapped, commit a violent act."

"Yes, Mrs. de L'Isle, that is *exactly* what I am saying." He gave a large sigh, thinking he had finally got through to her. "My ardent belief, backed up with evidence from my nearly fifteen years in the police force, is that *any* ordinary person who hasn't inherited the warrior gene, hadn't had a harsh upbringing, but who simply felt trapped, with no way out, can still commit a violent crime. Look at the serial killers Jeremy Bamber, Ted Bundy as you mentioned, and Jeffrey Dahmer and so many others. Their brains weren't wired in a weird way, and they had enjoyed a loving and nurturing upbringing."

"That's rather troubling, that we are *all* capable of murder." Jennifer shivered at the implications, but not believing she herself was remotely ever capable of murder.

"But most of us have a moral compass and don't feel the need to cross the Rubicon of despair and commit a crime. Perhaps the social issue is more how can friends or families, or the police, stop someone crossing the moral divide before it's too late. Like in the film *Minority Report*, starring Tom Cruise, where the 'precogs' police can arrest you before you commit a violent crime, on the basis that either you have a high propensity to commit a crime, or they catch you thinking about it."

"Yes, I saw it. Interesting. Does Mr. Jelleners have this warrior gene, out of interest?"

"We checked. He doesn't."

"But you have the gene and are not a murderer…well, I hope that you are not! At the very least, I must be careful not to annoy you in case you snap!" Jennifer laughed, rather too nervously.

"No, I am not, of course. Yes, I have the gene, and I did, however, have a very tough upbringing. My father was a drunk, and when he went bankrupt, he tried to commit suicide, which failed, and he was left in a coma. He eventually died. My mother was also uneducated, and her menial jobs weren't enough to keep me, so I was put in the care of the social services. And at school I was bullied for being black."

"That's dreadful." She paused, then asked, "Inspector, I hope you don't mind me asking, but the scar down most of the right-hand side of your face—is that a tribal scar from an initiation ceremony?"

"Hmm. Ah, yes, that. It's rather prominent still, isn't it? No. Tribal scars tend to be symmetrical about one's face. As you can see, this is only down one side." His lifted the palm of his left hand to the scar, and his long, slender fingers lightly brushed down the track of the three-inch scar from the top to the bottom in a caressing motion. Jennifer watched, and a tingle went down her spine.

"This scar was done by a bully a long time ago when I was a teenager. I was trying to help a younger boy who was being beaten up and got this beauty mark for my troubles." Kofi didn't sound angry; he was more matter of fact.

"Oh, I am so sorry, Inspector. Did you manage to save the younger boy from being bullied?"

"He did escape but died later in hospital—all rather sad—affected me terribly at the time, and coincidentally I decided to become a policeman and try and fight crime from that day on. I remember shocking my teacher, when asked what did I want to become, by replying, 'I think I will turn to crime, Miss.' She quickly corrected me saying, 'Solve crime, young man, not turn to crime, I hope you meant!'"

"What a nice, innocent remark, and such a very admirable profession, Chief Inspector," said Jennifer, oddly now remembering his more senior title and feeling very comfortable in his presence. "Your wife and family must be very proud of you."

"How kind of you to say. But sadly my wife died a few years ago now." Jennifer noticed the detective look down at the ground, raise his right hand to his mouth, and shake his head. She felt the need to enquire further. "Do you mind me asking how she died?"

He smiled at her and coughed to clear his throat. "No, not at all. It's no secret and was in the local newspapers at the time. I secured the conviction of a murderer—coincidentally, one who had poisoned his mistress." He paused to see if this remark sunk in. Jennifer seemed enraptured with his story and appeared to have missed the deliberate connotations left by Kofi. Damn! he said to himself. "His defense lawyers were very good, and in fact interestingly used the warrior-gene tactic with success and obtained a manslaughter conviction instead of murder. Consequently he only got a ten-year sentence, instead of life—which is up to thirty years."

"I see. How annoying for you," was all Jennifer could think of saying.

"But clearly the convicted man thought otherwise. He protested his innocence throughout his time in prison. He was released in seven for good behavior. However, the very first week he was out, he burst into my cottage and deliberately shot point blank in the face, in front of me, my beautiful wife, my soul mate. She died in my arms. He's back in prison, but this time for life. This was over five years ago now, so ancient history, although I think of her every day." Kofi took out a handkerchief and dabbed his eyes.

"Oh my God, Mr. Ghazini…sorry, Chief Inspector, that's simply dreadful. I am so very sorry. Will you marry again, do you think?"

"Mrs. de L'Isle, what woman in their right mind would have me?" he said, smiling but narrowing his eyebrows in despair.

Jennifer looked at him, thinking he was quite a catch for any woman. He saw a lot of her own husband in the inspector—both were incredibly handsome, very intelligent, kind, softly spoken, but with a forceful nature needed for their jobs, especially when solving complex problems or crimes. He was probably in his midthirties like Richard, she thought. "I suppose the horrendous hours you work and the type of work, combined with a murderous ancestry, might put a woman off, Mr. Ghazini?" said Jennifer, smiling and instinctively fiddling with her hair.

"Oh, not at all! The type of work, the psychology of understanding the human mind, the power I have, and my colourful ancestors—seems perversely to attract women."

"So forgive me for being so personal, but why are you not dating or married then? You are a good-looking chap, very smart and kind. Giving something back to society. You seem a good catch to me," said Jennifer, immediately regretting that last sentence she blurted it out.

"Mrs. de L'Isle, that's so kind of you, and I know I have been somewhat painful to you with all my questions about the Goldschmidt case, and now this afternoon about the Rebecca Falconer Jelleners crime. But I have a dreadful secret, Mrs. de L'Isle, which once known, puts most people off from having anything to do with me." Kofi looked down at his shoes, and started shifting his weight from one foot to the other. *Should I carry on with my explanation—is it too personal? But I want her to trust me and open up to me*, he thought.

Jennifer's mouth was wide open. Kofi suddenly noticed her small pink tongue against her white teeth, surrounded by her full, red lips. He felt attracted towards her. Her beauty, charm, and intellect were wasted on the philandering Richard. He desperately wanted to tell her that he had high suspicions that her husband was the murderer, but ethically of course he should not.

Kofi drew in some air and then sighed. "Mrs. de L'Isle, who would want to be the soul mate of, and be associated with, a man who has HIV?"

***

Kofi left Mrs. de L'Isle's house humming an operatic tune as always, but hoping that his chat with her had done what he had expected it to do—raising questions in her mind, so that the seeds of doubt about the integrity of her husband could emerge and cause her to confront Richard.

A few weeks earlier, Kofi had begun to think that the cocky Richard was perhaps a tad too confident and might be playing games with the inspector. Over his fourteen-year career, he had often gone out on a limb by just following his gut feelings. And they had always led to a successful conviction. He knew that the odious Chuck was the obvious prime suspect, and of course in fact had been charged with murder. But when he went through again the documentary evidence against Chuck, and having recently learned that Richard was an IT geek, it was clear that Richard could have planted much of it,—if he had so wished. He could have set up Chuck for a fall; he certainly was enjoying the benefits of having Chuck's role.

Kofi wanted to keep the pressure on Richard, and perhaps his wife would start asking him some awkward questions. Kofi was waiting in case Richard might make a mistake or say a foolish remark that might trap him or incriminate him. "Just a feeling I have about him," he said out loud as he walked to his car. His last resort was to wait until the trial and, using Richard as a witness, have the prosecution's QC ask Richard some awkward questions.

Mr. de L'Isle may think he's out of the woods, but he is definitely not yet, in my view, thought Kofi.

He yawned loudly as he sat in his car, driving back to the office. He was so tired and anxious to get the trial out of the way and not postpone again his long-awaited sabbatical.

CHAPTER 46
BLACKDOWN CLOSE

Jennifer was feeling exhausted after yet another day of drudgery looking after her three boisterous offspring. But now that her boys were finally tucked up in bed, her best friend, Isabelle, had popped over for a chat over a nice glass of wine. She always loved this part of the day, when she could finally relax before Richard came home.

"The detective seemed to be on some sort of fishing expedition, Isabelle. He asked me about Richard's mood before and after he went to the Jelleners' for that Sunday lunch, and whether he was his usual self in the bedroom—can you believe that?"

"Sounds ruddy impertinent to me. Why on earth ask you something so personal?"

"No idea, but I just hope they don't ask Richard such questions in the trial when he is called as a witness. Richard is always very cool under pressure—one of the things I admire about him," said Jennifer as she took a sip of her wine, "but if he feels he or our family or a work colleague is being insulted, he can lose his temper very quickly. He's quite frightening then."

"Yes, but what's Richard's mood got to do with the fact his boss argued with and then strangled his wife in a rage?"

"Actually I forgot to tell you. He mentioned that Mrs. Jelleners was first poisoned by some deadly type of puffer fish, which paralyzed her organs in a slow, painful death. It sounded absolutely dreadful and nearly made me throw up."

"Oh my God, that's awful. That husband is a sick man, and I hope he goes to jail for the rest of his life."

Jennifer slapped her head with the palm of her right hand. "Duh! Isabelle, I am a complete clot. I remember Richard and I going around to the Jelleners' house for dinner a few months ago now. Swanky, ostentatious place of probably eight to ten thousand square feet, with two acres of manicured land. The wife was, I have to say, very charming, down to earth, and a great cook. He was a pompous Yank. But what I was about to say was that for dinner, I am sure we had puffer fish as a starter!"

"Oh, jeepers creepers, you could have all been poisoned by Richard's boss—a Wako-style mass murder at Wentworth!"

"Actually his boss did mention it was a 'deadly delicacy,' which was the precise phrase he used. I don't like sushi, so I just ate the salad that accompanied it, but Richard loved it. Said it was thrilling to eat something that was both delicious and deadly. Seemed odd to me."

The Feather of Truth   Ian Campbell-Laing

"So, that's where the idea of poisoning his wife came from, I guess. Interesting, Jens. Seems like an open-and-shut murder case to me, don't you think?"

"Absolutely, and apparently, according to Richard, Chuck had a history of abusing his wife, including slapping her around a few times. So I can't stop thinking what on earth Ghazini was doing asking me these damn silly questions about Richard."

"Well, what else did he ask you, apart from Richard's mood?"

"Let's see. Oh yes, I think the first thing was when I mentioned that Richard was behaving normally before and after that Sunday, e-mailing business colleagues as usual day and night. Ghazini asked how did I know he wasn't e-mailing or texting friends?"

"So bloody what, Jens! He was on his iPhone as usual doing whatever he does every day, so hardly breaking news. What an weird question." said Isabelle, looking confused.

"And another thing he mentioned was that Mr. Jelleners was having an affair."

"Well, that's no big fat surprise, is it?" Isabelle laughed. "An arrogant, powerful, rich guy like that—they attract all sorts of women!"

"But when I asked him how did he know that, he said Mr. Jelleners had been spotted with a younger woman at his golf club, on a night he said he was dining with a powerful male Scottish client. He also said Mrs. Jelleners was having an affair as well, with someone handsome, about her own age. Well, that's no surprise also, given she hated her husband and she's a very pretty American woman."

"This is odd, Jens. Let me think. I have never met this Ghazini chap, but do you think he's a smart guy?"

"Yes, most definitely, he chooses his words carefully, and you get the impression his brain is working at a fast pace, always keeping a few thoughts ahead of you."

"How old is he?"

"Well, I guess mid-thirties, similar to Richard. He is tall and slim, obviously takes care of himself, and dresses well. He would be quite a catch for any woman. But his very deep voice always made me feel nervous, even though he always seemed to be trying to put me at ease."

"And is he successful at what he does?"

"God, I don't know, Isabelle! How would I know that?"

"Come on, you slow coach. The police publish statistics now on all of their detectives. We can look it up. Here, let me do it." She tapped a Google request on her iPhone: "Surrey Police stats…" Isabelle looked up and said, "How do you spell his name?"

"Kofi Ghazini, G-H-A-Z-I-N-I."

"What kind of name is that? Kofi sounds African, and Ghazini Italian!"

"I think he mentioned he was of Nigerian descent—two generations ago his grandfather came to the UK, something like that."

"OK, let's see...here it comes: Ghazini, K...Detective Chief Inspector...Cases, 200...Convictions, 200 (100 percent). Ranked...My God, he's ranked number one in Surrey Police, and number two nationally! 'Youngest policeman to attain rank of DCI ever! Joined force after earning triple first honors degree in maths, physics, and psychology at Cambridge where he won the prestigious Campbell-Conscience Scholarship.' Jesus, the guy's a modern-day genius Sherlock ruddy Holmes! And wait...if I click on his name...yes, up comes a picture of him, so let's see...OK, so he's a very good-looking black guy, nice smile—very dashing, in fact! Immaculately dressed for a humble, underpaid policeman."

Isabelle showed the picture to Jennifer.

"Yes, that's him. But must have been taken a while ago. He looks older than that now. In fact, he appeared rather tired and couldn't stop yawning when he came to see me. Must be the stress of his job."

"Well, I'd still sleep with him and wake up his senses, no question, Jennifer," said Isabelle, deliberately licking her lips and raising her eyebrows.

Jennifer ignored her provocative friend. "So what, so he gets his man, and he's good looking, so good for him!"

Isabelle was intrigued. "My point is, Jennifer, that this bright, good-looking Sherlock comes into your house, asking you a load of odd questions that don't seem to be getting anywhere, nor helping the detective, especially given they have charged the husband with murder and the trial date has been set. So why did he come to see you? He came for a reason, no question. Let me think...Let me check one thing more from his profile..." Isabelle used fingers from both hands to tap in a few more commands. "Yes, that's it."

"What's it? Isabelle, what are you going on about, you silly cow?"

"He came for one of two reasons..."

"Which are what, for heaven's sake?" said Jennifer, who found her best friend infuriating at times.

"He either wants to warn you about something, or he fancies you," concluded a beaming Isabelle.

"What? That's insane! Why the hell would he fancy *me*? He has only met me twice, and then to interrogate me. The first time I was pretty rude to him. And he wouldn't be interested in a simple mother of three boys who is permanently exhausted."

"Well, you admitted he was handsome, and I also checked—he is not married. Apparently, his wife died in a shooting five years ago."

"Yes, he mentioned that, and it clearly upset him. She died in his arms, poor man. Anyway, I agree that he's quite a catch, and he has a certain sexual magnetism about him, but I am happily married, and he never once made a flirtatious comment to me."

"He did ask you whether or not Richard was his normal self in the evening at bedtime, didn't he?"

"Yes, but he apologized and said he was just trying to establish Richard's demeanor or something like that."

"What-ev-er," said an unconvinced Isabelle.

"But why should he warn me? And anyway, warn me of what?"

"Let me think this through, aloud…Let's take each of the odd comments in turn. One: 'How do you know Richard was e-mailing work colleagues and not friends'…He is perhaps implying that Richard was e-mailing friends or texting friends…perhaps personal matters?"

"What? He's e-mailing work, not texting some fancy woman, Isabelle. After all I know Richard."

"As Ghazini said to you, how do you know that?"

"I don't. It's just that I trust Richard, that's all."

"Two; the reference to having an affair, with Mr. Jelleners being caught seen with some old tart and not a client. Richard is out at client dinners all the time, isn't he?"

"Yes. Recently, three or four nights in the week. He normally dines at the RAC."

"And how do you know he is with a client each time, Jens?"

"Because he tells me he is and who he's with, and I trust him, for God's sake. You sound like you are interrogating me like that Ghazini."

"I am your best friend, and that's what we do. So, here, let's do this. Give me the name of one of Richard's clients then."

"OK, that's easy. Sir James Campbell, who he sees probably monthly."

"Duh! Who happens to be a *Scottish* client, like Mr. Jelleners's client was, correct?"

"He happens to be Scottish, yes, Isabelle, but that's a coincidence."

"Rather odd that the inspector said *Scottish* though?" Isabelle leant her head to one side and looked at Jennifer in disbelief at her naivety.

"What-ev-er."

"And when did he last dine with him at his club? Any idea, Jennifer?"

"Oh, that's easy." Jennifer got up and went to her wall calendar and looked it up. "See, I make a note of every day he's dining, where, and with whom. Just an old habit I got into in case I need to speak to Richard. So let's see, last time was, I think…Yes, Sir James on Thursday, third April, at the RAC: over two months ago now, and no one since, see—no affair!"

"Now, is Sir James the same *Scottish* billionaire who made his money in fashion and music management and now hosts a weekly satirical TV show?"

"The very same. Why? Where on earth is this leading us and Ghazini warning me about something?"

The Feather of Truth   Ian Campbell-Laing

Isabelle finger tapped in more instructions and placed her iPhone speaker near to her mouth. She spoke in a not very convincing Scottish accent. "Good evening, is that the RAC in Pall Mall?"

Jennifer shouted, "What the?"

Isabelle mouthed to her "Ssshh!" and continued, "It is? Good. I wonder if you can help me, I am the PA to Sir James Campbell who dined at your club on Thursday the third April as a guest of a Mr. Richard de L'Isle who is a member of your club. Sir James asked me to call you and enquire whether or not he left his wallet at the club: it's a burgundy-brown small leather wallet—it will have his credit cards in it, of course. He simply can't find it, and I am calling all the places he visited whilst he was in London there on business."

"Isabelle, you are dreadful," whispered Jennifer, smiling at the small wallet reference.

"Er, yes, of course I will hold, thanks." Isabelle turned to her friend and held her hand over the microphone, saying, "They're checking lost property now for you, Jens."

"Oh yes, hello again. No, it's OK, I don't mind waiting."

"Isabelle, what are you trying to prove?" asked Jennifer.

"Ssshh! Oh dear, no such wallet has been found or handed in. I wonder which restaurant it could have been, then. Maybe it was at one of two pubs in London I know he visits, perhaps Dirty Dicks or The Spread Eagle? Would you do me one last favor, just to double check, can you put me through to the restaurant please? Er, no, I don't recall which restaurant Sir James dined in that day, but probably your signature one, which is the…Yes, that's it, the Great Gallery. I remember him saying that's the one."

Isabelle waited. "Thanks. Yes, I will hold while you put me through…Great Gallery, yes, hello…That's right…Yes, looking for a mislaid wallet of Sir James…Yes, I am his PA for my sins…Yes, he is most demanding, as you can appreciate! Yes, that Thursday evening of the third of April, he was, I believe, dining with a Richard de L'Isle…Yes, just the two of them I understand…So you can confirm that Mr. de L'Isle was dining there that evening…A reservation for two at seven o'clock? Yes, that sounds correct…Did Sir James leave his wallet that evening by mistake, would you happen to know? Oh dear, you can't see any record of the wallet being seen or handed in? I have got the right date, haven't I? Sir James was dining there that evening wasn't he, or have I, like a silly Billy, got the restaurants mixed up. Would you know?…What? You can't tell me whom Mr. de L'Isle dined with? Why ever not?…But…" Isabelle ended the call. "They won't tell me any more. It's 'confidential information,'" she said.

"Well, that's that then, isn't it, Isabelle? He was dining at the RAC as he said, and with Sir James, presumably."

The Feather of Truth Ian Campbell-Laing

"Yes, dining at the RAC but not *necessarily* with Sir James," said Isabelle. "If Sir James had been there, they would have said so surely, Jens!"

"Oh, come on, Isabelle, you're barking up the wrong tree with my Richard. He's very trustworthy. I should know; I am married to him, after all."

"Look, I am not saying he is or he isn't, but just be careful. Remember you just told me the inspector had mentioned that Mrs. Jelleners was having an affair. Why didn't he just say with whom? Was he protecting you? I just don't want you to get hurt, ever—you work so hard as a great mum and wife, and always so tired and never thinking about yourself. Someone has to look after you, Jens."

"Thanks, Isabelle. It's appreciated," said Jennifer, who was now getting tired of this topic. "Look, if I ever have any suspicions about Richard, I will come to you for help, that's for sure, but I think it's unlikely."

Isabelle had the last word. "Just remember, Ghazini came to you for a purpose, and that clearly wasn't to extract information from you about the Goldschmidt or Jelleners cases. He mentioned two very cryptic things. One, that Mrs. Jelleners was having an affair with a handsome man who was a similar age to him, and two, Mr. Jelleners had lied to his wife about meeting a Scottish client one evening for dinner when he was instead seeing his mistress. How old was Mrs. Jelleners, any idea?"

"Oh, gosh. At the dinner we had at their house, Richard's boss mentioned that his wife was twenty-one years younger than him. And I think Richard said once that he was in his mid-fifties."

"That puts her age at say in the mid-thirties. How old is Richard?"

"He's thirty-five."

There was silence.

"Look, Jens. In my mind, the detective was speaking in a simple code to you. He came to warn you about Richard, who coincidentally is also a handsome man, and who allegedly saw his Scottish client—i.e., his similar-aged mistress, whomever she is—for dinner, three days before Mrs. Jelleners was murdered."

Jennifer stared at Isabelle, trying to resist believing her logic. A tear emerged from Jennifer's left eye.

CHAPTER 47
TEDDINGTON, SURREY

Ten weeks later

The Rebecca Falconer Jelleners murder case, which would go to trial shortly, was still causing Kofi misgivings.

Even though he had Richard trailed and used undercover officers to sit at nearby tables at restaurants when he went to dinner and at pubs he frequented, Richard seemed to be acting normally: no loose talk, and the topic of conversation seemed to be always about work. He also didn't appear to be having another affair. So maybe, Richard was the man he claimed to be who had made a bad mistake but was trying to be a better husband. Or, of course he was on high alert and just being more discreet.

The evidence against Richard of potentially writing Chuck's incriminating e-mail, "who will rid me of my troublesome wife," and the gift of far too expensive a case of wine were just circumstantial. More powerful was the evidence of the Jehovah's Witnesses whom he had tracked down. But even together, it was still not enough to convict Richard as the true murderer.

But something was telling him that he knew that Richard de L'Isle *could* have done it and most likely *did* commit the murder. Richard had the means, the opportunity, and the motive. Anyway, it wasn't up to him: Chuck had to be tried by a jury of his peers, as decreed by the Magna Carta since the year 1215.

Chuck had refused to take a plea bargain, and Kofi expected the case to proceed quickly, with one of two conclusions by the jury within a few weeks: either the conviction of Chuck for murder—which was the prosecution's presumption that the husband intended and planned to kill his wife—or involuntary manslaughter.

Kofi's only hope now was that under cross-examination, Richard as a witness could perjure himself, his secret affair would become public knowledge, and sufficient doubt would be left in the jurors' minds to warrant a mistrial, with a case then being brought against Richard.

However, Kofi was pragmatic and knew that with the direction of a good Queen's Counsel, the jury would, in all probability, believe it was the husband, Chuck, and not Richard. Chuck would get a fair trial, but he knew Chuck would not do himself any favors, and his conviction was therefore pretty much a foregone conclusion.

So be it, he thought. Life wasn't always fair, but the wheels of the law had been put in motion, and someone would have to pay for Rebecca's murder. After all, he consoled himself, that pompous oaf of a husband had

The Feather of Truth   Ian Campbell-Laing

in fact previously assaulted his wife—very seriously, according to the wife's doctor—and Chuck should be punished somehow. Whether or not that meant life in prison, who was he to judge? And anyway, some would think perhaps bad apples like Chuck shouldn't be wandering around society at all. But, in his fourteen years as a detective, this case was the first one in which he had doubts about the true identity of the murderer.

He knew that he shouldn't play God when life appeared unjust. He reminisced again about the Juma boy dying needlessly, and he, Kofi, having to live with the stigma of being both black and having HIV in a bigoted, judgmental world. It didn't matter that Kofi had been infected with HIV from the thug's blood on the knife that had killed Juma, whilst Kofi had simply been trying to save the little boy. The world was unjust, and you just had to cope with it, he thought.

He hummed an operatic tune to himself: it always calmed him.

And then there was the Goldschmidt case, which was the second case that still bothered him. He had quickly discounted Richard's wife of having any involvement. Jennifer had simply discovered the body while walking her dog. She had raised his suspicions initially with her nervous and inconsistent answers. Then Richard called the police saying they were harassing his wife, and to leave her alone or he would make a complaint.

Richard's wife had clearly simply been nervous in the presence of the police. Kofi recognized that. It was quite understandable.

He thought how different Jennifer was compared to her husband. She seemed nervous in the detective's presence, yet Richard appeared completely at ease and even toyed with the police regarding Rebecca's murder.

Kofi considered how different Richard and he were. Doing good for society drove him, yet Richard, whilst openly appearing to be a good, hardworking, and loving family man, was in practice living an entitled, fraudulent existence. He had cheated on his wife and was clearly a control freak, driven by money and his own self-importance. They did, however, appear to share one past event in common, which Kofi had recently discovered from reading Richard's medical notes and which, if true, meant that Richard was a complete and utter coward as well.

CHAPTER 48
THE RAC

Richard felt invincible and rather smug from his promotion to Chuck's role and the threefold salary increase that came with it. Of course, Richard knew from his spying inside V-Trax that this was still only a fraction of what Chuck had been paid, but he was happy to bide his time. With Chuck's trial next week, and near certain conviction, Richard wouldn't anymore have to worry about whether or not he had gotten away with a flawless murder.

Richard also hadn't been contacted by Udo regarding hacking into V-Trax, so he assumed that he must have left no trace back to himself, but instead had skillfully exposed Chuck as the hacker. So Richard had gone back into the system once more and uncovered even more amazing confidential information, including some on Celsius. He would use that information when he felt the time was right. He was concentrating presently on keeping his head down, doing a good job, and not hacking off the demanding Celsius. He didn't want Celsius to regret promoting him.

With his increased wealth, Richard decided to upgrade his cherished Aston Martin for what he thought was the most desirable car in the world. No, not the Lamborghini Aventador, nor the impractical remake of the Ferrari Enzo, nor the beautiful Ferrari 668 Italia, but the newest McLaren, the MPX-20C. Richard enjoyed watching passersby stare with envy at his expensive toy.

The previous week, Richard had dinner with the RAC's chairman of the committee, Lord Canaan of Barnstable. Lord Canaan, who was also a client of VCb, had wanted to personally thank Richard for his generous gifts of computers for the library and tireless fundraising efforts for the club, both at Pall Mall and at their sister club in Surrey, Woodcote Park.

They sat in two high-backed leather chairs in a quiet corner of the Club Room, sipping their glasses of medium-priced red wine and devouring some delightful canapés. After discussing the recent Asian-caused turmoil in the financial markets, the chairman talked about future fund-raising plans to meet the huge costs of renovating part of the club. On the spur of the moment, enjoying his increased wealth and the attention given to him from his promotion, and being entertained by a lord, Richard announced that he would like to make a significant donation to the RAC.

"Oh, that would be most welcome," said his lordship, wondering how significant exactly.

"One hundred thousand pounds."

Lord Canaan took a quick intake of air and raised his eyebrows—the club's maintenance costs were astronomical, and funds were always rather tight. He exhaled and reached over to shake Richard's hand and warmly patted the top of it with his left hand. "That's extremely generous. Thank you, Richard." He then added, "For what purpose, if any, would you like to earmark the funds?"

Richard thought for a moment.

"To upgrade the two suites, Kent and Burma. The last time I stayed in the Kent, I noticed it looked a little tired, to be quite frank."

"No, you are quite right, and it's uncanny, because they were in our three-year strategic plan, but we didn't have the funds to fully upgrade them. Now it appears that we might. But I would have to check with the board to confirm that there aren't more pressing needs. However, I shall simply say that is the very reasonable condition that is specifically attached to the donation. That should do it."

As the lord reached for his half-empty glass, he was deep in thought. He knew of Richard's promotion at the bank and presumably much higher salary. He had an idea. "Richard, what may be of more interest to you is that within that plan, for which we have some funds, the committee wanted to create a third suite, by combining three existing double rooms, to become our largest and most luxurious suite."

Richard leaned forward in his seat. "Oh, yes, your lordship?"

The chairman wanted Richard to believe that he was part of the process of enhancing the club—despite not being on any of the subcommittees—in order to secure immediately his donation. "And interestingly, we are at the stage of researching a suitable name for this premier suite, which must be in keeping with the traditions and heritage of the club. Perhaps you may have some thoughts of a name, or could come back to me with something appropriate—after all, last year you researched our club's history and wrote an excellent book about the RAC."

Richard synthesized the deluge of information flooding his brain. "Yes, I would like to help in that process. Well, sir, let's see. We have of course the two existing suites named after Prince Michael of Kent as our royal president, and Lord Mountbatten of Burma. So let's step back for a minute. The club is the premier club in London, with facilities that rival five-star hotels. But we should always be thinking ahead of our competitors, and we have in many respects: after all, we were one of the first to welcome women as members, and yet we have also stayed firmly attached to our traditions and not let our standards slip, for example by ensuring a strict and appropriate dress code."

Richard was rambling slightly, trying to buy his tired brain precious time to come up with something clever.

Lord Canaan simply sat back in his chair, watching Richard carefully. "Indeed."

Then Richard's neurons connected - he had solved it. Perfect.

"Sir, I do need to give this more thought, but perhaps something to consider is this. Sir Winston Churchill was a member of the club, and in fact we are sitting on the site of the old War Office," said Richard, knowing the lord knew this, but he was playing with him. He now had a bigger plan for his own family.

"So, Churchill would be the name?" asked the chairman, raising his eyebrows in disappointment with Richard's apparent lack of imagination.

Richard shook his head. "No, not at all, your lordship. I think we need to think more holistically, by embracing the progressive nature of this traditional club and also incorporating the fairer gender."

The chairman was now intrigued. "Go on, Richard, a penny for them then."

"Sir, you may not be aware that Churchill was a secret fan of the former-beauty-queen-turned-first-female-spy in World War II, Christine Granville, whom he described as his favorite spy. And incidentally, her character was the basis of James Bond's lover, Vesper Lynd, in *Casino Royale*."

"No, I didn't know that. So, what had you in mind, Richard—to call the suite 'Vespa' to link in with our motoring heritage as well?"

"Actually I did think of that, but the Vespa motorbike is spelt with an 'a' at the end, whereas the character Vesper in the Ian Fleming film is with an 'er' at the end."

"But of course. Well spotted, Richard," the chairman conceded.

"So going back to the spy theme. Christine Granville sat on this very sofa where we are sitting, and where the British spies Philby and Maclean also anxiously reclined whilst plotting their escape to their handlers in Russia," explained Richard.

"So, perhaps 'The Granville Suite'?" asked the chairman, digesting the new information.

"Yes, sir. I think it has a certain merit, and should be a contender for the committee to consider: it neatly links in Churchill, a famous female spy, the site of the old War Office, and also, the name Granville, which I understand is rich in history going back to the Norman Conquest."

"Yes, worth considering, I agree. But, allow me very briefly to just access our strategic plan and see what funds were earmarked for the new suite, to see how much an impact your donation will have." He typed in some commands on his iPhone, and after a minute said, shaking his head, "Yes, I thought so."

The chairman paused. "I'm afraid, I think to assist in the decision of the name you propose, it might need higher funds." The chairman looked disappointed.

"Perhaps if my donation stretched to one hundred and fifty thousand pounds, would that secure the name, Mr. Chairman?"

The Feather of Truth   Ian Campbell-Laing

"That may do it. But I can't promise anything yet. All I will say is that it will have my personal support, and I will keep you posted, Richard."

"Excellent, sir. I leave that with you then, and thanks for an excellent evening and perfect wine." They both stood up and shook hands.

The chairman signaled to the nearest waitress, who immediately hurried over. "My dear, would you be so kind as to get Mr. de L'Isle a bottle of one of his favorite, high-end wines, and charge my personal account?"

Svetlana recognized the chairman and replied, "Certainly, sir. Right away." She turned to Richard. "Would that be a Chateau Margaux, 2018, Premier Grand Cru Classé?"

"Well remembered, Svetlana. It would."

Richard saw that some members had spotted him with the chairman, and he basked in the association with his lordship. "That's most generous and much appreciated, Lord Canaan."

"My pleasure, Richard, but knowing how busy you must be, might I trouble you for that cheque now, if it's not too inconvenient whilst you wait for your gift of wine?"

Richard thought that was rather cheeky, given all donations or bequests had to be accompanied by certain tax forms.

Richard wrote out and handed the cheque to the chairman.

"Good-bye, Richard, and thanks again."

Richard was chuffed at so small an amount—relatively to what he now earned—to secure his personal choice of name for the premier suite. And he hadn't had to mention, or rather threaten his lordship about, what he had read in the secret V-Trax file on the chairman's private life and shady business dealings.

As the chairman walked back to his awaiting limousine to take him to his Mayfair apartment, he also smiled. Over drinks and canapés, costing the club £250, he had initially secured a £100,000 donation—and by being cunning, and just for the price of a £500 bottle of wine that the club could write off as business entertaining for tax purposes, he had increased the gift by another fifty thousand. Not bad for ninety minutes' socializing, and through only having to use one of the two important facts he knew about Richard: during the conversation, he suspected Richard had an undisclosed conflict of interest in the suite name he had proposed, and that could push the donation price up a tad—the chairman had not accessed on his iPhone a moment earlier the strategic plan at all: he was aware that Richard's wife, Jennifer, had a rich ancestry, and on a hunch typed in "Jennifer Granville" on his Google search. Up it came:

> Jennifer Granville, met Richard de L'Isle at Oxford University, married, three children, lives in Haslemere Surrey… The Granville's could trace their history back to the Norman Conquest and were handsomely rewarded with land by the then king.

Secondly, he, like many staff at the club, was fully aware of Richard's infidelities in the bedrooms of the club, information about which also could force Richard to either increase his donation or make further ones down the line, in return for the staff's continued silent discretion.

***

The feeling of increased power and intellectual stimulation at work and having so much more money to spend intoxicated Richard. And now a suite was likely to be named in his wife's family name, to boot. He was also relieved that with Chuck's impending trial and near-certain conviction, he could soon put that nefarious chapter behind him. But he was still burdened by a total lack of physical intimacy at home, and Jennifer just refused to discuss the topic when he dared to bring it up periodically. As a result—he justified to himself—a few months ago he had embarked on another affair, this time with an American called Elisa Reynolds.

Elisa was one of the partners in a firm of headhunters that VCb used, and had recently relocated to Britain. Richard first met her when she came to his office to introduce herself as his new contact and to discuss three new positions he needed to fill in his division.

Elisa's beauty captivated him. At six feet two inches tall when standing in her three-inch heels, she was almost as tall as him. She had the slim and toned body of an athlete—which she was, regularly competing in and coming in the top ten of her state-level triathlons. She glided when she walked, with her long brunette hair gently waving enticingly at him with each step. Rebecca was the attractive, curvaceous, and full-bosomed girl-next-door; Elisa was the muscular, energetic, adventurous, strong tomboy across the other side of the track.

Today, on Friday afternoon, he and Elisa had just enjoyed a nice long lunch and a bottle of wine at his usual table in the Great Gallery restaurant. They spent an hour together afterwards, drinking more wine and making love in the Kent suite.

Afterwards, Elisa always took a shower to wash away her disgust at her whorish actions. *I have to do what has to be done*, she thought.

As Richard lay on his back, exhausted, sweaty, and limp, he observed Elisa come out of the bathroom naked with a white towel wrapped around her drying hair. She smiled a fake big grin as she saw him staring up at her. "See anything you like, lover boy?"

"Indeed I do, very much," he said as he feasted on her long, muscular legs, neatly cropped, thin landing-strip fanny, tight stomach muscles, and pert, small breasts.

"Good. Glad to be of service to my largest client!" She laughed at the double entendre.

Richard closed his eyes. Whilst he always had the stamina for such physical exertions, despite feeling a little drowsy from the wine, after the simple act of ejaculation, his body and mind automatically made him want to go into a deep sleep.

He thought about his two lovers. Rebecca had been an elegant lamb that Richard wanted to hold, cuddle, make love to, and have an intelligent conversation with on a range of interesting topics. Elisa was a lynx whose lasciviousness both dominated and controlled Richard. She took the lead in their sexual liaisons. She was someone who would stalk and jump her prey with ease and grace. But on an intellectual level, Elisa and Richard had nothing in common.

Elisa finished dressing, kissed Richard good-bye, and then left the club to take a cab to King's Cross Station. There she would get on the train to Cambridge to visit some friends for the weekend. Richard took a quick nap, and after a few glasses of cold water and a strong latte, had started to sober up.

He showered, dressed, and got into his McLaren, which he had parked outside the club in full view for the club members to admire, and for Richard to gloat. Next week, the club was to show the car in the rotunda outside the Great Gallery restaurant.

He knew he should never have embarked on another affair after the one with Rebecca. The whole episode with Rebecca had originally shaken him up, especially after what he had been forced to do to her and the baby. But he reasoned that it really was all Rebecca's fault. He wouldn't have had to murder her if she hadn't gotten pregnant – probably deliberately - insisting on having their baby and becoming overwhelmingly clingy and swamping him. But, pinning the crime on Chuck had worked out perfectly. The police had still been snooping around and asking questions, but he suspected that they were getting nowhere. He knew that by his easily passing the polygraph, and Chuck's flunking it poorly, after initially refusing to take it, had been the final self-administered blow for his boss's demise.

Chuck's trial was about to start. But Richard knew not to be complacent. He would be called by the defense as a witness, and Richard suspected there might be an ulterior motive behind it. He was nervous that his affair with Rebecca would be made public and his wife would probably divorce him. He had thought about it but hadn't quite made up his mind whether to deny everything or admit to a very brief fling. A denial would annoy Ghazini, because it was simply Richard's word against the detective's. The taped interviews with the DCI in Richard's office were inadmissible as evidence, given he hadn't been cautioned first. Alternatively, if he admitted to a brief fling, he could cite the pressure of work and Chuck stealing the bonus he should have had for himself. Then Jennifer would still read him

The Feather of Truth   Ian Campbell-Laing

the riot act, but in time probably forgive him.

This was really his only concern about the whole episode: whether his wife would find out about his infidelity, because with the overwhelming evidence against Chuck, who would surely dig a nice hole for himself if he took the stand, in all probability Chuck would soon be convicted, leaving Richard finally in the clear.

As he was sitting at the traffic lights on his way home, he saw a jam ahead. His McLaren was purring, and Richard's thoughts returned to the feline Elisa. After Rebecca, he would always use a condom because he could not risk getting someone pregnant ever again. Elisa had said she was still on the pill after dumping her previous unexciting and unadventurous boyfriend, but Richard had insisted. Richard had clearly learned one lesson, but not the most important one.

Richard with one hand started to text Elisa, using his throwaway, pay-as-you-go mobile phone:

Babe, gorgeous lunch, amazng aftrnoon. Safe travels to ur friends + hv a grt weeknd. H xxx

He had also decided to never use his own name in a text. She nicknamed him "Hardy" as an inside joke because that was how he always was with her, and also it was close to "RD," his first two initials. She told him that her middle name was Ruth, after her father's British mother: he referred to her in text messages as Babe—as in Babe Ruth, the American iconic baseball player who knocked his balls out of the park, as it were. Again, another one of their private, albeit childish, schoolboy humour jokes.

Hardy it was soooo gd—U r a generous and loving guy—Make me v satisfied...ur fingers found the sweet spot! U2 hv gr8 wknd. Thanks 4 pen, I watch it tomorrow! Babe xxxx

Richard smiled and started texting her again, still not worrying about spelling mistakes.

***

Elisa sat on the train and reached into her briefcase, searching for her trashy book to pass away the time. Then she saw in a side pocket Richard's silver pen, which he had used to record their lovemaking, and which she had told him she wanted to replay over the weekend. He had initially refused to let her borrow it, but after she'd knelt down before him, it didn't take much to persuade him.

She examined its elegant, polished-silver finish and saw the inscription from his wife to him. How sweet, she thought. What was also sweet to her was that she, Elisa, and not Jennifer, was sleeping with Jennifer's husband, and she would eventually get what she wanted from Richard. Her thoughts were interrupted by a loud announcement through the train's intercom.

"This is the 3:45 peak-hour London Midland train to Cambridge."

She started to write with his pen on the inside cover of her book.

To Elisa,
All my love,
Richard xxx

She leant back to admire her handiwork. Not quite as neat as Richard's, who knew how to write with the heavy italic pen, but not too bad, she thought.

Then, she heard the same announcement again, completely startling her. Those sitting nearby looked up and stared at her.

CHAPTER 49
TEDDINGTON

As Kofi's phone rang, automatically the final few bars of the opera *Madam Butterfly* to which he was listening went quiet. "Ghazini here."

"Sir, it's me. Sorry to bother you at home on your day off, but I just got off a call with the CPS team."

"Oh yes, Harriet? What do the Crown Prosecution boys want at this late pretrial stage?"

"The Defense Statement submitted to the prosecution has included some information unearthed by that smart PI, Robin Daniels—new evidence about Richard."

"Hmm. Oh really? You have my attention." Kofi started to pace around the room to help him gather his thoughts.

"Well, Daniels went back digging up Richard's past—when he was at Rugby Boarding School in Warwickshire. You may not know, but this famous school has a long history of training the students on a Thursday afternoon in their own Combined Cadet Corps. Students can choose between joining in year ten either the army, Royal Marines, or air force. Richard was spotted in year nine as potential officer material, and he was fast-tracked into the Royal Marines. He rose up the ranks, and at the end of his first year, he was already in charge of eight other cadets."

"Actually I would have guessed he would have joined the air force—I see him swaggering around as a entitled flying ace, don't you? But so what?"

"Well, I am coming to that. In the next year, he was in charge of a platoon of men and underwent rigorous physical and mental training exercises, including a mock capture and interrogation routine."

"Oh, really?"

"He was trained to survive being captured, including coping with the use of intense interrogation techniques and—"

Kofi interrupted her, "OK, so that's why he is so cool under the pressure of being questioned. But I suspect there's more to this, because whilst that demonstrates that he's resilient, it would not be enough in a court of law to raise a question about his integrity and honesty."

"No, it wouldn't, but he was also trained in the art of faking a polygraph when being interrogated by his captives...He scored the highest marks ever attained when fabricating to his mock interrogators about his fake identity! He's a professional liar, sir. He could have duped us all."

"Oh, damn, no wonder he did so well on the poly test. Anything else of interest, Harriet?"

"Yes, we understand that the defense team are building a very solid case as to why Chuck failed to pass his own polygraph."

"How so? Wasn't it all conducted within police guidelines?"

"Apparently there are mitigating circumstances. For instance, the video of the poly shows that the polygraph junior officer was pretty aggressive towards Chuck, and they ended up getting into an argument. All rather unprofessional."

"Really? I had no idea."

"And that's one reason why Chuck's heart rate, blood pressure, and sweating were above normal levels. The other is that Chuck, for two days before taking the lie detector, whilst he was in police custody, hadn't taken his antihypertension tablets. Likely that his test results will be inadmissible. That's a real pain for us, sir, isn't it given the recent law change that permits poly tests in murder trials?"

Kofi paused in thought. "Actually, maybe not. It may ultimately turn out to help us. Clearly, whilst the defense is attacking the prosecution's case, it's also as a quasi-insurance counter tactic introducing the possibility that Richard may be the real murderer."

"So, sir, perhaps the web of likely deceit is finally encroaching on this smug, entitled banker."

"Indeed. Thanks, Harriet. Cheerio."

Kofi sat down, took a swig of his warm beer, and said, "Remote: Act 1 of *Don Giovanni*," to start the opera whose main character was a young, arrogant, and sexually promiscuous nobleman. The first few haunting bars filled his sitting room. How apt, he thought.

The phone rang again. He sighed and tried to not sound annoyed as the music went silent again. "Ghazini here."

"Sir, this is Sergeant Yarrow. Do you have a moment?"

"Hmm. Sure. What's up, Yarrow?"

"It's our old friend, Mr. Jelleners."

"What? I'm trying to forget all about him! Has our arrogant Yank gotten into another fight in prison, which he seems to do each week? He's going to trial next week, so maybe he's getting a bit tetchy and winding up the other inmates more than usual."

"No. It's worse—much worse."

CHAPTER 50
WANDSWORTH, LONDON

The call immediately came through the speakers in Richard's car, which automatically turned down the music. It was one of his favorite tracks—"Free Bird," by Lynyrd Skynyrd—and it was just building up to the crescendo before the lead guitarist starts his instrumental piece after the words, which Richard was now singing out loud, "Oh Lord, I can't change…"

"Richard, here."

"Richard, sorry to bother you. It's Nigel Longtone in HR. I tried you in the office but couldn't find you. And tried leaving a message with your PA, but he's also not at his desk. Where are you?"

"Sorry, Nigel. I was just with a client for a working lunch at my club, and then I went to the library to carry on working on a project for Celsius. I was, in fact, just heading home; it's been a very long last few weeks in the new role. So, what's up in the world of HR? Someone resigned that I should know about? It can't be about comp, because it's too early to get the first cut of bonuses done, isn't it?"

"No, nothing like that, Richard. I have some very sad news. Is this a good time to talk?"

"Yeah, sure. What's up? God—is my family all right?" Richard felt a brief twinge in his stomach.

"Yes, they're fine. It's Chuck. I just got a call from a Detective Chief Inspector Ghazini a few minutes ago. You remember him?"

"Vaguely. Wasn't he the guy handling Chuck's wife's murder case? I thought it was all wrapped up and the case going to trial in…let's see…of course, next week. In fact, I am due to appear as a witness for the defense, but when I have no idea."

"The inspector called your office and kept getting no reply, so he was put through to me to take your call as I was passing your office. He informed me that Chuck was found dead in his cell less than an hour ago. It appears that he hanged himself."

Richard's mouth gaped open; then he grinned. "Oh my God. That's absolutely dreadful. Poor sod."

"Yes, it is dreadful for his family. Maybe Chuck knew he was guilty and couldn't face the public humiliation, Richard. Anyway, we will never know now, of course. I just thought you should know. I expect the detective was going to call you over the weekend with the news anyway."

"Yes, probably. Will you take care of liaising with the police and to notify Chuck's family, please?"

"Yeah, already in motion. I also sent an e-mail to Celsius on your behalf."

"Thanks, Nigel," Richard said. "Have a good weekend, my friend."

"You too, Richard."

After their phones were disconnected, Richard shouted out loudly and banged his hands onto the steering wheel. "Yes! Luvvly-jubbly! This is effing great news. The little shit of a man is finally dead. He won't stand in my way anymore." I assume the police will now back off for good and close the file with no further action, leaving a note that Chuck murdered his wife. And, I don't have to appear in court. Yes! Perfectamundo! He thought.

Richard was distracted by the conversation and enjoying driving his new toy, when his mobile pinged, displaying that a new text had arrived. He reached down to pick it up as he followed a detour on the road, leaving Wandsworth Bridge Road and driving onto Trinity Road, approaching a roundabout.

He glanced up and saw the car in front was moving forward into the roundabout. Then, with one hand, he replied to the text from Elisa and completed the last sentence:

Can't wait to see you next week also. H xxx

As his right foot pushed lightly down the accelerator, the engine revs increased, and the car surged forward. As he pressed "send," he took his eyes off the road, just for a millisecond, but long enough to not spot the Ford Prius car that had come around the corner to his right.

Richard looked up, and sunlight briefly shone in his eyes, reflected off the road, still damp from last night's rain. He reached over to pull the passenger visor down and saw he was much further along the road than he had imagined and was accelerating into the beginning of the roundabout, with the Prius just twenty feet away to his right. Then he heard a text message ping. In his distracted state, and with his body out of position, he jammed his right foot hard on what he thought were the brakes, but instead hit the accelerator again. He realized his error immediately and hit the brakes, hard, with a pumping action.

It was too late.

For Richard, in his now heightened state of alert, the whole event appeared to decelerate time itself. He watched his car slide slowly on the wet leaves towards the Prius, his foot stomping the brake but making no difference. The Englebrau family in the Prius screamed as the two-tonne McLaren rammed into the car's left-hand side with such force that it skidded sideways and smashed into the concrete wall central reservation. The father, Jonathan, who was driving, was trapped in the car and wedged against the roundabout wall to his right. The crumpled metal smashed through the deployed airbags and into his right arm and hand.

The Feather of Truth

Ian Campbell-Laing

Richard's face was too close to the dashboard. When the steering wheel airbag deployed, it was the size of a beach ball, and traveling at over two hundred miles per hour, it took less than one-twentieth of a second to engulf his face and chest and whiplash him backwards into his seat. The back of his head smashed into the headrest.

After the airbag deflated, Richard's head slumped to his left side. There was dust floating in front of him, and a smell of chemicals in the air that permeated his eyes and hands. He didn't notice that his face had abrasions, and his hands, burn marks. He felt nothing.

He didn't hear the screams coming from the passengers trapped in the Prius car, nor see the crowd that had gathered around the two cars. He had concussion.

Three minutes later, he slipped into a coma.

CHAPTER 51
SAINT GEORGE'S HOSPITAL, TOOTING, SOUTH LONDON

Five Days Later

Richard was sitting up in bed, his neck in a brace and three pillows supported his back and head. His hands and chest were bandaged. He had struggled to read just one page of *The Financial Times* on his tablet: his eyes were burning due to being unusually sensitive to the light.

Jennifer and their three children had been to see him every day, along with a few colleagues from work. He had twenty cards wishing him well and a supportive e-mail from Celsius saying he was very pleased with Richard's work in his new role, but requesting he take his time before returning.

He put down his mug of Tetley tea and glanced up to see his longtime friend Anthony Lea, QC, peek his head around the door.

Seeing Richard wearing dark glasses, he smiled and said, "Expecting fine weather, old boy?"

Richard smiled. "Ha, bloody ha! So, Anthony, how the devil are you, old chap? It's good to see you. What brings you out here, away from your luxurious office in the temple to the unpleasant bowels of South London?" He then laughed. "Do I see a cinnamon-encrusted, orange pomander hanging around your neck to mask the foul smell of the great unwashed of Tooting?"

Anthony briefly smiled at his friend's humour. Richard was always cracking jokes with him: it seemed to be Richard's release valve to let off steam. It was the same good old Richard. They had been childhood friends.

"I am fine Richard, but more importantly, how are you faring?"

"Much better. I have a bit of a headache, but the intense throbbing after the concussion seems to have gone for the first time this morning."

"Excellent, I'm glad."

Richard screwed up his face in frustration. "I just hate being stuck in here while they do more and more tests. I've got to get back to work. I have a new, demanding role. Oh my God, I am sounding like Chuck already!"

"Glad you are feeling better, but best to not rush things. The airbag saved your life, but the force with which it was expelled gave you a pretty serious knock to your head, whiplashing it back onto the headrest. You were completely out cold for a few days, which you shouldn't take lightly, and today is only the second day you are fully conscious."

"I know, I know, but I'm fine now. Really, I am."

"Well, Richard, I'm here to give you an update."

The Feather of Truth Ian Campbell-Laing

"What? You've come to announce that your Queen's Counsel's fees have increased yet again?" He grinned and added, "Don't tell me you've repented and repealed the lawyer's creed, 'A man is presumed innocent until bankrupt and can't pay his counsel.'"

"Nope, I'm working pro-bono for you, as you jolly well know. You're my best friend and always will be. Also, I haven't forgotten that because of your introductions, my chambers secured three very lucrative employee criminal surveillance claims cases defending your esteemed bank, which are proving most intellectually stimulating and financially rewarding. But that's not why I am here," said Anthony, shaking his head and trying to get Richard to stop larking about.

Richard looked at Anthony but decided to not comment on surveillance measures at his bank, given his knowledge of V-Trax. "Then you must be here to announce that you've proposed to your long-suffering girlfriend, Eva, and are restricting what I can say during my best man's speech?"

Anthony smiled even though this had hit a nerve with him, because his girlfriend was indeed getting impatient. "No, Eva and I are still very happy together, but we're not yet engaged. If we ever get married, then you know you will be the best man." He then looked sterner. "But yes, I would like to see your speech in advance."

"OK, I give up. Why are you here? Some developments after the car accident last Friday? Are the police going to prosecute me, or the Englebrau family going to sue me?"

"Yep, it's about the car crash, and you best remain seated, because I don't have good news for you this afternoon, I'm afraid."

Richard was impatient and couldn't see what the issue was. "OK, let's hear it. Look, it was just a simple car accident, and yes it was my fault. So I guess I will get some penalty points on my licence for careless driving or whatever it's called now, and my premiums will rise as a result of the insurance company having to fork out paying to repair the bonnet of my car and replace the totaled Englebrau's car. So no big deal. I am alive and still kicking."

Anthony walked up to Richard and sat on the end of his bed. "Richard, Mrs. Englebrau's daughter, Husn, is not. She died in the car crash."

"Oh, shit. She did? Why didn't anyone tell me? God, I am so sorry for her family."

"Yes, indeed. Husn was sitting in the rear left-hand seat. The impact caused her head to smash into the left-hand door, killing her instantly."

"Anthony, how much trouble am I now in, and what's the procedure, old chap?"

"Serious trouble. Let me explain. In cases of injury or death involving traffic accidents, the police do an investigation automatically, and the CPS then decide whether or not to bring a charge, depending on the seriousness

The Feather of Truth   Ian Campbell-Laing

of the offense and likelihood of a conviction."

"The death of the daughter is pretty serious, surely, even though it was obviously only a simple accident, Anthony?"

"Yes, it is, obviously. You could go to jail."

Richard shouted. "What? It was a bloody accident. I thought under the law you would just get banned for driving, or face a suspended sentence, or do some community service? Certainly *not* time in jail. What about my career, for Pete's sake? It would be ruined."

"Stop shouting, and calm down," Anthony said in his usual soft voice.

"How can I be calm? My life is potentially ruined, and you always take so long to explain the conclusion to your thoughts. Sorry," Richard said, now smiling, hoping he hadn't upset his friend.

"The courts don't give a fig about your career. They are concerned that a person has died as a result of your driving. Now, just hold on a minute, and let me explain. It's important for you to have all the facts, because it can get complicated with aggravating and mitigating factors all in the pot."

"OK. Go on then, but *please* be brief," Richard pleaded.

"So, under the UK law, there are three kinds of offences: summary, indictable only, and either way. The least serious offences are summary and triable only in the magistrates' court. The most serious are indictable and triable in the Crown Court only. Either-way offences can be tried in either court according to a process that is followed at a mode of trial hearing in the magistrates' court."

"Sounds complicated. How do you know which offense you will be charged with and which court hears the case?" asked Richard.

"Well, if you let me explain the process, it will become clearer."

Richard slowly rolled his eyes and looked to the ceiling. "OK, OK."

"Firstly, the accused always has the option to choose trial in the Crown Court. Despite the fact that sentencing powers are greater, this is often tactically the best choice, or thought to be."

"Why is that, Anthony?"

"Because juries tend to be less ready to convict than magistrates, and while sentencing powers are greater in the Crown Court, the judges see a larger number of more serious offences and potential penalties than magistrates, and often have a less draconian approach to relatively less serious offences. Magistrates are a pretty mixed bunch: it's a bit like a spaghetti western."

"What are you going on about, Anthony?"

"Didn't you watch any Clint Eastwood films? Well, to misquote one film: some magistrates are good, some bad, and others are plain ugly mad."

"That's hardly reassuring."

"It depends. If the accused is content to stay in the magistrates' court, the magistrates will consider if they can accept jurisdiction. If they think their sentencing powers are enough, they will proceed. If they do not think they are sufficient for the offence, they will pass the case up to the Crown Court."

"So, I could end up in the Crown Court anyway."

"Yes. But there's another consideration. Under the UK traffic laws, you fall under one of two areas, both of which are serious. The first is careless or inconsiderate driving, and the second, and more serious, is death by dangerous driving."

"Well, go on, explain the difference then."

"Under the Road Safety Act of 2006, the careless driving offences include, for example, jumping a red light, overtaking on the inside, driving too close to the car in front, and being distracted whilst turning on the radio. Relatively minor acts like that."

"Well, it's pretty obvious I fall under that one, as I was simply being careless, surely, Anthony?"

"Actually, no. I believe you would fall under the dangerous driving rules of the Road Traffic Act of 1988, as updated by the 2003 Criminal Justice Act."

Richard sighed loudly—he knew it would be quicker to just shut up and listen; he rarely succeeded in hurrying his legal friend.

"So, Richard, there are three levels of dangerous acts, the worst of which, level 1, carries a fourteen years' custodial sentence and a minimum disqualification of two years with a compulsory retest."

Anthony saw his friend look horrified, so he quickly added, "But this is for totally reckless behavior, like say, excessive speeding, having outrageously high levels of alcohol or drugs in your body, persistent driving offences, flagrant disregard for human life, and multiple deaths. So we believe you shouldn't fall into that category."

"I should jolly well hope not," said Richard, looking more relieved.

"The lowest, and least dangerous level, is number three. It is deemed when there was a significant risk of danger. Here, this would include driving above the speed limit, or within the speed limit but not appropriate to the conditions of the road. Also, conducting a brief, dangerous manoeuvre."

"Well, I don't think any of those apply, do they? I don't think I was speeding or conducting a dangerous manoeuvre."

"Well, you *might* be so assessed. For example, one might argue you were not driving in an appropriate manner according to the conditions of the road: after all, it had been raining the night before, and there were leaves on the ground, making the conditions too slippery for your speed. Also, you accelerated—albeit by mistake—instead of braking into the roundabout, so that might be deemed a brief, dangerous manoeuvre, Richard."

"And what are the level-three penalties then?"

"Still harsh. Starting point is a three-year custodial sentence, with a range—depending on the mitigating and aggravating factors—of between two to five years in jail."

"Anthony, oh Lord, that's pretty grim." He then quickly thought and countered, "Could you not argue that my actions were more akin to careless driving, like the example you gave of being distracted by turning on or off the radio?"

"We could have, but since 2007 texting is specifically mentioned as something which the Crown Prosecution would classify as death by dangerous driving, and not the lesser careless driving."

"Oh, shit. So a jail sentence is inevitable then?"

"Very likely, Richard. Sorry, old chap."

"Dammit, I'm probably ruined! But what are the mitigating factors in my favor? Any thoughts on that yet?"

"Yes, of course we've given that some thought, Richard."

"Sorry. Yes, do go on, thanks." Richard sighed.

"OK. So, in your defense, you have no prior convictions—just a disputed parking ticket—you weren't driving over the speed limit, you had only just bought the car, so you weren't familiar with its power, you injured yourself in the process, you showed immediate and genuine remorse to the victims, and—"

Richard cut him off. "I did?"

"Yes, you *will*. We will arrange for you to undergo a full medical, which will hopefully show some physical injury that, whilst it permits you to carry out your duties at work unencumbered, you still feel pain and have to take medication and undergo physiotherapy or something like that."

"Very good, Anthony, and the remorse part?" Richard looked down and took a swig of his tea.

"You should attend counseling, and a course like MATT."

Richard looked up, confused.

"It's *Mothers Against Texting and Talking* whilst driving. It's intense, but it would be very worthwhile to have completed it before the Crown Court case."

Richard suddenly thought he had spotted a flaw. "But hold on—what court case? I haven't been charged yet, have I, Anthony?"

Anthony smiled. "No, you haven't, *yet*."

"So why the rush then?" said Richard, flashing a smile revealing his white teeth and optimistic boyish grin, adding, "And, out of interest, do they always prosecute?"

"As I mentioned, the decision whether or not to prosecute an offence depends on a two-stage test contained in the Code for Crown Prosecutors. The first is that it is in the public interest to prosecute. The second is whether, on the available evidence, there is a reasonable chance the jury would reach a guilty conviction—deemed more than a 50 percent chance."

"So in my case, what would they do, prosecute or not? Your explanation is taking too long. For Pete's sake, tell me the bottom line conclusion!"

"In your case, as someone has died, and given the obvious public interest in deterring texting-while-driving behavior, the first part is clearly satisfied. The second part depends on what evidence exists that this was what you were doing."

"So, out of interest, how do you or they know that I was texting?"

"Even though the police haven't completed their collision accident report, my sources obtained a sneak preview of the draft, and it states that at the scene of the accident, you still had in your hand your cell phone showing the time you made your last text. Also, the driver in the car to your left saw you holding and looking down at your cellphone. He came forward as a Good Samaritan witness."

"How come he did that? Just my luck! Don't most people just walk away, preferring to not get involved?" Richard said with a knowing smile.

"Yes, that is the typical reaction of the general public, but when you drive such an ostentatious car, the public take note, and some can't wait to rub the driver's smug face in the mud—probably out of jealousy, Richard."

"So the prosecution has pretty persuasive evidence that I was texting."

"Yes, and I know that the police are working very closely with the CPS to ensure that the CPS prosecute you."

"How, so?"

"The police have made a specific recommendation, on the advice of DCI Ghazini, whom I understand you have met."

"Christ, not that ruddy plod again. Will he never leave me alone?"

"Evidently not," said Anthony, smiling.

"Oh shit, Anthony."

"Indeed. But I haven't finished the sentencing guidelines yet."

"Well, it can't get much worse," said Richard, but then added when he saw his friend's stern face, "It can?"

Anthony nodded. "Texting has grabbed the headlines of late and is now termed a 'gross avoidable distraction' and more likely to be a level-two category than the lesser level three. The penalties are harsher—it has a starting jail term of five years, with a range of four to seven."

"Oh God, I am definitely ruined."

"Not necessarily. There's much more to come. But firstly, I hadn't finished the list of mitigating factors in your favor. Husn, the daughter in the Prius car, wasn't wearing her seat belt, having just undone it to retrieve a new DVD from her satchel on the floor."

"She wasn't? That's against the law, isn't it?"

"Yes, it is, Richard. We may be able to use that. But I should caution that some judges ignore it, saying it doesn't affect your culpability."

"That seems unfair, given I am sure I read that wearing a seat belt doubles your chances of surviving a serious accident. In other words, she might not have died if wearing a seat belt, and then I wouldn't be in this pickle."

"I'm just pointing out the case law, Richard, so you can make an informed decision."

"OK, thanks, but hurry up, and let's start preparing our case, please."

"We already are, as I mentioned."

"So are we done then? Did you have any other news? No offence, but there's only so much law tutorial I can take in one day."

"Yes, two more things. Both are not great news for you again, I fear," said Anthony.

Richard's eyes widened. "What are they?"

"You obviously don't know that there have been other developments following the car accident. The father, Jonathan, had to have his mangled right hand amputated, because the dead arteries risked infecting the rest of his arm and potentially his body."

"Oh, my God, no I didn't know. Poor sod. When was that?"

"Yesterday, on Tuesday, and he's in a critical condition, given the amount of blood he lost. You better pray that he doesn't die, or you could then—if they deem his death a direct result of the car accident—have an aggravating factor of more than one death being caused. And that might at best push you to the upper jail term of a level two, of seven years, or at worst, given your flashy, ostentatious notoriety, and a harsh jury, slip you into a level one, which as I mentioned, is up to fourteen years."

"Shit, I didn't realize he was so critically injured. The nurse said he was badly injured, but she thought he should pull through and make a full recovery. I knew his hand had been trapped in the wreckage and it took a long time to cut him free. God, poor man, but more importantly, bloody hell, poor me! Jeepers creepers, I'm going to need you, Anthony, to get me out of this ruddy hole I've dug myself into. It was all just a stupid accident following a momentary lapse in concentration, for Christ's sake."

"Well, although he is on the critical list, we are miles away from that, provided his condition doesn't deteriorate. Anyway, as the collision accident report is only partially completed, we don't know if Mr. Englebrau was driving recklessly, or whether or not you or he were over the alcohol limit. They did some Breathalyzer tests at the scene of the accident, but I haven't seen the results yet. The department only seems to operate on certain weekdays. They promised to e-mail me the results later today."

"OK. Very good. And the second thing you wanted to mention?"

"Yes. Let me explain what Mrs. Inaam Englebrau, the wife, is now doing. The game she appears to be playing," said Anthony. "It's all rather intellectually stimulating for me, but I wouldn't want to be in your shoes. It's pretty grim."

CHAPTER 52
SAINT GEORGE'S HOSPITAL

Richard's heart started pounding. "What do you mean? How can it be any fucking worse than what you explained so far—given each of the three levels means a jail sentence, and you think it's a likely level two, and that means at least four years in the slammer?"

"Well, despite Mrs. Englebrau's upbringing in England, she was born in and remains a citizen of Iran and has retained her Muslim faith."

"Really? What does this have to do with the car accident and me? The CPS is prosecuting me, and she will be a witness; that's all, surely?" Richard said, not seeing any connection.

"Well, instead of a traditional British court, Inaam Englebrau has talked with a Sharia lawyer, and is offering you to be tried voluntarily under the laws of an Iranian court of law—and not within a British court of law."

"What? How can I, a law-abiding citizen of Great Britain, paying God only knows how much in taxes, and whose only prior run-in with the law was a disputed parking ticket, be tried under those arcane, foreign laws? It makes absolutely no sense!"

"Well, you can, but only if you so choose. Following a clause in the Arbitration Act of 1996, the UK government sanctioned a legal process for Sharia judges through the five Muslim Arbitration Tribunals located in the UK, which operate the courts for Muslims. These Sharia judges sitting on the Islamic tribunals have full legal powers, and their rulings are binding."

"Oh, my God! No bloody way, Anthony!"

"Actually, it literally is 'the way,'" said Anthony.

Richard was confused again, and raising his voice, snapped back at his longtime friend. "What way? What on earth are you talking about? Speak in plain English, for Pete's sake."

Anthony, as always, never raised his voice. "Well, if you calm down, old chap, I was about to explain. You obviously didn't know, but actually, Sharia means 'the way,' or sometimes it's translated as 'the path to the water.' It's a religious code of living for Muslims—akin to the Bible, which is a moral code for many Christians. Sharia law is based on the Qur'an and teachings of the Prophet Mohammed. Within the code are the so-called Hadd offenses, which are clauses that outline the recommended punishments for various crimes. Want to know more, Richard? It's quite fascinating and revealing, actually."

"Not from my vantage point. Don't they chop off children's hands for stealing bread or slice off your John Thomas for rape or sleeping with another man's wife, Anthony?"

"Yes, that's the crude perception from outside the Muslim countries, and is, in fact, sometimes true, but it can be more complicated than that. Theft gets prison and/or amputation of the hand or feet, for example, but—"

"That's OK," said Richard, interrupting. "I haven't stolen anything from Inaam or her family, thank heavens!"

"Unless she makes a case that by ending her daughter's life, you stole her daughter, Husn, from her, or you stole her husband's hand because it had to be amputated. A bit far-fetched, granted, but we need to tread carefully here, as these Muslim courts in the UK don't operate in the same way as the typical British justice system."

"Bloody hell, you are making me ruddy nervous, Anthony."

"And of course, sometimes it does appear to the West as somewhat draconian and over the top. For example, adultery quite often gets stoning. They put the respondent—usually the woman, even if the man was the accused—in a pit of sand up to her neck, and the public throws stones at her head until she dies. Can take hours to die."

"Yes, I've seen footage of it. Quite horrible," said Richard. "Didn't I also see on TV maybe ten or fifteen years ago now, a Sudanese lady punished by getting forty lashes for wearing trousers to work and in public?"

"Yes, I think she worked for the United Nations. But also, for any of these stoning or amputation punishments, you can also get public lashings beforehand, mainly to deter others. Many don't survive these lashes," said Anthony, getting unusually animated.

Richard shook his head and sighed nervously. He felt hot and sweaty.

"But, as usual, you keep interrupting me. The discussion about these physical penalties is totally irrelevant, Richard."

"Why's that?"

"Because you are a British citizen, and such acts as flogging, amputation, and stoning are against all human rights legislation to which the UK has signed up, and it simply couldn't happen here on British soil."

"OK, thank heavens. But what would be the penalties that these tribunals can dish out then for death by dangerous driving, Anthony?"

"We don't have a precedent yet—the tribunal previously only arbitrated on matrimonial and domestic disputes. It's only earlier this year that its powers have been extended to cover criminal law such as serious traffic offenses."

"So it's a bit of unknown lottery then?"

"Yes, but we are researching this further to see what precedent has been made in Iran itself. For example, recently, a case of dangerous driving by a man incurred seventy-four lashes. But of course you can't be given that. We are trying to establish whether or not you would be given a jail sentence or a fine as retribution, or both, and if so, how much."

"But do you think if jail was given, it would be more than the four years the CPS would hand out under a level two, Anthony?"

"No, so far we believe from our research that the tribunal would be more lenient that the Crown Court—the tribunal has never handed out a jail sentence. Anyway, let's leave the tribunal aside for a moment, because Inaam's lawyer presented us with two other options, so three choices in total."

Anthony paused, then continued. "So choice number one is, as we described, to voluntarily go to the tribunal. Once you go and you agree to have her case as applicant against you as respondent tried there, then their ruling is binding and irrevocable."

"OK. So we keep that in the back pocket then for now, Anthony."

"Yes. Her other two choices also don't involve going to a British court of law."

"Well, that's decent of her, isn't it?" But when he saw Anthony's frown, he added, "Oh God, what's her proposals?"

"She clearly thinks you are a man of means, and it doesn't take a genius to go to *YouTube* and join the many thousands who have gloated watching the video of the smashed-up bonnet of your expensive McLaren car with the personalized number plate, COO 1."

"Well?"

"Her proposal for choice two is for you to make a one-off payment to her family for restitution of the death of her daughter and loss of her husband's right hand. Her lawyers have stated that they are confident that the CPS would then either step aside and take no further action, or at worst, issue a two-year community service order."

"The CPS would back off?"

"Under this government, there is a determined move to give more power to the victim and spend less public money on costly trials—which often fail to convict the accused—or incur huge incarceration costs. The CPS would instead likely simply charge you with the lesser offence of texting, and that now carries an automatic ban from driving for three years, a five-thousand-pound fine, a suspended prison sentence, and a mandatory course on dangerous driving one day a week for ten weeks, where you sit and listen to parents who have lost their loved ones from cellphone-distracted driving accidents, like the MATT I mentioned earlier."

"What's the amount she wants, for me to avoid being charged by the CPS or joining her at the tribunal?" demanded Richard, getting impatient.

"Ten million."

"*What?* Ten million fucking quid? That's absolutely bloody ridiculous! Her daughter died because she wasn't wearing a ruddy seat belt. Everyone else survived the car accident, for Christ's sake! Yes, the father lost his

The Feather of Truth   Ian Campbell-Laing

hand, but ten million for that is outrageous and egregious. No British court would grant that amount in fines or restitution, surely?" Richard shouted.

"Yes, I also think it's unfair. But think for a minute…You would be avoiding the CPS, which has an almost near certainty of a lengthy jail sentence. Think of it as the price of your liberty."

Richard thought that there was a principle at stake here, which he needed to defend, and so decided to not mention his new, much higher salary. "I don't have anything like that amount, Anthony, in liquid cash. You know that it's all tied up in the house, VCb unvested stock, and trust funds. And I am not selling my McLaren. I've only just bought the two-hundred-thousand-Great-British-pounds beast, and it's being repaired, as we speak—which is going to cost me another twenty grand in deductibles and higher premiums."

"She will know how much the car cost you, and details of your extravagant lifestyle, including recently flying in a NetJets private plane to Italy to buy a vineyard. And she will be aware of your wife's family's high net worth—she will have done her research, and know that Jennifer's dad could write such a check with relative ease."

Richard spoke slowly, starting in a calm manner, but with increasing volume. "Anthony, there is an important precept here underpinning fair play and justice. I'm not guilty of dangerous driving or manslaughter, just stupid, careless driving, and I should just lose my license for a year or two and do some community service. And, I was not directly responsible for the daughter's death, because she wasn't wearing a seat belt. I am surely only guilty of causing Mr. Englebrau to lose his hand, correct?"

"In a British court of law, Englebrau's hand is assigned a range of values, depending on whether it's central to his livelihood—for example if he were a painter, or if it had been of lesser importance to his work. But, either way, the amounts are small. In the UK, broadly under the Criminal Injuries Compensation Scheme—which the civil courts would follow—the tariffs mandate that one hand is worth thirty thousand pounds."

"So, she should be claiming from me thirty thousand quid in damages for the loss of her husband's hand. What's his profession? Don't tell me he's a successful artist who paints with his right hand?"

"He's a leading heart surgeon."

"Oh God, poor man! Was a leading heart surgeon, I guess? That ups the ante of the claim then, doesn't it?"

"Yes. Case law would indicate maybe a few hundred grand, given his position, and providing he wasn't in any way responsible for the accident. For example, as I said, if he had been drunk, that would change matters."

"Hardly seems a fair amount to his family," Richard admitted.

"No, it's not. In the US it's based on your income. A hand is two hundred and forty-four weeks' compensation, so nearly five years of

The Feather of Truth   Ian Campbell-Laing

income—so that, as a top heart surgeon earning say a million dollars a year—is, around five million. So, thank heavens the accident was in the UK!"

Richard thought back to his cheapskate comments about his now deceased boss, Chuck, whose actions in swindling Richard out of a proper bonus initiated the start of this whole sorry affair with Rebecca. But now the tables had turned in Richard's favor, and skinflint Britain had come to rescue Richard's hide.

"Would they reduce the compensation for any disability insurance his family had taken out on his hand?"

"Yes, in the US, they would. Here in the UK, sometimes they do, but some case law shows they don't always. It depends. But my PI chappie, Robin Daniels, has already checked. Mr. E didn't have any."

"That's rather bizarre, isn't it, to not have any, Anthony?"

"In fact he did have coverage up to when he turned sixty-five, four years ago, now. However, I assume that many years ago, when he took the policy out, he probably assumed he would retire at that age."

"So, it seems I have three options. A, voluntarily go to the Sharia tribunal and play Muslim roulette, but where it should lead to the lowest likely sentence, and probably not a custodial one; B, pay a settlement of ten million to Mrs. E, and not go to the tribunal or Crown Court; or C, go to the Crown Court and face a jail sentence of between four and seven years, with probably compensation of a few hundred grand, correct? None of which are particularly appealing."

"Actually, there's a fourth option. I hadn't finished with Mrs. Englebrau's proposal. As I mentioned, it came with two options, the first was to pay the ten-million lump sum. The second proposal is that you voluntarily agree to lose your own right hand, like her husband lost his."

"What the f?" Richard shouted.

"Richard, let me finish, please. And if you agree to it, then there is a reduced restitution payment of two million pounds. In other words, she is valuing your hand at eight million Great British pounds."

"God Almighty in Heaven, save me from this evil woman. That's perverse."

"Quite the contrary, it's certainly not perverse to Muslims—not at all. In their eyes, and given their long traditions, it seems very fair to them. An eye for an eye, and all that. In your case, a hand for a hand. And blood money is part of their rich religious history."

"What do you mean, Anthony?"

"Under their faith, they believe that the soul of a man is in his blood, which cries out to heaven for atonement when it's been shed."

"OK, I can understand the logic in that, given our own country's medieval past."

"Richard, also attached to that last option is a condition that you voluntarily go to Iran to have the amputation done."

Richard shouted, "No, bloody way, Anthony, this is just not fair. In a British court, I would not lose my hand, and I would be paying her one hundred thousand, or maybe two hundred thousand, tops."

"Probably, but you will also likely be going to jail as well, remember."

Richard swore and shouted, "I am not going to Iran under any circumstances, because I don't know anything about their medical profession, and also, once there they can do whatever they like with me. I am not a blithering idiot and won't fall into that trap."

"Calm down, old chap."

"Oh, bloody hell!" Richard said. "Anthony, let me think for a second." Then he went into deep thought and closed his eyes.

Finally he opened them and said, "Aha, I have solved the problem of the ten-mil payment. Surely, old chap, it's covered by my insurance, who will have to pay up because I am covered fully comp."

"Come on, Richard, of course we thought of that right at the start. But it was remiss of me not to have mentioned that we looked at your fully comprehensive motoring policy under your insurer, Armadillo, and coincidentally you do have cover of up to ten mil in the case of a death."

"OK, so the insurers pay the ten, matter solved. What's the big problem?"

"Nice try, but there's a clause in it specifically saying that they don't pay out anything if the accident involved you in any way breaking the law. Your texting of your latest fancy woman whilst driving broke the law, Richard."

"Aha, but I was only breaking the law *if* Detective Ghazini or the Crown presses charges against me *and* secures a conviction for my texting?"

"Not so. The report says you were texting, which is against the law. Whether or not the CPS prosecute you subsequently is irrelevant."

"But I could fight the report in a court of law and question its efficacy?"

"Yes, you could, and the prosecution would bring up who you were texting and why. Your word against theirs. They would simply get the records of who you were texting and find the time of it and put two and two together to prove it. If you hadn't been texting whilst thinking with your dick instead of your brain, they would have paid up. Ten minutes of amorous texting could cost you ten million quid. It's harsh, I know!"

"Anthony, let's go back to her offer and me going to the tribunal in the UK. We are absolutely sure that even though it is based on the Sharia law of Iran, I cannot be given *any* physical punishment, correct?"

"It's likely that the Sharia tribunal would ask Mrs. E for her own views of restitution, and a hand for a hand is what she would probably demand. Her husband lost his hand, so you lose yours. She may also, based on a case in Iran last year, request that you could lose your right ear, if they could prove that you were also listening to a voice mail on your mobile and that also contributed to the crash. But as I mentioned, this is for Muslims in Iran, not British citizens. Such an act would be decreed torture, and the UK does not allow that on British soil, or for British citizens to be deported to a country where they believe this inhumane act could be carried out. So they can't legally amputate your hand or ear on British soil or demand you be deported to Iran to have that done. So that's simply *not* an issue."

"But hold on, whilst the tribunal can't do that legally, what's stopping them doing it behind the government's back and then saying, 'Oops, sorry'?"

"That's ridiculous. Relax. You cannot as a British citizen be forced to lose any limb, period."

"That's a relief."

"However, overall it's *not* looking good. Sorry, old chap. You were having an affair, and whilst illegally texting, caused a car crash, which injured and killed people. That's very serious. So it's going to turn out to be rather brutal. My job is to try and ensure you don't go to jail—which is going to be a tall order if you choose to go with the CPS."

Richard was nervous. He now resigned himself, knowing that, whatever was the best outcome, he would still suffer greatly. "A somewhat brutal affair indeed, Anthony."

"As affairs often are. As your counsel, let me sum up and add a few more thoughts for you to consider overnight. Option one, go to the Crown Court, where we stress the mitigating circumstances, and hope you get the lowest of a level two category, which is four years. And, if you plead guilty up front, you get a third off your sentence, which then reduces it to two years and eight months. You would be out in less than one and a half years, because you get another 50 percent reduction for good behavior. That's just the blink of an eye in the grand scheme of life."

"Still grim, and would ruin my career."

"Perhaps. Let's look at the choices under Mrs. Englebrau's proposals. Option two, offer to pay her a reduced amount, say half—i.e., five million pounds, and perhaps meet in the middle at £7.5 million. Get father-in-law to cough up on behalf of his adorable son-in-law. Pay it and walk away with your right hand intact, and no jail time served, but probably community service and so on." Anthony paused.

"Option three, negotiate with Mrs. E to allow some British, and not Iranian, surgeon to chop off your left hand—and not your right hand, and offer to pay, say one million pounds in restitution instead of her two million pounds. I don't recommend this option, obviously." Again he waited for it to sink in.

"Option four, take the lottery of the Sharia tribunal and pray they will be lenient, but be mindful that whatever they pronounce is binding as if administered by a UK court of law. And bear in mind that their sentence must be carried out, typically within thirty days of sentencing, often sooner. And carry it out they will."

"Which is likely to only be a payment of a monetary penalty and disqualification from driving for a period?"

"Yes, we believe so."

"Thank heavens. That's very reassuring news that I won't under any circumstance be forced to lose any body part, Anthony, and I can probably avoid jail by going to the tribunal."

"*Probably* avoid jail—remember we don't have any precedent here. But bear in mind that when attending the arbitration tribunal, or indeed if you went to the Crown Court, the Sharia judge or prosecution will probably bring up the affair, which might mean of course that you could lose your job, jeopardize your career, and may have divorce proceedings filed by your wife. Then you wouldn't see your family as much as you would have liked. And, so-called colleagues and friends will turn out to be 'fair weather' by never speaking with you again. You will lose a great deal," said Anthony.

Richard looked up to the ceiling, wondering why he had been so very stupid to get into such a mess. *Consequences,* he had always told his children, *think of the consequences.* And he had ignored his own advice.

"Anthony, where's the hand of the government in helping me here? That's what I want to know. It's all heavily weighted for the victim and not the accused, it seems to me."

"The law's the law."

"If I chose the tribunal route, and they surprise us and give me a harsh sentence, is there any appeal to a higher court or intervention by the British government, Anthony?"

"No appeal, and it's unlikely the government would overrule or intervene over a court's decision. A spokesperson may comment, but nothing more. And, what will come out into the public domain of a British court or the Sharia tribunal will be that you were having an affair and the 'sexting' caused you to be distracted, which directly led to the crash. Unfortunately, the prime minister, Malcolm Quigley, has been most vocal here. He's squeaky clean as far as washing in public one's family's dirty values. Remember the last MP in his cabinet who had an affair? Mr. John Rodgers-Smith, the secretary of state for the arts? He was dismissed from his post by Quigley immediately and publicly humiliated for displaying unacceptable moral family values, following the revelation that he had had six mistresses, many concurrently."

"So nothing we can do, even though I'm a good citizen, pay my taxes, and I contribute to numerous charities?"

"Well, not publicly, no. And I doubt privately. Let me step back and spell it all out for you. There are two complications for you. First, either the

The Feather of Truth   Ian Campbell-Laing

British or Sharia courts would eventually learn from where you were driving—a boozy lunch and then some intimacy in a bedroom, all during work hours, and to whom you were sexting—your mistress, the stunning American beauty Elisa. The adultery would be made public, and your wife, Jennifer, would find out about the affair. And any other affairs that you've had would probably surface, too!"

"Allegedly had, Anthony."

"What-ev-er! As I said, our prime minister hates immoral behavior."

Richard felt suddenly weak, and the pain in his lower stomach had returned.

"But the second complication is the key here, and why you won't get any political help. It's all about oil, anyway, as you know. It's always about the oil. Economists and geologists calculate that the world's current oil supplies will run out in less than twenty-five years, and unless new sources are identified, or alternative energy becomes feasible, we are all doomed. It's not really about the people and the Qur'an or any of that stuff, you know that, right, Richard? The real issue here is oil and its politics."

Richard couldn't make the connection from oil to his driving accident sentencing. "What do you mean, the real issue is oil and its politics?"

"You must surely read the papers? British Petroleum is bidding for some of the rights to extract and refine some of the oil within one of the largest oil fields, discovered a few months ago in Iran. The Americans, the Ruskies, and the Chinese are also all bidding. Whoever is granted rights will share in the estimated six trillion dollars of retail oil discovered."

"Six trillion? Cripes, that's staggering! Even after the costs of extraction, surely that would solve most of those governments' debt problems in one go?"

"Precisely. Of course, the Americans, who are trillions in debt, would love to get in on this, but given their recent change in foreign policy and accompanying hostility to Iran, they have little hope of getting any share of the action. And Britain, being seen to be in bed with the Americans on so many political fronts, is struggling to get a slice of the pie. However, Niall Cruickshank, the foreign secretary, has been conducting secret and apparently promising talks with his Iranian counterpart. But if the UK prime minister pisses off the president of Iran any further—by constantly denouncing Iran's nuclear enrichment program, highlighting humanitarian abuses, and going out of his way to ensure no British company trades with Iranian corporations on Britain's blacklist—then Britain won't get any rights either. And many jobs, as a result, won't be created for the next ten years."

"Good God, Anthony, how did I get caught up in the middle of a political game like this?"

"More things are connected than you know. You presumably know of

The Feather of Truth   Ian Campbell-Laing

the four folk from your bank who strayed into Iran last month and have been held as spies—the so-called VCb4?"

"Yes, of course I do. In my new role, they ultimately report to me. It's all a sham. They were on a humanitarian exercise. In fact I ponied up twenty grand for their charitable work to help them get to their goal."

Anthony looked down at his notepad and nodded. "John Whitley, who's a Brit; Anna Lo is of Chinese descent but based in New York; Andrew Stonedene was born in Britain but is now an American citizen; and Olga Polzin is a Russian living in the USA. So, you can imagine, given the nationalities of the VCb4, similar pressures are being felt by the president of the People's Republic of China, the president of the Russian Federation, and the American president at this time. So you see, there is a bigger picture here than just the Englebrau family and your hand. There's much more at stake, my friend."

"The VCb4 and I are simply the sacrificial lambs, aren't we, Anthony?"

Anthony nodded. "So, the government is unlikely to question any tribunal ruling given down to you, however draconian—save torture, Richard which they shouldn't permit."

"Shouldn't or wouldn't permit torture? There's a massive difference."

Anthony looked embarrassed by his slip-up. "Sorry, I meant wouldn't, of course."

"Anthony, it's OK," Richard said. "Yes, I'm a pawn, and it's clearly oil that makes the political world go around. I do now remember back in 2009, at the height of tensions between Libya and Britain, the government returned the Lockerbie bomber, Abdelbaset Ali Mohmad al-Megrahi, to Libya as a free man. It was on the grounds that he had terminal prostate cancer, when in fact the press alleged that it was more to ensure that the talks between various British oil companies and Libya—granting exploration rights to Britain worth some nine hundred million pounds and other oil deals worth fifteen billion pounds—which had stalled, could then be kick-started."

"You're right, Richard. I also recall seeing on TV a documentary with Jack Straw, who was the justice secretary at that time, saying that it was in the overwhelming interest of the UK to return to Libya, this man, al-Megrahi. He meant, of course, in the overwhelming financial interest and jobs, and screw the poor families who had lost their loved ones at Lockerbie. At the end of the day, every man and every political person has a price of how much the government considers he or she is worth. Contrary to what we ordinary folk think, there *is* a price on a life, and it appears to many in the public, myself included, that the price paid by the Lockerbie victims and their families and friends didn't justify the oil rights. I agree that it's a harsh political unwritten reality that most governments probably adopt when it suits them."

"OK. So, Anthony, in practice, in order to likely avoid jail, that leaves just one avenue open to me: the Muslim tribunal. Can we hide the fact I was having an affair and sexting on my mobile?"

"No, as I thought I mentioned, it's in the police report. And they have already interviewed Elisa, who confirmed seeing you that afternoon."

"Why did she grass on me?"

"They threatened her with being an accomplice to the accident and distracting you while driving."

"Who on earth threatened her like that?"

"Richard, it was at the command of DCI Kofi Ghazini. He was most insistent, we understand."

"Christ. Bloody Ghazini's back in my life yet again."

"And with a vengeance, it seems," said Anthony.

"These are all grim choices, Anthony. God, what if the husband dies in hospital, on top of all of this mess?"

"If Mr. Englebrau dies, you could spend between seven and up to fourteen years in the slammer. But we are not there yet because Mr. Englebrau, I understand, is now stable in hospital, Richard."

"Shit, even a short spell in jail would be horrendous to go through and probably would ruin my career. That, together with the public knowledge of my affair with Elisa, would definitely ruin my marriage. Let's at least hope the hospital keeps him alive."

"Quite so, Richard. Two other things, old chap. Firstly, Mrs. Inaam Englebrau wants our answer about her three option proposals by the end of this week on Friday, by six p.m. at the latest, or she helps the Crown Prosecution Service build a case and publicly goes for your jugular."

"Christ, we don't have much time. And the second?"

"DCI Ghazini wants to see you, again. I saw him in the waiting room just before I came in, and he mentioned he wants another word with you."

"Oh, heavens. What about—any idea?"

"He didn't really say, but he said a very odd comment to me. He looked down at my shoes and said to himself out loud, 'Hmm. Slip-on shoes, with a buckle. Interesting.'"

CHAPTER 53
SAINT GEORGE'S HOSPITAL

As Anthony sat on Richard's bed, he thought back. He had known Richard for thirty years, since they were five years old. They had gone to the same schools. From the Kensington Little Angels Pre-Prep School, Summerfields Prep School in Oxford, and Sheriff House at Rugby Public School in Warwickshire. After that, Richard studied at Oxford University, went to MIT in the United States, and then entered banking. Meanwhile Anthony, after going up to Cambridge, followed in his father's footsteps into advocacy.

Richard continued in his own thoughts. At least I am not a Muslim in Iran. There, I would be flogged and have my hand and ear amputated, for sure. And how times change; what was viewed as an enjoyable afternoon's family entertainment—throwing Christians to the lions in the Colosseum of Rome in AD 100—became illegal three hundred years later. And whilst most of society now views Africans as having equal rights to their white brethren and the owning of slaves as abhorrent, in the sixteenth century, it was seen as an important source of financial trade, necessary to enhance one's own balance of payments. So, at any point in time, each government's attitudes evolve at their own time period of common sense.

Richard was conciliatory. He looked up and spoke to Anthony. "To be fair to Iran, these Islamic current-day punishments are nothing compared to what Britain used to do in mediaeval times, and in fact, not that long ago in our own country, as I'm sure you know. So, despite my own predicament, to give Iran and others their dues, we are wrong to criticize these countries' laws or their religious pronouncements. It's somewhat hypocritical."

"Yes, quite so, Richard, quite so," Anthony said, deep in thought and only half listening. He and his team had so much to do preparing for whichever option Richard chose.

"Here in the UK, we had public floggings twice a week for minor crimes and misdemeanours," said Richard. "You could watch a ten-year-old child be hung in public for stealing a handkerchief or for poaching rabbits. You could be hung for stealing five shillings, which is around a fiver today, or arson, or being outdoors at night with a blackened face. Instead of today's family Sunday roast beef meal, followed by an afternoon of watching reality TV shows or sports, back then it was the roasting of a murderer on the fire. Or, the family would watch a nice, live hanging or flogging outdoors," Richard rambled on. "But oh, hell, Anthony, what am I going to do?"

"Richard my dear, oldest, and closest friend, I think I have a plan on what option we should go for and how to play our hand. It's a bit risky, but may just work. I need to think it through and do some more research overnight. If we get it wrong, it might exacerbate the situation. But we need Mr. Englebrau to remain in his current stable position."

"I trust you," said Richard. "You're all I've got, old chap."

Anthony stood up, and, instead of hugging each other in a European embrace, they shook hands firmly, the only physical contact British males typically permit. "I'll see you tomorrow, old friend, and we can discuss our response before the Friday deadline. Just hang in there. I'll get you out of this with all your delicate bits and pieces intact. In the meantime, you get some rest, and get your strength back, Richard."

Anthony left the room and closed the door behind him. He got into the lift just as Genevieve, his assistant, was exiting it. He put his hand out to stop the lift door closing. She had a red face and was out of breath.

"Anthony," she said, breathing out heavily, "oh gosh, thank heavens I got hold of you."

"What's up, Gen?"

"Mrs. Englebrau's lawyer just called your office, and I took the message. I called your cell phone, but it went into voice mail, so I came as soon as I could. She has just changed the terms of the offer, and you should call her lawyer to learn what it is."

"Oh God, why would she do that? Has something happened to her husband? Please don't tell me he has died?"

"Yes, he has, about thirty minutes ago. There were complications after the amputation, and he lost so much blood. He apparently suffered a massive heart attack. Should we tell your client, Richard?"

"Absolutely not—not yet. He has enough to worry about. Let him get some rest today. I'll tell him tomorrow morning when I see him. We have much work to do now. And there goes my plan. Can you see the sister on this ward and ask her to ensure Richard is not made aware of Jonathan Englebrau's death until I see him tomorrow, please?"

"Sure," said Genevieve.

"OK. See you back in the office. Damn!"

CHAPTER 54
SAINT GEORGE'S HOSPITAL

Mrs. Inaam Englebrau rushed back to the hospital, after the ward sister on duty had called her on her mobile phone. She had only been away from the hospital twenty minutes to run some errands. When she got back, her husband was dead.

She screamed out, "No! No! No!" She looked at her husband and thought to herself, I will never forgive myself for leaving your side. You, Richard de L'Isle, are the sole reason my daughter is dead, and now you've taken away my dear husband, too. I won't ever forgive you! I will show you the way to hell and the path to the water source, as the Qur'an dictates. You are to die drowning under Sharia law.

Inaam held her husband's left hand and wailed over his body. Already, it seemed that his hand felt cold, and the room, despite having the heating on, suddenly felt icy. She shivered.

After a while, she dried her eyes, and picking up the phone by the side of her dead husband's bed, dialed "0" for the hospital operator.

"Can I be put through to Richard de L'Isle's room, please? He's at this hospital, but I have forgotten what room—sorry."

"Sure, ma'am. Who should I say is calling, please?"

"I'm a friend of the family…er, say it's Mrs. Kind."

"Sure, putting you through now, Mrs. Kind."

Inaam heard her phone pulsating out the number, an electric heartbeat. Finally it was picked up. Her own heartbeat was pounding in her chest. She was angry but nervous; she disliked confrontation.

"Hello. Richard de L'Isle here."

"I have a Mrs. Kind for you on the line. Putting you through now, caller."

"I don't know a Mrs.—"

"Yes, you do, Mr. de L'Isle," Inaam said rather too quietly.

"Sorry, I can't quite hear you, but I don't think I do, madam. What's this about, please?"

Inaam cleared her throat and spoke louder and with more conviction. "My name in Farsi means 'kindness.' Does that help you?"

"Farsi? I think you have the wrong number, madam, sorry," insisted Richard, about to put down the phone, thinking it was a prank call.

"Farsi is the common language of Persia, the ancient country that included Iran, Mr. de L'Isle," Inaam explained, as her voice grew stronger.

"What?" said Richard, perplexed. But then he understood. His body froze in time. Blood drained from his face. He started perspiring heavily.

The Feather of Truth — Ian Campbell-Laing

He knew exactly who it must be if she was from Iran. Who else would phone him at the hospital in this way? It was obvious, now.

Calmly and assertively, Inaam spoke into the phone. "Yes, Mr. de L'Isle, my name is Mrs. Inaam Englebrau, and I am your nemesis, your worst nightmare. Not only have you murdered my daughter, Husn, which by the way, means 'beauty' in Arabic, but you have just murdered my dear husband, both for which I will show you no mercy whatsoever. He died in the intensive care unit less than an hour ago because of your selfish actions. I loved my daughter and my husband dearly, Mr. de L'Isle. You have robbed me of two of the three people who mean more than anything in this world to me."

"Oh my God, Mrs. Englebrau! I'm so dreadfully sorry. It was an awful accident! I am so, so sorry. Words cannot describe—"

She interrupted his pleas, raising her voice but not shouting. "Save your pathetic, arrogant, entitled, middle-class excuses for the Crown Court. You are going to jail for a very long time."

Richard heard the phone go dead. As information flooded his brain, he quickly felt sick. His head was spinning. He looked around the room through his sunglasses, but his vision was blurred. The walls seemed to be moving inwards towards him, then rushed away from him. He tried to get out of bed, but his muscular arms felt weak. He tried to grab the side of the table next to the bed to help himself up, but his moist hand slipped, and as he attempted to steady himself, he got caught up in some of the wires that were monitoring his blood pressure, heart beat, and oxygen levels. He tried to grip the table but instead pushed it over, its weight taking all the wires with it, ripping them from his body. He felt faint, his skin clammy and hot. He sensed a tingling down the side of his right arm and side. And his stomach pains had returned again.

As his legs gave way, the side of his head slammed into one of the corners of the upturned table. Everything went blank. The monitor in his room started ringing two different alarm signals as Richard slipped into unconsciousness, again.

PART FOUR

Where Do We Come From? What Are We? Where Are We Going?

Oil on canvas, 1897–98
Paul Gauguin, artist
Museum of Fine Arts, Boston, Massachusetts

CHAPTER 55
MUSLIM ARBITRATION TRIBUNAL, LEYTON, EAST LONDON

Five weeks later

The doctors determined that Richard had appeared to not have suffered any long-term ill effects after briefly going into a coma at the hospital. They had signed him off as fit—physically and mentally—to face trial: his mind was fully alert, his schoolboy humour had returned, and they had removed his neck brace, bandages, and sunglasses. The abrasions on his face and burn marks on his hands from the car accident, whilst healing well, were still evident. There was a scar on the right side of his face from his fall.

Richard sat anxiously at the left-hand table in the front of the long room, his hands resting on its wooden top, and his index fingers lightly tapping a nervous, irregular beat. He was dressed as he would be for work—everything immaculate and coordinated. Prebattle nerves took hold of his stomach and cramped his abdominal muscles. He felt like he was going to be sick.

He was flanked to his left by Anthony and on his right by Mrs. Khulood Siddiqui, a leading female Sharia lawyer. At the adjacent table to the right were Mrs. Inaam Englebrau and her two Sharia lawyers, one female and one male.

Inaam felt confident, righteous, and determined to secure revenge and justice for her husband's and daughter's deaths. Out of respect for the court, she was wearing an Iranian veil, the hijab that covered her hair and shoulders. She chatted quietly to her lawyers.

The three Muslim judges, known as qadis, entered the room from a side door wearing their official robes: grey gowns with open sleeves and two white linen bands hanging in front of their necks. They took their seats on the raised platform in front of Richard and Inaam. As required by the rules of the Muslim Arbitration Tribunal, there must be at least two judges, one a scholar of Islamic sacred law, and the second a solicitor or barrister from England or Wales.

On the senior qadi's right was a female British barrister, and on his left, a male Islamic scholar. Sheikh Faiz Faqui, who was both a qualified barrister and an Islamic scholar, addressed those in the room with a deep, soft voice, and in perfect English. "The applicant and respondent should now please stand before this tribunal."

Inaam and Richard pushed back their chairs, making a noisy scraping sound on the floor, and stood up with their hands folded in front of them.

"As applicant, do you confirm that you are Mrs. Inaam Englebrau of Wandle Road, Tooting Bec, London, and do you understand that you are under oath now and during the whole proceedings?"

Inaam and Richard had been advised on how to address the qadi. "Yes, respected judge, I do."

"As respondent, do you confirm that you are Mr. Richard Heathcote de L'Isle of Blackdown Close, Haslemere, Surrey, and do you understand that you are under oath now and during the whole proceedings?"

"Yes, respected judge, I do, also."

"Good. Then you may both sit down."

He waited until they had done so. "Let me say at the outset, that this tribunal appreciates the speedy acceptance by both the applicant and respondent for the date of this case being brought forward nearly a month, following a space opening up in our schedule."

He paused. "Also, because this is both the applicant's and respondent's first time before a Sharia court in England, I think it would be helpful if I made clear the objectives and powers of this court, which is referred to as a Muslim Arbitration Tribunal.

The overriding objective of the tribunal is to ensure that the proceedings are conducted in accordance with Qur'anic injunctions and prophetic practice as determined by the recognized schools of Islamic sacred law, and as fairly, quickly, and efficiently as possible. Members of the tribunal have responsibility for ensuring this, in the interests of the parties to the proceedings and in the general public interest.

This tribunal was established in 2007 under the Arbitration Act of 1996, with the intention of providing a viable alternative for the Muslim community seeking to resolve disputes in accordance with Islamic sacred law, without the costly, time-consuming, and often unnecessarily adversarial litigation seen in other courts.

The tribunal operates under Section 1 of the Arbitration Act, which states that 'the parties should be free to agree how their disputes are resolved, subject only to such safeguards as are necessary in the public interest.' As such, it must operate within the framework of English law, but it does not constitute a separate or parallel Islamic legal system.

He paused again, then continued.

"Let me just explain this important point a little further. This tribunal is not part of the court system of the UK. It is simply a venue where two parties can amicably settle their disputes, without going to a formal court.

Previously, and with much success, this tribunal has focused on issues concerning forced marriages, domestic violence, family disagreements, and commercial and debt disputes. However, today, following a recent amendment to the Arbitration Act of 1996, this tribunal welcomes the opportunity to adjudicate on the death by dangerous driving complaint which we have before us today. This is the first such serious traffic complaint upon which we have been asked to arbitrate."

As the senior qadi spoke, his head moved gently left and right, with his eyes looking to the front where Richard and Inaam sat and reaching to the back of the hall to capture everyone's attention in the room. He sat upright, leaning slightly forward, and rarely looked down at his handwritten bullet point notes on his yellow pad.

He paused again, and then continued.

"Also, previously, disputes before this tribunal have been between those only of the Muslim faith, but today we preside over a case where one of the parties is of a different religion. This tribunal welcomes and treats equally faiths of all denominations.

Until recently, our pronouncements were not binding in law, merely in honor only, and this tribunal could only make recommendations. Today, this tribunal's pronouncements may be followed through by other UK courts and used as case law in the land."

Sheikh Faqui spoke slowly and deliberately kept pausing to allow his comments to be digested. He knew how much was at stake for both the applicant and respondent, both of whom were unfamiliar with these proceedings. "There is one proviso. Namely, that the applicant and the respondent must both agree to the tribunal arbitrating over their dispute. This is their right, without any obligation on them. The applicant and respondent are both free to leave this court immediately, if either one does not so agree, and then other British courts will take over the judicial process. Pending such an agreement, any pronouncement for the applicant and respondent that we make is then binding. There is no appeal, save under the MAT Rule 23, namely that of a judicial review with the permission of the High Court. However, it would be negligent of me if I don't point out that no reviews have ever been so granted by the High Court." He noticed that in the room everyone was listening attentively.

"Any findings, decisions, and sentencing must be carried out within the specified time limit, either here in the UK, or in the applicant's country of birth, namely Iran." His peripheral vision noticed the respondent, Richard, whisper something in his QC's ear, who then shook his head. "The applicant and respondent will shortly have time to privately converse with their lawyers before anything is binding."

The senior judge continued, "Usually, such tribunals are held in private, but under the MAT Rule 17, both parties accepted the admission of the public to this dispute, and members of both parties' families are most welcome here this morning."

The hall held room for one hundred people. With the religious feelings that this case had created, behind the applicant and respondent sat crowds of relatives and the press. It was packed to capacity.

"But as you will see, no cameras are permitted at this tribunal." His voice lowered slightly, and the muscles in his face tensed. "Unlike some daytime TV courts in the USA, and unfortunately increasingly so in this country, this tribunal is a solemn place of law." He looked to his right and then left as he focused on the two participants before him. "Mr. de L'Isle and Mrs. Englebrau, now please confer with your lawyers, if you have any questions so far."

Inaam spoke to her lead counsel, "I fully understand. I have no questions. Let's proceed." But she thought to herself, *My only apprehension is whether I did the right thing by offering de L'Isle the option of coming to the tribunal or whether I should have gone with the CPS route that virtually guarantees his imprisonment. I hope I don't come to regret that decision.*

Inaam's leading counsel nodded her head to the senior judge in agreement and indicating that her client was ready.

Richard talked quietly to Anthony and Mrs. Siddiqui, holding the palm of his right hand over his mouth so that his words could not be heard or interpreted by Inaam or her lawyers. "So far, with one important exception, what the judge said seems fine, and as you briefed me. But let's be very clear. Anthony, both you and Mrs. Siddiqui have advised me that whatever punishment is dished out—for example, if it involves chopping off my hand—then the British High Court will step in and not permit such a barbarous act either on Britain's soil or in Iran, correct? It's bloody important that I am not mistaken about this, because it seems at odds with what the judge was just saying."

Anthony replied, "Yes, yes. Richard, chill out. As I keep telling you, under the Human Rights Act of 1998, and as a member of the EU, Great Britain does not administer torture. And, under the British Nationality Act of 1948, and their subsequent amendments, a British citizen like you is exempt from being forcibly deported to another country where the UK believes that citizen may experience torture. Torture would definitely include any flogging, stoning, or amputation."

Richard wasn't yet convinced and remained nervous. "Exempt under any circumstances, so that you are absolutely 100 percent bloody sure that I cannot be forcibly deported?"

"Yes," said Anthony, firmly.

"So why, for Christ's sake, is the judge talking about punishment in the 'applicant's country of birth, namely Iran,' then?"

"I don't know, Richard," said Anthony.

Richard opened his eyes wide in amazement. "What sort of ruddy answer is that?"

"Look, so far, these courts have only been used for Muslim respondents and applicants and for cases of matrimonial disputes and their ilk. They

The Feather of Truth   Ian Campbell-Laing

have forced deportation of guilty respondents back to their country of birth, namely Iran. But that can't apply to you as a British citizen, born and bred," stressed Anthony, hoping this would placate Richard.

Richard had an odd feeling about this judge. Whilst the qadi was obviously intelligent and appeared sincere, he wondered if he was just a little too slick. Richard had a peculiar feeling that he just didn't trust the judge to be fair and impartial and do the right thing for a non-Muslim. His palms felt clammy, and he was perspiring. He felt his cotton shirt stick to his armpits and lower back. He leaned forward and loosened his shoulders. He wiped his hands on his trousers and took out a handkerchief and lightly dabbed his forehead to remove the glistening moisture.

Richard still looked concerned. "But you would advocate that I should still go through with this Muslim tribunal, even though to me it seems not much more than a lottery system with unknown case law, instead of the British courts?" asked Richard.

"This judge was brought up and educated in Britain and is known for being lenient," said Mrs. Siddiqui. "As your case is the first of its kind in the UK, we have no MAT precedent to know precisely how it might go. But that said, we believe that he is more likely to set a fair sentence as a marker and to encourage more cases like this to be brought to the MAT. So our feeling is here you will get more lenient punishment and are unlikely to be given a custodial sentence."

The senior qadi thought it was time enough and, looking at Richard's legal team, coughed to bring the proceeding back to order. He also glanced at his notepad to check he hadn't missed anything.

Richard took in a deep breath and exhaled loudly. The walls were closing in again. He hated not being in control of his own destiny. He looked over to Inaam and saw her smiling with her lawyers. That made him feel uncomfortable. He looked at Anthony and leant over to him, putting his hand on his shoulder.

Sheikh Faqui coughed again, slightly louder, still tolerating this delay. Once they had agreed to the binding nature of the tribunal, he would speed matters up.

Richard looked at Anthony and nodded his head. He briefly thought back to his childhood where Anthony and he would always look out for each other, no matter what. Their loyalty to each other was absolute. Richard had Anthony in his will to look after his children if anything happened to him and Jennifer. That was enough for Richard. But he shivered slightly when he recalled from the back of his mind a very selfish, uncourageous act he had done when he was younger. Would God now choose to punish him as retribution? He felt imprisoned already, with no choice but to proceed.

"OK, OK. Let's roll the Islamic dice."

The Feather of Truth   Ian Campbell-Laing

Anthony nodded his head in agreement. But he was far from certain. He felt slightly apprehensive. All he was confident of was that Richard would not be, could not be, deported.

Mrs. Siddiqui smiled and nodded to the judge that Richard was ready.

The senior qadi nodded back his acknowledgment.

"Will the applicant and respondent please stand." They did. The room's chatter died down to a few "Ssshh" sounds.

"Mrs. Inaam Englebrau, as applicant, you have brought this case to us for arbitration under Sharia law, the pronouncements of which, if agreed by you and also by the respondent, would be binding. Do you accept this condition?"

"Yes, respected judge, I do."

"Mr. Richard Heathcote de L'Isle, as respondent, do you also agree for this tribunal to arbitrate under Sharia law, the pronouncements of which, if agreed by you and the applicant, would be binding on you both?"

"Yes, respected judge, I do also."

He smiled back at them. Good, finally, he thought. "Thank you both for putting your trust in our system. You may now both sit down."

There was a sudden burst of noise in the room. All present knew that there was no turning back from this path.

The senior judge looked up and waited for silence. The whispering subsided, quickly, respectfully. "The procedure now is somewhat different to a traditional British court of law. My learned colleagues and I have read your individual submissions, the respondent's plea for leniency, and the many letters supporting his good character and as a model family man. We note too his generosity in supporting charitable and other good causes." He paused and saw that Richard was smiling at this favorable summary.

"Most of the facts of the case before us are not in dispute. The respondent, due to a lapse in concentration when driving his sports car—due to taking his eyes off the road whilst physically using his mobile phone to text—caused an accident involving the Englebrau family, which then resulted in the immediate death of Mrs. Englebrau's daughter, Husn, due to head trauma. Her father, Mrs. Englebrau's husband, Jonathan, was trapped in the wreckage, and his hand so badly injured that it had to be amputated a few days later. Mr. Englebrau, had he lived, would never have been able to continue practicing his career as a leading heart surgeon. He died a few days later of a heart attack, probably as a result of the trauma of the amputation, but we will come to that point later. The collision accident report notes that neither the respondent nor Mr. Englebrau had alcohol levels above the permitted amount when driving. Is there any disagreement so far, by either the applicant or respondent, regarding the facts I have presented?"

Inaam's counsel shook her head.

The Feather of Truth — Ian Campbell-Laing

Richard's Iranian lawyer raised her hand.

"Yes, Mrs. Siddiqui?" said the qadi, surprised at a question, so soon.

She stood up. "Respected judge, on behalf of the respondent, we would just like to ensure two matters had been taken into consideration by the tribunal. Firstly, you and your respected colleagues are cognizant of the fact that the daughter's death—while tragic—was ultimately caused by her not wearing a seat belt and which is also against the law in Britain. Tests have shown conclusively that, had she worn her seat belt, she would have doubled her chances of surviving the impact, and thus may have likely lived. And secondly, the coroner's report indicated that Mr. Englebrau's death from a heart attack, cannot *for certain* be linked to, or be assigned as directly resulting from, the amputation of the hand, and hence not with any certainty be directly attributable to the car accident."

"Mrs. Siddiqui." He smiled, rather patronizingly, and spoke as if to a bright student who wasn't listening to her professor. "We have read the statements in full, so we are of course fully aware of both your assertions. And I have more comments, many more comments, to make. In connection with your first point, actually, I was just coming to that part of the summary."

"Thank you, respected judge," said Mrs. Siddiqui, who was not at all intimidated by the seasoned judge. If she had a point to make, make it she would. She sat down.

The qadi continued. "While Mr. de L'Isle caused the accident, it is clear that had the daughter been wearing a seat belt, she probably, but no one can say definitively, would have lived. Both her parents are at fault here. In Sharia law, and in accordance with pronouncements of the Royal Society for the Prevention of Accidents, the onus is mainly on the driver, and hence the father in this case, to ensure her seat belt was fastened. However, we have determined that given this modern age of equality, especially here in Great Britain, this should be a joint liability between Mr. and Mrs. Englebrau.

"Finally, when considering any restitution or monetary penalties, we have taken into account the applicant's and respondent's schedule of assets and income statements for the last five years, and their life insurance monies due."

As the senior judge looked down at his notes, Richard whispered to Anthony, "Hold on, why are they taking into account any life assurance policies that I have? I get it that they need to know about any monies she is to receive on the death of her daughter and husband, but why me? If they taking into account monies that Jennifer will get on my death, are they implying I am to die? For Christ sake what's going on?"

Anthony held his hand over his mouth and replied, "Ssshh, Richard. Don't be so absurd."

The Feather of Truth   Ian Campbell-Laing

The senior judge heard the whispering, looked up from his notes and sternly caught Richard's eye.

Richard held up is hand, shook his head and mouthed "Sorry".

"As I was saying," continued the judge.

Even though the judge had a calm, almost soothing voice, the atmosphere in the room was tense with anticipation. With the publicity of this case, the sentencing outcome was bound to be controversial and stir up factions between the two faiths involved. Neither community would be satisfied, and an amicable resolution was unlikely.

"My learned colleagues and I have deliberated over this case," said the qadi, and then turning to Mrs. Siddiqui, looked at her, saying, "based on all the evidence presented to us, and unlike in a traditional British court, we do not conduct lengthy examinations, cross-examinations, reexaminations of evidence and witnesses. Nor do we permit slick PowerPoint presentations or visitations to the crime scene. This process, under Sharia law, is much quicker. I will briefly consult with my colleagues before sentencing."

The three qadis huddled together, forming a triangle of whispers and nodding of heads.

Richard thought that it was quite evident that before arriving at the tribunal, the judges had predetermined his sentence. Despite applying deodorant this morning as always, today he could feel the heavy sweat under his armpits still clinging to his shirt. He reached under each armpit to wipe the sweat away using one of the remaining small, less damp parts of the shirt. He found it odd that he felt far more nervous now than during the poisoning of Rebecca, for which, if he'd been caught and convicted, he could have spent the rest of his life in jail. He couldn't recall the last time he was this nervous. He now reached forward to pick up his glass of water to clear his parched throat and heard the clinking of the ice.

Mrs. Siddiqui held Richard's hand and Anthony put his hand on Richard's forearm. Richard pulled away from them.

The qadis stopped talking and looked towards the tables where the respondent and the applicant sat. The audience started whispering, "Ssshh."

Richard leant forward ready to get up from his chair.

"Mrs. Inaam Englebrau, please stand," said Sheikh Faqui.

Inaam and Richard both looked confused. She had no idea why she was being asked to stand, given she was the applicant and not the respondent. She looked at the lawyer to her left and shrugged her shoulders. She did as instructed, and stood up. Richard sat back in his chair, and crossed his legs.

"The tribunal is sorry for your loss. Your daughter and husband's lives were snatched away from you and from this world before their normal time. We genuinely feel your grief. However, this tribunal must address your and your late husband's lack of responsibility for ensuring your daughter, Husn, was wearing a seat belt. Not only was this breaking British law, it was morally reprehensible, because your daughter might have survived. But more importantly, we must address this issue because our records note that you and your husband have been previously cautioned, twice, by the police for failing to ensure she was wearing a seat belt."

Inaam looked down, blushing.

The qadi continued his admonishment of her. "In a traditional British court of law, you would today have been prosecuted by the police and may have been given a custodial sentence. Although I would expect that sentence would have been suspended given the loss of your husband, and it being his primary responsibility as driver of the car. Whilst we are bound by the principles of Sharia law, we are also mindful of British law.

However, the tribunal is also aware, Mrs. Englebrau, that your son, who survived the accident, made it clear that his sister, Husn, briefly undid her seat belt to retrieve a DVD from the pocket of the seat in front of her, just before the moment of the impact. He also said that you and your husband were recently very strict about seat belts, and his sister knew this. This, in our minds, has reduced severely the onus on Husn's parents, and we have taken this into account. But we need to make an example here, to highlight the importance of wearing a seat belt and remind those upon whom it falls of their responsibilities in this regard. So, we must consider what is best for the greater good of society as a whole and to act as a deterrent to others. I am sure no one disagrees with that principle."

Sheikh Faqui paused, took a deep breath, exhaled, and then spoke in his usual firm tone, but slightly louder than before. "This tribunal sentences you, Mrs. Inaam Englebrau, as applicant and an Iranian citizen, this day of Tuesday, the seventh of October, 2025, to be temporarily deported and incur ten lashes in a public place in Tehran, Iran, in two days' time, namely on Thursday, the ninth of October. At the conclusion of this tribunal, you will be taken into our custody."

Inaam's face went white, her mouth gaped open, and then she fainted. She would have crashed down as a dead weight onto the floor had her lawyer not reached over and caught her in his arms.

Richard looked at Anthony in disbelief. And terror. Oh God, this is going horribly wrong, he thought. Mrs. Englebrau's sentence was surely an incipient prelude as to what was likely to follow for his treatment.

Sheikh Faqui quickly added, "The tribunal will adjourn to assist Mrs. Englebrau to regain her composure. Please give her some water. Clerk to the tribunal, we will reconvene in twenty minutes."

CHAPTER 56
MUSLIM ARBITRATION TRIBUNAL

Bloody hell, thought Richard, and then he blurted out to Anthony, "My God, they don't mess around when it comes to sentencing. But Iran! She's being extradited to Iran! Christ, will they do that to me?"

Anthony and Mrs. Siddiqui said nothing, but exchanged a quick, anxious glance. They feared the worse for Richard. This judge was firm, but hardly fair. To make an example of her, he had just sentenced a woman of good character, who had only had a few cautions from the police before, to ten lashes in public five weeks after she had lost her daughter and husband. She clearly wasn't aware that Husn had taken off her seat belt; otherwise she would have insisted she belt up again immediately. The lashes would be brutally painful, especially for a woman. And she also faced the humiliation of the public punishment. She could even have a heart attack and die. It would be comparable to a spectator sport, and hundreds—maybe thousands—of people would turn out to see the lashing.

Inaam was now sitting back in her chair. As she sipped some cold water, her lawyers held her steady around her shoulders. She knew she had to accept her punishment; this was the law and decision of the tribunal. What gave her strength now was her faith and knowing that she could not, especially in public, let her family down. Also, she wanted to hear what Mr. de L'Isle would receive, predicting that he would get a similar harsh treatment.

The three qadis filed back into the room.

Inaam stood up again, her legs a little wobbly.

"The sentence on the applicant is complete," said the judge.

As was traditional, after sentencing, the convicted person always thanked the judge to acknowledge that this was God's will.

"Qadi Faqui, Insha'Allah," *Judge Faqui, God's will be done*, said Inaam in a firm, defiant voice, adding, "Jazakullah Khair." *Thank you. Allah will reward you.*

"You may sit down now, Mrs. Englebrau."

He paused until she was sitting still. Then, looking sternly at Richard, he said, "Will the respondent please stand and face the tribunal."

Richard slowly got to his feet, his body weighed down by his foreseeable imminent doom. He steadied himself by placing his shaking right hand on the table. He briefly put his left hand on Anthony's shoulder. He then took a deep breath and, standing erect, moved his hands so that they were folded in front of him, as before. He had faced a mock interrogation during his

The Feather of Truth   Ian Campbell-Laing

school army days, which had at the time felt utterly realistic. Then, he had the courage to persevere in the face of such adversity and fear. But today, this was for real. This was not an army exercise in mind games; this was reality and life. Just like when he had faked the polygraph when questioned about the Rebecca murder inquiry, he now needed to stay calm and in control. He relished that the world was watching and would record this moment—it gave him inner strength.

The qadi briefly looked down at his notepad. He looked up and started his summary of the evidence. "The first consideration we have to make is establishing the severity of the crime; any subsequent sentencing is then a separate matter under Sharia law. This tribunal has never before arbitrated on such a case as this, and we are thus mindful of, but not necessarily beholden to, case law in the traditional courts of England. There, it is clear that there is quite a wide range of driving that can properly be described as dangerous, and the appellate courts have emphasized that while the tragic consequences are very important, the main consideration in determining what is an appropriate sentence must be the culpability of the driver, as judged by the gravity of the careless driving involved, and the surrounding circumstances."

On hearing "careless driving," and not "dangerous driving" Richard smiled, and Inaam understood perfectly what this implied. "Oh, no!" said Inaam to her counsel, loud enough for the qadi to hear.

The judge paused and looked down at his notes again. His teeth squeezed closed, his jawline moved outwards, and the veins on his temple visibly expanded. He looked at the applicant and stared at her. "If I may be permitted to continue?" He paused. "A momentary distraction, but selfish lapse in the respondent's judgment has caused the death of two innocent persons: the daughter immediately, and a few days later, the husband of the applicant.

It is clear to the tribunal that the respondent was committing three misdemeanours whilst driving: firstly, by texting on his mobile phone, the respondent was carrying out a gross avoidable distracted act; secondly, by accelerating hard into the roundabout, the driving was not appropriate for the conditions of the road, which were wet and slippery; and thirdly, accelerating rather than braking into the roundabout constituted carrying out a brief dangerous manoeuvre."

In unison, Richard quietly said to himself, "Shit, it's *not* careless driving, then," and Inaam whispered, "Perfect, it's at least dangerous driving; he's in trouble now. Maybe he's going to jail after all."

"And texting being a gross avoidable distracted act, is a level two, or what is termed a 'substantial risk of danger' category. We have looked at the various factors that the courts have held should be considered, in order to place this case at its appropriate point on the scale of cases of causing death by dangerous driving. In other words, are there mitigating factors that would reduce the sentence within a level two, or on balance are the aggravating factors sufficient to move this higher within a level two or indeed push into even a level one, the most serious of offences? But, we are not bound by these categories; instead we merely make reference to them. This tribunal has far more discretion than that which is available to the traditional courts. In addition, this is an arbitration, and so the views of the applicant are most relevant."

"Uh-o," Richard whispered as his heartbeat increased. "Here we go. I knew he wasn't on my side."

"We have noted that it is considered by those that compiled the collision investigation report that, had Husn Englebrau been wearing a seat belt, she would have, in all probability, escaped serious injury."

"Good," Richard whispered, pleased that the qadi had accepted that important mitigating point in his favor.

"However, we do not see that as reducing the culpability of the respondent's driving—although it is yet another illustration of the importance of always wearing seat belts, whether travelling in the front or the back of a vehicle."

"Damn," Richard said rather too loudly, such that the judge stopped and looked up.

"Sorry, did the respondent have something to say?"

"No, respected judge. My apologies," replied Richard quickly, and saw a stern look from his lawyers.

"We accept, in this case of arbitration, that there are present the following relevant mitigating factors: the respondent's previously good driving record, absence of previous convictions, and acceptance to appear before this tribunal in a timely manner. In addition, his good character as demonstrated by the social enquiry report and the reference from his employer and many others, and his unfamiliarity of the power of his car, which was new to him.

The respondent has also stated that he has demonstrated great remorse for his actions, through voluntarily attending relevant psychological counseling and action groups, including Mothers Against Texting and Talking whilst driving. We are not wholly convinced of his efficacy here, and believe, like many accused, instead of being sorry for their alleged crimes, they are more sorry for their predicament."

Ouch, thought Richard. This is going to be very grim.

"In addition, we see no evidence of any physical or mental disabilities in the respondent as a result of the accident. He has even recently returned to full-time work and clearly is able to perform his very onerous duties."

Richard shook his head. He was losing on points.

"Of the aggravating factors, we do not accept the respondent's statement that he was momentarily dazzled by the sun reflected off the wet road. In addition, and very significant, is that there is more than one death here, because we do not accept that there is no causal link between Mr. Englebrau's amputation (which was directly caused by the collision) and his subsequent heart attack. Thus, his death, in our view, directly forms part of the respondent's culpability."

Richard knew he was now doomed. His head briefly looked to the ceiling for comfort and inspiration. He found none.

"The applicant is fully entitled to *quisas*, or restitution for the loss of her husband. We have also noted in the applicant's submission that Mrs. Englebrau requested the following punishment for the respondent. One, that Mr. Richard de L'Isle be banned from driving for the rest of his natural life. Two, that Mr. de L'Isle pays restitution of twenty million pounds in compensatory damages to the Englebrau family, within one month, in lieu of the loss of the Englebrau family income. And three, that Mr. de L'Isle loses his left hand, the one that used the mobile phone to text just before the collision."

There were gasps from the members in the audience, especially from Richard's family.

Even though Richard was fully aware of these written demands by Mrs. Englebrau, hearing them again in court caused him to hyperventilate. He looked at the judge, took a deep breath, and exhaled very slowly.

"Under Sharia law, the pathway of retribution, more commonly referred to as 'an eye for an eye' and which, bizarrely, some westerners view as barbaric, is often deemed appropriate when considering punishment. Not so long ago in Britain, in medieval times such physical punishment was the norm. But, again, and it is relevant here also, we must consider what is best for the greater good of society as a whole in this present day, and to act as a deterrent to others."

Richard's cheeks went red. His chest was tight, and as his diaphragm pushed upwards, he felt he was suffocating. The suspense was torturous. Richard just wanted to know the verdict. What worried him most was the "eye for an eye" and "act as deterrent" comments. He prayed he would not lose his hand, but was comforted by the thought that the British prime minister would never permit such a barbaric act to be carried out here or in Iran on a British subject. But he knew he was a political pawn, able to be sacrificed for the greater good of the oil deal Britain needed from Iran.

Richard shuffled his feet, and tightened the muscles in his legs once again, to prevent them collapsing. *Be steadfast*, he said to himself.

The qadi continued. "The texting with your left hand on your mobile phone, just moments before the car accident was a selfish affair that caused your loss of concentration. Using a mobile phone, whether to take or make a call or text a message, whilst driving, is illegal under British law, and you may be separately charged for this act outside this tribunal."

Richard was well aware that the judge had deliberately used the words "selfish affair" for the act of texting, and was sure that he had placed an emphasis on the word "affair." He knew that Jennifer would focus on these words. And of course, DCI Ghazini would be pleased it was now in the public forum. But ever the optimist, he started thinking of damage control with his wife and how he could deny everything about a physical affair and position it by explaining that the judge meant "an affair" simply as in "an event." Then his thoughts went back to the present. Deal with one issue at a time, Richard, he reminded himself.

The judge paused, took another deep breath, and exhaled. He was now ready to deliver his final sentencing. "Mr. Richard Heathcote de L'Isle, this tribunal delivers the following sentence to you, as respondent, this day of Tuesday, the seventh of October, 2025."

Richard was shaking and heavily perspiring in the cold, air-conditioned court room.

CHAPTER 57
MUSLIM ARBITRATION TRIBUNAL

"We disqualify you from driving or applying for a driving licence for a period of ten years. Thereafter, you will be required to pass the extended proficiency-driving test and prove to this tribunal's satisfaction that you are responsible enough to be allowed on the road again and are not a risk to the public.

"Secondly, under *tazir*, our rules of compensation, you will pay Mrs. Inaam Englebrau the sum of three million pounds in restitution, one month from today; that is, by Tuesday, the fourth of November.

"Thirdly, and this comes in two parts, one of which is an option, so please listen carefully. The first part is that you will receive forty lashes, in a public place in Tehran, Iran, in two days' time, on Thursday, the ninth of October, and then—"

Some in the room gasped and then started whispering loudly.

"What? You can't do that!" Richard shouted, interrupting and pointing at the judge. He then turned to Anthony and, jabbing his right-hand index finger at him, shouted, "You advised me they can't deport a British citizen and carry out torture. You promised me that. What the hell's going on?" Richard's face was bright red.

"If I may be permitted to finish, Mr. de L'Isle, there are two more important points that I do still need to make," said the judge, frowning.

Mrs. Siddiqui's hand shot up.

"No, Mrs. Siddiqui, you may not speak. You are very well aware of the protocol of this tribunal."

Frustrated, Mrs. Siddiqui said nothing, but just put her head in her hands in total confusion.

"As I was saying before being rather rudely interrupted," said the judge tersely, "you will receive forty lashes, and then later that day in Iran, you will have your left hand amputated by a qualified orthopedic surgeon. You will then be permitted to return back to your country of citizenship, Great Britain."

The noise in the room rose immediately to a deafening roar. Some were shouting "Yes! Yes!" Others, "That's barbaric! No way!"

Richard's mouth opened in shock. He turned around to seek out Jennifer.

The judge raised his hand for quiet. The noise subsided. "In addition, regarding the second part, if you can continue to concentrate just a little longer, Mr. de L'Isle, and face the tribunal?"

Richard turned back and stared ahead in horror—the colour now draining away from the outside of his cheeks. His head was spinning.

Inaam smiled with delight, banged her fist on the table and shouted, "Yes! Yes! Yes." Justice had been done. She smiled at her lawyers and shook their hands.

The qadi then proceeded, "Finally, regarding the second part," but he was drowned out by Jennifer, who now jumped up from her seat and screamed, "No! No! No!" She tried to run up to her husband's lawyers but was blocked by the tribunal clerk.

She shouted at them, "This is a fiasco, a sham, a bloody set-up. Anthony, you cretin! What on earth were you thinking of when advising my husband to come to this court? This isn't arbitration. This is an iniquitous annihilation of my husband's rights!"

People in the room started talking loudly again.

The judge raised his voice and held up his hands again. "Silence in the back. Mr. de L'Isle, you will soon, but not yet, have the customary opportunity to address the court, but somewhat more respectfully than your wife's unacceptable outburst."

Richard could not immediately find the words to speak. Then, he breathed deeply, leaned forward, and pressed down the tips of his fingers onto the table. His knuckles were white. He looked at his old friend Anthony, and his eyes drilled into his. He then took his time; he was speaking up for his life. He knew the public spotlight was illuminating him. He was spiritual but not religious: he now appealed to whatever higher being was watching over him. He spoke slowly and carefully.

"Respected judge, yes, I would indeed like to address this court. And no, it can't wait. I am shocked by the severity of the punishment for an innocent mistake, an accident, for Pete's sake, and one that occurs every day by many motorists. It was a lapse of concentration of less than one or two seconds, yet you wish to physically scar, financially steal, and publicly defame me for the remainder of my life. It was not deliberate, and it was not premeditated. People who know me have attested that I am a very good, honorable person, with an impeccable record. I have already provided to this court evidence of many people who have corroborated my good standing in society. My brief actions in that car that afternoon were not evil or egregious, but a simple, stupid, careless mistake."

"Mr. de L'Isle," the judge began, but Richard wasn't listening. This was a matter of principle.

"It's not my fault that the daughter wasn't wearing her seat belt; had she been, she would not have died. And you have no medical proof that the husband's death was directly attributable to my actions."

"Mr. de L'Isle," the judge raised his voice but was ignored by Richard.

"Consider the person who incorrectly checks out your grocery item by scanning it by mistake twice. A simple mistake, a single momentary lapse of

The Feather of Truth   Ian Campbell-Laing

judgement, with a simple remedy; pay the customer a refund on that additional item not purchased and perhaps give them their first item free of charge."

"Mr. de L'Isle, you may not—" started the judge. Richard interrupted him yet again. Mrs. Siddiqui grabbed Richard's sleeve in an attempt to stop his rambling, in case the judge amended the sentence to something harsher.

Richard ignored the tugging on his sleeve and shrugged her off to carry on. "Respected judge, consider the person on the *Herald of Free Enterprise* passenger ship, whose job in 1987 was to electronically shut the rear gate where the cars are housed. That person committed a simple mistake, a single short lapse of judgment, and thought he had shut the gate, but he hadn't. He was distracted, tired, and I don't think he was drunk. No different to the checkout person in the grocery store. But in this case, water flooded in, and nearly two hundred people died. He was not sent to prison. He didn't have his offending hand amputated. They all realized it was a simple mistake, albeit with tragic consequences. He did pay a high price, namely having to live with what he had done for the rest of his life. I should imagine he was a broken man, and his life had no purpose or meaning. Esteemed judge, sir, I appeal to your sense of conscience and fair play. Please at least commute the amputation, which is harsh and quite frankly barbaric, for this, a first offence and one which will never be repeated."

The judge stared at Richard and pointed his right index finger at him. "Mr. de L'Isle, your counsel should have told you that speeches during and after sentencing are not allowed, nor under our MAT rules are they appropriate. In fact, your diatribe is wholly disrespectful. It is also rude for any respondent to either lecture the judges or complain to them. I will be shortly waiting for your closing words of gratitude; otherwise, we may amend the sentence to account for this tantrum." He paused and then added, "I hope we have made our views most clear."

Mrs. Siddiqui yanked Richard's sleeve, pulling him down somewhat inelegantly towards her face. She curtly whispered in his ear, "What the hell are you doing? For heaven's sake, shut up and be more respectful, or he will throw the book at you. Do you hear?"

Anthony leant over and implored Richard to listen and act accordingly. Richard was nothing if not determined, though. He wanted to take back control, at whatever the cost.

He freed himself of his lawyer's clutches and stood upright again. "Respected judge, please, I beseech you to reconsider this harsh and unfair sentence. I warn you that otherwise it will have unintended consequences. My voluntarily going to arbitration instead of facing the Crown Court as is my right, as you know, was and still is extremely controversial in the public's eyes. And the flogging and amputation will surely pit Christian values against Muslim ideals. Mark my words, respectful judge, you could also be in deep trouble with the UK and European legal systems, which will not permit any torture!"

The qadi had heard and had enough.

He shouted to make himself heard above the chatter in the courtroom. "Silence, Mr. de L'Isle! How dare you threaten this judicial tribunal. In your ignorance, you will not be aware, but we had already granted you leniency by reducing the lashes from an initial eighty to forty, given the amputation that will proceed later that day. However, your disrespect for this tribunal after you had agreed to arbitration with no appeal is wholly unacceptable and contemptible. I will consult with my learned colleagues before commenting further."

The judge looked furious—his face was red with anger, his veins again pulsating out from his neck. There was a huddling between and a nodding of heads by the three qadis.

"Mr. de L'Isle, this tribunal has decreed that you will receive an extra forty lashes, doubling it back to the original eighty."

There was a shriek from some in the courtroom. The judge continued. "These additional lashes are a direct result of your disrespect for this tribunal. However, I hadn't finished with the sentencing. There is one further matter, which you clearly, in your hasty, self-entitled arrogance didn't hear, and that was regarding the second part of the sentence."

Those present in the court shushed again. The qadi waited for silence. "I am perfectly aware that under various humanitarian laws, human rights acts and so on, Great Britain does not permit what it defines as torture on its soil, nor does it permit deportation to another country for that act to be administered. And flogging and amputation clearly come within this definition."

He paused again. He looked around and saw confused looks in the room, and the chattering started up again.

"That is why that part of the sentence is an *option* for the respondent to consider voluntarily accepting. What I hadn't got to, because I have been constantly interrupted, was the second part, which is this, and why we spent so long outlining the case of dangerous driving and the aggravating and mitigating factors. So, to complete this part of the sentence, uninterrupted, the respondent has the option to either *voluntarily* be deported to Iran for the eighty lashes and hand amputation, or accept a custodial sentence in a British prison of…" He deliberately paused for effect and looked down at his notes to ensure he had the full attention of the room and to have total control of the previously raucous proceedings. The room was silent.

"Ah yes, for a level-one category, the most serious risk of dangerous driving, and which has a range of between seven and fourteen years, we originally had decided a ten-year custodial sentence, Mr. de L'Isle."

There was shouting now in the back of the room. Richard's mouth gaped open. He could not believe what he was hearing. He didn't think the tribunal would or could hand out any jail term.

"But, given your unacceptable and disrespectful outburst, and those of your family, and to make an example of you for the greater good of society, we now increase this to the maximum tariff of fourteen years."

Jennifer shouted out, "Oh my God!" and then collapsed.

"Let me say one more thing, before I am again interrupted. The contempt you and your wife have shown to this court, had you done so in Iran, would have been far more seriously dealt with: under our Islamic *hudud* laws, you both may have been found guilty of a slanderous attack on Islam—a most severe charge—which can carry the death penalty. I will now allow you to confer with your lawyers and let you decide if you wish to voluntarily accept the temporary deportation for your eighty lashes and amputation, or if not, then the fourteen-year custodial sentence will stand. I will give you thirty minutes, after which I expect your answer."

The qadis left the room.

CHAPTER 58
MUSLIM ARBITRATION TRIBUNAL

Richard sat down with his lawyers and strained above the loud chatter in the room to hear what they said. He breathed deeply, his forehead resting on his upheld hands. He sighed, knowing his battle was lost. Both his lawyers had deceived him. He felt trapped again. Mrs. Siddiqui warned him that he had to honor the court's sentencing, or he could get harsher punishment still—even stoning, as the judge had mentioned. Richard had no choice. He was in the hands of the prime minister and any higher spiritual being now.

The qadis filed back into the room, and Richard stood up.

"Have you made a decision regarding the optional part of the sentence, Mr. de L'Isle?"

"Yes, respected judge, I have. I have chosen the voluntary temporary deportation."

There were gasps in the courtroom.

"Very good. Thank you. So you will not now be given a custodial sentence. So, in summary—because it's been a while since I started pronouncing the sentence, which had a litany of interrupting soliloquys—Richard Heathcote de L'Isle, as respondent, you have been sentenced to the following:

One, disqualification from driving for ten years, effective today, and a reapplication; two, a payment of three million pounds to the applicant effective in one month's time; and three; temporary deportation to Iran to receive eighty lashes and for the amputation of your left hand. You may now address the tribunal, in a manner that befits the seriousness, respect, and authority of this process."

Richard placed his hands together below his churning stomach. He looked straight ahead and stared at the qadis in turn and then rested his gaze on the senior judge. He knew his words would be recorded and made public.

"Yes, respected judge, it's most clear. My sincere apologies for my outburst, and please understand that I sincerely meant no disrespect to this tribunal or to Islam. Thank you, respected judge, for the sentence. God's will, will *certainly* be done," said Richard, defiantly. He slumped back into his chair, a defeated man, for the first time in his life.

The judge said, "You may now sit down, Mr. de L'Isle, although it appears that you have already done so. This concludes the sentencing. The respondent will immediately be placed into the custody of this tribunal."

Jennifer de L'Isle had recovered, but was still red-faced and shaking. She jumped up again and screamed at the judges, "What type of primitive justice is this? You should be ashamed of yourselves!" Then, jabbing her fingers and pointing at Richard's counsel, she shouted at Anthony, "What are you going to do? You have to appeal to the prime minister, for God's sake! I'm going to the press! This is bloody barbaric! Richard is right: Christians and Muslims will attack each other as a result—you buffoons."

Jennifer turned to Mrs. Englebrau, who looked shocked at her tirade of abuse. Jennifer shouted at her, "You wicked, evil witch! You won't get to spend the money because, you pathetic woman, the lashings will probably kill you!"

"Quiet in the court! Quiet in the court!" shouted the clerk. Judge Faqui then said, "Mrs. de L'Isle, your outburst does you no credit. If I hear one more word from you, I will have you taken into custody in the cells below to allow your hot head to cool down."

He paused and saw that Jennifer had sat down and had her head in her hands. "This arbitration tribunal is dismissed. Please take into immediate custody both the respondent, Mr. Richard de L'Isle, and the applicant, Mrs. Inaam Englebrau."

In the back of the courtroom, the Iranian journalist who had been texting the details of the sentence on his cell, pressed "send." A few seconds later, Iran's minister of foreign affairs smiled at reading the good news. He would inform Jamal Ahmadi, the president, immediately. Wonderful! He thought.

At the back of the courtroom sat Sir John Roland, head of the Department of Iran and special representative for the Middle East, and next to him, Baroness Petersbridge of Hindhead, legal adviser to the Foreign and Commonwealth Office.

"Oh, shoot," he said to Lady Petersbridge, "now the sh'ite has really hit the political fan."

CHAPTER 59
BLACKDOWN CLOSE

Jennifer was sitting at home in her kitchen with Isabelle. She poured some strong breakfast tea into two mugs, and set out a plate of assorted McVitie's biscuits and Jammie Dodgers, the ones with the delicious strawberry jam in the middle.

Jennifer was distraught and exhausted from a restless night without Richard in the house. "I'm still in shock at the sentence they gave Richard yesterday morning. Why can't the British government intervene? Richard may be no angel, but he's a British citizen and a good man who pays a lot of taxes to this country. They should never have let him be deported to Iran for the public flogging and amputation. It's bloody barbaric, for Christ's sake. I don't know where this country is going, but it's on the wrong path."

Isabelle gently placed her hand on Jennifer's. "Yes, but Richard *chose* that option. He clearly decided that being in the clink was far worse for him and his family. I checked, and a fourteen-year sentence with good behavior still meant he would serve at least seven. But think what the other inmates would do to a middle-class, wealthy pretty boy like Richard! Also, he would definitely lose his job and miss you and the growing up of your kids. I know the torture is awful, but he deemed it less painful in the long run. I think he absolutely made the right decision. Remember, under the tribunal, there's no appeal process to a higher court."

"I just don't know. I just can't take in what's happened. He will be a cripple."

"No. He will be just like any other war veteran—fighting a war to protect his family, if you like—but who has lost a limb and has to move on with their life. Remember, he caused the death of two people. He has to have some punishment. But, look, have you seen the support on the blog you wrote? Hundreds of thousands of people on Facebook, Reddit, and Twitter have said they disagree with what's happening, and they support you. As we predicted it's pitting Christians against Muslims in Britain, and already caused some riots. Soon, someone may get injured or even die, for heavens sake."

"Well, Richard may be the first, if he doesn't survive the lashing tomorrow in Vanak Square in Tehran. I've read that many people have collapsed and died. The beatings are extreme. I feel sick just thinking about it. I don't know how he'll, or we'll get through this, Isabelle."

"That's why I think they put him and that cow, Mrs. Englebrau, on an Iran Air flight within two hours of the sentencing—to get them away from Britain and to make sure they couldn't escape. This isn't justice, but somehow, you will get through this, Jens," said Isabelle, smiling and patting her hand.

The phone rang, and Jennifer picked it up. "Hello? Jennifer here."

"Hi. It's Anthony," said the lawyer, trying to sound upbeat.

Jennifer scowled. "Oh, what do *you* want? Did you speak to the Foreign Office or the PM, Anthony?"

"I tried, God only knows I tried, but neither office would take my call."

"God help Richard, it's all lost then! Damn!"

"I did have a conversation with Sir Scott Sherrins, the head of the Civil Service, who went to university with Richard and is also a member of the RAC, to try and gain some leverage, though."

Jennifer raised her eyebrows, hoping for good news. "And? What did he say? Can he help?"

"Maybe. He firstly mentioned that the PM and Foreign Office won't be seen to publicly intervene and the ruling of the tribunal must stand. However, he added that they might of course be trying to do something behind closed doors."

"And they may not. Either way, Anthony, I blame you for ill advising my husband and the ruddy mess we find ourselves in."

"Jennifer, I gave what I thought was the best advice at the time, and Richard accepted it. He was going to jail if he went to the Crown Court anyway."

"Yes, but only for a few short years. But because of you he had to choose between fourteen years or flogging and amputation. Great result, Anthony! You advised him incorrectly, and he took that advice based on his friendship with, and trust of you. I have nothing further to say to you. Good-bye, and never phone me again."

Jennifer slammed down the phone and shouted out, "Goddammit, this is so ruddy unfair!"

After a while she dried her eyes with a small handkerchief kept in the sleeve of her sweater and said, "Anyway, over the last week, whilst waiting for the tribunal to begin, I have been very busy becoming familiar with that witch's family. I am trying to understand why she did what she did. She knew what she was doing—that Richard would get this kind of sentence. Well, I've discovered a few interesting things these past few days."

"Oh, really? Like what, Jens?"

"Well, as you know, last year I did a search on Ancestry.com and uncovered the family history of my Granville side of the tree, and the year before, I started some of Richard's de L'Isle side, and I put it all into a binder. Seems a long time ago now."

"Yes, I do remember now. Didn't you uncover that one of Richard's ancestors was one of the torturers of Guy Fawkes when he was held in the Tower of London after the failed attempt by those chaps involved in the

The Feather of Truth   Ian Campbell-Laing

Gunpowder Plot to blow up the Houses of Parliament?"

"Yes, Geffrye de L'Isle worked in the court of King James I, and in 1605 was one of three torturers involved in extracting a confession from Guido Fawkes. He reported to Sir William Waad, who was overseeing the proceedings. Geffrye was a well-educated man and also was the person who drafted the confession and forced Fawkes to sign it."

"Cool—so Richard's ancestors were torturers!"

"Not sure 'cool' is the right word, Isabelle. Geffrye apparently kept the quill pen used in the signing, and we're trying to trace where it went. It's perversely bizarre that one of Richard's ancestors was a torturer, and now tomorrow Richard is to be tortured."

"Perhaps God is punishing your family for Geffrye's acts, and centuries later Guido Fawkes is getting his revenge," said Isabelle, excitedly.

Jennifer looked curiously at her best friend, who, like Jennifer, wasn't remotely religious, but was surprised that she enjoyed watching gruesome TV shows like *Hannibal*. Although the stunningly handsome actor, Mads Mikkelsen had something to do with it, she was sure.

"In fact I've uncovered some other murderers on Richard's side of the family, which is a little worrying."

"Jens, that's awesome! But I am sure we all have some ancestral wicked skeletons in our closets. Perhaps it's God's way of punishing generations later—i.e., Richard. Anyway, what did you find out about the Englebrau's? Anything interesting?"

"Not really. Her husband, Jonathan, was Swiss German: his father was German, and his mother Swiss. He served in the Swiss army from 1978 to 1984, then moved to England, trained as a doctor, rose up in the ranks to become a successful heart surgeon. He was sixty-nine years old, much older than Mrs. Englebrau. But he was very fit and still working as a heart surgeon. Then, of course, the car accident happened, and he lost his hand, and then his life. Tragic, I admit."

"I feel sorry for Mrs. Englebrau that she lost her little daughter, Husn, and her husband, all in the space of less than a week," said Isabelle. "But the sentence that Richard had to choose between—fourteen years or flogging and amputation—doesn't seem fair either. However, as you said if he had gone the usual route of the Crown Court, as a level two with mitigating circumstances, he might have got four years tops."

"It's not fair, Isabelle, but even four years in jail would have devastated us all," whimpered Jennifer, with tears forming in her eyes. She sniffled slightly, and inelegantly, and rather loudly blew her nose. "Anyway, back to our nemesis, Mrs. Englebrau. She was born in Iran, but her family moved to England. She went to the prestigious London School of Economics to study law but never went back into the profession after having her two kids. Despite living most of her life here, she retained her Iranian citizenship. I

The Feather of Truth — Ian Campbell-Laing

guess she's got dual citizenship. Her grandfather, Massoud Behzad, was a painter and artist who was trapped in the rubble during the 1978 earthquake in Tabas in Iran, which killed thirty-five thousand people. One of the worst in history by all accounts, Isabelle."

"So where is this leading?" Isabelle was impatient with Jens, who always took a while to tell a story and often got sidetracked.

"His right hand was mangled when the rubble fell on him, but apparently a local doctor managed to save it, and he continued to paint for many years to come. Massoud had a son, who was Mrs. Englebrau's father, called Farbod, which in Farsi literally means 'right.'"

"Maybe they named the son after his right hand was saved?"

"I doubt it, but anyway, who knows or cares, Isabelle. I hate her and her family for what they are doing to Richard and our family."

"Hold on a minute, Jens. Didn't you…or was it Richard who said something earlier this year when we all had dinner, after we went through your family tree research, about Richard's grandfather, Ben? Something about having a watch with the inscription on it 'To Ben, many thanks,' and some name that I can't recall, but wasn't the date 1978? I remember the 78 because coincidentally it was the number of my locker at our old school, Saint Paul's."

"Gosh, I can't recall, but yes, Richard has kept a watch from his grandfather. I never was able to research his grandfather much because he was such a secretive man. We just knew he was a successful surgeon in the UK, and that he spent a short spell in Iran."

"Where's the watch now?" asked Isabelle.

"It's usually in Richard's bedroom with all his other fancy watches. He wears it on the sixth of each month, as a tribute to his grandfather who gave him the watch on the fifth of April, Richard's birthday, as a twenty-first birthday present. Richard treasures it highly."

Isabelle smiled at the usual sidetracking by Jennifer, but didn't make a remark about it. "Was Richard's grandfather a doctor in Iran, around the time of the earthquake?"

"Ben rarely talked about that time abroad. We just assumed he had such bad memories, so we didn't press him. And then with the boys being a handful, I got distracted from my research."

"Distracted, you? Surely not!"

"Thank you, Isabelle."

"Maybe it's just a coincidence, but there can't be many Bens in Iran, especially a Ben who was a surgeon in Iran at that very same time! Come on, chop, chop—go and get the watch!"

Jennifer went upstairs and fetched the watch from Richard's closet.

She sat back down at the kitchen table and read the inscription on the back.

The Feather of Truth   Ian Campbell-Laing

"Bloody hell, Isabelle, your memory is sharp as a button. It says, 'Ben, with thanks,' and it's from Massoud, 1978."

"That's the same name as Mrs. Englebrau's grandfather, right?"

"Yes, it is. But I know that Massoud is a very popular Arabic name, so probably just a coincidence."

"Maybe, maybe not, Jens. Is Richard's grandfather, Ben, still alive?"

"Yes, although we haven't seen him for a few months. He's in the Glebe House Hospice in Caterham, an hour or so away from here. Although he's physically frail, his brain was completely sharp the last time we met him. Poor soul, his body is deteriorating with a muscular degenerative disease he's had for a few years."

"Let's call him right now. It's still only seven in the evening. He may still be up."

"Good idea."

Jennifer reached for her address book. She found the number and dialed it and heard the phone ringing. She put it on speakerphone.

"Hello, Glebe House. Matron speaking."

"Hi. It's Jennifer de L'Isle here, Richard's wife and Ben de L'Isle's granddaughter-in-law. How is Ben today?"

"Mrs. de Lisle, he is not too bad today. But, to be honest, his mental faculties now seem to be slowing down, and he is a little depressed. I was going to ring you this week after seeing your husband on the news yesterday. I am so sorry about the trial and everything."

"Thanks. When Richard returns from Iran, we'll come up and see Ben. Has Ben been watching the news—is he aware of what's going on?"

"No, he hasn't. A month ago, he said he was bored listening to the TV and radio, saying the news was too distressing. He prefers to read a little and listen to the classical music DVDs you gave him. We didn't want to upset him by mentioning his grandson's trial."

"I agree. I don't think he would be able to handle it. But can I speak with Ben? It's quite urgent. And please, continue to not mention the trial to him."

"Yes, surely. He was wide awake when I brought him his cup of cocoa ten minutes ago. He has a nap in the early afternoon, and that seems to help him stay awake until around nine o'clock. So now is a very good time before we turn out his lights in a couple of hours. Hold on, I will transfer the call to his room and walk upstairs to alert him. Just wait a moment, please."

***

Glebe House Hospice, Caterham, Surrey

Matron walked up the stairs. She reached Ben's room and saw him listening to his music and gazing out of the window.

"Ben, hello."

He turned his head towards her. "Hello, Matron."

"How's your cup of cocoa this evening, Ben dear?"

"What cocoa?"

"The cocoa I brought you ten minutes ago, just before seven, like I do each day, you silly man!"

"You do?"

Matron sighed. The old fool had a fragile short-term memory, not being able to remember things that happened five minutes ago, but he could recall in detail events that occurred fifty years ago.

"I have Jennifer on the phone—you know, your grandson Richard's wife. She wants to say a quick hi to you."

"She does? Oh, good. When are she and Richard coming to see me again?"

"You can ask her, but she said to me perhaps in two weeks' time, after Richard is back from an overseas business trip." Matron pressed the accept button on Ben's phone and left the room.

"Hello. Ben de L'Isle here."

"Hello, Grandpa Ben. How are you? It's Jennifer, Richard's wife."

"Hello, Jennifer. I am well, or so they tell me. Are you, Richard, and my great-grandchildren coming to see me soon?"

"Yes, probably in a couple of weeks—Richard's away on business presently. If that's OK."

"Yes, let me check my diary. Yes, I seem to be free that day!" He chuckled.

"Grandpa Ben, I need to ask you something. Did you tell me awhile ago that you worked in Iran when you were practicing medicine as a young surgeon?"

"Oh gosh, that's a very long time ago, now. My God, I haven't thought about that era for a while. Let me think. Yes, I remember. I had a practice in Harley Street in London, and was devastated by the news of the Iranian earthquake after I saw pictures of the dying and injured on TV. Two colleagues and I packed our bags, and I cancelled our operations in the UK for a month and flew to Iran to lend a helping hand. God, that brings back memories. The destruction was unbelievable. Why do you ask? It must be, what, forty or fifty years ago now? I don't really watch the news anymore, so has there been another earthquake?"

"No, there's not been an earthquake. I just came across the watch you gave Richard many years ago in his closet. He still wears it on the fifth of each month in your honor, and for important meetings. I was doing some more research of our family tree and wanted to ask you about the watch."

The Feather of Truth   Ian Campbell-Laing

"Oh yes, that watch. The only watch I was ever given by a stranger. A beautiful Omega timepiece, if I recall. Yes, it was an Omega Seamaster watch that he said he had purchased in 1967. Must have cost the dear fellow a fortune! But didn't I give it to Richard for his twenty-first?"

"Yes, and he treasures it. Do you recall who gave it to you and why?"

Ben paused and thought back all those years ago. "Yes, I can picture him still very vividly. I and the rest of the small team of doctors were working in the makeshift operating tent, helping the wounded. Stitching back partly severed hands and fingers. Sometimes we were able to save a person's hand or fingers, sometimes not. It was heartbreaking and backbreaking work, with the constant threat of the authorities putting us into jail, or of being lynched by a public that was at the time very anti-British and anti-American."

"So, who gave you the watch? The inscription on the back says 'Ben, with thanks, from Massoud, 1978.' Do you remember who he was?"

"Yes, I certainly do. Our team had arrived about three days earlier, and it was my first successful operation there. We managed to stitch back the partly severed three middle fingers of the man's right hand. He was probably thirty years older than me. He regained nearly full use. It was so satisfying to accomplish this, and he was so pleased, he hugged me. A week later, he gave me the watch he was wearing after he had it inscribed. Yes, I remember Massoud, a delightful, softly spoken Iranian artist. I was chuffed that he could work again with his right hand and fingers. I still have a painting somewhere that he also gave me many years later. It was a watercolour of the street in which he lived with his family before the earthquake. He also said that in the war, the Germans caught him passing off reproduction master oil paintings as originals. Quite a character he was."

Jennifer smiled at Isabelle. "Grandpa Ben, thanks. That's very helpful. Do you remember his surname?"

The line went quiet as Ben thought back all those years. "I remember him telling me he had a son called Farbod, which in Farsi, he said, translates to mean 'right.' Which was kind of nice, as it was the right hand of Massoud whose fingers we managed to save. Massoud said that it was 'right' to give me the watch after what I had done, even though his family hated the West and didn't want him to give me anything.

Yes, I do recall his name; it was Massoud Behzad. His surname in Persian means 'of good and noble birth,' and he said that meeting me was good, and his giving me the watch was a noble thing for him to do."

CHAPTER 60
10 DOWNING STREET, LONDON

There were two meetings being held at 7:00 a.m.: one in the prime minister's private office, and the other in the study. Both were discussing Iran and Richard de L'Isle.

In the study sat Sir John Roland, Baroness Petersbridge, and Jennifer de L'Isle.

Sir John and Lady Petersbridge sat in the two leather armchairs, either side of the two-columned fireplace. No fire was lit; instead it contained a glass vase with white and yellow tulips. Facing them sat Jennifer. Between them was a walnut table, upon which were a telephone and a silver service of tea. Jennifer briefly stared above the fireplace and looked at the portrait of Lady Thatcher: it seemed to depict a rather soft and gentle image of the Iron Lady.

Sir John brushed his silver hair back with the fingers of his right hand and started the proceedings. "Thank you all for coming, especially so early in the morning. Mrs. de L'Isle, thank you also for your call to the FCO yesterday evening. You did the right thing. Since that call, a team of researchers have gone through your information, and it's clear it is accurate and may be of help to Richard."

Lady Petersbridge continued the conversation. "It's a remarkable coincidence that your husband's grandfather, Dr. Ben de L'Isle, did indeed help Mrs. Englebrau's grandfather, Mr. Massoud Behzad, nearly fifty years ago after Massoud was injured in the Iranian earthquake of 1978. He sewed back his severed fingers, enabling him to continue work as an artist for the rest of his life. May I see the watch that Massoud gave Ben that year?"

"Certainly." Jennifer took out a small black cloth from her handbag and passed it to the baroness.

Lady Petersbridge examined the gold Omega watch. She saw the inscription on the back. "It's a beautiful timepiece and marvelous heirloom, Mrs. de L'Isle, and appears to show precisely what you indicated to us."

Sir John said, "So it seems genuine. Good." Then looking at the baroness, he added, "We may be able to use it as leverage for Mrs. de L'Isle's husband, agreed?"

"Yes, I believe so, Sir John."

Sir John frowned. "However, Mrs. de L'Isle, we don't think the usual diplomatic channels will be appropriate here. In fact, I'm sure they won't, given the hostilities and suspicions between our two nations. And we are of course, running out of time."

"So, what do you think will work?" Jennifer enquired.

"We think that a woman-to-woman discussion is what's needed here to make a breakthrough—an appeal to female reason, if you will," said Sir John.

"Fine. Lady Petersbridge, when will you be talking to Mrs. Englebrau?" asked Jennifer; relieved she wasn't going to be directly involved.

"Sir John and I are recommending that *you* call her, Mrs. de L'Isle, and very soon."

"Bloody hell! Oops, sorry." Jennifer blushed.

"No need to apologize. We've heard far worse, Mrs. de L'Isle. So, just speak your mind," said Lady Petersbridge.

"Well, I hate that woman. I may not be able to do it. Also, I detest the limelight."

Sir John sighed. "Mrs. de L'Isle, you need to curtail your anger. As, we understand, so does Mrs. Englebrau; she holds a great deal of contempt for your husband, who caused the death of her precious daughter and her dear husband. No one outside this room ever needs to know that this call took place. It will be made in private, with no one else present, here in this room."

"Christ, what am I to say to her? The last and only time I spoke to her was at the end of the tribunal where I called her an evil witch! Should I appeal to her just because her grandfather and Richard's helped each other out over half a century ago? I doubt she will buy it, Sir John."

"Actually, we believe there's a fighting chance that she will," said Lady Petersbridge. "You and she are both reasonable women, caught up in all of this. I don't think she is an evil person at all. Her more radical Muslim brothers are merely influencing her. Are you willing to give it a try? We'll be here with you, and it may be the only chance Richard has of saving his hand."

"You mean right now? God, I need to compose myself and think what I am to say. If I blow it, Richard will be punished today. Heavens, I…"

Lady Petersbridge reached forward, gently placing her hand on Jennifer's shoulder. "Precisely why we need to make that call now. He is due to be flogged at 15:30 hours, Tehran time, which is midday our time. That's less than five hours' time. And later this evening, he will have his left hand amputated, probably around 20:00 hours, but all depending on how well he holds up from the flogging. The FCO has arranged for Mrs. Englebrau to be on the line at the prison in Tehran where she is being held, in"—she looked at her watch—"fifteen minutes. Earlier this morning, she agreed to take your call."

Jennifer took a deep breath and breathed out slowly. "OK. This is so sudden, but yes, I will make the call. But, I need to gather my thoughts." Jennifer tried to forget that she was, in her own mind, "just" a mother of three boisterous children. She now instead had to think of herself as her husband's ambassador. He had always been strong for her, and now she must do the same for him.

Lady Petersbridge turned to Sir John, raising her eyes and cocking her head towards the door.

Sir John took the hint. "I'll just pop over to the PM's private office and check how the other meeting is going."

Jennifer closed her eyes and thought about what she was going to say. She felt anxious and totally unprepared. She always so depended on Richard's strength, and now he was in her hands. She felt pressurized and not up to the task assigned to her.

Lady Petersbridge said nothing and, grabbing her iPad, scrolled down to read the latest BBC news, in case something more had been written about the de L'Isle-Englebrau case. There was plenty.

Then, the baroness accessed the meeting app, which had automatically, through voice recognition, recorded the conservation in the room. She went through the transcript so far to ensure it was edited correctly.

After five minutes, Jennifer opened her eyes and looked down at the official notepad and pencil that the baroness had placed in front of her. On the notepad, an address was printed: Office of the FCO, King Charles St, London SW1A 2AN, United Kingdom. She wrote down three points and then numbered them one, three, and two, respectively, according to their importance. Sir John returned just before the call was due to be made. He asked, "Mrs. de L'Isle, are you ready?"

"Yes, I am. Let's get this ugly business out of the way."

The conference line had already been set up. Lady Petersbridge spoke into the phone in front of her. "Conference line four, dial Evin Prison, Tehran, Iran, please."

A prison official who was expecting the call answered the phone. He spoke perfect English. "This is Evin Prison. Mr. Rouhani speaking. Who is this, please?"

"This is London. My name is Sir John Roland, and I head up the Department of Iran and am the special representative for the Middle East region. Thank you for taking the call, Mr. Rouhani. I have with me, as agreed, Baroness Petersbridge of Hindhead, our FCO legal adviser, and Mrs. Jennifer de L'Isle. Is Mrs. Inaam Englebrau also ready to be on the line, please?"

"Thank you, Sir John. Yes, she is sitting here with me. I have on a conference line, also as agreed, Mr. Saeed Ebrahimi, who is the head of the UK Department within the Ministry for Foreign Affairs, and Mr. Hadi Ghorbani, the prosecutor general of Tehran."

Sir John spoke. "Good. Thank you. Shall we make a start?" He raised his eyebrows at Jennifer, expecting her to speak first.

"Mrs. de L'Isle, this is Mrs. Englebrau. Please quickly say whatever it is you have to say to me, and then promise to never call or contact me ever again." Inaam spoke quietly and matter-of-factly, with no emotion.

Wow, thought Jennifer, what a dreadful start. She briefly looked up at the portrait of Margaret Thatcher and was reminded to stick to her conciliatory script. "Good morning. This is Mrs. Jennifer de L'Isle speaking, but please call me Jennifer."

"No, I would prefer to call you Mrs. de L'Isle. Please, we have not formally met, apart from when you shouted disgraceful insults at me at the tribunal."

Jennifer's chest was rising and falling quickly, but she continued to speak slowly and did not get rattled. "I quite understand, and yes, you're right, that does seem more appropriate. My outburst at the tribunal was totally uncalled for and not becoming of the good name of either a Granville or a de L'Isle. I have regretted what I said ever since then. However, let me say, Mrs. Englebrau, that I share in your pain for the loss of your daughter, Husn, and of your husband, Jonathan. I have read that they were very good people. I know that this is a very difficult time for you, especially after being sentenced yourself by the tribunal. If it's any consolation, I thought your sentence very harsh."

Inaam began to raise her voice. "I do no seek, nor do I need your sympathy, Mrs. de L'Isle. I require only revenge for your husband's careless act. Nothing more. I bear you personally no grudge. I too have done my research, and despite you calling me an evil witch and hoping that I don't live to spend the restitution monies fairly and rightly awarded to me by the tribunal, I have read that you are a decent woman, mother, and wife as well. But that does not matter, and you are wasting my precious time. I hate your husband, who took away the two people who were most dear to me, and not only has the tribunal deemed I am entitled to have revenge, but morally, and under my faith, I believe I am also deserving of it."

Jennifer hadn't anticipated this level of hatred and hostility. She paused before speaking again, and glanced at her notes. She felt hot, and her head was throbbing. She wondered what tack she could take to change the direction and ameliorate the tone of the call.

"Mrs. de L'Isle, the phone has gone quiet. Did you hear my last words?"

"Yes, Mrs. Englebrau, I heard them all, loud and very clear."

"Well then, what is it that you wish of me, because I don't think we have anything in common or much more to say?"

Jennifer smiled. She suddenly thought of something not on her notepad. "Actually, Mrs. Englebrau, I think we have much in common."

"The only thing we have in common is that we are both women. Period. The first difference is that you have a husband, and I do not. The second is that I have also lost my daughter, and you have not. Please get to the point, Mrs. de L'Isle, because you are beginning to irritate me, and in only a few short hours, God has decided to punish me further and humiliate me in public. I am to be shamed for an act committed by your husband."

"Mrs. Englebrau, you may have researched me, but I doubt you will know that my first husband, Gordon, died of pancreatic cancer less than two years after we were married, and only six months after being diagnosed. We were both very young and very much in love. So I *do* know what it is to lose a husband, a best friend—a soul mate if you will." Jennifer paused but heard no reaction from Inaam.

"The second thing you do not know about me, and in fact neither does my husband, Richard, is that when Gordon was diagnosed with cancer, I found out I was pregnant with his child, a baby girl. The stress of his illness and his subsequent death took its toll on me, and the pregnancy developed complications. Our daughter had to be delivered by cesarean section but was stillborn after only twenty-five weeks," said Jennifer. She paused as she wiped away a tear that had formed in her right eye. "So I do not need to be lectured by any woman about losing people who were special and dear to me. I do not intend to be sharp with you, Mrs. Englebrau, and I know I am raising my voice, so apologies, but these two deaths were very difficult for me. They still are. Every time I see a little girl, or someone who would have been the same age as my precious unborn girl, it causes me much grief. Her and my husband's deaths were just accidents, or perhaps fate intervening, if you will—as was your loss."

There was silence at the other end of the line in Iran. Jennifer felt hot and upset. Her hands were shaking, and she wondered if she had been too harsh or very tactless, and now had blown it. The baroness put her hand on Jennifer's shoulder, and Jennifer carried on after clearing her dry throat, and taking a small swig of a glass of water. "I, too, do not wish to have your sympathy. As you say, it is not appropriate, as we do not know each other. In fact, I rarely bring up my loss and had no intention of mentioning it today, until your comment. No, the purpose of my call is unrelated and something quite different, actually." Jennifer paused and then added, "Are you still on the line, Mrs. Englebrau? The line has gone quiet."

Inaam said softly, "Yes, Mrs. de L'Isle, I am still here."

"Good, thank you. The purpose of my call was simply that I wanted to bring something to your attention that I believe you have a right to know. After that, we need not communicate with each other ever again, as you requested earlier."

"What is it that is so important at this crucial hour before my public disgrace today?"

"I understand your grandfather, Massoud Behzad, was a painter and an artist of considerable talent, but who got trapped in the rubble of the Iranian earthquake in 1978 that killed many thousands of people. Is that correct?"

The Feather of Truth   Ian Campbell-Laing

"What? That's so long ago now. How do you know about that? Yes, he was, and nearly forty thousand people died. He was lucky to survive. What's that got to do with your husband, Mrs. de L'Isle, and what he has done to my family?"

Jennifer took a deep breath, exhaled, and said, "My husband's grandfather, Dr. Ben de L'Isle, was a very good doctor, and—like your husband—a surgeon, in fact. He had a thriving business in Harley Street. But in 1978, Ben and a small team dropped everything and went to Iran to help out in the local hospital. They answered the humanitarian call. They felt compelled to go there and offer their services free, for a month. In fact, they stayed three months."

Inaam was getting impatient and raised her voice in frustration. "So? That's ages ago. I still don't see the connection, Mrs. de L'Isle."

"Ben did some very good work out there, amidst a great deal of hostility from some local Iranians that resented his western presence. As I am sure you know, at that time in Iran there was great unrest, political turmoil, and mob rioting in the streets, including attacking the British Embassy. It was a brave humanitarian move by Ben to turn up in Iran and offer to help out the local people. He was literally risking his own life to save others.

Ben never, ever told anyone—not his son, nor his grandson, my husband Richard—about his experiences in Iran, because the horrors he saw gave him nightmares. But we found out only yesterday evening that he repaired the three fingers of a man who was trapped in the rubble. His team spent over twenty hours nonstop sewing back the partly severed fingers, attaching complicated, tiny nerve endings in a hot, sweaty hospital with no sanitation, very little food and water, poor light, and little anesthetic. And, amidst the constant worry that the mob would take his own life, as they had done to other doctors before he had arrived."

"So?" said Mrs. Englebrau.

"The person whose fingers Ben sewed back and who, as a result of Richard's grandfather's surgery, was then able to continue his career as a painter and artist, was your grandfather Massoud Behzad."

There was silence on the end of the line in Iran. Then, Inaam said, "Oh, please, Mrs. de L'Isle, with the power of the Internet, you could have researched so much of this and simply invented the connection. You are surely making this up to try and save your miserable husband's punishment at the eleventh hour. How despicable of you, Mrs. de L'Isle. And you call *me* a witch? That's what you really are. I think this conversation should end right now. I need to prepare myself for God's public punishment shortly. I suggest your husband does the same. Mr. Rouhani, I am finished with this call."

Jennifer started to panic, quickly adding, "Not true, Mrs. Englebrau. I have concrete proof, please listen just a minute longer."

The Feather of Truth — Ian Campbell-Laing

"What proof exactly?"

"Richard has in his possession a watch that is inscribed on the back, 'Ben, with thanks, Massoud.' And beneath that, the year, 1978. I spoke to Richard's grandfather yesterday, who has never spoken to anyone about this before, but who now confirms the story. Your grandfather gave Richard's grandfather that watch as a thank you for saving his fingers. Our families are linked in history, and in kindness, whether we like it or not, Mrs. Englebrau. And if I am not mistaken, your Christian name, Mrs. Englebrau, Inaam, means 'kindness' in Farsi, doesn't it?"

Silence.

"Mrs. Englebrau. Are you still there?"

There was the sound of a woman crying on the other end of the phone. Then Mrs. Englebrau spoke. "Mrs. de L'Isle, my grandfather told me a story that you could not have possibly known, about a doctor who was not a Muslim, but a brave, hardworking Englishman whose name he never divulged to me, but to whom he once gave his precious watch as a present. He described the watch and its meaning to me. Do you have the watch with you now?"

"Yes, I do."

"What type of watch is it?"

"It's a gold Omega Seamaster, Mrs. Englebrau."

"Will you please open the back of it?"

"Hold on a moment." Jennifer struggled but could not find out how to open it. She passed the watch to Lady Petersbridge, who found the clasp and with her long nails opened it and then passed it back to Jennifer.

"If you are telling the truth, you should now read to me what words are on the inside."

"OK, I have it opened now. I have never before seen the inside, so please give me a second. There are no words inside, but there appears to be a diagram or perhaps the outline of a picture."

"It is correct that there are no words. Turn the watch to let the light shine on it and move it around. What do you now see?"

Jennifer quickly peered inside. "It looks like near the top there's an oval shape with some very small vertical lines inside, and underneath some wavy lines. Three wavy lines I think."

"Yes, that is what my grandfather told me. The three little wavy lines represent waves of the sea. Look carefully at what is inside the oval—which represents the land—next to the sea, Mrs. de L'Isle. Is there anything?"

"Let me see. It's very small, and the vertical lines I can now see are in fact italic letters."

"Go on, Mrs. de L'Isle."

Jennifer passed the watch to Sir John; he examined it and, on her notepad, wrote down,

NIB?

Or *NJB?*

"It's so small, Mrs. Englebrau, and my reading glasses aren't that powerful. I think it's perhaps the three initials NIB or NJB."

"Not quite. Look more carefully, Mrs. de L'Isle, please."

The baroness grabbed the watch and peered at it. She then took the notepad and, using Sir John's italic pen, crossed out what had been written and wrote, *MIB*.

"No, you are right. It's a bit clearer now. I think it's MIB, Mrs. Englebrau."

"Yes, that would be right. Grandpa Massoud Ibrahim Behzad said he put his initials on the inside, too small for most to see immediately."

"What is the significance of the land and the waves, Mrs. Englebrau?"

"The watch was definitely my grandfather's. He only once mentioned the operation on his three fingers to my mother, who later relayed that story to me. She said that the three little waves represented his fingers that would otherwise have been taken away from him." Inaam paused before adding, "And during my research of you, Mrs. de L'Isle, if I am not mistaken de L'Isle is of French origin and means 'from, or of the Island,' is it not?"

"Yes, it is, but I don't make the connection, Mrs. Englebrau."

"Neither did I until now. He definitely engraved the back of the watch before giving it to Dr. Ben de L'Isle. The inscription 'To Ben, with thanks, Massoud' and the three waves of his fingers warmly protecting the de L'Isle island was his tribute of thanks to your grandfather, no doubt. No question in my mind now that you have the authentic watch. I owe you an apology, Mrs. de L'Isle, for my previous terse behavior."

"Mrs. Englebrau, you actions were totally understandable given your loss and my outburst at the tribunal. No apology is necessary. It is I who must apologize to you for the horrid names I called you, especially in public. As I mentioned earlier, I very much regret my outburst: I did not mean to insult you, or your faith or your noble country."

"Mrs. de L'Isle, may I take a moment to get some water and call you back shortly, please?"

"Thank you. I would like that."

The line went dead.

Jennifer was absolutely exhausted and breathing heavily.

Lady Petersbridge checked that the line was dead. "Line clear."

"Very well handled, Mrs. de L'Isle. Very well done indeed!" said Sir John.

They all chatted and waited for the return call. After ten minutes, Sir John left the room. Finally, over an hour later, the phone rang, just as Sir

John returned. Lady Petersbridge saw the number was from Iran, pressed the OK button, and took the phone off mute. She nodded to Sir John.

"Sir John here."

"Sir John, this is Mr. Rouhani of Evin Prison again. I have Mrs. Inaam Englebrau with me. Do you still have Mrs. de L'Isle with you?"

"Yes, sir, I do. We are all here, as before, and thank you for calling us back."

"Mrs. de L'Isle, I apologize for the delay in returning the call. My mind is in turmoil, as you can imagine. This has not been easy for me," Mrs. Englebrau said.

"Mrs. Englebrau, I fully understand."

"My personal wish is for your husband to not lose his hand later today. I had no idea until we spoke that it was your husband's grandfather's extraordinary skills and bravery that saved my grandfather's own fingers, as evidenced by the story he told my mother and the watch in your possession. He only mentioned it was an Englishman. He never gave my mother his name. Today's revelations have caused a paradigm shift in my anger towards your family. Your family has helped mine, and it is right that I now help yours and save your own husband's hand."

Jennifer opened her mouth in amazement before she said, "My God, Mrs. Englebrau! That is very kind and indeed noble of you. Thank you." In the room, Jennifer and the others all shared looks of relief.

Then a somber voice spoke, in perfect English with no hint of an Iranian accent, said, "Hello. It's Mr. Hadi Ghorbani here, the prosecutor general. The reason why we took so long to call you back is that we have been thinking of the implications of Mrs. Englebrau's request. I took the liberty to call a respected Shariah lawyer here who sits as a judge in the Tehran courts and also to one of the judges who works at the London Muslim Arbitration Tribunals. But the feedback is not promising."

"What on earth do you mean, Mr. Ghorbani?" asked Jennifer. "If this is the will of Mrs. Englebrau, then surely the tribunal must recognize it?"

"No, Mrs. de L'Isle, that's not how the courts work under Shariah law. Once sentencing has been pronounced, there is no appeal—apart from a judicial review with the permission of the High Court, which is not relevant here—and nothing will stop the pronouncements being carried out, short of the death of the person who was sentenced."

Jennifer was now in tears and looked to the baroness for support. She quickly spoke. "Mr. Ghorbani, Lady Petersbridge here, the FCO's special legal adviser. Had Mrs. Englebrau been aware of these new facts, it is likely she would not have sought in her applicant's statement, the amputation of Mr. de L'Isle's hand, and hence, the court would probably not have included it in one of its options of sentence, surely?"

"Lady Petersbridge, yes, it is certain that I would have amended my request to the Muslim Arbitration Tribunal court, as you so say," said Mrs. Englebrau.

A new voice interjected, "Hello. It's Mr. Saeed Ebrahimi here, head of the UK Department within the Ministry for Foreign Affairs. The tribunal was presented with evidence at the time, and they acted on it. So there is no possibility to change the sentence today. It seems harsh, I know, but there it is. The will of Allah, through the tribunal acting at that time, must be carried out in full."

"Gentlemen, I thought under Shariah law, the intervention of the head of the judiciary in Iran could commute a sentence?" said Sir John.

"Yes, sir, you are technically right," replied Mr. Ghorbani, "in exceptional circumstances, that is true. But this is also not a quick process. And it has never happened under the circumstances we have here."

"What if we appeal to the supreme leader himself, to whom the head of the judiciary reports? Would that speed matters up?" asked the baroness.

"No. We considered that, but going over the head of the judiciary might exacerbate matters."

"What about if we arrange for our prime minister to call the president of Iran himself?" said Sir John, giving it his last shot.

"Well, I wouldn't recommend that, given he has no influence over the judiciary. They report to the supreme leader, and—"

"Yes. Mr. Ghorbani, I suspect you were going to say that the president and the supreme leader's relationship is not exactly rosy, presently?"

"I couldn't possibly comment on such matters, Sir John."

"Quite so."

Mr. Ebrahimi sighed. "I am sorry, Mrs. de L'Isle, but your husband must be given his eighty lashes in public this afternoon, and then tonight, must lose his left hand. *In sha'llah*. It is the will of God."

CHAPTER 61
ROYAL SURREY HOSPITAL, GUILDFORD, ENGLAND

Later that afternoon, Jennifer had gone to the hospital in preparation for her husband's anticipated return to the UK after his ordeal in Iran.

One piece of good news had emerged after he had been sentenced: once Richard was on his way home, he would be immediately put under the care of Dr. Caleb Moore, one of America's leading trauma specialists, and who coincidentally was the visiting overseas professor at the hospital.

Jennifer had met Dr. Moore in his office at the hospital and discussed the level of care Richard would likely have in Iran for the twenty-four hours immediately following his flogging and amputation before being flown home. They concluded that too much was at risk from an unknown medical team, uncertain quality of suitable equipment, and being in a hostile country. So, she had arranged for a private jet to take Richard from Tehran's Imam Khomeini airport back to Britain within an hour of his amputation. Dr. Moore and his team would be on that plane to ensure that Richard was properly stabilized.

Dr. Moore had discussed with Jennifer his approach to Richard's recovery. "Mrs. de L'Isle, cases like his work algorithmically. After taking his vitals, phase one is to stabilize your husband. A patient like this would be quite unstable, so he would likely be sedated, chemically paralyzed, and intubated with a respirator, immediately. The cardiac rhythm would be assessed, which for simplicity purposes, I would say, is stable. This we will do immediately on the plane journey home."

Jennifer was alarmed. "Christ, you will paralyze him?"

"Yes. His body will be in shock, and so we need to put him in a semi-unconscious state for him to be able to start the recuperation process in the most efficient and effective manner."

"Aha. Like how the trauma doctors did for the racing driver Michael Schumacher when they placed him in a medically induced artificial coma and lowered his body temperature to reduce the swelling in his brain?"

"Precisely. Michael had a traumatic brain injury, and Richard will likely have traumatic body injuries. For phase two, access needs to be obtained. A triple-lumen catheter would be inserted into the right jugular vein. That allows the team to give him IV fluids, medication, and blood if needed. A Foley catheter would also be inserted into the bladder. As the lines go in, blood and urine would be collected and sent for analysis."

"Will you do that on the plane also?"

"Yes. During the six-hour flight home, we have all the technology on board to do all of that. It's a specially designed plane. Phase three is then early interventions once he is here at the hospital. My team, based on the results of the primary survey, would give broad-spectrum antibiotics and IV fluids. He would likely get vancomycin, one gram intravenously every twelve hours, as well as ceftazidime, two grams every eight hours. They would also give him two litres of normal saline 'wide open' to rapidly bring up his blood pressure. Sometimes we use 'pressors,' but that may be too complicated."

"Once he's back here, how long do you think it will be before he is able to leave hospital and come home?"

"We can't tell until we have examined him and seen how he is reacting during the first few weeks. But what I have described is only the first part. We would then go into the secondary survey, soon after he arrives here. Richard would be given a rigorous exam, and issues noted. He would then be sent off to radiology for CT scans to the chest, abdomen, and pelvis. Plain film X-rays would be done to look for breaks. Then he would be transferred to the surgical ICU."

"He would need to go to the intensive care unit?"

"Yes. We would monitor him for any issues of concern over the coming days and weeks. For instance, loss of blood supply to lower limbs. Vascular surgery would assess and either repair or amputate."

Her mouth gaped open. "Amputate his legs?"

"It has been known for those receiving the full eighty lashes, but uncommon. It's more typical after two hundred or so lashes. But, as I said, these are areas we need to monitor closely. Secondly, we would look for and treat any sepsis or osteomyelitis of the bone."

Jennifer's head was pounding. "Christ, this is more serious than I could have ever imagined."

"Mrs. de L'Isle, that's why it is called trauma. But my team and I are here to ensure he makes a full or near-full recovery. We would continue treating him with antibiotics for six weeks, maybe two months, and periodically your husband would be sent to the OR for debridement—i.e., removal of dead tissue at the sites of the lashing."

Jennifer started to cry with fear.

Dr. Moore bent down and rested his hand on her shoulder. "Mrs. de L'Isle, let me say that, while I must point out the risks, I have had a 100 percent success rate in restoring patients in similar circumstances to near previous health. So at this stage, you should not fear anything. Let's see how he is when he arrives here. Remember he is in peak physical shape, has a strong, positive mental frame of mind, and as you mentioned to me, survived mock interrogations when at school."

"OK. So is that the treatment in detail?" said Jennifer, not sure if she could absorb any more of this gruesome discussion.

"Nearly. Finally, we would assess for rhabdomyolysis. When cells are damaged, they leak electrolytes and creatine kinase into the blood, which affects heart and kidney function. If present, we treat with fluids and possibly hemodialysis."

He paused and looked at her. He was pleased that she had stopped crying. "The intubation that I mentioned would probably last three to five days. As sedation is lifted, he would receive morphine for pain. The first week will be critical, most certainly."

***

The next day

Jennifer saw her husband being wheeled into ICU on a stretcher by two orderlies, with Dr. Moore following behind. She shot up from her chair. "Dr. Moore, I am so glad you arrived back safely. How is he faring?"

"Oh, hi, Mrs. de L'Isle. He has been *very* badly beaten, but we have stabilized him for now. It's too early to say until we have run more tests and seen how he reacts over the coming weeks. His back, buttocks, and upper part of his calves are swollen and raw from the canes ripping through the outer epidermis, then penetrating deep into the inner dermis layers of collagen fibers and reaching some nerve endings.

Having examined the strokes from the two canes, I can advise that they appeared to have been deliberately planted for maximum effect. The officer on the left, who was right handed, landed his forty blows on Richard's back between the highest lumbar vertebrae, L1, and the lowest thoracic vertebrae, T12, of his spine, where the subcutaneous fat is typically thinnest, and hence he had more chance of reaching the nerve endings to cause maximum pain. The officer on the right, who was left handed, appears to have had the role of inflicting pain over the largest area possible, from the shoulder blades, the top of the buttocks, to as low as behind the knees. Richard's supreme fitness and mental state prevented him from the indignity of collapsing, but his lean body, with only 10 percent body fat, did not protect his body from deep punishment. But what is a surprise was the condition of his left hand, because..."

Jennifer interrupted him. "Oh heavens. My poor Richard, what have they done to you? Can I come into ICU with you, Doctor?"

"Yes, of course. But I warn you, he's not a pretty sight."

CHAPTER 62
THE RAC

Two weeks later

Richard was in a cab on his way from the hospital to have dinner with Elisa. Richard had told Jennifer he needed to see his recruiter to discuss some important hires he wanted to make in his department. He reasoned to her that it was important for him to appear in public. He promised her and the doctors that he would be gone from hospital for only a few hours.

Whilst he had made good progress since being taken out of the induced coma a week ago, he was still heavily sedated with morphine, and Jennifer and the doctors were not happy about him leaving their care so soon, even for a couple of hours. But Richard was insistent.

She was thankful that at least his first public appearance was lunch that day at the hospital canteen with her, his wife. Whilst Richard was clearly feeding off the public attention, she didn't enjoy the new scrutiny her family were having. Reporters had turned up at their home, seeking interviews and statements. She had received bags of mail: some praising her for supporting her husband, but many others promising to take revenge on her family for insulting their Muslim faith. She wanted it to all go away. One hand written letter had caused her to cry. It was from Mrs. Englebrau, who had replied to Jennifer's letter thanking Inaam for her help during the phone call with the FCO. Inaam had now reached out to her, offering for them to meet for lunch in a public place to show forgiveness by their families and display unity between their two countries and their two faiths. This was now planned for next week, at the RAC.

As Richard went through the events a fortnight ago, the muscles in his face tightened. He was only able to sit down or lean back in a chair for short periods of time. So, Richard knelt on the floor in the back of the cab, holding onto the handle of the door with his right hand.

Richard shifted his weight from one knee to the other, feeling the coarse, thick, carpeted floor of the cab press into the thin cotton trousers of his suit. As he closed his eyes, he reminded himself that there was a principle at stake here, and he wanted to show the public how strong he could be and how proud he was to be British and a de L'Isle.

He was determined to sit at his regular table of the Great Gallery restaurant, no matter how much pain and throbbing he would have to endure. Earlier that day, at lunch with Jennifer, he had only lasted forty-five minutes before the pain took over, and they left the hospital canteen soon after only finishing their starters. And the walk to and from the canteen was dreadfully slow and painful. He hadn't appreciated how much one uses and depends on one's back muscles for just carrying out simple tasks, like walking and getting up or sitting down.

The image in last weekend's papers flashed into his mind, as he saw his photo on the front page of the *Sunday Times* magazine. He was standing in the square in Iran, his hands handcuffed in front of a wooden post, with a bamboo cane striking his naked, bloodied back at the moment of impact.

He shuddered as he remembered that afternoon so vividly. Even with the heavy-duty drugs he was now taking, the excruciating pain took over his mind, preventing him from concentrating on any subject he chose to think about and slowing his perception of time passing.

Elisa was making her own way to the club from her Kensington office and had earlier that day asked him if he was sure that he wanted to dine at the club tonight—she was worried that it was so soon after his ordeal, and wondered how she would cope with the publicity. She wanted their affair, which amazingly had not appeared in the press, to remain a secret.

"Yes, sweetheart, I do," he said on his throwaway phone. "I want to show what the de L'Isle's are made of, and of course I can't wait to see you again," he had replied.

He continued the journey on his knees, praying for relief of his pain. Without opening his eyes, his mind kept drifting back to and focusing his thoughts on his time in Iran.

At Evin prison, Richard was issued with the standard prisoner's uniform: dark blue trousers and a light blue shirt with a badge on the breast. He couldn't sleep the night before, lying on a dirty mattress in his cold, solitary-confined cell. At 5:30 a.m., he was given breakfast, which consisted of warm black tea with mint and *sobhaneh*, a piece of flatbread, some butter, feta cheese, and jam. Whilst not hungry, he knew the importance of eating now. And once he started eating, the prison food tasted surprisingly good. He noticed a camera in the corner of the ceiling of his cell. Of course even in this prison, which had a reputation for being one of the harshest, he was a priority prisoner, and no doubt with the world watching, he had to be given a good meal and would be under twenty-four-hour surveillance.

At 10:30, a medical officer came to examine him in his cell. In perfect English he said, "You are fit to receive your punishment, Mr. de L'Isle, which will commence at three-thirty this afternoon."

Soon afterwards, he was taken downstairs to a basement where an Iranian-built white Khodro diesel van awaited him. Six officers inside guarded him for the ten-kilometer, twenty-minute journey to Vanak Square, passing along the Chamran and Modares highways and Africa Boulevard.

In a small, windowless holding room in a building adjacent to the square, at midday he received a large bowl of *khoresht*, lamb stew with rice.

The Feather of Truth   Ian Campbell-Laing

He knew he must eat it, to keep his strength up and not let his blood sugar level drop, or he might pass out. The pain in his stomach had returned, and he didn't feel like eating, but he chewed it slowly and forced it down. It tasted very good.

At 3:20 p.m., the same medical officer came into the room and checked his blood pressure and heart one more time. He pronounced him fit for his punishment.

Two guards came into the room. One of them handcuffed his hands together in front of him, and the other motioned him to walk ahead of them upstairs to the square. As the door opened, the warm, outside air rushed into the cold atmosphere of the building and onto his face and chest. He heard the noise from the crowd in the square ahead. He held his head up and walked forward. A third guard joined them and took his arm. Richard roughly pulled his arm away. "I do not need to be held. Got it? I am British, and I want to walk unaided!"

The official standing by said something in Farsi to the guard, who shrugged his shoulders and released Richard from his grip.

As he entered the square from the side passage, he saw the spectacle before him. There must have been a few thousand people crammed into the area, all talking at once. It was clear they were all excited. When they saw Richard step into view, the noise erupted to a deafening level, and they started chanting rhythmically and raising their fists in the air. It was as if he was entering the old Roman amphitheatre, like a gladiator about to fight a lion. But they weren't there to cheer on a conquering hero or root for a respected slave trying to earn his freedom—rather, they were there to taunt a hated Christian westerner who had committed a fatal crime against a Muslim family. They literally wanted blood and to witness suffering. They wanted to see weakness in this unwelcome visitor to their sacred country.

Richard saw in front of him, in the middle of the square, a thick, brown wooden post planted upright in the ground. Standing nearby was an official and three soldiers. That morning, he had been told the protocol. He knew what to do. He didn't need any instruction.

"Let's just bloody well get on with it, now," he said aloud as he walked upright towards the post. He noticed a bank of TV crew standing on a raised platform filming his every move. He straightened his back and looked around into the crowd, on the left and then the right. They were eager for the spectacle to begin—the chanting had increased in volume, and the fist pumps grew more intense.

He stopped a few feet short of the post and held out his hands. One of the guards undid his handcuffs, and Richard took off his shirt and placed it on the ancient wooden tray held by one of the soldiers. The crowd saw a pale westerner who was slim, toned, and muscular, but with very little body fat to cushion the blows. The noise level increased further.

He now saw come into his view the same medical officer standing nearby. Richard stepped forward and placed his arms around the post, hugging it. The guard then rehandcuffed him. Richard shuffled his feet in the dirt in order to get into a comfortable, firm position. He did not want the indignity of slipping and needing to be helped back to his feet. He then gently placed his forehead on the post, near the top, and rested it on the thin, grey muslin cloth that was wrapped around it. He reminded himself that the last thing he needed was to whack his face on the post and knock himself out, which one unfortunate person had done the month before.

The official, a Shariah lawyer, raised his hands and waited for the crowd to calm down. He waited patiently, until the sound level had dropped sufficiently so that he could be heard. In Farsi he read out the crime and punishment from the open book held in his hands.

Richard stood firm and kept his eyes open. From the corner of his left eye, he saw a bank of camera lenses. Millions around the world were clearly watching this spectacle. They had come to be entertained. Richard prepared himself to enter into a semitrance—just like he had done during the mock interrogation at his school—to be able to block out the pain. Eighty lashes, normally in quick succession, would probably all be over in less than three minutes. A blink of the eye in the grander period of his life.

The medical officer approached him with a rubber, six-inch-long object shaped like a dog bone that Richard was to put into his mouth and bite onto. Richard shook his head and clamped his teeth shut. The medical officer held up the bone, and the crowd screamed with delight at the thought of this westerner foolishly refusing it. He knew he must not open his mouth in case he bit into his tongue, or worse still, bite completely through it. He knew he must grit his teeth and not scream out.

The sun was directly in his eyes, and he couldn't see the people in front of him. All was a hazy blur. But when he turned his head, he could see those to his side. The chanting was starting up again.

Then he saw and heard what would pervade his mind forever—the "whooshing" noise of the cane. He looked to his right and saw a soldier swishing a bamboo cane a yard long and half an inch wide. He was practicing his swing. *Whoosh, whoosh!* To his left, he heard the same sound from the second soldier, also limbering up. Behind Richard, the official had finished speaking. He closed the book and balanced it delicately on top of the upturned fingers of his right hand, as if making an offering to the gods watching above. He scanned his eyes from the left to the right of the square and raised his left hand, signaling all to be quiet.

This is it, Richard, he thought. Your time has come. Do not waver or crumble. You have the weight of Britain on your shoulders to not show any emotion. You will emerge a stronger man as a result. Your mettle is being tested today, so don't let yourself or your family down.

CHAPTER 63
THE RAC

Richard struggled to get up from his knees and out of the cab. His cheeks and forehead contorted in pain.

Bill, the familiar porter, greeted him in the lobby. "Mr. de L'Isle, so good to have you back at our club, and so soon. I hope you are recovering from your ordeal?"

"Yes, thanks, Bill. Appreciate you asking." Richard managed to now stand more upright, and he walked very slowly towards the stairs. He laboriously lifted one leg slowly up onto the first step, and then after wincing in pain, rested a moment before taking the next step. He glanced up and saw Ivano the maître'd at the top of the stairs. He came down to greet Richard.

"Mr. de L'Isle, it's an honor to have you dine with us tonight. Let me take you to your usual table. Your lady guest has been waiting for you, and your usual G&T is ready for you to taste. I suspect you need it."

As he followed Ivano, members looked up at him and started whispering, some pointing. Richard held his head up high and smiled. Soon, some started clapping, and within less than a minute, the whole room was standing up and clapping. The applause moved Richard. This is what he had wanted and had waited for—adoration. He raised his right hand in acknowledgement, and shook hands with some members as he slowly made his way to the table.

Richard paused when he saw Elisa, not just because of her beauty, or because she always dressed so elegantly, but tonight she wore her favorite dark-blue-coloured Chanel suit—which was only for very special occasions. Coincidentally, it had been Rebecca's favorite designer suit, but in a different colour. She was sitting at his usual table, the one where of course he had entertained his other mistress many times. She raised her eyebrows, moved her head back slightly when she spotted him, and gave a little wave with her hand: just like Rebecca used to do. He had forgotten how sensuous Eliza was. But in his current condition, he wouldn't be able to make love to her as he used to, for many months to come. And given his ordeal, he had wondered if she might be repulsed by his physical appearance, once she saw him naked again.

"So, the conquering hero returns! Richard, how are you after your horrendous ordeal?" she said, smiling at him.

"Popular! I appear to be today's news, Elisa." Richard shook her hand and carefully eased himself into the seat opposite her, trying not to look in too much pain. Richard winced, trying to get comfortable. "Been here long,

The Feather of Truth

Ian Campbell-Laing

Elisa? Sorry I'm a tad late. Traffic was busy down the A3."

"No problem. You texted to say you were running half-an-hour late so I arrived just a few minutes before you, just enough time to nip into the ladies' room and freshen up before I sat down. See, I've only just started my cocktail, so perfect timing, sweet pea." She knew that people were watching them and listening to their conversation, so she whispered the words "sweet pea." She looked down at the table as she spoke, finding it difficult to establish eye contact with him.

As he took a large swig at his gin and tonic, always placed on the table before he arrived, Elisa checked her watch again. 7:30 p.m. Good, she thought. Still plenty of time.

CHAPTER 64
THE RAC

After an hour, Richard asked, "Everything all right, Elisa? You've hardly touched your food all evening. Something bothering you, sweetie? We are fine, aren't we? Nothing to worry about, is there?"

"Oh, haven't I? Well, you know me, I never eat much—don't have much of an appetite at the best of times. Keeps me slim for you though. Nope, everything is fine, and we are fine." She sighed and ran the fingers of her right hand through her hair, which she then tucked behind her ear. "I suppose it's just the whole Iran thing that has been so stressful for me—I was so worried about you, but also to be honest, that attention may be coming my way. After your tribunal hearing, as you know, rumors circulated about to whom you were texting, which caused you to crash your car. Various names came up, but not mine—well, not yet."

"Well, plod knows about us, doesn't he?" said Richard looking angry.

"Plod?"

"Policeman plod. Ghazini, for Pete's sake. You told him, correct?"

"Er. Yes I did admit to our affair. But only after he threatened me with being an accessory to your texting which caused the Englebrau car accident, and that I could go to jail. I had no choice, sweat pea. He promised to keep it confidential, so I hope no one hears about us."

Richard sighed. He was not in the mood for a blame game argument with her. "It will soon pass, Elisa. Then I will be yesterday's news, and we can go back to where we were. Oh, did you remember to bring my pen that I lent you a few weeks back?" He lowered his voice, adding, "I think you wanted to replay some of our lovemaking—did you?"

Elisa whispered, "Yes, I did, and it was very good. Oh, damn. Sorry, I knew I had forgotten something. It's back at my apartment. I will bring it when we next meet. Or I can come to your hospital with it tomorrow, if you like?" Elisa looked down at her unfinished plate of scallops; they tasted a little undercooked. Her heart was pounding.

"Yes, OK. Pop by the hospital tomorrow morning, but avoid between ten a.m. and midday—that's when Jennifer usually visits. I don't like not having it on me, and I should delete such stuff. Bit risky having it on my pen—you never know who could access it, even though that person would have to know how to do that.

She continued to look down. "OK. Will do. And of course I understand how you cherish it, given it was a present from your wife. Yes, important that you have it with you, definitely."

Why is she rambling on so, fidgeting and not looking me in the eye? He wondered.

The Feather of Truth
Ian Campbell-Laing

Hawker came over. "Any room for dessert, sir, madam?"

"Not for me, but Richard, you go ahead. You normally have the cheese board, don't you?"

Richard gave a bloated-face look. "Er, I am kind of full, so maybe I won't this time."

Surprised, Elisa looked up quickly at him. "Oh, go on! I'm sure your doctor said you must keep your strength up and have loads of protein and fruit. I insist. Hawker, we'll have the cheese board, thanks, and perhaps I will, for a change, have some with you, Richard."

"OK. That's the spirit, Elisa," said Richard, not having any energy to argue with her over such a trifling matter.

A few minutes later, when the cheese board arrived with an array of soft, pungent cheeses, biscuits, and a few bunches of large, green grapes, Hawker was about to explain the sources of the different cheeses, but Richard waved him away.

Elisa still felt hot, and her heartbeat wouldn't climb down. She breathed in and out slowly. She saw that her lover was checking his e-mails on his iPhone, and not looking at her. She looked up at him. "Richard, can I ask you something?"

"Sure, Elisa." He put down his iPhone onto the table and smiled at her. "Whatever you want. Are you sure that everything's all right? You seem distracted tonight, for some reason."

She leant forward. "No, I am fine. When we started our relationship, we said we would have no secrets between us, correct?"

Richard noticed that her voice was quieter than usual, and she spoke quickly. "Absolutely. No secrets at all," he replied, nodding his head.

"And we would trust one another implicitly. No matter what."

"Yes, correctamundo."

"And we would always be truthful with each other?"

He sighed and rolled his eyes. "Yes, yes, yes, we did."

Despite being so nervous, her inner anger at him continued, and tonight she wanted to deliberately bait and test him—very dangerous though she knew that was. She cleared her throat and spoke. "You know, the Feather of Truth, and all that."

He stared at her, his temples pulsating. What a peculiar phrase to use, he thought—only he and Rebecca had ever discussed the Feather of Truth. Rebecca, who had a degree in ancient Egyptology, had described to him how souls, before entering the afterlife—known as the Field of Reeds—first had to pass through a trial in the Hall of Truth. There, the heart of their souls would be weighed against the white Feather of Truth. If their heart was lighter than the feather, then they would go into the afterlife. If heavier, they would experience a fate worse than death: being eaten alive by Amenti, the goddess of the dead—who had the head of a crocodile, the body of a lion, and the backside of a hippo. Rebecca and he had a pact—to promise to be truthful to each other and never tempt fate by lying. Something's up here—careful, Richard. Elisa, you are very smart, but not bright or particularly well educated. So, I wonder how you would know of that rather unusual phrase?

He changed his facial expression to one of looking interested in what she was saying. "What's on your mind, Elisa? Out with it. Yes, we are always truthful with each other, aren't we?"

Elisa leant forward more and whispered, "Were you upset with me, the last time we met, when I wasn't in the mood to make love to you, and after I snapped at you, saying that all we do is have sex and spend so little time talking?"

Richard was distracted when he saw Svetlana, the serving lady, come up to the table and discreetly top up their wine glasses. Her hair was done in a ponytail, and as she turned to Richard, she gave him a flirtatious smile. He smiled back at her, briefly looking in between the buttons of her blouse. Then he turned back and laughing said to Elisa, "Wow! Is that all that's bothering you?"

"Yes, that's it, but I was thinking about it the other day. Please answer the question. Did it?"

"Well, now you ask, yes, I must admit it did hack me off, initially. But I soon got over it, and anyway I thought we do chat a lot. Didn't we have a long chat about American politics the time before last? Also, look here this evening. I've made time for you even though I am in unbearable pain, and we're chatting aren't we? Happy now?"

Elisa looked down at her plate. "Well, sort of."

Richard looked to the ceiling, then leant forward, staring at her. "Well, what *else* is there? Even though we have only known each other a few months, I know you well enough that you want to ask me another question. So go ahead. Fire away. I have no secrets, not from you or anyone."

"Actually you are wrong. We all have secrets. Even me. But since you ask, yes, I have another question for you." As Elisa gripped tightly her napkin on her lap, her knuckles went tense. She looked up at Richard and, staring into his eyes, spoke quickly to get her question out of the way. "OK. Have you been seeing anyone else, whilst we've been going out, Richard?"

Richard was stunned and annoyed. She had never asked this question before. Something is going on, he thought. He knew that during his fling with Rebecca, he had not seen anyone else, but with Elisa he had been a naughty boy with two others. He justified his philandering on the basis that they were fleeting, hadn't lasted long, and Elisa wasn't remotely for the long term. Either way, he had been very discreet where and when he saw them, and at times only when Elisa was meeting clients. So he wasn't sure how she would know about them. Was she spying on him? Stay cool, Richard.

The Feather of Truth — Ian Campbell-Laing

There's no reason she knows anything. She's just paranoid and bluffing. And anyway, why should I care what she thinks? She's unlikely to want to reveal her relationship with me and cause embarrassing damage to herself.

"Elisa, what on earth has gotten into you? It must be the stress of worrying if the press will find out about us, and all that. Look I am only seeing you, OK. That's settled then?" He crossed his arms and sat back. He immediately winced in pain and sat upright again. "Damn, that hurt," he said, annoyed that she had caused him unnecessary pain.

She whispered. "Of course you are being unfaithful to your wife, but you said she had lost interest in sex for years. So, you haven't ever been unfaithful to me then, Richard, that is what you are saying, correct?" Elisa kept staring into his eyes, trying to judge whether or not he had a conscience, a soul, a sense of morality. She needed to know—before her next act.

He raised his voice and looked sternly at her. "I *have* answered your question. Topic over. Finito. Got it, Elisa?" He returned to his e-mails.

She looked up at him. Recently, and especially now she feared him. She knew he could have a temper in the office, and she didn't want to be the brunt of it. She had now heard all she had wanted to hear. Yes, she knew he was blatantly lying to her, and yes, the matter was certainly over, as he said. Like all whores, she wanted her payment. But to get it, she must now perform one final act, as she had planned. That was her duty.

She exhaled and smiled warmly at him, and, sounding cheery and upbeat, she said, "OK. Good. Sorry. I *was* being paranoid. Not sure what the matter is. All the stress probably, just as you said. Well, I don't know about you, but I am still hungry. I think I will have some grapes. Oops, I nearly forgot. Must take my evening vitamin."

She leant over to her left-hand side and with her right hand reached into her black Kate Spade leather shoulder bag, which was hanging off the arm of her chair, to retrieve her small china pillbox. With her left hand, she felt into the inside side pocket and picked up the stalk of the two grapes she had prepared with surgical precision, earlier downstairs in the ladies' room. As she turned to her right to face him, in one sweeping motion her right hand placed the pillbox onto the table in front of Richard, whilst her left hand, palming her prepared grapes out of view, reached to the cheeseboard for a similar-looking stalk with two grapes.

"Remember you bought me this Faberge pill box as an birthday present, Richard?" She reached forward and pushed it nearer for him to examine it.

Richard looked up. "Yep, I sure do. It's exquisite, isn't it?" he said, nodding, just relieved that the unexpected but brief interrogation seemed to be over.

As he examined in his right hand the beauty of the painting on the box, she said, "Now let's see, which grapes shall we have?" Elisa's left hand

The Feather of Truth   Ian Campbell-Laing

rested on the cheeseboard, with the grapes underneath her palm and out of sight. With her fingers she picked up the stalk of her two grapes under her palm and dropped them onto her lover's side plate.

Elisa added, "And let me chose some for me as well. Let's see. These look nice and juicy also." She selected a stalk with two grapes identical in size and colour to the ones on Richard's plate. Meanwhile, Richard opened the box and reached inside and selected a blue pill and gave it to her. She took it from him, popped it in her mouth, and sipped a mouthful of water from the tumbler in front of her. She held out the palm of her right hand, and he gave the box back to her.

"Thanks." She then leant to her left and placed the pillbox back into her shoulder bag. She smiled: at school she was teased because of her height and her very large feet and hands, but now she was pleased for the concealment her hands bestowed. She looked up at Richard, who was now looking down at his iPhone again.

"Come on, eat your grapes. They look delicious." She pushed his plate nearer to him. Richard wasn't listening to her babbling and didn't look up—he was trying to concentrate on replying to an e-mail from Celsius.

Elisa had one last question to ask, so she could witness what reaction it would bring. "Richard, something else has been bothering me."

"What is it now, Elisa?" He was wondering why she was in a peculiar, pensive mood. As he quickly scanned his e-mail reply and pressed "send," he decided he didn't want to have any physicality with her tonight. His body ached, and his mind was flooded with her incessant chattering. He put his iPhone back on the table in front of him. He just now wanted to get back to the hospital, have his meds and gets some sleep.

"Why did your boss murder his wife. Did you know that they were both having affairs, Richard?" She then gulped down some more red wine, sat back in her chair and smiled at him.

He shot her a stern look. "Elisa, darling, I can't take much more of this. I don't know what you are going on and on about. All these questions, when I am in such pain from the torture. I can hardly sit still, as you know." He writhed about on his chair, trying to get comfortable. "Ah!" he groaned in pain. He grabbed his iPhone, tapped in some commands, and placed it to his neck. Immediately 0.2 ccs of salicylic acid, entered his bloodstream. Soon, the pain should subside, temporarily.

"Sorry. I'll be quiet. But only if you are a good boy and eat up your grapes. They will do you the world of good." She leant forward, and, picking up the two grapes by their stalk from his plate, she dangled them in front of his mouth.

He opened his mouth to receive the gift, just like a child does when being fed by its mother. Then he abruptly closed it just beforehand, and one of the grapes bashed into his lips.

"Oh, come on, grumpy chops! Just before you went to Iran, you used to do things to me with grapes that sent us both wild, sweet pea!" she said flirtatiously and looked for the reaction. She hoped she had been subtle in her comment by masking it with "sweet pea." He had said he liked her to call him that.

Richard blushed slightly, hoping no one was listening. But he became more confused, thinking he had only done that sexual act with Rebecca, and not Elisa. *But maybe I did, maybe not. I am in such pain and so drowsy from the morphine, that perhaps I am not thinking straight.*

"Hey, sure, I will have the grapes in a moment, but I must get up to rest my backside and take a leak." He slowly got up and touched her shoulder lightly. "Will be back in a sec. Can you order me another G&T, please?"

"Sure, will do. Don't be long."

He slowly went down the small flight of stairs to the hall porters, trying to sieve through the last hour or so of information and acts. *Something's very odd. Elisa seemed to be making a big thing about showing him her pillbox and nagging him to eat the ruddy grapes. And the "Feather" comment. How could she know about that secret pact, which he was sure only he and Rebecca shared?*

"Hi, Bill. Anything going on tonight?"

"Nope, all is well here."

"Oh, OK."

As Richard turned to go downstairs to the restroom, Bill added, "Oh, I forgot, I'll make sure the guest gets the package that was left for him. He hasn't picked it up yet."

Richard stopped and turned around, "Sorry, what package?"

"Oh, it's this one here." He pulled out from the pigeonhole labeled "Z" an oblong white envelope and passed it to Richard.

Confused, Richard took it. It was addressed to "Mr. Zanan". He felt its contents: a five or six long and an inch wide, solid object wrapped inside bubble-wrap.

Staring at the envelope, he continued to feel its contents. After half a minute he said, "Oh, yes. *This* package. Sorry, Bill, I'm being a bit dim tonight. I'm in some pain at the moment and not thinking straight."

"I can well understand that," said Bill as he reached out his hand to take the envelope back.

Richard held on to it. His mind was sifting through what was going on.

"Quick question, Bill. When did my lady guest arrive tonight, any idea?"

"Oh, I'm not sure, maybe forty-five minutes to an hour before you, but I couldn't be certain."

"Not just a couple of minutes, then?"

"Oh, no, much longer than that Mr. de L'Isle."

"And did she go directly to our table, would you happen to recall?"

"No. When she arrived, I saw her go straight downstairs, presumably to hand in her coat and freshen up in the ladies room."

"And I bet that she took an age getting ready, like she always does?"

"Indeed, sir. She came back up, oh I'd say about fifteen or twenty minutes later, perhaps."

"How can you be sure of the times, old chap?"

"Well, your guest arrived at just after half-six which is when our evening shift starts and I was being debriefed on the day's activity. Then I had a call from a member, which we always log." He turned and scanned his logbook. "Yes, here it is, the call ended at six fifty, so twenty minutes later. And just as I put the phone down, it was then that I saw her walking up the stairs, and she gave me that envelope, for Mr. Zanan who is guest and due to dine here later tonight. Then she went up to the restaurant. And if I recall, you arrived just before half-seven, correct?"

Richard's mouth gaped open. He was starting to piece together the meaning of this evening's events. He paused. He knew now what was contained in the bubble-wrap. And he guessed who must be Mr. Zanan.

"Hold on Bill, just a sec. There's been an *almighty cock up*."

Richard googled a request on his iPhone. He smiled at the answer.

"Sorry, Bill. This is all my mistake. Change of plan, if you don't mind. What a clot I am. *This* envelope was for me, in case I couldn't make it tonight in time for dinner. There's *another* package for that guest, which I like the clot I am forgot to bring with me. My head's not up to speed at the moment with all my meds and the pain I'm in. It's all my fault really. Look, you want to earn a quick five hundred notes to get me out of a jam with my lady friend?"

"Well, I don't know if I am supposed to let you have that envelope, given it is not addressed to you."

"Bill, *come on*, you can trust me, surely? Look it it's in Elisa's handwriting, I recognise it, and I asked her to do it. But she got the two mixed up."

"Well, given you do so much for the club, yes, I know I can trust you. What would you like me to do exactly? I won't do anything illegal, mind."

"Course not, it's just a humorous gift from one member to his guest."

Richard stepped closer and whispered instructions into Bill's ear. Although Bill looked surprised by the odd but seemingly innocent request, he readily nodded in agreement.

"OK. I will do that right now, sir. I think I know where I can find one."

Richard reached into his jacket and removed his wallet, and whispered, "Here's three hundred now, and I will give you another two hundred quid tomorrow, if that's OK?"

"Perfectly." Bill quickly put the money into his back pocket.

Richard went down one flight of stairs to the restroom.

The Feather of Truth — Ian Campbell-Laing

Elisa was fidgeting with her napkin, waiting for Richard to return. She thought he was taking longer than he should, but she then reasoned he had to walk slowly given his flogging.

Her mind turned back to seven weeks ago, to the afternoon Richard had had his car accident with the Englebrau family. Earlier that afternoon, she had seen Richard for lunch and then intense intimacy upstairs in the bedroom suite at the RAC. As she sat on the train on her way to spend the weekend at her friend's home in Cambridge, what made her jump and the other passengers look surprised was hearing from Richard's pen the train conductor's announcement be repeated, as she inadvertently turned the pen on and activated the last words it had recorded.

She then inserted Richard's recording pen's USB connection into her laptop, and plugged in her headphones. She could only just cope as she heard each spoken word that the pen had captured of two individuals that week in April, six months ago now. As the words played out, they were also being displayed on her screen.

Once she had arrived at her friends house, she went into the study. She had to keep wiping away her tears of anger and disgust as she scrolled down the seventy-five-page transcript on the screen. The recording had started when Richard had said good-bye to a Mr. Paul Ruggiere, a security guard at Richard's bank.

She cringed as the familiar words came to life. The night Richard had said to his wife that he was seeing his most important client, Sir James Campbell, at his club, was a lie. Instead he was seeing his mistress, Rebecca.

Whisper: "Hello, darling, don't get up. You look ravishing."
"So do you, Richard."

Then later, Rebecca's soft voice:
"Richard, you are the father, obviously. I am only making love to you, you daft Brit!"

"Of course I want to have our baby. Don't you too, sweetheart?"

And then Richard's final words to Rebecca, three days later in his mistress's house, as she lay dying, poisoned by Richard, the man she loved:
"Good-bye Rebecca, my dear. I did love you, but your pregnancy left me with no choice. I am so very sorry. Hopefully, your pain will end soon. Forgive me for what I have done. I know I will be judged by the feather of truth and go to hell for this."

The final surprise for Elisa were the last words from Rebecca not heard from the audio pen, but appearing on her laptop screen in front of her, oddly in a lighter typeface barely visible:
"Richard, how could you do this to me? I loved you with all my heart.

Please do not kill our baby. Please do not do that. You couldn't do that, surely, could you? PLEASE…"

Elisa was confused and didn't know how this could be, because Ghazini had said to her that from the autopsy report, Rebecca was unable to move or talk during the last few hours of her life. Richard had clearly been in the room when these words were spoken, and if so, why hadn't he replied? He was talking to himself and to Rebecca as if he knew she was already in a coma and couldn't hear him. It was as if Rebecca had been thinking those thoughts while still conscious, and somehow, quite remarkably, the audio pen had recorded them. How that could possibly happen, she did not know. But it frightened her. She hadn't appreciated, until she had done more research, that some sophisticated computers could now decode one's brainwaves of thought and record them for everyone to see. There was nowhere to hide in the world anymore. Not even in your thoughts.

One of the last few sections of the recording, was of Richard talking to one of his male colleagues from work when dining at the RAC:

"Jules, nope, Elisa is definitely not the one for me long term. She's just for fun, old chap. She's gorgeous looking and amazing in bed, but pretty dim. We don't have much in common. She bores me with her tittle-tattle conversation. I will probably end it, because there are so many other more desirable and intellectually interesting fillies around."

Elisa had felt disgusted, betrayed, and afraid.

Then she replayed the recording of him having sex with another woman the day after making love to Elisa.

As she saved the transcript as a pdf document so that it could not be overwritten, in walked her friend Wendy. She quickly dried her eyes.

"Hi, Wendy. Can you do me a favour?"

"Sure. What is it? Have you been crying?"

"Just a bit: usual boyfriend nonsense. Don't worry. I am over him. But, if anything happens to me, can you make sure my laptop gets safely to DCI Ghazini at the Surrey, and ask him to take a look at the pdf document saved as Capital letters, 'R-D-L' then the number '1'?"

"Ghazini and RDL1, sure. But what could happen to you?"

"Probably nothing. It's just a precautionary measure, Wendy. And the password to the laptop is 'sweetpea101.'"

"OK, if you say so." Wendy tapped in the details into her iPhone. "See you down for drinks in an hour, then." She left the room.

Elisa had then started to think how she could gain revenge. Clearly the most obvious action would be to simply hand over to Ghazini, Richard's recording pen and let the law takes its course. But then a thought so chilling occurred to her, it made her squeeze her shoulders together and shake. If

Richard could murder in cold blood a woman and their unborn baby for whom he had expressed his undying love, could he, would he, do the same to her, Elisa, if he ever decided he didn't want her around? By handing over the evidence that would get Richard convicted, she would be Richard's target for the rest of her life. Would Ghazini be able to always protect her against Richard – even if he was sent to prison, or worse, after he was released after serving his time?

The alternative of not handing over the recording pen, might be equally unpleasant. Ghazini, a week ago, quite coincidentally and unannounced, paid a visit to her in her office to update her on her sister's murder case. He had informed her that whilst they had gathered more evidence against Richard, it was all still circumstantial. The detective described again to her the painful death Rebecca had endured and added that if Elisa had any evidence of Rebecca's murderer, however apparently insignificant, it was her duty to disclose that to the police now. He clearly believed that she had some evidence, because he then made a veiled threat to her, saying "Just so that we are clear, withholding important evidence after the fact in a murder enquiry is a very serious offense and could land you in jail."

Then she realized that the recording evidence may not be admissible in court. If so, not only would Richard escape justice but he would surely seek deadly retribution against her.

She faced a dilemma: both her options were fraught with danger.

Finally, an hour later over her third glass of wine she had come up with a third option which neatly ended the debate going on in her head: she would take matters into her own hands, and secure absolute protection against any further nefarious actions by Richard. With her thoughts starting to formulate a plan, as she powered down her laptop, she didn't notice the faint outline on the screen:

*"Elisa, are you sure you wanted to take **that** course of action?"*

Elisa was nervous, but furious and determined to make Richard pay for his lies to her. She just hoped Ghazini would understand her actions.

After the inspector had left her office, Elisa was shaking. Without telling the inspector specifically about the pen, she called him up at the station and offered him a deal—in two days' time, she would have one last supper with Richard at his club, during which she would leave at the porter's station, in an envelope addressed to Ghazini, the evidence that would help convict Richard. But she asked that the inspector not pick up the envelope until after she had left the club at nine o'clock. In return, she required in writing that the inspector would never disclose who gave him this evidence, he would not pursue any accomplice charges against her regarding her texting Richard before his car accident with the Englebrau family, and he would provide her with police protection against Richard until she returned back to the United States a month later. He readily agreed but asked her what was the specific evidence against Richard. All Elisa would say was, "It's a damning tape recording." He agreed, with just one small change to her plan.

Now, tonight whilst she waited for Richard to return from the mensroom, she drained her glass of wine, and scanned the BBC news on her iPhone.

She looked up as Richard entered the restaurant and briefly chatted with Ivano, who then nodded his head and smiled. Soon after Richard had slowly eased himself back into his chair, Svetlana, the server, whilst stretching to refill Elisa's wine glass, accidentally spilt some red wine over Elisa's shoulder bag. Svetlana immediately apologized but looked very shocked as Richard got very angry and made a scene. Elisa turned to her left and examined her shoulder bag and was relieved when she saw that luckily the wine had not appeared to have spilt inside. Ivano offered to take the bag and arrange now for one of the staff to remove the stains on the outside. Elisa held onto the bag, and looking up at Ivano said she would get it dry cleaned herself and send the RAC the bill.

Richard took a swig of his G&T, and smiled. It tasted so good, and gave his brain a kick start. He waived away Ivano.

Elisa turned around and reached for the grapes from Richard's plate, and presented them to him, again. He opened his mouth and accepted the first grape and started chewing it.

She smiled as he chewed. "When you feel up to it, say in a few weeks, Richard, perhaps we can resume our intimacy? Given your condition, I've got some ideas about how we can be creative!"

"Can't wait!" He spoke in between bites of the grape that was releasing its warm fluid into his mouth. It tasted ever so slightly sharp. Maybe it's a tad unripe, he surmised.

Elisa dangled the remaining grape by its stalk near his mouth. "Here, have the other one." To please her, he closed his mouth over the grape, tugging it away from the stalk. This one tasted better, he thought. He chewed and then swallowed it.

"Elisa, in answer to your question earlier regarding Rebecca's murder, I also thought it was an open-and-shut case. All the evidence pointed to Chuck—whilst very drunk and getting angry with his nagging wife, whom I understand was refusing to have sex with him—he snapped in a moment of rage and poisoned her. He later strangled her in a final act of anger, for good measure. Period. Well, that's what the police told me, and what I understand was written in the local press as well. Seems straightforward to me, anyway."

Richard looked at Elisa's plate of grapes. "Look, I've eaten mine. Now you have yours. They look nice and juicy, also."

"Sure." She readily removed one of them from the stalk, opened her mouth, and popped it onto the back of her tongue. After chewing it, she ate and swallowed the second one.

She dabbed her mouth with her napkin and resumed the conversation about Rebecca. "Oh, OK, Richard. I hadn't read anything about it in the press." She sighed. "Yes, you are probably right. You boss was a sociopath and snapped." She looked at her watch. It was five minutes to nine. "Come on, we best be going. Didn't you say you have to get back to the hospital not later than nine thirty for your evening meds? It's probably around a half-an-hour cab ride, isn't it? And I really need to get home, as I have a long day of meetings tomorrow."

Richard looked upset. "Aw, I thought we were going to have some oral intimacy tonight? Remember I said that I have the key to the Kent suite."

"Nope, not tonight, but tomorrow, I promise, when I come and see you in hospital. Can you wait until then?"

Richard sighed and smiled. He was now in such pain, he wasn't bothered. He said, "OK. Yes, let's go. You are right. I really need another shot of painkillers, that's for sure."

"And, sweetpea, I *will* bring your pen to the hospital tomorrow morning, around eight before I go to work."

"OK. Great. Thanks, Elisa."

They got up to leave, with Richard allowing his mistress to walk in front of him. He didn't see her on her iPhone, texting someone. He shook some more hands on the way out. Bill went to the cloakroom on the floor below to retrieve their coats and helped Elisa and Richard into them.

Outside in the cold air, Richard spotted a cab coming around the corner. He held out his hand and flagged it down. It stopped by the curb in front of them. He leant forward as the cabbie's window came down. "Three Goswell Road, Barbican, please. Thanks."

Elisa stepped up to Richard, who was holding the door open for her. She looked into his eyes. "Thanks, darling. It was a nice evening. See you tomorrow." He bent down to as usual kiss her passionately on the lips. She turned her head slightly, and instead she pecked him on his cheek.

She stepped into the warm cab, and he closed the door after her. She didn't look back to see him waving. She took out a handkerchief from her shoulder bag and wiped a tear that had formed in her eye. She was still shaking.

Richard saw a free cab coming towards him and held out his hand to flag it down. The cab stopped about ten feet away from the entrance to the club, and out stepped a lady who then reached over the driver's window to pay. "That was perfect timing, thanks," he said to the cabbie. "Royal Surrey Hospital, Guildford, please. Need to be back before nine thirty, if you can, please."

The Feather of Truth   Ian Campbell-Laing

"Sure," replied the woman cabbie, adding, "You're my last job of the night, so do you mind if we drop off my friend in the back? He lives just a couple of miles away from here, and it's on the way."

Richard peered into the rear of the lowly-lit cab to see a tall man in a light grey overcoat with its beige collar turned up, wearing a hat, and sitting on the right-hand seat with his head turned away looking out of the window. Richard didn't really want company but was too weary to complain.

"Sure, no problem. Be happy to oblige." Richard stepped into the rear, closing the door behind him, and flopped down onto the left-hand seat. My God, how he ached. He couldn't wait for his bedtime shot of painkillers.

The cab started moving. Richard heard the familiar clicking sound of the doors automatically locking, and the small red light being illuminated showing the occupant could not exit the cab before the cabbie had been paid and had released the locks. The light in the back of the cab turned off.

In the darkness Richard thought it odd that the man to his right hadn't the courtesy to introduce himself, or thank Richard. No matter. I want some peace and quiet anyway. Richard closed his eyes. He was exhausted.

CHAPTER 65
WEST END CENTRAL POLICE STATION

Richard sat in the windowless room, no larger than ten feet long by five feet wide. The walls were painted white, and there was a small desk with three chairs. Richard was told to sit in the small, grey, flimsy plastic one, deliberately forcing him to have his back to the corner of the room. His closed his eyes, as his thoughts went back to the cab journey just ten minutes previously.

The man to his right in the dark cab turned to face Richard and, after taking off his hat, spoke softly, in a deep voice that reverberated within the cramped space, stressing each word, "Rich-ard, Heath-cote, de L'Isle."

Richard recognized the voice of his nemesis immediately—DCI ruddy Kofi Ghazini—and opened his eyes. He screwed up his face in annoyance. My, my, how busy a little bee had been his unfaithful mistress, Elisa, he thought.

The detective continued, but this time in a formal manner. "Richard Heathcote de L'Isle, I am arresting you for the murder of Rebecca Falconer Jelleners. You do not have to say anything. However, it may harm your defense if you do not mention, when questioned, something upon which you later rely in court. Anything you do say may be given in evidence. Do you understand the charges against you?"

Richard did not respond.

"DI Gilmore," Kofi said, turning to face the lady cab driver, "I think we can take that as a 'yes.'" Kofi smiled: tonight, finally the smug Richard would be brought to account.

Richard turned and faced the Inspector. All Richard replied was, "Arsehole!" He then closed his eyes. His mind was trying to unscramble the information that was flooding his brain. My boss had been charged with the murder but died in prison awaiting trial, so what new evidence could they suddenly have linking me to the murder?

Back in the interview room, Richard now opened his eyes. To his right sat DI Harriet Gilmore in a comfy chair. In front of him was a larger, equally comfy empty seat, which of course Kofi would occupy. Richard's self-administered injection was helping to alleviate the pain, but he knew it would soon wear off. He resigned himself that he faced a very long night: he had read about the interrogation of suspects in murder cases and the protocol used to extract confessions. But he still managed a small smile, eager to prove his superior intellect against the detectives. He assumed that Kofi would presently be watching Richard from another room and would know that Richard was in extreme discomfort following his ordeal in Iran. The detectives currently had the upper hand.

Richard sipped at the cup of stewed tea that had just been brought to him. "Ugh," he said. It was lukewarm.

He then sat in silence. Harriet smiled pleasantly at him. He ignored her and pretended to sift through his e-mails, whilst he continued to think.

The door opened, and, stooping to clear his head under the doorway, in walked Kofi. He was carrying a large blue mug in his hand. He was old school; as he reached forward with his index finger, he pressed "record" on the machine that sat on the table.

"This is DCI Ghazini and, in attendance, Detective Inspector Gilmore at West End Central Police Station. Time 21:15 hundred hours Thursday, October 16, 2025. Interviewing the suspect, Mr. Richard de L'Isle of three Blackdown Close, Haslemere, in connection with the murder of Mrs. Rebecca Falconer Jelleners. The suspect has been cautioned and read his rights. He has indicated that until his lawyer has arrived, he will not be answering any questions. I have informed the suspect that the tape is now recording." Richard knew, having watched numerous TV detective series like *CSI*, *Joe Kenda the Homicide Hunter*, and *Dateline*, that he was being video recorded as well.

Kofi saw Richard look bemused at the presence of an old-fashioned tape recorder. He said, "Yes, we are all being videoed as you suspect, so this little device is simply a backup should the video fail—it's something we always do—after a bad experience a colleague had a while ago. And, DI Gilmore's iPad has an inbuilt voice stress analyzer."

Richard said nothing but noticed that Kofi's blue mug had an award stenciled in gold on it: **#1 Detective**.

Kofi sat back and crossed his leg over his knee. His deep, soft voice filled the room. "Hmm. So, Richard, we meet again."

Richard didn't like the friendly tone of calling him by his Christian name instead of the more formal Mr. de L'Isle. He didn't say anything. He knew that this was now a game of wills—having asked for his lawyer, he didn't have to answer any questions, but if he did, the answers couldn't be used against him. And of course, once Anthony arrived, he would ensure that Richard said very little anyway. Richard felt confident, but he knew Kofi was in no hurry and was experienced.

Forty-five minutes passed with nothing more said. The detectives stared at Richard, who simply ignored them and carried on with pretending to check his e-mails. Kofi made a large gesture to look at his watch, despite a large clock on the wall in the room showing that it had just struck ten o'clock.

"Can we get you anything, Richard?" asked Harriet.

Richard coughed to clear his throat. "It's time for my medications. I would like to take them now with a glass of water and visit the gents." Richard reached into his pocket and placed on the table a small cylindrical box of pills—his emergency supply.

Kofi thought to himself, Good. Now we have established some communication, finally. "Richard, I can appreciate that you are in some physical discomfort after your recent visit to Iran, but you will understand that I need to check these pills are what you say they are, and prescribed by your doctor."

"Of course they are, Inspector. See, look, they have the name of Dr. Moore on them and are addressed to me, for Pete's sake."

Kofi was pleased that Richard was agitated. "I am sure that you are right, but I need to check first—it's simply standard procedure designed to protect both you and us. What if they turned out to be sleeping tablets, or something worse? We couldn't have you take them at this time, could we now?" Kofi grinned. One of the most rewarding aspects of his unpleasant job was interviewing: plowing through a minefield of lies, misdirections, and half-truths and setting his own snares and traps in order to get to the truth and secure an incontrovertible confession or the welcome release of an innocent suspect.

"Inspector, they are a combination of anti-inflammatory and painkillers, as you would ruddy well expect. But, for Pete's sake, yes, please check them. But be quick," said Richard, raising his voice and pushing the pillbox closer to Kofi.

"Thank you. Harriet, would you be so kind as to take them to the MO and get his approval that Richard can take his medication at this time."

He leaned forward and spoke into the microphone. "DI Gilmore leaving the room, time 22:01 hundred hours."

Kofi and Richard sat in silence for thirty minutes. Just as Richard was about to ask where on earth were his medications, Harriet walked back into the room. She nodded to Kofi and placed the medication case in the middle of the table.

Kofi leaned forward. "Time 22:32 hundred hours, DI Gilmore returning to the interview room, placing Mr. de L'Isle's medication case on the table."

As Richard eagerly leant forward to take the box, Harriet spoke, holding her hand over it. "Hold on, Richard. Firstly, my apology that this took a while. Our MO was busy dealing with an urgent case. He has examined your medications, and you may take two white tablets and one blue one now. Would you allow me to take them from the container for you, please?"

Richard stared at Kofi and raised his hands in astonishment. "What? That's ridiculous! I want and need all of them, not just one blue. That's the additional pain killer, for Pete's sake."

"That's all the MO has allowed you to have." Kofi shrugged his shoulders dispassionately.

"Christ, this is deliberate harassment." Richard breathed in deeply and exhaled loudly. He knew he couldn't fight this. "OK, OK, let me have the three, please, now."

"DI Gilmore is taking out the tablets, placing them on the saucer, and passing a tumbler of cold water to the suspect."

Harriet bent down and whispered something in Kofi's ear.

Kofi looked annoyed and tersely whispered back, "Well, get them to search again—she said it would be there for us to collect at nine o'clock!"

Richard concentrated on taking his medication, drained the glass of water, and then resumed to fidget in his uncomfortable chair. He closed his eyes again. There was another period of silence, finally broken by Kofi when the clock struck eleven.

"Richard, we have waited for your lawyer to arrive for nearly two hours. I don't think he is coming tonight."

"He will be here, just mark my words," said Richard, jabbing his right index figure at Kofi.

Kofi smiled. "Oh, like he was for you during your Sharia tribunal, where you got a very harsh sentence for what we all thought was an innocent lapse in judgment?"

Ouch, thought Richard. The detective knows how to rile a person. Certainly, Richard had been initially disappointed with Anthony, but on reflection thought the tribunal had predetermined his sentence anyway. He believed that Anthony had done all he could have done. And of course, Richard's outburst in the court had exacerbated matters. Richard now blamed himself.

Kofi looked Richard up and down. He was clearly very uncomfortable in the deliberately hard, small plastic chair, literally with his back to the corner of the room, unable to leave. He smiled thinking, That's why they call it being "arrested," from the French word arret, meaning "stop." The suspect, when arrested, stopped having his freedom, deliberately. He judged the time to be right to get things moving along.

"It's getting late, Richard, so do you mind if we make a start before your lawyer gets here? We just have a few questions, more for clarification purposes, and some facts which I think you'd be interested to hear. If we can get on with the questions, the sooner you can be back in your hospital room. But first, let me say again how sincerely sorry we all were at the police station about your recent painful experience in Iran."

"Utter bollocks you were, plod," Richard shouted. He knew the game the detective was playing. He had read that under the common Reid nine-step interview technique interrogators use, the first stage was to be nice and pleasant, and then wade in and confront the suspect with incriminating evidence. Richard knew he should wait for Anthony, but he was getting very tired and wanted to leave within an hour in order to get back to the comfort of his bed. There in the hospital, he could regroup and could have all the painkillers he demanded. Also, for some odd reason, his stomach and the sides of his chest had started to throb. He had previously experienced some stomach cramps and nausea, but the doctors had said that was a minor side effect of the heavy-duty painkillers. But this was a more intense pain that he hadn't experienced before.

After a few minutes, Richard couldn't resist asking, "Why did you reopen the case that I thought was closed, Inspector? I was advised it was an open-and-shut case, with Chuck charged and due to appear in court."

Kofi moved forward, encroaching on Richard's personal space and meeting him eye to eye, just like Richard had done to him in Richard's office many months ago. "Hmm. Are you saying that you are waiving your right to a lawyer, Richard?"

Richard paused. There was no turning back if he said yes. But the burning sensation in his back, on his legs, and buttocks was now too much to bear. The medications would take about fifteen minutes to kick in, but he reasoned that during that time, it was easier for him to have the distraction of conversation than sit in the agony of silence.

"Inspector, let's just say until my brief arrives, I would be interested to know what new information you have that could possibly be of any interest or relevance to me."

Kofi considered this opportunity. He weighed up the risk of the whole interview being deemed inadmissible as evidence. He knew once the lawyer turned up, Richard would clam up completely, and the element of surprise would pass. His instinct advised him to proceed, but cautiously.

"I know you murdered Rebecca Falconer Jelleners and her unborn child. It was obviously only either you or her husband. The evidence overwhelmingly pointed to her husband, Chuck, but it got me wondering if it was deliberately planted there. You attended the prestigious MIT University and clearly are very adept with technology: being able to tap into your bank's V-Trax system, you could easily find a way to manipulate and plant evidence against your boss."

Kofi waited to see Richard's reaction, but there wasn't any. Richard was more concerned about how the inspector seemed to know that he had broken into the V-Trax system. Although Richard was fairly certain the bank would not wish to publicly air what he knew about V-Trax, he was now nervous about what could happen to him, given the research he had recently done that showed that the last person to penetrate the system had died in unexpected circumstances. Why hadn't Udo Wassermann at the bank contacted him or had one of his henchmen come after him? Maybe they were biding their time because they knew he was to be charged with murder, and hence the bank could just let that play out?

The Feather of Truth   Ian Campbell-Laing

Richard was annoyed with himself for earlier getting angry with the inspector—that was foolish, given he was being videoed. He now remained calm and matter-of-fact. He must concentrate from now to not overreact, but still enjoy the sparring with the detective and try and outwit him.

"Inspector, what makes you so sure it was me that killed her, and not her arrogant husband—who after all, confessed to having regularly abused her in the past, was known to dislike women in the workplace, and belittled many women in and outside the office?"

"Your reply and last few comments just helped prove it," said the smiling inspector, also enjoying the joust.

"What last comment? That her husband had abused her in the past? She told me that many times and showed me the punch and strangulation marks herself. I also told you that before, in my signed statement."

"No, it was the unborn child comment I made just a few moments earlier, but which you didn't challenge. You made no reaction to that because you already knew she was pregnant with your child. That's why you murdered her and the baby and blamed it all on your boss. Very neat of you, Richard, to murder two human beings and get away scot-free, and get promoted to your boss's job, to boot! You purloined not just the perfect murder, but the perfect promotion, as well. Congratulations."

"You have no evidence supporting that. And anyway, isn't an unborn baby of a few weeks old called a fetus and technically not a human being yet, and thus has no rights?"

The inspector was amazed at Richard's coolness and disregard for the murder of an innocent human life. But he would now play the first of his ace cards and retain the upper hand. He glanced at the tape recorder to see the red light, signifying it was still recording. The video would also show Richard's posture of crossing and uncrossing of his arms: all useful evidence.

"Actually, Richard..." He paused. "Rebecca was *not* pregnant at all."

"What? But she told me she was...and the autopsy report...er..." As the colour drained from the capillaries of his cheeks, Richard knew to stop speaking.

"Precisely, Richard. As I said, I knew you thought she was pregnant. She must have told you she was, and that was the good news she had for you. And I deliberately left on my desk—when I interviewed you again at the station—the top page of her autopsy report that I knew you couldn't resist glancing at when I went to the other side of the room to refill my coffee mug. I had underlined the section that showed she had heightened levels of the human chorionic gonadotrophic, or hCG hormone, in her body, and which I knew you would research when you got back to your office or home. You would have searched 'high hCG levels and pregnancy,' and it would have come up that such levels were typical for women who are pregnant. Doubtless we can find that search you performed on your laptop, which would be an odd action for you to perform in normal circumstances, wouldn't it? Yes, her pregnancy kit unfortunately must have showed a false-positive reading."

Richard glanced around the room, not speaking, but thinking intently. Fifteen–love to the Inspector, Richard thought.

"And what you clearly don't know is that high levels of hCG are also common in persons suffering from severe depression. In reality, she was still depressed being with her husband and saw a way out for a new life with you. You justified her murder because she announced she was pregnant and wanted your baby. Richard, you murdered her totally unnecessarily."

CHAPTER 66
WEST END CENTRAL POLICE STATION

Richard paused to consider the consequences of his actions. He was already well down the communication road, having broken his silence. He reasoned that he hadn't admitted to anything and concluded that until his lawyers arrived, whatever he said was inadmissible.

"Inspector, that's very interesting, but hardly enough to convict me. You know that it's all speculation, based on hearsay and coincidental, flimsy evidence. You will have to do much better than that."

Kofi raised his arms as if to deliver a sermon to his flock. He then placed them on his lap and re-crossed his legs. He was in no hurry. "Hmm. Well, let's see if we *can* do better, shall we? It wasn't until after Chuck's suicide in prison that her best friend, Dawn, remembered something important, and mentioned to us of the existence of a diary kept by Rebecca. We eventually found the diary, carefully hidden in a sewing box with a false bottom at the back of the top shelf in their utility room—an area her husband was unlikely to ever look. A diary entry was made the morning after your last dinner date with her at your club. She wrote how much she loved you and wanted to spend the rest of her life with you, and how thrilled she was to be pregnant with your baby, Richard. She went on to say that you were also pleased, although a little apprehensive, but something was frightening her and she wanted to leave a note to Dawn, just in case. She was frightened of her husband's reaction to the news that you and she were having an affair, and that she was having your baby. She was petrified of her husband's violent temper. Little did she know of what you were capable when you felt trapped and had no way out, and that it was you who she should be scared of, and not of her husband."

Richard gave a loud, bored sigh. "Really, Inspector, none of that is true. You must write a crime-thriller novel. I am sure the housewives of middle England would love to read such tosh."

The baiting didn't at all bother Kofi: in fact it amused him and suited his line of questioning. "There was another diary entry on the morning of her death that was also interesting."

On cue, from the inside of her jacket pocket, Harriet took out and unfolded a photocopy of the page in Rebecca's handwriting. "DI Gilmore is taking out of her pocket a copy of the said diary entry." Harriet read it aloud to Richard, in a slight American accent, which made Richard twinge slightly.

Waiting for Richard to arrive. Hope he likes his birthday pressies, and that my pain-in-the-butt husband doesn't kill him when Richard tells him of our affair and that I'm pregnant with Richard's baby! Will be a big day. Will write an entry later tonight after Richard has left and the dust has settled!

Harriet then said, "DI Gilmore is passing to the suspect a copy of the entry."

"Here, read it yourself," she said.

Richard stared ahead, showing no emotion.

Kofi pressed on. "That's pretty damning, isn't it? But do you know what finally made me realize it was you, Richard? Not just the IT skills you have in faking searches by Chuck on his wife's laptop, nor re-creating the documents incriminating Chuck, but instead an interesting combination of English literature, the shoes, your hands, the blinds, the wine, and the tears."

Richard rolled his eyes again, looked to the ceiling and then shaking his head, said, "Oh, per-lease, what now? We've been over the English literature and wine discussion already when you interviewed me in my office."

"Yes, we have, but we didn't conclude on it. Chuck was highly unlikely to have written that incriminating e-mail. Yes, it was on his PC, but he lacked your English literature knowledge, and whilst he may have overheard the phrase, he clearly didn't understand it. With your IT skills, you could easily have re-created and changed an existing e-mail of his. We know that now."

"Hypothetical and circumstantial, Inspector."

"Yes, it is, on its own. But let's briefly look at the wine you took as a gift from his cellar."

"So what that he couldn't recall which wine case I took? He was very drunk and tired, as you well know."

"But, what's clear from our discussions with him is that he said he would never have offered you *that* case, the most expensive one in his cellar."

"He's mistaken."

"It made me think that perhaps you were getting back at him in some way. But why? For what? And so we went back to Rebecca's diary, and there it was: an entry about how you were severely disappointed with the bonus your boss had given you. You referred to him as an 'asshole who had stolen your bonus.'"

"All either circumstantial or hearsay."

"'Maybe, maybe not. But there's *always* one thing that slips up a criminal, but luckily for us, in your case those weren't the only ones."

"Utter tosh. A jury would find those two flimsy anecdotes irrelevant."

"Maybe, maybe not. But, do you recall the Jehovah's Witness family who came to the Jelleners home that Sunday afternoon?" asked Kofi.

"Yes, I do, and I made a statement to that effect."

"Yes, you did. We tracked down the family and interviewed them. They made some very interesting and helpful observations. The little six-year-old girl says that you definitely wore buckled shoes, because she noticed the silver buckle sparkle in the afternoon sunlight."

"So ruddy what?" said Richard, raising his voice slightly in frustration.

"That style of shoes you later confessed to not wearing, and your wife has also confirmed to us you have never ever worn them. So, it was a slip-up, as it were, putting on Chuck's slip-on, buckled shoes, Richard. I suspect you improvised your original plan of ensuring the soles of Chuck's shoes had fragments of crushed pearls, given the meticulous planning you had done with everything else. Instead of taking his shoes in your gloved hands and smashing down on the pearls, why not wear the shoes and walk on the pearls, as Chuck would have done? Seems like a win-win for you."

"What rubbish!"

"Not rubbish at all. And when forensics couldn't get a match of your sock fibres inside Chuck's shoes, it made us wonder. Perhaps you put on one of Chuck's socks over your own, and later destroyed his sock?"

"Utter fantasy."

"Maybe, maybe not. But the fastidious Rebecca organized her husband's clothes drawers. He always had fourteen pairs of socks, underwear, and handkerchiefs: one of each day for two weeks. But do you know what we found when we counted the socks? There was only thirteen!"

Richard rolled his eyes. "Complete tosh, and anyway, why would they believe a six-year-old over me?"

Kofi remained calm. He was enjoying himself, slowly moving his chess pieces around, getting the reaction his wished for from his adversary. "They may, they may not. It simply adds more doubt in the jurors' minds, that's all. Just as the father of the family mentioned that when you stood at the door, oddly your hands were not visible. Normally at least one hand would be seen, and also one might gesticulate with a hand as one spoke, especially on seeing an unwanted visitor at the door. You did neither: perhaps because you were wearing gloves—Chuck's gloves—and didn't want the family to see them."

Richard shook his head and pursed his lips. "Sorry, Inspector, this is all rubbish and just speculation." But he thought, That's probably thirty–love to the inspector in this game of back-and-forth jousting.

Richard stretched his arms to improve his circulation, and suddenly gave out a yelp. "Ow! Christ, that hurt." He bent his body to his lap, which then stretched his inflamed back. "Aaaggghhh!" he winced again.

"Are you all right, Richard?" asked Harriet, genuinely concerned.

Richard continued to talk from his bent position, his voice slightly muffled. "My stomach. God, it's really aching, and my sides are throbbing.

Maybe I ate something at the club. What did I have? Oh yes, the ruddy scallops—maybe they weren't fresh. That was stupid – although Elisa also had them. May I have that second painkiller *please*, Detective Chief Inspector?"

"Our MO didn't allow it, you know that." But then Kofi, knowing how unsympathetic this might look in a court of law, quickly added, "However, given the circumstances, and that the time now is 23:45 hundred hours, DI Gilmore will now leave the room to ask for permission for an additional painkiller to be given to the suspect."

Harriet got up and left the room.

Kofi waited for Richard to recover and sit upright again and then offered him a bottle of water.

"Thank you." Richard smiled appreciatively.

"Hmm." Kofi said. "Now, about the blinds, Richard. Given you said your hosts were asleep—and they must have been for you to have answered the door to the Jehovah's Witness family—only you could have closed the blinds and overridden them, because we checked, and they were set automatically to do so at sunset."

Richard was cautious. This was unfamiliar ground again. "I have no idea when the blinds went down. Maybe Rebecca or Chuck turned them down—I can't recall. Sorry. But, so ruddy what?" He shrugged his shoulders.

"No, you said they were both asleep at that time, so it couldn't have been them."

"How do you know the time exactly of the blinds? Maybe the drunken Chuck woke earlier than he said and turned them down, or Rebecca did and then went back into her morning room?"

"You won't know this, but the little girl who saw you wearing Chuck's buckle shoes accidentally dropped her toy rabbit on the ground near the car as they left. The father, after realizing this a few minutes later, drove back to the house to retrieve it. It was his wife who then saw the blinds in the morning room slowly reopening."

"Oh, I do recall them saying that they can come down and up automatically. As you mentioned, Inspector, something about sunrise and sunset?" added Richard. "Maybe you are mistaken, and they reprogrammed them for earlier. So who's to say—and anyway, who cares?"

"No, we checked. The program was set for all blinds to open at sunrise and to close at sunset, and sunset wasn't for another two hours that day. And the mother distinctively mentioned that *only* that room's blinds were opening. All the other rooms already had their blinds up. So *you* must have opened that blind yourself by pressing the morning room's *M* button."

"Well, if that was the case, surely my fingerprints would be all over them."

"Not if you were wearing Chuck's gloves, or the latex gloves of the kind that you keep in your fancy sports car, Richard."

"Again, pure speculation, Inspector," said Richard, crossing his arms and shifting his weight again.

"Maybe, maybe not. Maybe the woman in the car was mistaken in seeing the blinds in just one room opening, or maybe she wasn't. But why would she invent that? Instead, maybe the jury would think perhaps you were initially closing the blinds in the morning room, which had a light on next to Rebecca's armchair, so that no one outside would see what treacherous acts you were about to perform on her. And then after those acts, you reopened the blinds so that from the outside, nothing would look amiss." Kofi smirked and added, "Yes, maybe the jury wouldn't buy it."

Kofi paused, then continued his theory. "But again, it's slowly all adding up to doubt concerning your testimony. That's what it does, and after a while, the tide of doubt becomes the tsunami of injustice, including when considering the tears."

Richard winced again, and they both heard his stomach grumbling. He decided to stand up. His back, legs, buttocks, and now his sides and stomach were pounding. That position didn't help either, and he buckled down again in pain, again. Probably now, forty–love to the detective he admitted to himself.

Harriet came back in and passed Richard the additional painkiller and some water. He bent down to take it, holding on to the table with his right hand for support.

Richard spoke again. His voice was strained and quiet. "What tears? What on earth are you going on about now, Inspector? I am not crying, even now when in such pain, Inspector. I rarely do."

Kofi remained seated and looked up at him, allowing him to stand so as to not disrupt the conversation flow. Kofi said, "I am sure someone as heartless as you doesn't. It's not your tears to which I was referring, Richard, but those of your mistress, Rebecca Falconer Jelleners."

Richard studied Kofi. *Was this yet another trap he is laying for me? He's relentless.*

Kofi carried on. "It was DI Gilmour here who noticed a light smudging of Mrs. Jelleners's mascara, which had formed a slightly different-coloured line down her cheeks when looked at in the floor light. She tasted some saltiness on your lover's cheeks and alerted the pathology lab. The autopsy mentioned that Mrs. Jelleners had indeed residues of salt in her closed eyes, her tear ducts, and on her cheeks. We have concluded that she had been crying that afternoon as she lay dying."

Richard laughed loudly and then winced from the accompanying pain of the muscles in his back contracting. "Well, no shit, Sherlock! She was probably crying out of fear of thinking she was about to be murdered by

The Feather of Truth — Ian Campbell-Laing

her arsehole of a husband, don't you think, Inspector Clouseau?"

Kofi leant forward and calmly said, "My, my, you are an irritated man and getting angrier as you painfully tie yourself in knots. Again, you should be careful what you say. In your office during our taped conversations, and on your statement, you advised me that you liked your boss, and yet now you seem to hate him. Inconsistencies are powerful weapons in my world, all over which a good legal cross-examiner would jump. No, the tears she had shed contained certain proteins in them, which tears of fear do not have. These protein tears are due to sadness, Richard."

Richard snapped back, raising his voice. "I've never heard such crap in all my life. Surely, tears are tears are tears are tears."

"No, the experts, of which you are clearly not one—thank heavens, for once—say they are very different. Apparently, when one cries and produces tears, the biochemists in the pathology labs can analyze the tears and determine if the tears reflected one of three different actions: firstly, as a result of emotional stress; or secondly, if they were due to fear; or instead thirdly, if they were due to, say, an external body irritant like a hair or a chemical in the eye."

"So, what tears did Mrs. Jelleners have just before she died? Fearful ones of dying, I should ruddy think, don't you?" Richard decided to sit down again.

"The report says that initially, she exhibited some fear tears hormones, probably when her body's organs started shutting down, and she was clearly in great pain, but completely immobilized and unable to move. Then on top of those tears, there was evidence of an extraordinary high amount of emotional stress or sadness tears in her tear ducts. Their residue was after the fear proteins had been created—because they were above them, with cells that were younger than the fear proteins cells. There were no antibody proteins, so no irritant in her eyes."

Richard winced again as he listened to the lecture. He now felt a throbbing in his head. Probably a migraine after all the incessant questioning. The smart detective was wearing him down and taking full advantage of his weakened physical state.

Richard struggled to remain calm. "So she was fearful and emotional, so what?" He laughed. "I would be if I thought I was about to die, wouldn't you?"

"Richard, you surprise me. You are bright but not always smart. You've not grasped it yet, have you? So, Rebecca was initially frightened of what was going on with her aching body, and then, after becoming paralyzed with fear, eventually did not fear dying at all. We don't think that she was frightened when being strangled or punched by you. She was, instead, quite calm but very sad. It was as if she was witnessing an act that upset her dreadfully, but about which she was paralyzed to do or say anything."

"All very interesting theory, but it's quite simple. The act that was upsetting her was her ruddy husband poisoning and then strangling her, surely, Inspector."

"No, we don't now think so. The bottom line was that Rebecca died a very, very painful death, about which you know full well, because it was you who researched on her laptop the actions of the deadly ground-up grey grains of the toxic liver of the puffer fish. You did that remotely and then backdated the date to when she was out of the country to ensure it would not look like her researching her own potential suicide, but only when her husband was in the house, and thus nicely incriminating him. Very, very neat. We have only recently found out that it's possible to do this. Probably less than a handful of IT geeks in the world could do this, of which you are one, as demonstrated by your G-H0st computer program. Unfortunately, we found that out only *after* Chuck's suicide in prison. It also helped that a few months earlier he had cooked the puffer fish delicacy for his dinner guests, of which you were one. That was very, very clever of you to use that particular poison. It implicated your boss rather well."

"All utter nonsense, Sherlock," said Richard, who decided to stand up again, and now looked down at Kofi.

The detective ignored Richard's baiting.

"From the protein analysis, we and the forensics team, together with the pathologist's autopsy report, have pieced together the last moments of your mistress's death."

"Oh puh-leeze, Inspector, this is all too fanciful, and I am getting weary of you. My body aches from the barbaric punishment in Iran, and my brain hurts from your incessant questioning and harassment."

"*You* talk of harassment? Let's picture the scene. The last scene of Rebecca Falconer Jelleners's tragic life."

"If you insist, Inspector." Richard rolled his eyes, looked to the ceiling, and appeared bored and nonplussed. He slowly sat down and then ran the index finger around and around the top of the rim of his mug of tea in a hypnotic motion. He needed to think and digest this evidence against him.

Kofi took a deep breath and exhaled. He was entering the final stretch before the crucial phase of the questioning. He had to handle this carefully. "Hmm. Richard, you entered her morning room for the last time. You did not know she had initially cried tears of pain, as the neurotoxin from the few small grains of puffer fish's liver that you ground up and sprinkled over her food took effect. The poison blocked the transmission of the nerve impulses into each organ, causing paralysis. As each organ shut down, it then froze the muscles in the eyes, the chest, and stomach. She would have felt great pain and a heavy weight on her chest and stomach. As her lungs got tighter, she would have felt like she was suffocating but unable to gasp for breath. Also, the lab detected urine in her panties, suggesting that, whilst

The Feather of Truth   Ian Campbell-Laing

paralyzed with fear, she involuntarily wet herself, adding to her discomfort and sense of feminine indignity.

When you came in to punch her stomach, slap her face, and strangle her in order to make it look like her husband's acts—in precisely the same areas of her body she showed you her husband had done previously—you saw that her eyes had remained open, without blinking. You knew then that her nervous and muscular systems had shut down, so that she could not move her body.

She may have appeared to be in a coma and near death to you, but her brain was functioning perfectly, as was her hearing: because the toxins do not attack these two areas. She almost certainly could hear you in the room as you walked around; she would be able to smell your presence and listen to you if you talked to her or spoke aloud to yourself. I do know that at the time of your final moments with her—which was probably around sixish before you left the house, and not the eight o'clock that showed on her watch that you altered and smashed—she was crying emotional tears, because the man she loved was murdering her and their unborn baby. She was silently crying out to you, pleading with you, begging you to stop. She was a devout Catholic and devoted to you. The pathologist stated that as the pain in her stomach became unbearable and the suffocation of her lungs made her feel like she was drowning, she would have been fully conscious until her very last breath, with her heart being the last organ to shut down. I wonder what were her last words that she tried to speak to you?"

Richard, on hearing the pain Rebecca had gone through, felt that his stomach, sides, buttocks, and upper part of his legs were going through something similar. He wished that he had taken the hospital's advice and stayed in bed in the ward. None of tonight would have then happened. He probably wouldn't have been arrested, even. Well, maybe at least I could have delayed it a day or so, he thought.

Kofi paused. He looked at Richard staring at him: a silent protest from a worthless man. "Richard, she literally died of a broken heart. You needlessly broke it, and her family and I will never forgive you. You are a despicable, callous murderer, Richard de L'Isle."

Richard turned and stared ahead, remaining impassionate. He wondered why the painkillers were not ameliorating his discomfort. He wondered if it was because of the painkiller he had taken at the restaurant, which could be playing with the lining of his stomach. The doctors at the hospital had told him to not take it. But, he had taken it before, and he hadn't had a reaction. Or he thought perhaps it was the scallops. He wanted to leave, but this inspector was proving a worthy adversary, and he knew this was going to be a long night. All he could say was, "Please do take up writing fiction. I can't wait to read your first novel, Inspector. It will be too unbelievable for words."

The Feather of Truth   Ian Campbell-Laing

"Have you no shame, sir?"

Richard, in the face of an inconvenient truth, as usual chose to deny and go on the offensive. He baited the detective. "Inspector, the expression 'How many angels can dance on the head of a pin?' comes to mind, because that is how I now feel: tired of debating something that is completely irrelevant and has no value to me. But then again, your education may not stretch to such phrases."

Kofi leaned forward, his face very close to Richard's. "You, sir, are a pompous, wealthy, arrogant, overeducated, self-entitled shit. My education is on a par with yours: I went to the Dragon Preparatory School in Oxford; and you at Summerfields Prep, our rivals. You went to Rugby; I went to Portsmouth Grammar, one of the best schools in the land. You went to Oxford, probably using your family's wealth and connections; I got into Cambridge on the prestigious Campbell-Conscience scholarship. In fact, given your privileged background, compared to my family's humble beginnings, and considering that the colour of my skin is black, I suspect I had to prove myself much harder to be accepted. I then simply chose to go into a profession that adds something to society, whereas you took the path into banking, typically because of greed."

"Oh, really? You think you're in such a noble profession? There are many crooked cops." Richard knew that this was such a lame thing to say and regretted it immediately. He was finding it increasingly harder to concentrate.

"As in every field, there are some bad apples. You love to deflect the truth, don't you? It is still amazing to me how cavalier your attitude is. I think you are a sociopath, whom you will know is someone that outwardly appears quite normal and sociable, but underneath can be a ruthless murderer. I have been rather successful in catching and putting away *every* murderer whose case I have been given to solve. I will make it my life's ambition to convict you and ensure you are locked up for life. You will soon learn that you will have nowhere to hide!"

"Inspector, I request to go to the men's room to take a leak."

"Denied. We haven't finished yet," replied Kofi tersely and loudly, adding, "By the by, one other interesting piece of evidence at your club also assisted us. You wrote down on a piece of paper, 'where,' 'when,' and 'how,' which reminds me of the assassin in the *Day of the Jackal* film. Your wife confirmed it was one of your favorite films, and that you had a copy of the original and the remake on your laptop."

"What are you going on about now? Can't you piss off and leave me alone? You have arrested the wrong person, as I keep telling you, and as my lawyer will reaffirm. In fact, where the fuck is he?" Richard shouted.

"You wrote down on the RAC notepad those three words, didn't you? But the pad got wet when one of the servers spilt your drink on it. She must have taken a shine to you and retained it."

"I threw it…" Richard stopped. He was again being trapped.

"Yes, you did throw it away, but that was from the second pad. We interviewed the serving lady who retained the first pad that got wet after she accidentally spilled a drink on it. As I said, Richard, each one piece of evidence might not be enough to convict you, but with so much circumstantial evidence against you, and then once you add motive, means, and opportunity, the jury would now surely convict someone as flashy as you, with ease."

Richard knew his long-held secret was out and the Inspector had everything he needed to bring a case against him and possibly convict him. But where was his lawyer, Anthony? Clearly he had got delayed in arriving. And why weren't his meds acting to dull the pain?

Kofi wasn't done yet. "I was also thinking about your grandfather Ben, many years ago, who had a very comfortable position as a Harley Street surgeon. However, he went off to Iran and, despite death threats by a small portion of the Muslim community, who resented the British and American relief efforts after the devastating earthquake of 1978, worked tirelessly in appalling conditions to help the victims, sewing back fingers and hands. Your grandfather was a brave and courageous man, and you and he are poles apart: he saved many lives in his career, whilst you directly took two of them away, and were instrumental in the suicide of a third, and the death of a fourth. What an appalling legacy for your children and your proud heritage with a de L'Isle lineage that goes back to the wars of the Norman Conquest. It pains me to think of what a waste you made of your life."

Richard remained silent, missing the reference to 'the death of a fourth'.

"But thankfully, there's one piece of evidence that we will shortly have that's *not* circumstantial at all."

Richard said, smiling, "And that is, what, precisely?"

You haven't won the game, the set, or the match yet, Inspector, he thought.

CHAPTER 67
WEST END CENTRAL POLICE STATION

Kofi briefly left the interview room to take a leak.

At the inspector's mention of the harsh conditions his beloved grandfather had endured in Iran, Richard's thoughts went back to the flogging and how he had to fight so hard to stay composed and not scream out.

Richard briefly looked at DI Gilmore and then closed his tired eyes as he now remembered hearing the official counting after each stroke; the words pronounced as *yek* (one)…*do* (two)…*se* (three)…He saw the hatred in the eyes of the two soldiers wielding their bamboo canes. Luckily, the official had ensured that the punishment was administered within strict Shariah law. The two soldiers had to hold a copy of the Qur'an under their arm to ensure they couldn't raise their cane too high or get too long a backswing. Even still, the muscular, young, and fit officers were able to unleash hell onto Richard. He nearly passed out.

The only way he could keep going, and not collapse was his determination and his ability to blank out part of the pain, by being in a semitrance and thinking of a pleasant place in his "mind palace." This was on the beach under the shade, in Barbados, sipping his favorite, signature ice-cold gin and tonic. His school army training had served him well.

He had been waiting to hear the word هشتاد *haeshta;d* which would sound like "hash targ," signaling his eightieth stroke, and it would be all over. But he couldn't hear anything over the noise of the crowd that had screamed after each blow.

The medic came to him and checked his heart again.

Richard had lost count of the number of strokes and assumed they probably checked him halfway through. If so, he wasn't sure he could take the remaining forty.

The official said something in Farsi, and the two guards approached him. They uncuffed his wrists. Richard clung to the post, trying to steady himself and ensure he didn't collapse to the delight of the crowd. Maybe he had endured the eighty lashings, and it had simply gone quicker than he thought, given the two soldiers didn't pause between their blows.

The official said something else in Farsi, and the medical officer turned and approached Richard, speaking in perfect English as before. "The punishment is complete. You have had your eighty strokes. We will take you to the hospital to clean up your wounds and prevent infection, before we later amputate your hand."

"Thank you, Doctor," said Richard, as his body pressed hard against the post. He breathed in and pushed himself away from the post and tried to stand upright. As he stumbled and nearly fell over, the crowd bayed for him to collapse. He managed to steady himself. The crowd noise abated.

Richard remembered being handed back his prison shirt, which he struggled to put on. One of the guards tried to help him, but Richard gently pushed him away.

"Don't touch me. I am a British citizen and a de L'Isle. I can do this myself." His words were heard around the media networks covering this live event. He later heard that fifty million people had watched the flogging and that double that would watch the amputation, which was to be held later and again in public.

It seemed to take an age for Richard to put on his shirt, and then he walked slowly back to the building. They hadn't needed to cuff him—no one after that ordeal would be able to put up any resistance or run. The networks focused on his defiant face and then, lastly, the back of his light blue shirt that had soaked up his red blood, giving it a purple tinge.

In Britain he was mainly being hailed as a brave man who had endured the first part of a wholly outrageous sentence for a careless mistake. They thought he should only have had a light prison sentence. Muslims had an opposing view: the original punishment was appropriate, and anything less would be a travesty. They would have liked to see him get far more lashings, endure the amputation, and then also serve a prison sentence in Iran. They were eager to later watch his amputation as a final act of redemption.

The Muslim crowd then started chanting in Persian, "More, more, more!"

Back at the holding building next to the square, they led him to the hospital wing, where he was examined. He stripped down naked and pictures were taken of his back, buttocks, and legs. He turned his head to the mirror attached to the wall and saw a dreadful sight: his back, buttocks, and upper parts of the back of his thighs were raw and covered in blood, which was dripping onto and staining the white tiled floor. The canes had torn through layers of skin and ripped at the bare flesh. He saw the crisscross of red lines and some short red dots where the tip of the cane had found its mark. The swelling had already begun, and any movement he made felt like he was bumping into the sides of a sharply studded hot cauldron.

Richard was slowly helped onto a soft-padded table and lay on his front. A nurse cleaned his wounds and then applied a cold, petroleum-based antiseptic solution. It stung sharply. Now that he was out of the public spotlight and the media gaze, he screamed in pain.

She then quickly dressed his wounds and applied various ice packs to hasten the healing process.

The medic then spoke to him. "Mr. de L'Isle, you are strong, and will be all right. I know you are in great pain, but the injection I am giving you now is a strong cocktail of painkiller, antiseptic and anti-inflammatory drugs. Over the next few days, the process of your body healing itself will cause your back to swell further and turn a bluish-black. In a week or so, it will become yellow, but then after a couple of months, it should start to settle down. The scars, I am afraid, will remain for a very long time. In this bag are the drugs you are to take twice daily for the next week."

"Doctor, thank you for your help, and to you, nurse. It's appreciated. I feel no animosity towards you. I never intended to harm any of your people or insult your faith, or indeed your great country with its amazing history. My grandfather, you know, was a doctor also, and loved your country."

"It's our pleasure. You may think us barbaric, but I am here to help you get better."

"Ah!" he screamed again. "Actually, I totally respect your customs, despite in the UK we would never do such an act." Richard corrected himself, "Well, not in modern times, er, or rather not with the public knowing about it."

"Nurse, help me get him to stand up, whilst I check his heart again."

Another nurse handed Richard a warm broth—a mixture of black tea, small pieces of goat meat, vegetables, medicinal herbs, and some rice. "You need to drink this, Mr. de L'Isle; it will help you regain your strength before tonight's operation on your hand."

"Thank you, nurse. You are so very kind."

***

Richard's thoughts came back to the reality of this evening at the police station. He opened his eyes and sighed deeply as he saw the inspector had returned and was sitting very comfortably in his chair, his hands clasped together and resting on his crossed legs, apparently in no hurry to let Richard leave. Richard could see the steam rise from his fresh, hot mug of coffee.

The inspector, seeing Richard open his eyes, continued. "Richard, we are so very different, aren't we? Black and white, yin and yang. You take life, when I try and protect it. And, we found out an interesting fact about your ancestors."

"Oh yes? What did you uncover, Columbo, that could be of any interest to me at this present time?"

"That similar to my ancestors, the de L'Isle's also had relatives who committed murder."

Richard screwed up his face in surprise. "You don't say? How weird is that. Well, those genes weren't passed down to either you or me then, were they?" Richard then tried to smile, but he was too tired to do so.

"I suspect actually that some were, including the so-called 'warrior gene' that children inherit from their parents. I inherited it, and so, I would guess, did you."

"Oh really? I have read about that unusual gene—quite controversial isn't it—it imbalances the enzymes in the brain that control emotion and anger, which may give the carrier the propensity to act violently when provoked or trapped, or some such stuff and nonsense."

Kofi's tone remained calm, but he had had a long day and wanted to wrap this up shortly. "Quite correct, although I think it may not be 'stuff and nonsense', as you crudely put it. Some psychologists believe that not only do you need that gene but also a harsh upbringing, which you advised me that you had, Richard and which we share in common. That combination when combined together with a situation when one feels trapped, caused you to snap and decide to commit the most heinous crime, that of murder. You felt you had no choice but to cross the moral divide. Isn't that so, Richard? Isn't that how it happened, how I described it?"

In walked the desk sergeant, looking flustered. Harriet spoke into the microphone. "The sergeant has just placed a white envelope in front of DCI Ghazini."

"What was the holdup, Sergeant?" said Kofi not showing his annoyance.

The sergeant bent down and whispered in Kofi's ear. "Sorry, sir. They couldn't locate it at the porter's hall pigeon hole. It had been mistakenly put under 'R' for Mia Reynolds instead of 'Z' for Zanan, as you had requested."

Kofi shook his head and said quietly, "Idiots. Well, at least we finally have it and can wrap this up."

Kofi then smiled.

Richard looked at the detective without speaking, refusing to react when he saw the envelope. He was still mulling over Kofi's last words to him. Richard never thought he was previously capable of murder, until put into the position Rebecca had placed him where he had felt trapped with no way out. The inspector was clearly an astute man. But did it mean that he, Richard, all along had been genetically programmed as a murderer-in-waiting, so to speak, so that when provoked, he was capable of carrying out that heinous crime? Am I a monster, a freak? He began to wonder.

CHAPTER 68
WEST END CENTRAL POLICE STATION

Kofi deliberately now kept his voice softer, at a less deep octave, and more welcoming. "Richard, I do sincerely believe that any ordinary person, even without the warrior gene, given the right, or rather the wrong circumstances, has the inherent ability and capacity to do an extraordinary act and kill another human being, no matter who they are."

He paused but received no reaction. "People have murdered for much less than what I suspect you feared you were about to lose. You had a secret, which, like all potential killers, you wished to remain hidden. You were prepared to commit murder to keep that secret out of the public domain and away your family's knowledge in order to protect your family's good name and your career. In fact, upon reflection, I think the reason you seemed distracted to me when we met at the RAC that evening you dined with Mrs. Jelleners was that she had just told you she was pregnant and, being a devout Catholic, insisted on having your baby. You excused yourself and had a dilemma of Morton's Fork dimensions. Am I not correct, Richard?"

Richard knew to not respond directly and incriminate himself any more.

Kofi smiled at Richard. "You look surprised, but are you really? Perhaps your expensive education didn't advise you of Morton. Let me explain him to you and why the phrase 'Morton's Fork' now seems apt."

Richard took the bait. "I know the phrase, Inspector. I am not dim or uneducated!"

"Well then, enlighten us." The inspector knew to allow the suspect at this stage of the interview the chance to feel good and self-important.

"But of course, Inspector. John Morton was the archbishop of Canterbury in the fifteenth century and a tax collector for the king of England. He determined that a man living modestly must be saving money and hence could afford to pay taxes to the king. Conversely, someone living extravagantly was obviously rich and could also afford to pay taxes. Either way, you pay the taxes. It's akin to the phrase 'between the devil and the deep blue sea.'"

"Correct. You are as always, well read, Richard. You may also know the phrase 'between a rock and a hard place,' which describes a dilemma of two equally unpleasant outcomes. In your personal case, you could choose firstly to allow your mistress to have the baby, and endure the wrath of your boss, who would surely find a way to ensure you never worked in the industry again, and of your wife, who would divorce you, take custody of your children and take most of your assets, which we understand are held in trust."

Richard raised his eyebrows and looked up at Kofi, wondering how he knew about his family's trust assets that allowed Jennifer, whose family was much richer than Richard's, to keep all the assets she had brought into the marriage if they ever got divorced.

"Secondly, Richard, the alternative of this dreadful dilemma was to commit the ultimate crime of murder, and at worst if got caught be sent to prison for life, or at best forever look over your shoulder in case you were found out. Sincerely, Richard, I suspect this dilemma was difficult initially for you to make and caused you some fear."

Richard had no intention of confessing or placating the policeman. "I have no idea what on earth you are going on and on about." But as usual he couldn't resist answering back and taunting the detective. "But in connection with fear, Inspector, do you have any fear?"

Kofi snorted quietly through his nose and smiled. "Hmm, oh yes, of course I do. Fear that I won't do my job properly and fail to catch a criminal and not ensure he or she pays their debt to society. And to be quite honest, I still have a fear that one day, someone whom I put away behind bars, or their friends, will take their revenge on me, like they did to my poor wife. But that's by the by. I know you felt you had no choice but to poison your mistress. If only she had agreed to an abortion, then the problem would have literally been flushed away. Am I not correct, Richard?"

Richard said nothing.

Kofi was wondering if he would ever get this arrogant suspect to confess. He decided to change tack one last time. It was now well after midnight, and Richard had been held for nearly three hours.

"Richard, I would like something confirmed in my mind, something that has bothered me for much of my life." He saw Richard's eyes rolling with mock boredom again. Kofi waved his hand. "No, hear me out, Richard, because this has nothing to do with Rebecca's death, nor your punishment in Iran, but someone else and which coincidentally I suspect has affected us both. It relates to the 'fourth death' I mentioned earlier, but which you didn't pick up on."

Richard was intrigued but not in the mood for yet another story. "What on earth now, Inspector? Is there no end to your rambling? I want to be released right now. I am not speaking with you anymore. I have asked for my lawyer, and until he arrives, I am keeping stum."

Kofi ignored his plea. "I think when we were both fifteen years old, we may have met, briefly."

"I don't think so. I would have remembered *you*."

"Richard, picture the scene of this crime, which was in Shepherd's Bush, in South London where I went to the local comprehensive school. I had to cross a run-down neighborhood to get back to my home. That day in April,

The Feather of Truth   Ian Campbell-Laing

I saw a thirteen-year-old skinny African boy named Juma being set upon by white, slightly older bullies, three of which were laying into him with their boots and fists. But, there was one person standing by and just watching." Richard's eyes looked bemused, but then his mouth opened slightly.

"I went to Juma's rescue, he then escaped, and so the three thugs set upon me. Most of the scars they inflicted on me have healed, apart from this beauty mark on my face here. The words they used in hate against me will, however, stay with me until it's time for me to pass into the next world. After Juma later died of his wounds, I wondered what happened to that 'watcher boy,' who was never caught by the police. And now I know. You know who he is, don't you, Richard?"

"Nope. No idea what you are going on and on about, as usual, Inspector plod."

"He's sitting in front of me now. It's you, the coward that you have always been when under pressure."

"What tosh, Inspector. That could not have been me. I have never been to Shepherd's Bush."

"Oh, really? Then how come I know that below your left breast you have a small, V-shaped port-wine stain? I saw that mark when, during the scuffle all those years ago, I reached out to you to intervene and help me, and as I fell down, I pulled at your school shirt, ripping it, and saw the mark. Instead you watched me being beaten up and then walked away. Please open your shirt, now. I need to see if it's true."

Richard, using his right hand, slowly opened two of his shirt buttons to reveal the very mark. "Purely a coincidence, Inspector. You could have looked up my medical records where this mark will be noted, and invented your heroic story. No proof at all."

Kofi ignored his denial. "Good. I can now lay that ghost to rest in my mind, Richard. Now, let's play this one final game, because this is all just a game to you, isn't it?"

"What more can you do to me, given I am in such pain? We both know that you can't guarantee my conviction. I will outgun your pathetic lawyers and leave sufficient doubt about your purely circumstantial evidence. Whatever you have just won't hold up in court, and you will be wasting the taxpayers' money. The worst you can do to me is advise my wife about my affair, something I will simply deny. Your word against mine."

Kofi laughed. His adversary was weakening and severely wounded. "Actually your word against mine, and the evidence of Rebecca's diary entries and Dawn, her best friend. You had forgotten about that and her, haven't you?"

OK, Richard conceded in his mind. First game of this match to you, Inspector.

Kofi paused. "Think about this, Richard. In our lives, there is always

The Feather of Truth Ian Campbell-Laing

one moment that stands out where we can follow one of three paths: be a hero, or commit an evil act, or be guilty of passive inaction. Once chosen, your action stays with you forever. In your short life, Richard, you have had two opportunities to be a hero, and you chose the coward's way out. Firstly by being a bystander and letting Juma be beaten to his death and watching me get beaten up also. Then, more recently, crossing your moral Rubicon and choosing to kill your innocent mistress and what you thought was her and your unborn baby. You may not think so presently, but you are fortunate that you now have a third time in your life to redeem yourself, where you still have a choice in your actions. Will you finally now have the courage to do what's right in the face of adversity and fear, to lift this weight off your shoulders, and to confess openly now of your murderous actions against Rebecca Falconer Jelleners?"

Richard sat in silence. Then he blurted out, "Where in God's name is my ruddy lawyer? And for Pete's sake, why do you wear odd-coloured socks, man? What kind of weird statement are you trying to make, apart from appearing colour blind?"

Kofi smiled at the little things that were still gnawing at this prima donna murderer's sense of entitlement. "Hmm. Aha, yes. 'Richard of York gave battle in vain."

"You're completely mad! What are you going on about, Inspector?"

"The choice of the colours of my socks is not random or ill thought out, but quite planned. I have seven pairs of socks for the week, one for each of the colours of the rainbow, and hence the mnemonic: red, orange, yellow, green, blue, indigo, and violet. But—"

"OK Inspector. So as today is Wednesday for fuck's sake, why aren't you then wearing yellow socks on both feet?"

"Now, now. You asked the question, so have the courtesy to listen to the reply instead getting irritated and interrupting me. You may not know that the ancient Greeks believed that there was a connection between the seven colours of the rainbow, the seven musical notes, the seven days of the week, and the then-known seven planets in the sky."

"So ruddy what, Inspector?"

"And like the seven musical notes, I like to play my socks in the set order of the rainbow to produce a colourful melody. So, on Monday I wear one red and one orange sock; Tuesday one orange and one yellow; Wednesday one yellow and one green; and so on until Sunday, then it's violet and red."

"You're really weird, Inspector."

"Most definitely I am, Richard. And as you will surely know, what's interesting also is that a rainbow is in fact an optical illusion. What you see as a colourful object is not there at all—you're seeing what you want to believe is there. As a catcher of criminals, my job is to create order out of chaos. What I eventually see is not usually what is initially presented to me. Eventually, I *always* see through the illusion that the murderer has created."

Richard stared at the inspector and sighed.

Kofi leaned forward and said, "The time is nearly half past twelve. We will stop the tape and allow the suspect a loo stop, and then we can open this envelope and reveal its contents. DI Gilmore, can you make a call now and find out when the suspect's lawyer is likely to arrive, please."

CHAPTER 69
WEST END CENTRAL POLICE STATION

Thank God that's over, thought Richard.

He sat on the toilet in the police station. He was exhausted. His body had cramps all over. He was alone in the men's room with an officer standing immediately outside and within hearing distance. He noticed that the windows had thick grey bars on the outside. He was too weak to even try and escape. Anyway, escape wasn't his style.

He thought about Rebecca and the needless murder, given she wasn't even pregnant. But he quickly comforted himself with the knowledge that she would have certainly made a great scene about breaking up and would have hounded him or trapped him into getting her really pregnant. Also, he had implicated Jelly, which was righting a wrong about the meager bonus his boss gave given him, which was so satisfying. And then he got Jelly's job.

What I did had to be done, thought Richard. It was for the greater good—my family's greater good. Anyway, politicians and soldiers do this all the time, and nothing ever happens to them. Even so, having been told by Ghazini that his de L'Isle ancestors had this warrior gene, which was hereditary, he now wasn't even sure who he really was.

He was escorted back to the interview room. Only Harriet was sitting in the room. She spoke as he sat down.

"Richard, we have just learned that your brief, Anthony Lea, has been involved in a car accident on his way to this police station."

"Oh my God, is he all right?"

"Yes, he is. He's a bit shaken up—his car was rear-ended at around ten o'clock this evening, and he suffered some whiplash. The local A&E is holding him there for another hour before releasing him. Then he will come here directly."

"Oh, OK."

Richard decided to turn his cell phone on and check any messages. Not surprising given the hour, he hadn't any. He pressed the buttons on his iPhone to send a text message to his wife.

Jens, darling. I am being held in custody by flatfoot Ghazini! It's ridiculous. Of course I had nothing to do with Mrs. Jelleners' murder. It's absolute tosh. They just need to try and convict someone after Chuck's suicide. They only have flimsy circumstantial stuff because I was at the house when he poisoned and then later strangled her after I left. It's all rubbish. Once Anthony gets here, it will be all sorted you have my word. Love Rxx.

Harriet asked him. "Richard, I should have asked you before, but I see your left hand completely intact. How on earth did you get your amputation commuted?"

Richard looked down at Harriet and for the first time thought she was rather attractive. "No idea, but perhaps our PM and the president of Iran had a chat and decided it was immoral. Who's to say?"

However, Richard had a pretty good idea.

***

After his sentencing at the London tribunal, he was taken down into a holding cell to await temporary deportation to Iran. He was allowed to keep his possessions, which included his laptop.

There, he sat on a wooden bench and suddenly recalled during his initial search of V-Trax in his office in April, that amongst the list of the clients under "A" was the president of Iran. Using G-H0st, he quickly hacked into V-Trax and searched the confidential client file for "Ahmadi, Jamal." He read the summary and smiled when he came to the "Leverage" section. It showed evidence, allegedly uncovered by the Chief Auditing Office of the Iranian Parliament, of corruption by the president: he was about to be accused of diverted oil revenues to his personal offshore account which should have instead been deposited with the Iranian Central Bank. Just before going public with these findings, the chief auditor was sent to Evin Prison and never seen again.

The file also contained some useful Iranian cell phone contact numbers, one of which Richard now copied into his throwaway cell phone.

Richard asked for permission to make one call, in private. The tribunal official agreed, but only for three minutes maximum. Richard dialed the number and set the timer on his cellphone to 180. He had a feeling of déjà vu with that number.

"Hello, who is this?" asked the Iranian man in Persian, not recognizing the calling number.

"Mr. Mehta?" asked Richard. "Is this Mr. Akbar Mehta, Iran's minister for foreign affairs?"

"Who are you? And why are you calling me on my personal cellphone, from what appears to be a London number?" He now spoke English, but his voice sounded nervous. "And how did you get this confidential number? There are very few people who know of it."

"Mr. Mehta, my name is Richard de L'Isle."

"Ah. I know of you of course." The minister smiled. "And yes, I am the minister. But what do you want?"

143...

"Good. I wondered if you might have time for a very quick chat."

"I am not sure I should be talking with you. It's against the protocol of my office. I should only be dealing with your foreign minister."

"The information I have, Minister, which you will find very useful, has forced me to bypass my country's Foreign and Commonwealth Office, because I do not trust them to help me in my plight," said Richard very calmly, but knowing the potential danger.

"By your plight, you mean your voluntary temporary deportation to our country to have your sentence from the tribunal carried out, I presume?"

"Yes, precisely."

116...

"And what information do you have that could be so important and so useful for me?"

"Minister, I don't have a lot of time. Less than two minutes. I wish to make a deal with you. I am prepared to have the lashing given to me in accordance with my sentence."

"Young man, that's very noble of you, but you have no choice in the matter."

"Actually I do, and the information I have concerns your president. Please listen a moment, sir."

Richard waited. His heart was now racing. He knew he only had one shot at this. And it could backfire.

76...

"And what information could you possibly have on our esteemed president, who has the highest of moral values?"

Richard quickly described what he had.

60...

"I simply don't believe it, young man. This accusation is totally outrageous. I think this conversation is over." The minister was about to cut off Richard's call.

"Minister, please just hear me out, and then consider my proposal after our call."

"I'm listening."

"I promise to never reveal into the public domain, or privately with anyone, including any official of the British government, that damning information I have on your president, and which could cause him and your country severe embarrassment, especially in a year in which he seeks reelection and needs outside assistance in extracting the recently found gigantic oil field reserves. For my silence, I must have assurances my amputation would be expunged."

41...

The minister laughed. "I don't have authority to intervene in a tribunal's decision to commute or cancel the amputation—and even if I did, and what you say is true, which it isn't, what assurances do I have that you would keep your word?"

33...

"Minister, the president has such an authority—talk it over with him. We have to trust each other. If you amputate my hand, a file containing some very interesting information will be sent to three people, one of whom is Niall Cruickshank, our country's Foreign Office minister, for him and our prime minister to use as leverage, as they please."

"That sounds like a threat, not a bargaining discussion to me, Mr. de L'Isle."

"It's just a fact. However, if you don't amputate, and I am released back into the UK unharmed apart from the lashings, then should I divulge this information on your president, I suspect you would organize a hit man to take me or my family out," Richard said solemnly.

12...

Richard waited.

8...

"And what possible excuse could we make for not carrying out the tribunal's sentence in full? There will be a public outcry."

"That's for you to figure out."

2...

The tribunal official entered the holding cell and said, "Time's up, Mr. de L'Isle. Please end the call now."

***

Now back in the interview room at the police station, Richard started sweating heavily. The pain in his stomach was now unbearable. He looked at Harriet, and then suddenly she went out of focus. He also felt dizzy, and a force was rising up from his stomach, making him want to throw up. His chest felt tight, and he started gasping for air, thinking he was drowning. Maybe I have miscalculated? He wondered.

He leant forward and with a loud shout, "Ugghhh!" expelled the contents from his stomach, narrowly missing Harriet, who had jumped from her seat just in time. His body carried his momentum forward, and he knocked the side of his face against the table as he crashed to the floor.

"God, Richard, are you all right? You look awful." She bent down and shouted at him. "Richard, can you hear me?"

He didn't move.

Harriet stood up and thumped her fist on the red alarm button on the wall.

She knelt down and cradled his head in her hands and looked into his eyes. They stared back at her without blinking.

She checked his pulse. She looked at her watch for fifteen seconds. She felt only a count of ten. "Shit," she said.

Kofi brutally swung open the door, which smashed into the wall with a loud thud. "What the hell's going on?"

"He's been violently sick and collapsed on the floor. His heartbeat is very weak."

Kofi knelt down by the other side of Richard. He shone his mini light pen into Richard's eyes. No reaction.

Harriet shouted. "I'll get the MO." She shot up and ran out of the room.

Kofi put his ear nearer Richard's mouth and could just hear a faint rasping and gurgling noise, as if he was drowning and struggling for air. Kofi thought it was similar to the noise made during the death rattle, and if so, perhaps he was witnessing the last hours of the suspect's life. Kofi knew that Richard had been in pain, but just assumed it was mainly due to his punishment in Iran. And the stomachaches that Richard had complained about throughout the interview were simply as Richard had himself said, probably because he had eaten some poorly prepared fish earlier that evening. But then it dawned on Kofi that perhaps the fish that Richard had eaten wasn't just scallops, but something far more deadly.

"Richard, can you hear me?" shouted Kofi. He gently slapped Richard's cheeks. No reaction.

"Watcher boy, don't you bloody die on me now, you damn coward! Richard—you are not escaping facing trial for murdering your mistress, you bastard!"

CHAPTER 70
BARBICAN, LONDON

Elisa endured an increasingly uncomfortable journey in the back of the cab, since leaving Richard earlier that evening after their dinner at the RAC. The slight stomach ache she had experienced at the start of her journey had, forty minutes later, transformed into an extremely painful cramp, far worse than any period pain she had endured. Given she was on the pill, she knew that wasn't the source of her intense discomfort.

She was now relieved to be back in her apartment. She closed the front door but forgot to lock it. She let her shoulder bag fall onto the floor. Holding her stomach with her right hand, she picked up her laptop from the hallway table, and shuffling her feet painfully slowly towards the kitchen she struggled to carry it under her left arm.

Eying the nearest kitchen chair, she steadied herself, but her energy deserted her and her laptop slipped out of her hand and crashed onto the tiled floor.

She slumped down rather inelegantly onto the chair, and reaching over to the medicine drawer took out two aspirin. She spotted a half empty glass of water on the table, and drained it.

She began to feel nauseous and rather light headed. She thought it was simply due to the stress of the evening. And, she admitted, having more wine than she was used to probably didn't help. She would pay that price tomorrow with a hangover, for sure. But, she thought, managing a thin smile, Richard would by now be in much more pain than her during his questioning at the police station.

After seeing Richard finally devour the grapes she had prepared with surgical precision earlier that evening in the ladies' room, she knew she had tonight poisoned him using the same toxic grains of the liver of the puffer fish that he had given to his previous mistress, her sister Rebecca. Justice was now complete, and her fears about Richard taking retribution against her soon would evaporate.

Within a few hours, Richard, whilst at the police station being questioned, would slowly die the same agonizing death her sister had suffered.

She was sure that there was no linking her to the poisoning of Richard at his club, because she had flushed down the toilet the syringe and plastic jiffy bags of poison. Of course, the inspector would not be happy that Richard had died, but she had been very apprehensive that a case against Richard may not be watertight anyway—the recording pen she had placed in an envelope for Kofi may not be admissible as evidence. No matter, she

The Feather of Truth — Ian Campbell-Laing

thought. Richard should pay not only for murdering her dearest Rebecca, but also he should suffer for belittling me behind his back and making love to two other women while he was going out with me. The detective would surely conclude that perhaps Richard had administered the poison himself and taken the coward's way out through suicide to avoid the public humiliation of a trial, followed by a lengthy jail sentence.

A sharp pain now went down the left-hand side of Elisa's lower back, where her kidneys resided. She screamed. She slowly got up, and with her left hand holding her back, she struggled to get to her bedroom. She managed to slowly undress into her white cotton nightdress, put her iPhone into the charging stand on the bedside table, and flopped on top of her bed, too exhausted to get under the covers.

An hour later, she was still awake, in too much pain to be able to sleep. She remembered thinking that her scallops tasted a bit underdone – she knew that eating them raw could cause severe stomach pains.

As the right side of her face rested on the pillow, she watched her electronic clock witness the time passing slowly. It was now one o'clock in the morning, and over three and a half hours after she'd arrived home. Her temperature had risen, and she had been sweating profusely; her nightdress was soaked through and clung to the outline of her body. Her iPhone rang, but she was unable to turn her body or lift her arm up to reach for it. Her whole body felt paralyzed, yet she could hear and smell. She heard the message being left.

"Mia, it's Inspector Ghazini here. Sorry it's rather late, but I need to speak with you urgently. One of my sergeants picked up the envelope you left for me at the RAC. But I am confused. I thought you told me it would contain damning recording evidence that would incriminate Richard? Well, all that was in it was a white feather! Please call me as soon as you get this message. We are questioning Richard, and he has denied everything, as expected, so with just the circumstantial evidence, I can't hold him for much longer—we need watertight proof of his guilt, which you promised you were going to give us."

Elisa was also confused and anxious. Why wasn't the pen in the envelope where she had left it? After all, she saw the porter place it in the "Z" pigeonhole, just as Ghazini had requested, before Richard had arrived at the club.

Her eyes swept across her bedroom. She tried to understand what was going on. She went through the evening with Richard, looking for clues. She remembered Richard's eyebrows had risen when she taunted him during dinner by mentioning "the feather of truth." She knew that was a risk, but she couldn't resist it. All evening Richard was in pain, understandably, and got quite irritable with her. He was often distracted on his iPhone; well, that was pretty usual. He had gone to the men's room just

The Feather of Truth   Ian Campbell-Laing

once; again pretty normal, albeit he took a while, but he was obviously having to walk very slowly, after his ordeal in Iran. He had chatted with the maître'd—as he always did. Oh yes, then the serving lady had accidentally spilled wine over her handbag, and Richard got very angry. Yes, he seemed to overreact, but he often did. Nothing seemed out of the ordinary, apart from the white feather in the envelope. Must be some sort of joke. But about what? She was perplexed. Oh, well, she would go to the RAC first thing in the morning and talk with the porter and find out what had happened to the pen.

Her attention was drawn to a text message that had just lit up on her iPhone, from an unknown sender. There were no words, just a picture of two green grapes, with a white feather pierced through them.

She stared at it, her face screwed up.

Suddenly she was now mortally clear about the significance of the feather, and the reason for her discomfort. She tried to scream as loud as she could, "No! No! No!" but no words came out.

When ostensibly visiting the restroom, she now knew that Richard must have found out about the envelope with his recording pen inside. He must have removed the pen and replaced it with a white feather, as his lethal calling card. Her heart started pounding as she realized that his chatting to Ivano was him setting up the wine spillage distraction to allow him to switch the grapes from his plate onto hers and vice versa. In the corner of his eye, whilst e-mailing on his iPhone, he must have seen her palm and then plant the grapes from her shoulder bag onto his plate, and suspected something was up.

A tear formed in her left eye, and it slowly ran across the bridge of her nose and onto the pillow. She knew the slow death that awaited her—she had researched it, of course—the same that Rebecca had experienced from the effects of ingesting the small grains from the puffer fish's toxic liver, more deadly than ricin or cyanide, and with no antidote.

Obtaining the grains had been surprisingly easy for Elisa—she had a friend in the restaurant business—but her own death would not be. Elisa's organs would now shut down one by one as the neurotoxins took effect. She was fully conscious, and she could hear her laboured breathing, her brain and ears being the only two organs the toxin wouldn't reach. Her plan to take justice and avenge the death of her older sister, Rebecca Falconer Jelleners, had turned back on her in a deadly embrace.

Mia Elisa Falconer Reynolds knew she would die soon, possibly within an hour or so. The cunning double murderer, her lover Richard, had won and would live. Rebecca had always looked out for her when they were growing up, but now she had failed her dead sister.

The Feather of Truth — Ian Campbell-Laing

***

Blackdown Close

Back in Haslemere, the same evening that Richard had been arrested, Jennifer was also in turmoil. She had uncovered two secrets relating to her husband. The first of her discoveries was related to Richard's ancestry. She now had evidence that he was not a de L'Isle at all.

She had uncovered that he had been born with the name Dick and abandoned that day by his mother, a Miss Olive Organ. The father was unknown. However, John and Mary de L'Isle, who were friends of one of the doctors at the hospital, and who were unable to have children of their own, adopted Dick. They kept their adoption a secret from Richard and tried to bring him up as if he was their own. Richard had always said to Jennifer that his childhood was harsh, but her recent research showed it was nothing of the sort. His adopted parents showered attention on him and sent him to expensive boarding schools where he excelled and had many friends. His loving parents were no stricter on Richard than any other normal parents would be. Richard was obviously making up his harsh childhood for fun or sympathy—but it was simply a big, fat lie.

She knew that the proud Richard would be devastated if he knew he wasn't a de L'Isle. She decided she certainly wouldn't be the one to divulge his real ancestry—well, not for now anyway.

Her second revelation was that Richard had a secret all spouses dread to find out—something more sinister. And it all made sense now, why the inspector had come to visit her. He had indeed been trying to hint to her about Richard, but she was too blindly in love with and trusting of her husband to see it.

Unknown to Jennifer, Isabelle had this evening also been at the RAC when Richard was meeting Elisa, a woman from a firm of headhunters that Richard had told Jennifer was crucial for work. Isabelle had suspected Richard was not telling his wife the truth and had persuaded an old friend of Isabelle's who was a member at the club to take her there for dinner. There, Isabelle, wearing a wig and sitting with her back to Richard and just a few tables away from him, was nicely within hearing distance of the philanderer and his mistress.

During dinner, Isabelle had sent to Jennifer pictures of Richard and Elisa together, including Elisa feeding Richard some grapes. She also texted her:

> Jens, they are definitely an item—discreet but occasional lovey dovey moments, including some talk about sex they have had. I suspect that the person he was texting causing the car crash was this floozy. Sorry, but the inspector and I have to protect you.

CHAPTER 71
BARBICAN, LONDON

At three o'clock in the morning, the police entered into the apartment of Rebecca's sister, and found her dead. Her nightdress was damp, clinging to the contours of her slim body; her eyes were open, glazed over, and staring at her bedside table; her mascara was smudged. Her right hand lay on her stomach.

Kofi picked up Mia's iPhone from its bedside charger and placing a small gadget next to it, unlocked the eight-digit password. He scrolled down to find her last calls and messages.

He recognized the number of the most recent call—he replayed it. It was from himself, asking her to phone him urgently to explain why the envelope contained only a white feather and where was the real evidence.

The second-from-last text message was from a number unknown. He clicked on it, and saw a picture of a white feather piercing two green grapes.

Her cell had one final text message, also from an unknown number:

> Elisa, babe. Such a revealing, and satisfying dinner. Am still being held at the police station—and as you will know, you busy little poisonous bee—have been charged by Kofi Zanan Ghazini with your sister's murder. Was sick as a dog, probably from the scallops I had eaten. I passed out, but now am awake again. MO thinks I had a minor stroke, following all the stress I've been under, but that I should make a full recovery. Good palming effort by you, though! Truthfully, enjoy your abiding sleep on a bed of feathers. H xxx

Kofi passed Mia's iPhone to Harriet for his assistant to examine the texts, and said, "Hmm. What on earth has been going on this evening?"

He reached into his wallet and took out the business card of Mia E. Reynolds. "Clearly the sender 'H' is Richard, and he knew that his mistress, Mia, who was known to him by her middle name of Elisa, was Rebecca's sister. And he discovered my unusual middle name. Interesting."

"Sir also, Richard, by using an unknown number— probably from one of those pay-as-you-go cellphones, and signing 'H' not 'R', indicated that he still wished that his affair with her remain a secret from the public."

"Well *we* obviously knew of their affair: our geeks traced the source of the text to Richard's phone that distracted him—causing him to have the accident with the Englebrau car—back to Mia. Then when I subsequently questioned Mia, she eventually admitted to being a whore. She was quite cut up about her actions of sleeping with the man she believed had murdered her dear sister. But she did it solely to record any careless pillow-talk by Richard confessing to murdering Rebecca."

"Rather distasteful sir, but somewhat understandable. But I'm not sure I understand what's going on here either? How did Mia die? And where is the incriminating recording evidence that was meant to be left at the RAC?"

"Hmm. Let's piece this all together by examining the facts and potential misdirections. So, Mia contacted me two days ago saying she had obtained a recording of Richard's guilt, but insisted on a last supper with him before she hands it over to me. But why have that last meal with a man who murdered your sister, when she could have more easily and far less riskily given me the evidence right now, so that we could arrest him at his hospital?"

"Well, Mia is rather feisty and obviously a competitive and determined lady. And she considered that meeting him in such a public place as the restaurant of the RAC, was not risky. Instead, what she needed for her own satisfaction, was to see him one last time, and look into his lying eyes, but in an environment where they weren't being intimate, and she wasn't being disgusted by her sexual actions?"

"Yes, I like that idea. Her last image of him, if your will. But let's go back to your initial two questions. How did Mia die and where's the ruddy recording evidence. Let's deal with the second question first."

"Assuming sir, that she *did* have the evidence of Richard admitting his guilt, and she *did* leave it in a white envelope at the RAC pigeon-hole marked for your attention, to be collected by you after she and Richard left at 9 o'clock, then someone must have intercepted it?"

"By Richard of course, Harriet. And he must have replaced it with a white feather, to taunt us and her."

Kofi re-read the taunting text from Richard and glanced at the picture of the white feather piercing the grapes.

Harriet saw Kofi then look down at Mia's body. The way she was holding her stomach, and her glazed look reminded Harriet of how Rebecca had looked after being poisoned.

"Are you thinking what I am thinking, sir?"

"Very likely, young lady. The 'palming' and 'poisonous' references seems clearer to me now. Do they to you?"

"Absolutely. Here's how I think it went down last night. Richard became aware of the existence of Mia's damning tape of his murderous pillow-talk confessions, so he readily agreed to meet her for dinner to find out where she had hidden the tape and kill her. During that meal, he poisoned her just like he did her sister, but this time by palming the grapes he previously had poisoned onto her plate to eat. This man is sick, sir. After murdering Rebecca, he has an affair with Mia, and at some stage finds out that she is Rebecca's sister, so he knows she's out to catch him slip up. He toys with her by continuing to sleep with her, then murders her as well. He's a very cunning, philandering serial killer."

"Hmm. Nearly. But his text to her, talks about *her* palming, not him."

"Aha, sir. You're right."

Harriet thought for a few seconds, and then had it. "So, Mia requested the last supper in order for *her* to poison Richard, but during that meal he spotted her palming the grapes and somehow he switched them, causing Mia inadvertently and unwittingly to poison herself?"

"Yes. I think's that's more likely. Autopsy will confirm any poisoning."

"But why did she need to poison him if we were about to bring him into custody and ultimate charge him? And how did he find out that the grapes were poisoned? And where is the recording evidence now?"

"Harriet, slow down! So many questions. Your last two questions I think are linked. Here's my hypothesis. Yes, Richard somehow found out about the envelope addressed to me—probably from one of the friendly porters spilling the beans, and he took out the recording tape that was inside. He knew then that Mia had set him up to be arrested, and so he was on even higher alert. Then he must have spotted her swapping his grapes for hers and he put two and two together to realize they may be poisoned. He must have distracted her and swapped them back. And he has kept or rather probably destroyed the recording evidence, unfortunately."

"Damn, sir. And if Mia intended to poison Richard, but ended up mistakenly poisoning herself, would it be ruled an unwitting suicide, or could Richard be charged for causing, or rather, not preventing her death?"

"Hmm. That's an interesting question. His text to Mia simply refers to her poisonous actions. And the feather through the grapes picture could be interpreted as anything. Whilst we believe that he knew she was poisoning herself, we'd need more direct evidence of his mens rea, or guilty purpose of mind before the CPS would take on and support the case."

"So that just leaves the question of why did she feel the need to poison her lover, when we were so close to arresting him, sir?"

"Hmm. Perhaps she didn't trust us to get a conviction of Richard."

"Because the recording evidence might not be admissible?"

"Yes, perhaps. And given her demeanor when I last saw her in her office, she looked petrified. Maybe she didn't believe me, when later during her call to me, I gave her my word we would protect her from Richard taking retribution on her."

"Sir, we can't hold Richard much longer with just the circumstantial evidence against him for Rebecca's murder, can we? What should we do?"

"We search Mia's apartment for any evidence of a recording!"

They scoured each room. His eyes focused on Mia's damaged laptop lying on the kitchen floor.

"Hmm. Harriet, please get an IT geek to recover whatever's on the hard-drive. Maybe Mia had the sense to make a copy of the recording. And let's interview all of the staff that served Richard and Mia dinner last night, and find out which hall porter accepted the envelope."

Kofi yawned and then sang from the opera Don Giovanni: "Dell'empio che mi trasse al passo estremo qui attendo la vendetta". *Here am I waiting for revenge against the scoundrel who killed me.*

He walked back to the bedroom, and looking into Mia's eyes he said, "Hmm. It's potentially a double murder enquiry now. Rebecca and Mia Elisa, Richard de L'Isle *is* your killer, and I promise you both that some how we will obtain the revenge you and your family deserves."

He sighed, gave out another loud yawn and thought, Sabbatical postponed, again. Damn.

TO BE CONTINUED…IN BOOK TWO…

'Cold Revenge'

ABOUT THE AUTHOR

Ian Campbell-Laing was born in Dublin, Eire, where his father was studying to be a pediatrician. He grew up in Surrey, England.

Ian has spent his entire career in the financial services industry. In 2005, the bank for which he worked relocated him to the United States, where he and his wife and son have lived ever since.

After becoming fascinated by psychology and human behavior, he decided to write crime fiction and study for a masters in psychology.

The Feather of Truth is the first book in Ian's DCI Kofi Ghazini series.

Printed in Great Britain
by Amazon